He Was Weird

By Michael D. LeFevre

 New Generation **Publishing**

Contents

Special Thanks

My wife Tina, who once again, had to endure me spending long evenings in front of the computer.

All of my proofreaders:

Dawn LeFevre- Chapters 1-4 and provided technical advise on chapters 12, 25 and 29

Thomas Huggins- Chapters 5, 7-20, the first half of 25, 36 and 38

Elisabeth Pearson- Chapter 6

Martin Pearson- Chapters 21, 23, the second half of 25, 26, 27, 33, 34 and 37

Jake Pearson- Chapter 22

Michael Gosling- Chapters 24, 28

David Watson- Chapter 29

Laurie Rutherford- Chapter 30

Sonya Shiers- Chapter 31

Nicola Totterdell- Chapter 32

Sam Welbourne- Chapter 35

To all my colleagues at Gloucestershire Group Homes for all their support

Jello Biafra- Former lead singer for the Dead Kennedys

and now a political spokesman. His speech on school shootings was an inspiration for me in writing this book.

Foreword

Nearly every time I read about a school shooting, (Dunblane, Scotland and Newton Connecticut being the exceptions), the first thought that pops into my head is, "This could have been me." Statistics suggest that seventy five percent of school shooters were victims of bullying and had I carried out a school shooting, I would have been included in that group. For three years, from the October I was in fifth grade until the same month of eighth grade, I lived in a town were I was bullied, humiliated and teased mercilessly almost on a daily basis and only ended when I moved out of that town.

"He Was Weird" is based on the three years of hell I suffered when I lived in that town, the difference being I never shot up the school. Many, but not all, of the things the main character suffers in the story, I suffered when I lived in the town. Although if I included every incident, I could have easily written one hundred more pages. I would have loved to have named and shamed the town where it all happened and named those who put me through so much misery, however, if I did, I would be sued. In that respect, the bullies win again. Saying that, I do leave clues to the identity of the town and individuals and those who wish to do so can probably figure it out. Unfortunately, for legal reasons, I wouldn't be able to confirm it.

When I began writing the story, I decided right from the start to give the main character Asperger's Syndrome and a condition known as DAMP (Deficiencies in Attention, Motor skills and Perception.) The thinking behind this is two fold: one) I believe that I have the conditions to a lesser degree. Having worked with adults and children with these

9

conditions, I see myself in many of the things they do. Because of that, the second reason is that I strongly feel that more awareness is needed about them, especially as they go hand in hand. A major common thread with them is that the sufferer tends to think inwardly and become so caught up in their own little world that they don't perceive social norms and their actions are considered "weird." This makes them a prime target for bullies and other aggressors. Hopefully, this story will make people more aware and sympathetic to those who have them.

Finally, why wasn't it me? Why not me? Even though I did move out of the town, I did have three years to plot and carry out my revenge. The biggest reason was that I had no access to guns or any money where I could go out and purchase them. Besides, I can't think of anywhere, even in America, that would sell guns to a thirteen year old. Additionally, my experiences occurred back in the early 1970s. At that time, school shootings only seemed to happen in large inner city high schools and were almost always gang related. The thought of shooting up a school never entered my head. This is a reason why I set the story in modern times.

While I hope you all enjoy reading "He Was Weird," I also hope that it will open your mind to the many issues brought up in it. There is much scope for discussion and debate and I hope the story is a catalyst for both.

Chapter 1

The First Week

He almost missed the sign as his mother's car drove past it. Through his black horn rimmed glasses, ten year old Marvin Leversee read, "Ramsgate Bridge and Causeway" as the car made the final few miles to Ramsgate. He was excited moving to his new home. Marvin had spent most of the summer at his grandparents' house in Ramsgate, New Jersey where he had lots of fun going to the beach and going fishing with his grandfather. Now Marvin was ecstatic about having the best of both worlds where he could do that every day throughout the summer.

As the car continued over the series of roads and small bridges, Marvin's excitement about his new home nearly blinded him to what he was leaving behind. Back in Woodhaven Heights, he had a good number of friends and was well liked by many in the school. He was on the local football team and started at offensive tackle in his last game. But that didn't seem to matter to Marvin at the precise moment. All he could think about was how much fun he was going to have in the summer.

Mr and Mrs Leversee had just spilt after eleven years of marriage. They had married very young, he was twenty, she was eighteen. Furthermore, Marvin's father was in the navy was still and was serving when Marvin was born a year later. Mr Leversee did leave the navy when Marvin was two and the family moved to Philadelphia where being a Seabee in the navy landed him a good job working construction. They lived in Philadelphia for six years before moving to

Woodhaven Heights when Marvin was eight.

Unfortunately, Mr Leversee also liked his drink and this was the main problem in the family. Although his job paid well enough to afford a nice house in Woodhaven Heights, Marvin's father preferred to use his pay check to buy the bar a round instead of paying the mortgage. After eleven years of marriage and the threat of foreclosure on the home, Mrs Leversee decided enough was enough and took Marvin, his five year old sister Leslie and his 6 month old brother Douglas and moved to her parents' home in Ramsgate.

It was only natural that Marvin would want to explore Ramsgate the moment the car pulled up to his grandparents' house, but he knew that his grandfather would never let him get away with not helping unload the car and removal van. Therefore, Marvin dutifully, if not enthusiastically helped unload and when both vehicles were empty, he spent the next two hours setting out his own bedroom. When all of his clothes were hung up or put in drawers and his toys tidied away neatly, Marvin felt a sense of accomplishment. Unfortunately, it was too late for Marvin to explore his new home and had to be content with simply riding his bike around the block.

Marvin awoke the next morning full of enthusiasm for his first full day in Ramsgate. He had slept soundly the previous night, probably owing to the fact that he had worked hard helping his mother move in. This day, Marvin would see his new school and although school wasn't something Marvin was looking forward to, it was one more way of saying that he was now living in Ramsgate.

Mr Quartz, the principal of Confederate Avenue School, was a round but serious looking man who was dressed very smartly in a light grey suit. He looked to be in his mid forties and had very little hair. He offered a gracious hand to Mrs Leversee and said a warm "hello" to Marvin and Leslie. Mr Quartz proceeded to tell them about the school including important things such as start and stop times and when lunch would be served. Marvin was especially glad to hear that he had a three-day weekend, as school would be closed on the Monday due to a teacher-training day. When he finished, Mr Quartz left the family in the capable hands of the school secretary.

Sitting authoratatively behind her desk, Mrs Webberman, the school secretary, wrote down all of the information provided by Mrs Leversee. Once all of the required information was taken down, Mrs Webberman looked over her large round black glasses and informed them, "That's everything for now, you can look around the school as everybody is at lunch right now."

Taking the cue, Mrs Leversee led her children out of the office. Hearing the sounds of children coming from that direction, they had a look at the school's gym. Inside, there were many children eating their lunches. To Marvin, it looked like a zoo with children being very loud and throwing objects across the room at one another. It was nothing like the structure, quieter regime at Woodhaven Heights. The staff there would not have tolerated the behaviour and at least they had tables to sit at. Mrs Leversee must have been thinking the exact same thing because she immediately granted Marvin's request to come home for lunch.

Confederate Avenue School was a red bricked, two story building of two long corridors with classrooms dotted along both sides of both corridors. While they walked along the corridors, they discovered that the lower grades were on the first floor with the upper grades occupying the second. All of the classrooms they passed by were empty except for the very last one on the second floor. A very large woman with short grey hair and bifocals over a very angry looking face met them coming out from behind the door. She wore a prudish looking dress that looked like it was straight from the 1920s and her blouse was buttoned all the way up to a neck that could have compared to that of an offensive lineman.

"What are you doing here?" the woman barked.

"We're just looking around, these two are starting here on Tuesday," Mrs Leversee explained.

The woman gave the three visitors an indignant look before muttering a soft "Oh." Then pointing to Marvin she asked, "What grade is he in?"

"He is in fifth grade, this is Marvin," Mrs Leversee politely answered.

"Hello Marvin," she said in an unwelcoming manner.

Seeing the name on the "Miss Erichetti" on the classroom door, Mrs Leversee ventured, "Are you Miss Erichetti?" She pronounced the "ch" in the way it was normally said.

The teacher gave Mrs Leversee another ugly look. "Miss Erichetti," she growled pronouncing the "ch" as it was a k.

Dumbfounded, Mrs Leversee led Marvin and Leslie away an out of the school. "I hope you don't get her for a teacher," she said to Marvin as they walked to the car. Marvin nodded in agreement. When they got home, she told her parents about the school and Miss Erichetti. Upon hearing their daughter's account, Marvin's grandparents also hoped that he wouldn't have Miss Erichetti as a teacher.

Marvin pushed the prospect of a new school to the back of his mind and enjoyed the three-day weekend. On Saturday, his grandfather took the family out for one last boat ride before ceremoniously watching it taken out of the water for the winter. Unlike the summer, the boat ride seemed less scenic, even a little grim on the cloudy October day and it definitely felt much colder. Nevertheless, Marvin still enjoyed the ride, going under the bridge and out into the inlet that separated Ramsgate New Jersey from Bay City New Jersey.

The Sunday was spent watching sports with his grandfather. First, they cheered the Arizona Diamondbacks to victory over the Baltimore Orioles in game seven of the World Series. After that they had the misfortune of watching the Philadelphia Eagles get hammered by the Oakland Raiders despite having a 10-0 half time lead. Monday was spent riding his bike and entertaining his sister.

Finally, the day to start at the new school arrived. Like most ten year olds, Marvin wasn't exited about the prospect of going to school. However, he was full of expectation. He remembered when he had been the new boy at Woodhaven Heights Elementary School and had good memories from it. The children in the class gave him a card, which read, "Welcome to Our School" and was signed by everybody. Furthermore, all of the boys were quick to try to make friends with him. So, no one would have blamed Marvin for thinking the same thing when starting at Ramsgate.

Confederate Avenue School stood a foreboding site as the car pulled up to it. Just like the previous Friday, Mrs Leversee took the children in to the office. Mrs Webberman, obviously buried under the morning rush, motioned for them to wait outside the office. They waited over half an hour before the secretary was ready for them. After a few formalities, she announced that she was going to take Marvin and Leslie to their respective classes. There was only one Kindergarten class in the school so showing Leslie to her class was straightforward. It was different for Marvin because there were two fifth grade classes. Marvin's hopes were raised as he followed Mrs Webberman up the stairs at the opposite end of the school from Miss Erichetti's classroom.

"This is Mrs Neil's classroom, she's the other fifth grade teacher," Mrs Webberman stated as she approached the classroom door. However, his hope turned to despair, as the secretary's pace didn't slow down as she walked past the door. His heart sank as he followed her down to the end of the corridor.

"This is your class," she informed when she stopped outside of Miss Erichetti's classroom door. "I believe that you've already met your teacher, Miss Erichetti." With that, she opened the door and let Marvin in.

All eyes were on Marvin when he walked into he classroom. Miss Erichetti's eyes seemed to be burning a hole right through to his very soul.

"This is our new pupil, Marvin Leversee," she announced.

No one said a word, but Marvin still felt uneasy about the eyes on him. "Your desk is over there," she informed pointing to an empty desk. "George will help you with what you need."

Marvin found his desk, his name already on it, and sat down. The boy identified as George came over to assist him. George Lane was practically the same size as Marvin. He had a decidedly Irish look about him with dark, curly red hair and freckles. George helped Marvin sort out all of his textbooks and presented him with a list of extra spelling words to copy into his spelling book.

Everything was a big blur as Marvin definitely felt out of his comfort zone. Miss Erichetti seemed to act as if Marvin had been in the class since the beginning of the year and began teaching away. He tried his best to follow along with the math lesson but the material was new to him. Therefore, it was no surprise that when Miss Erichetti finished explaining the lesson, Marvin put his hand up to say that he didn't understand everything.

Miss Erichetti let out a scream! "Weren't you paying attention?" she inquired. Then wagging her finger at him, continued, "You are making a bad first impression, Leversee."

Peculiar noises sounded around the classroom as some of the pupils held back from laughing out loud. Marvin sank down in his chair as low as he could. He hadn't been in school an hour and already he had been humiliated.

Fortunately, his ordeal didn't last long. Math period ended and it was time for the morning play period. Marvin listened attentively as the two captains read out the batting orders and positions in the field for kickball. He was pleasantly surprised when his captain, a boy named Todd LeMatt, put him at third base and kicking seventh.

The math lesson was soon forgotten as Marvin immersed himself in the game. Standing at third base, he didn't have any balls kicked to him in the first inning. However, he did get to make a play in the second inning when a teammate threw a ball to him in an attempt to get a girl who was running to third base out. The girl made it to third base before Marvin caught the ball, but the girl overran the base so he turned around and tagged her out with the ball. His team cheered and Marvin was happy that he had made a good play.

Not long after, his team came in from the field and Marvin soon had his chance to kick the ball. Before the ball was rolled to him, he noticed some loose stones on the ground, so he quickly cleared them away with his foot. Unfortunately, some of the children watching noticed and one girl remarked, "He must think he's a bull and is going to charge."

Ignoring it, he signalled to the pitcher he was ready and he rolled the ball to Marvin. Charging forward to kick the ball, he, momentarily forgot where he was and thought he was back playing football for the Woodhaven Heights Tigers. As he kicked the ball, Marvin let out a roar. He was so concentrated on making it to first base; he did not notice the looks he was getting from many of the children. He did get safely to first base and then to second before the third out was made. Sadly, he did not get another chance to kick as Miss Erichetti signalled the end of play period shortly after that.

The rest of the morning went by without further event. Marvin went home for lunch and fielded the expected question from his mother on how the morning went. He told her about the math lesson and Mrs Leversee declared, "That's not fair, you've only been there a day, she can't expect you to pick it up just like that." She emphasised her point by snapping her fingers.

Marvin merely shrugged at this and set to devouring his lunch and going back to school. Once at school, he had several minutes before lunchtime officially ended. He kept to himself as he didn't know anyone. However, two boys came over to where he stood. The shorter of the two was a boy named Steve McGuire and was also the captain of the other team at play period. His blonde hair reminded Marvin of a character out of the reruns of "Daniel Boone." The other boy introduced himself as Alan Fishman.

"Why did you do this before you kicked the ball?" Steve McGuire asked him making a sweeping movement with his foot.

Marvin's mind jumbled with trying to best explain

that the stones were in his way. Involuntarily, he answered, "I was trying to clear a runway so I could kick the ball."

"What, you were trying to clear a runway?" Steve repeated in a sarcastic tone.

Then Alan Fishman asked using the same sarcastic tone, "Why did you roar?"

Thoughts suddenly rushed around in Marvin's head as how to answer. He worried that if he told them that it was what he did playing football for the Woodhaven Heights Tigers, it would have heaped more patronisation on him. Therefore, he simply shrugged and replied with a soft, "I don't know."

"This is you," Alan suddenly remarked. Then without a second's hesitation, he began dragging his foot on the ground the same way in which Marvin had done that morning. A split second later, Alan charged forward and let out a roar as he kicked an imaginary ball. Marvin watched the demonstration unimpressed, but he took it to heart that he was being made fun of when he should have commented on how ridiculous the boy looked. After the little performance, the two boys walked off and did not press Marvin any further.

The rest of the afternoon went by without any hitch. Even having the homework assignment of writing questions for a social studies chapter he hadn't been there for didn't faze him. When the bell rang to go home, Marvin was simply glad that he had made it through his first day.

It would have been forgiven for Marvin to think that school was going to be ok. His first day wasn't too bad and the second day seemed to be going pretty well, especially after he quickly caught onto what he was supposed to be doing for reading. After that, he sailed through the rest of the lesson and he even was able to pick up the math work fairly easily.

That all changed when play period came around. That day, they were playing bat ball. Marvin had played it before, only according to the rules of kick ball, only the batter punched the ball instead of kicking it. The method played in Ramsgate was completely different with only two bases and the fielders lining up in rows and it was obvious that no one was going to explain the rules to him. As a result, the lack of clarity sent Marvin into a state of confusion.

He did try to glean some of the rules when his team was up to bat first. However, when it was his turn to bat, he thought he could bat the ball along the ground. The other team was quick to tell Marvin that he was out for doing this. Looking perplexed, someone on his own team finally explained that he had to bat the ball beyond a certain point. He still thought it would have been better if it had been explained to him earlier.

Worse was still to come as the bat ball game went on. Two innings later, when his team was in the field, a girl on the other team batted the ball and started running. One of his teammates passed him the ball and seeing he had a clear shot at the runner, took a step and threw the ball at the runner to get her out. The ball hit its target and Marvin thought he had made a good play.

"You stupid jerk off!" a taller boy with blonde hair named John Lodge bellowed at him.

"Keep away from the ball," scoffed a darker, heavier boy named Keith Wenger.

"I thought that's what you did to get her out," Marvin replied confused.

"I thought that's what you did to get her out," Keith Wenger repeated in a squeaky voice and in a condescending tone.

Then Todd LeMatt finally explained the rule to him. "You are not allowed to hold or run with the ball," he indicated.

All Marvin could do was whisper a soft "Oh" although inwardly, he wished that someone had bothered to explain this to him before the game started. Fortunately, there were no further incidents the rest of play period or the morning for that matter. When the bell rang, Marvin ran the nine city blocks from the school all the way home without stopping until he got home. To him, Marvin thought he had broken some kind of world running record.

He did the same on his return to school for the afternoon, running nearly the entire way. Having put the incidents at play period behind him and the fact there was no sight of Steve McGuire or Alan Fishman on the playground, he felt more positive. In the midst of children playing around him, Marvin kept to himself, feeling pleased at the distances he had running to and from home. To him, it was a world running record.

Unfortunately, despite of his attempts to stay anonymous, there were others in the playground who were determined to seek out the new kid. Soon, Marvin was surrounded by a large gang of kids all asking questions of him. The scene began to unnerve Marvin and a rush of anxiety surged through him. It was made worse when he had to explain where Woodhaven Heights was at least ten times to inquisitive children. The whole situation became a blur and combined with his earlier running feat proved a dangerous combination.

A tiny voice inside him warned Marvin that he should keep his mouth shut, but he couldn't help it. He found himself blurting out, "I broke the world's running record."

"Oh yeah!" snapped Danny Hamer, a boy in Marvin's class.

"Record for what, being the slowest runner in the world," added another boy whom Marvin did not know.

Before he knew it, Marvin found himself in a race with Danny Hamer. He knew he had no chance of winning having seen Danny's athletic prowess at play period. Therefore, he desperately tried to explain what he really meant, but no one wanted to listen. Reluctantly, he ran the race around the kick ball diamond where Danny easily beat him.

"You broke the world's running record," chided a boy after the race.

"That wasn't what I meant," Marvin began to explain.

However, the boy, along with all the others, walked away without giving Marvin a chance to explain. Fortunately, he didn't have to endure the humiliation very long as the bell rang, signifying the end of lunch.

Once inside the classroom, Marvin quickly forgot about the events of lunchtime. However, he had a new worry as the social studies lesson began. One by one children began asking their classmates questions they had written as a study guide for the test on the Friday on a chapter Marvin hadn't been there to learn. So he sat quietly at his desk, secretly hoping no one would ask him any questions.

The plan seemed to be working perfectly as no one called on him to answer any questions for the first half hour. Then a girl with long brown hair and matching round glasses named Amy Lornstein asked her question, "How tall is the statue of liberty?"

Marvin, again shifted in his seat in an attempt to hide, but Amy seemed to zero in on him and picked him to answer. He momentarily shifted his weight from side to side while he tried to think of an answer. Marvin had only seen pictures of the statue of liberty and had no idea of how tall it was. Furthermore, his concept of height and distance had always been way off. But, if he had been there to learn it, he would have remembered as Marvin had an ability to retain statistics like that.

"Uh, I say about thirty feet," he finally ventured already knowing that he was most likely incorrect.

A raucous laughter erupted in he classroom. Miss Erichetti immediately rose to stifle the noise. "Alright, he hasn't been here to learn it, so give him a break," she commanded, barely able to keep herself from bursting out laughing. The teacher's words did quell the uproar, but it left Marvin feeling miserable for the rest of the day.

Feelings of gloom began to dissipate the further away Marvin walked from the school. That was until he passed two girls in his class, Judy Reese and Liz Clover, who started to follow him.

"How tall is the statue of liberty?" the blonde Judy asked her darker haired friend in an obvious patronising tone.

"I say about thirty feet," Liz answered in the same tone.

Then shoving Marvin in the back, Judy goaded, "I call you out, do you accept?"

Liz then copied her friend. "Do you accept?" she asked giving Marvin an equally hard shove in the back.

Having decided that Marvin was an easy victim, the two girls continued to push him in the back for the next several blocks. Inwardly, Marvin was yearning to turn around and punch both of them. However, Marvin was told never to hit girls. This confusion left him not knowing how to respond so he simply took it. Feeding off this, Liz then tried to knock Marvin's books out of his hand, but Marvin must have seen it coming and tightened his grip on his books, thus thwarting her attempt. Liz tried several times to do this but each time, Marvin held onto his books. Her last attempt brought her up close to him compelling Marvin to gently push her away.

"Push me again and I'll break your glasses!" Liz screamed in his face.

"You do and you'll pay for them," came Marvin's reply. Then sensing an opportunity to get one back continued, "Maybe I'll break them myself and blame it on you."

"I'd like to see you do it," Liz challenged with a sneer. With that, she and Judy turned down a different road walked off leaving Marvin to walk the rest of the way home feeling very upset.

The moment he got home, Marvin told his mother and grandparents what had happened on the way home form school. His grandfather praised him for not hitting the girls, but his mother wasn't so understanding.

"If those girls bother you like that again, you turn around and slug' em," she commanded sternly.

"But you told me never to hit girls," Marvin began to protest.

"I know," Mrs Leversee conceded. Then she reassured, "But they have no right to push you or hit you like that, so if they do it again, I say slug' em."

Marvin understood exactly what his mother meant, so he said no more about it. While he was glad that he was now allowed to hit those girls if they picked on him again, inwardly, he hoped that it wouldn't come to it.

This thought was still with him when he went to school the next day. Upon his arrival, some familiar faces in the playground called Marvin over. Standing among the boys he knew was someone he'd never met before.

"This is the new kid, his name is Marvin," John Lodge said to the new figure in an attempted introduction.

The new figure looked at Marvin with little interest and then introduced himself as Andrew Blumenthaw.

Andrew stood several inches taller than Marvin and had black hair, which disguised his large nose. It was clear that the way the other boys seemed to regard Andrew with a hint of awe, that he was the "star" of the class. This was proved when Liz Clover came up behind Marvin and made another attempt to separate Marvin from his books. Upon her unsuccessful attempt, Andrew told Liz to "get lost" and Marvin, "not to take crap from her."

Andrew's apparent friendly attitude to Marvin suddenly changed when John Lodge informed him, "Marvin here says he broke the world's running record."

Marvin immediately found himself in a running race with Andrew, without getting the opportunity to explain what he had meant. Against his will, Marvin raced against Andrew and was beaten by a considerable distance. Like the previous day, there were comments about Marvin's "running record" and like the previous day, Marvin was denied the opportunity to explain what he really meant.

Ringing school bells killed the fear of more hassle on the playground. To the delight of the entire class, there was a substitute teacher for the day. Therefore, Marvin felt more relaxed without the intimidating presence of Miss Erichetti making reading and math much more enjoyable that morning.

When play period began, Marvin was relieved that the two captains had decided to go back to playing kickball. Marvin launched himself into the game even though he was put out in left field. He was full of enthusiasm when it was his turn to kick the ball. Remembering not to let out a roar, Marvin charged forward to meet the ball rolling towards him. However, at the very last moment, Marvin decided that the ball was bouncing too much for him. Slight confusion entered his mind as to what to do. If he put his foot out to stop the ball, he could be accused of trying to bunt and be called out. But, he was going to fast to move out of the way. Coming to a decision, Marvin did the only thing he thought possible, he leaped over the ball. Besides, he had seen someone do it in Woodhaven Heights and nothing was said.

This was not going to be the case in Ramsgate as kids on both teams muttered their disapproval. "What does he think he's doing?" he heard one girl ask.

"He's trying to be a hotshot," Keith Wenger replied as if to answer the girl's question.

There were a few other comments made, some even encouraging Marvin to do it again. He put those out of his mind as he waited for the ball to roll to him again. This time, the pitch was suitable and he gave it a good kick that got him to first base. The next boy up kicked the ball deep enough into the outfield that Marvin so he could round second base and make it to third. His teammates thought so too, but as he was speeding towards third base, Marvin saw out of the corner of his eye, the ball heading to the base as well. It was going to be a close play. In spite of the playground being tarmac, he thought the only thing to do was what his friend Jimmy McFarr would have done in the playground in Philadelphia. He slid into third base.

Even though Marvin was safe at the base, it still prompted comments from his team. Most were on the lines of, "I can't believe he slid" and quite a few "Wows" and even a "Cool" from the voice of John Lodge. It seemed most of the children were amazed that Marvin would attempt such a feat. But the only person to say anything directly to Marvin after he scored a run on the next kick was Keith Wenger who remarked, "You think you're such a hot shot because you slid into the base." However, he walked away before Marvin could respond that he was only trying to avoid being out.

On his next turn to kick, Marvin resisted the calls from his team to jump over the ball or slide into a base. However, on his third time up, he didn't like the first two balls rolled to him and feeling the encouragement from some of the kids on his team, jumped over them both. He also felt the need to slide into second base, as he feared it was going to be a close play. After the person up, he found himself on third base with the bases loaded, a situation where he would have to run when the ball was kicked. Some of his teammates, led by John Lodge, began encouraging Marvin to slide into home. John even instructed him to "slide all the way home" with captain Todd LeMatt nodding positively behind him. Unfortunately, the girl up only kicked the ball a very short distance and Marvin was out at home. He wouldn't have made even if he had slid all the way home.

At the conclusion of play period, it would have been natural for Marvin to be on a high. He had played kickball quite well that morning and had received several compliments. However, that all changed when the boys were sent to the bathroom following play period. The second Marvin entered the boys' room; Andrew Blumenthaw was there to confront him.

"If you jump over the ball again, I'm going to beat the shit out of you," Andrew threatened.

"I only did it because I didn't like the pitch," Marvin began to explain.

"No, he did it because he's trying to show off," Keith Wenger's voice rang out from somewhere in the lavatory.

Seeming to agree with the voice, Andrew reaffirmed his threat. "If I see you do it again, I'm going to take those glasses off and punch your eyes out."

Feeling alone and intimidated, Marvin did not say anymore. He already knew that Andrew had a reputation for being a good fighter, which was probably why he was the star of the class. Furthermore, he seemed to have the backing of all of the boys in the class, including some of those, like John Lodge and Todd LeMatt, who had been egging Marvin on just a few minutes earlier. Marvin felt decidedly isolated.

The rest of the morning came and went and Marvin's journey home and back at lunchtime was uneventful. Back at school, he tried to become anonymous again in case people would start on him again about his "running record." Again his attempt was in vain as two boys he had never met approached him. One was quite tall and very thin, the other, slightly shorter than Marvin and had a rounder face that was punctuated by a cheesy grin.

"You're that new kid," the shorter boy identified.

Marvin nodded as the taller kid added, "I know your name, it's Marvin, Marvin Leversee."

Again, Marvin nodded his confirmation as the two boys regarded him for a second before the shorter boy asked, "Are you related to Jim Lebversea, the second baseman for the Reds?"

Marvin hesitated for a moment. He had been asked this question many times and each time, he answered in the negative. However, after the last time he was asked it in Woodhaven Heights, someone suggested that he should say he was related to the baseball player for a laugh. Marvin decided it was time to play that joke.

"Yes, he's my cousin," Marvin said behind a devious grin.

"Really?" was all the shorter boy could say, while the taller boy just smirked. Marvin braced himself for some sort of comeback, but it never came. The two boys simply walked off leaving Marvin on his own.

When the two boys were well clear, Marvin breathed a sigh of relief that the encounter hadn't been too traumatic. He hoped that he would be left alone for the remainder of the lunchtime. He couldn't have been more wrong. Not long after, some other unknown boy came over to him.

"I heard that Jim Lebversea of the Reds is your brother," he said.

"No, I said he was my cousin," Marvin corrected already beginning to regret making the joke.

"Well they said you said he was your brother," the boy informed pointing to the two boys who had just been talking to Marvin.

First, Marvin asked their names and the boy identified the shorter boy as Jimmy Brown and the taller one as John Woolmore.

Upon learning their names, Marvin shrugged and reiterated, "No, he's my cousin."

Watching that boy walk off, Marvin braced himself for an onslaught of children asking him if his cousin played second base for the Reds. Fortunately, that onslaught never came and he breathed a sigh of relief when it was time to go in from lunch.

He thought he might have dodged a bullet that afternoon when nothing at all was said to him. That was until the final few minutes of the day. The class had watching a film about early famous explorers such as Columbus and were discussing it after. Having just learned about it back in Woodhaven Heights, Marvin volunteered his own explorer.

"I know of one who did reach the east by sailing west," he ventured.

"Who was it, Jim Lebversea?" teased Andrew Blumenthaw. His entourage of friends joined in with him laughing and repeating the name.

The substitute took a minute to calm the class back

29

down and then gently asked, "Who was it?"

"Magellan," Marvin stated matter of factly, impressed at his own answer.

"Yes, Magellan, good," the substitute congratulated.

The rest of the class didn't seem to impressed at Marvin's display of knowledge. After all, this was the guy who thought the statue of liberty was only thirty feet high. More than one child sent a patronising sneer his way. Marvin decided it was best to lay low for the remaining minutes of the day, so he sunk down in his chair as low as he could. It worked as no more attention was shown to him.

Friday marked the end of Marvin's first week at Confederate Avenue School in Ramsgate. He thought, "One more day and then two days off for the weekend." At first, he thought it might be an easy day as the school watched a play put on by one of the third grade classes. The play was okay and as expected, the class showed their appreciation by clapping. Marvin clapped too, but influenced by a popular television programme, he continued to clap along with some other pupils in the hope of being the last one clapping at the very end. A boy sitting next to him cautioned Marvin that he should stop clapping and that, combined with the fact that quite a few other children shared the same the same intention, Marvin ceased his clapping. But upon re-entering the classroom, Miss Erichetti still had a rant.

"I'm far from happy with some of you," Miss Erichetti hissed as she began goose stomping about the room like a storm trooper when the class was seated. "You there, Leversee!" she shouted looking directly at Marvin. "I saw you clapping for far too long at the end. You clap for so long and the you stop. You don't try to get the last two or three claps at the end." She emphasised her point by clapping her hands three times.

Then she continued her assault upon Marvin. "You are new, brand new!" she yelled. "The last thing you need to do is to single yourself out with behaviour like this!"

After she had verbally stripped Marvin down in front of the class, she ranted at the rest of the class for a few more minutes. Although in this new rant, she didn't single any other child out. Marvin sat through the whole rant bewildered.

"Surely clapping too long isn't a serious crime," rushed around in his mind. He concluded to himself that it definitely wasn't grounds for being dressed down in front of the entire class.

Once her rant was finally over, Miss Erichetti proceeded to hand out the social studies tests. Marvin hoped that he wouldn't have to take the test as he hadn't been there to learn the chapter, but he knew he was wrong when the teacher plopped a test paper in front of him. Marvin thought it best not to argue, especially after the ticking off he had just been given, so he struggled with the test. Most of the questions were completely foreign to him and he tried his best to answer, but when he handed it back at the end, Marvin was sure that he failed.

No one came to interrogate Marvin at lunchtime and he was grateful. Furthermore, his mother agreed that it was unfair for him to take a test he hadn't been there to learn the material for. All Marvin wanted to do was get through Friday afternoon and go home and enjoy the weekend.

The Friday afternoon first appeared as if it was going to be easy as the class was told it would be a double PE lesson with the other fifth grade class. Once they were changed and outside, Mrs Penhaligon, the PE teacher, informed both classes that the PE lesson was going to be a soccer game between the two classes.

Immediately the two classes divided themselves according to classroom loyalties and bait the other class with taunts of how their class was going to win and the other class going to lose. Naturally, Marvin joined in with his class. However, it was Mrs Penhaligon who stopped the taunting session and got the classes lined up to play.

Unlike the bat ball game on the Wednesday, the PE teacher at least explained the rules. She informed that the children standing on the two lines opposite from one another would be the goalies, while the three children in the middle would try to score. They would rotate after so many minutes. When the rules were explained, Mrs Penhaligon blew her whistle to start the game.

At first, things seemed to be going well, especially as Marvin didn't get a ball kicked at him requiring him to make a save. After several rotations and both sides exchanging two goals, a shot was directed at Marvin. He easily caught the shot, but he found it difficult to throw the ball back into play as all three of his teammates in the middle were closely covered by their opposite numbers. The situation began to send confusion in Marvin's mind and he hesitated as he did not want to give away a goal. Finally, one boy in the middle came in very close instructing Marvin to roll the ball onto his foot. Unfortunately, as the boy dribbled the ball, he lost possession and the other team scored from it. Although no one said anything directly, Andrew Blumenthaw gave Marvin a look as if to say it was his fault.

Worse was to come when Marvin finally rotated out into the middle. Twice, he mistimed his kicks and completely missed the ball. These misses now brought oral castigation from Andrew. Above the noise of the two classes, Marvin heard Andrew yell, "You stink!" and he was sure that comment was meant for him.

Even though sometime later after Mrs Penhaligon stopped the game to lecture both classes about shouting out things like, "You stink," it didn't stop Andrew from repeating it the next time Marvin went out into the middle. When Marvin was called for a handball that he couldn't have possibly avoided, it validated in Andrew's mind that Marvin couldn't run, throw, kick or catch. Marvin could only begin to realise what consequences Andrew's opinion would have on him.

The game ended with Mrs Neil's class victorious by a 10-7 count, although all of Mrs Neil's class would forever insist it was only 10-6. The loss only soured Andrew's mood, although he didn't seem to blame Marvin solely for the loss. Wound up by the taunting of the victors, he challenged the boys from Mrs Neil's class to a football game after school. After the classes returned to the classrooms following PE, Miss Erichetti spent a half hour jack-booting around the classroom and pontificating on how she disagreed with the idea of the two classes being in competition. At least it took that time away from doing any schoolwork.

Miss Erichetti decided to end the week by giving the class a spelling test. She was caught off guard when Marvin put up his hand to inform her that he had not been given a test booklet. The teacher went to rectify it, but was distracted and forgot what she was going to do. Therefore, when she was ready to begin the test, Marvin had to again inform her that he still hadn't received his book.

"Why didn't you tell me sooner, am I supposed to remember everything?" she barked from behind her bifocals.

Marvin didn't say anything, but he knew in his mind that it wasn't his fault. This didn't stop half the class from snickering and he felt humiliated yet again.

The spelling test led to the end of the day and as it was Friday, the end of the week. Out in the playground, Andrew Blumenthaw was organising the football game against Mrs Neil's class. The game was to take place at the Ramsgate field where the Ramsgate Colts played their football games. Andrew made sure that his friends from both classes were going to be there.

After all the arrangements were made, he went hopefully over to Andrew and eagerly volunteered, "I'll play."

Andrew gave him a disdainful look and huffed, "You're not playing, you're not good enough."

Marvin didn't know whether to argue or cry. He did go very quickly in case the latter happened. He walked home feeling very sad and resentful. He could have played, but he wasn't being given the chance on the basis of one soccer game. As he walked home, Marvin found himself wishing he was back in Woodhaven Heights. It had only been a week, but already he hated Ramsgate. What he didn't know was that there was worse to come for the children of Ramsgate had all the ammunition they needed to use against him.

Chapter 2

It Gets Worse

Most ten-year olds hate going to school after the weekend and for Marvin, this was especially true. He was dreading the idea of facing Miss Erichetti and pupils like Andrew Blumenthaw and those horrible girls, Judy Reese and Liz Clover. The closer he walked to the school, the more inward he withdrew himself.

Once inside, he realised his fears were right. Miss Erichetti began the week by ranting how poorly everyone had done on the social studies and spelling tests. Normally, getting only ten words wrong out of a total of fifty-five would have been a good score, it was eighty percent correct. After all, Marvin had only been at the school for a week. That made no difference to Miss Erichetti who made everyone who didn't get one hundred percent right feel like a failure by making every child in the class write each word they misspelled twenty five times.

Marvin had some consolation in the afternoon when the class got the social studies tests back. His thirty-four percent correct didn't surprise him, but he was glad to see that Miss Erichetti wrote "Doesn't Count" on the bottom of the test paper. She quietly explained to Marvin that it was due to him not being there for the unit. This didn't stop kids like Keith Wenger from giving him funny looks whenever Miss Erichetti pointed out a silly answer someone had put down like Christopher Columbus being a writer. When Marvin claimed innocence at this, Keith Wenger simply breathed a "Yeah, right," in a disbelieving tone.

After a few days grace, one lunchtime in the

playground, Marvin suddenly found himself surrounded by a group of fifth graders, many of them from Mrs Neil's class. The ringleader was a boy named Andy Millenberg, whose long hair and high-pitched voice at first had Marvin believing he was a girl.

"So, you say that you set the world's running record," Andy spat at him in a patronising tone. "What are you, some sort of speedy runner?"

Marvin began to explain, "No, I was just happy that I ran from school all the way home. It must be a mile and a half, and without stopping."

"So how's that a world record?" Andy returned curtly.

Marvin answered, "I didn't think anyone had ever run that far before."

Obviously, his explanation had fallen on deaf ears given the expressions surrounding him. Proof of this became even more apparent when Andy began calling Marvin "Speedy Gonzales." But while he was doing that, Jimmy Brown, who had approached Marvin the previous week, stepped in with a comment of his own.

"He also says that his cousin is Jim Lebversea, the second baseman for the Reds," Jimmy informed the others.

Immediately, Marvin regretted following the advice he had been given some months earlier about playing a joke. However, he believed it would be even more troublesome for him to reverse himself. Besides, it wasn't hurting anyone. Therefore, Marvin affirmed, "Yes, he is."

The answer brought back a renewed verbal barrage from Andy Millenberg. "First you say that you set the world's running record and now you say that your cousin is Jim Lebversea, the second baseman for the Reds."

Marvin simply nodded, but he knew that his

explanation about his running record was being ignored. Disbelieving faces with hostile scowls pressed closer, sending him into a state of panic. Andy Millenberg led the procession of accusations of "liar" and taunts of "weirdo" now directed at him. Marvin wanted desperately to explain his side of things, but the stress of the hostility he was facing prevented the words he was trying to form in his mind from coming out of his mouth. Besides, the fact that anything he said wouldn't be listened to by the surrounding mob compounded his stress. As a result, he froze and withdrew into himself hoping it would all go away. He was only saved when the bell rang ending lunch.

More grief was to come Marvin's way the following day as even more boys from the fifth grade surrounded him. Earlier that day, he had mentioned that his grandfather had won a senior citizens' miniature golf tournament. Unfortunately, he made the mistake of using the word "champion" when he told some children in his class about it.

"You say that your grandfather is the world champion of miniature golf," Andy screeched in his high voice as the crowd once again pressed on Marvin.

Before Marvin could venture an explanation, another boy jumped in with, "That's just another one of his lies!"

Marvin desperately tried to explain that his grandfather had simply won a tournament at a mini golf course in Ramsgate, but once again, the mob wasn't interested in listening. They were simply going to believe what they wanted to and nothing he could say was going to change that. Feelings of extreme anxiety were pushing him into a fight or flight situation. However, he saw that neither was possible. His mind overloaded and feeling powerless, he withdrew deeper into himself trying hard to ignore the taunts being hurled at him. Fortunately, for the second time, the bell saved him.

But, it didn't end there. At the end of the week, during the class Halloween party, the subject of horror movies came up. Marvin had always loved horror movies and with his wild imagination had come up with many ideas for his own. However, when he conveyed his ideas to his classmates, they seized the opportunity to heap more ridicule upon him. This time the ringleader was a boy named David Fitzpatrick.

David Fitzpatrick was a just a weed of a boy, but he managed to surround himself with powerful friends like Andrew Blumenthaw. This gave him free reign to use with mouth without reprisal. He was a typical rich kid, his father being a lawyer. He had been on crutches for six months with a broken leg following a bike accident and used this to gain sympathy when it suited him. Marvin remembered one occasion when Miss Erichetti had scolded him, he suddenly developed a limp.

David coaxed Marvin into naming some of his films that he had made up. He made great amusement out of one title Marvin had given called "General Custer versus Frankenstein" and continued to egg Marvin on more. Not realising he was being set up for more patronisation, Marvin proceeded to make a grave error: he revealed a plan by him and an old friend in Woodhaven Heights to make a movie of their own called "Earth v Mars" and send it to someone called Dr Fright, who hosted a programme that showed horror films on a local television station every Saturday.

To David and many of the others listening, this was solid gold. The children around him goaded him to tell more about it and again, Marvin's inability to transfer what was in his mind to his mouth made things worse. The mounting pressure put on him by David Fitzpatrick and his co-conspirators caused Marvin to say that the movie director had turned them down, but not explain that the movie director would have been his friend's father and that the whole thing would have been filmed using an old home movie camera that was in his attic. He was only stopped when Miss Erichetti made a comment about Marvin's imagination, but it was too late; the class had more ammunition to use against him or at least proof he was a total liar.

"I saw that film, "Earth v Mars," but I didn't see you in it," chided one boy when Marvin returned to school on the Monday.

"Tell us about "Creature Feature,"" added a fourth grader.

Before Marvin could point out that "Creature Feature" was on a different station to "Dr Fright," he was again surrounded by a mob and pushed into a fight or flight situation. With the mass of children all trying to ask questions at once, he desperately tried his best to explain that the movie was simply a fantasy idea of two nine year olds, but they weren't interested. Worse, the overload in his mind prevented him from explaining about the home movie camera and the movie director was his friend's father. The crowd was simply bent on humiliating Marvin once again.

Marvin tried his best to keep his mouth shut, but the children of Confederate Avenue School soon found other things to tease him about. One day, he wore his Cub Scout jacket to school. It was simply a light blue jacket with the official CSA badge sewn on it, but that didn't matter. Marvin may have been a proud Cub Scout in Woodhaven Heights as were many of the boys living there, as were many of the girls who joined the brownies but in Ramsgate, it clearly was different. There was an obvious antipathy towards the scouts and upon seeing Marvin in his jacket, kids like David Fitzpatrick and Judy Reese started on him straight away.

"Oh he was a Cub Scout," teased Judy.

"Aw, the little sweetie," added David making a limp wristed motion.

For the next few days, children would all call Marvin either "Cub Scout" or "Cubby." Unable to stand it any longer, Marvin ripped the patch off his jacket.

Mrs Leversee was less than impressed when she saw that Marvin had removed the Cub Scout patch from his jacket. "Why did you rip off the Cub Scout patch?" she demanded.

"They were calling me cubby," he replied, the anxiety already beginning to mount up inside him.

"So you ripped off your patch just because some kid called you "cubby," she reiterated. "Does that mean, if someone doesn't like the colour of your sneakers, you're going to throw them away or if someone says something about your black hair, you'll dye it blonde?"

With anxiety rising a high level, he did not answer, but his mother went on. "You were proud to be a Cub Scout and you shouldn't stop being proud just because of a few kids."

Again, he didn't say anything as the anxiety and fear of more lecturing from his mother prevented him from stating that children in Ramsgate hated Cub Scouts.

Marvin's persecution wasn't just limited to the playground at lunchtime. One morning, during a game of kickball at play period, when he slid into a base, he was immediately branded "mentally retarded" by a girl named Kim Havers. She then informed him that he needed to see a psychiatrist. Since Kim was the most athletic girl in the class, many of the other children jumped on the bandwagon and branded him mentally retarded as well.

The effects of the taunting Marvin was getting in the

playground began to manifest itself in the classroom. He found it increasingly more difficult to concentrate at the best of times, but with everything he was experiencing, it was nearly impossible. This caused him to miss parts of assignments being explained and not do the work properly. However, Miss Erichetti showed no mercy and simply concluded that he was being lazy and uncooperative.

She attempted to "help" Marvin by writing letters home to his mother. When that didn't produce the results the teacher expected, she took him to see Mr Quartz. Together, teacher and principal decided that Marvin would bring his work into the principal every morning so he could see that the work was done. Marvin's work did improve as a result.

This didn't stop Miss Erichetti from ridiculing Marvin in other ways. In one instance, the boys in the class were told to line up alphabetically by last name to present their work to the teacher. Marvin first attempted to line up in front of John Lodge who pushed past him, as did all the other boys behind. Marvin didn't want to make a fuss and being new, he thought he would be at the end anyway, like it had been done in other schools. In Marvin's mind, he wasn't doing anything wrong.

Miss Erichetti saw things differently though. "Since when does L come at the end of the alphabet?" she asked in her condescending tone.

Stammering, Marvin replied, I...I thought that because I'm new, I go at the end."

"You thought because your new, you go at the end," she repeated with a sneer.

The class needed no prompting in laughing hysterically and as he walked past Andrew's desk, he heard Andrew say "Daaarrrr," just loud enough for him to hear. Marvin would have liked to explain that it was done that way in his other schools, but he already knew that Miss Erichetti would respond with, "This isn't any of your old schools." He instead slinked back to his seat and tried to sink down low to hide from the humiliation.

Another occurrence happened a few days later when Miss Erichetti decided to know about all of Marvin's previous schools and when he attended. In Gestapo like manner, she questioned him for the information. Surprised as to why she wanted to know all this played in Marvin's head as he did his best to answer. The anxiety caused by Miss Erichetti's intimidating interrogation resulted in him making a genuine mistake. He stated he started school at Woodhaven Heights in third grade, implying that he had started at the beginning of the year, when in fact, he moved there in the November.

He thought know more about it; except that Keith Wenger decided to cross-examine him in the playground that lunchtime. For some unknown reason, Keith talked about a memory from third grade. Marvin said that he had a similar experience at the beginning of third grade.

"Was that in Woodhaven Heights?" Keith asked.

"No, it was in Philadelphia. I didn't move to Woodhaven Heights to the November," Marvin explained.

Keith's face went blank for a second as he calculated dates in his mind. Then putting the evidence together, he bellowed, "You lied to Miss Erichetti!" Then, shoving Marvin square in the chest continued, "You told her you moved to Woodhaven Heights at the beginning of third grade."

Bewildered that Keith was making a big deal out of it, Marvin tried his best to explain. "I wasn't an intentional lie, I made a mistake," he said.

"Bull!" Keith yelled. "You're a goddamn liar!"

Keith had already made his mind up and walked away saying over his shoulder that he was going to tell Miss Erichetti. Marvin couldn't believe it, especially because she was always getting on Keith about his behaviour. He knew from things Keith said that he hated the teacher, so he couldn't fathom why he would grass him up.

Grassing Marvin up was exactly what Keith did and Miss Erichetti wasted no time in ticking him off in front of the entire class for giving her a "bum steer." Normally, the class would have been amused at the idea of someone getting one over on the teacher, but they seemed to side with her. Marvin was not allowed to put forward a defence and it was just more evidence for the class to think that he was an out and out liar.

Worse was still to come. One lunchtime, five fourth graders jumped on Marvin for no explicable reason. One boy even punched him a couple of times. When he managed to shake himself free, the anger began to build up in him. However, his mind became overloaded as to hit back or not. In sheer autistic frustration, Marvin snatched his glasses off his own face and hurled them across the playground. This was something he did when he was extremely angry but did not know how to vent it. When his glasses landed, Marvin went over to pick them up with his attackers and a safety following behind.

"What do you think you're doing, chucking your glasses across the playground?" the safety demanded to know.

Before he could answer, the tallest of his attackers stepped in with, "If they're broke, it's not our fault, you threw them so you can't blame us."

"You made me do it, you all jumped on me for no reason," came Marvin's reply.

"It's no reason to chuck your glasses and then try to

43

blame it on these kids. I should take you to see Quartz," the safety interjected before anyone else could get a word in.

Marvin shook his head even though he knew the skinny girl wearing a safety's belt could not physically take him there.

"No need to take him to Quartz," another boy interceded. "If he blames us, we'll just beat him up after school."

The safety gave Marvin a sinister grin as if to say that she should let them beat him up, but in the end, she told the fourth graders to stay away from Marvin in case they "hurt" him.

Marvin walked away, but his ordeal was far from over. The safety spread the news all over the playground as to how he chucked his glasses across the playground and try to blame it on little kids. By the time the school lined up to go in, all of the fifth grade knew of the incident and they delighted in letting Marvin know they knew. What was worse, another safety, a girl named Jamie Horrowitz, informed him that she was going to take it upon herself to tell Miss Erichetti.

Jamie was true to her word and told Miss Erichetti all about Marvin throwing his glasses and blaming it on little kids. The teacher's reaction was predictable.

"I can't believe he'd do that," she huffed. I've had a lot of problems with that child." Then looking his way added, "He'll be staying after school."

She proceeded to write his name on the board next to two other boys who would also be staying after school.

The moment school ended and the rest of the children had cleared the classroom, Miss Erichetti lambasted her detainees. First, she derided Andrew Blumenthaw, who rivalled Keith Wenger on the number of telling offs from her and then turned her attention on the other boy. Guy Rialto was a shorter version of Andrew and was in collusion with him in disrupting lessons earlier that day. Marvin did inwardly smile when the teacher gave Guy a dressing down because he had called him a "girl" at play period.

She paused a moment before turning her attention on Marvin. "I have had somebody reported to me by a safety and I can't remember when the last time that happened." Then looking directly at Marvin stated, "And he's a new boy." This prompted both Andrew and Guy to turn around and look at him, but she then demanded to know, "What happened in the playground?"

"I wasn't doing anything," Marvin began. "These kids just started beating on me and I got mad."

Seeming to pay him no heed, Miss Erichetti continued to berate him. "You don't touch anybody when you're on that playground," she growled pointing to the window.

Marvin wanted to desperately respond, but he wasn't going to get the chance. Instead she further berated, "You have been the subject of a lot of teasing and much criticism. But I think that you often invite trouble."

He could see Guy and Andrew slyly nodding and smirking while Miss Erichetti was speaking. It was clear that Marvin's side of the story was going to be ignored as all the teacher cared about was that her unblemished playground record was now tainted. His only relief came when she went back to lecturing Andrew and Guy, thus wiping the smirks off their faces. When the three were finally freed from their detention thirty-five minutes later, Marvin was relieved that there were no fourth graders waiting to beat him up.

School wasn't the only place in Ramsgate where Marvin ran into problems. Some days he would take his football and ride his bike to the Ramsgate Sports Ground where organised baseball and football games were played. There, he would play out his own fantasy football games. To many people, he probably looked strange throwing passes to himself and even tackling himself, but he didn't care. Safe in his own little world, he would play out his games with himself as the star player. His games were so realistic to him that his team was known to lose on occasion.

One particular day while he was playing such a game, a large group of children asked to join him. Marvin agreed, especially as he didn't recognise any of these kids from being at his school. It turned out they were from the local Catholic school, Blessed Mary Virgin, but that didn't matter. He was just happy at the prospect of having made some friends.

Teams were chosen and the game commenced. At first, things looked to be going well. It was an enjoyable game with each team scoring a touchdown. Then things suddenly changed. Marvin was given the opportunity to be a running back. The first time he carried the ball, he was tackled almost immediately and the same thing happened the second time. Only this time, Marvin realised his team didn't seem to be blocking for him. So, it was no surprise that he didn't want to carry the ball a third time.

"We'll block for you," the team captain promised when he asked Marvin if he wanted to carry the ball again. The rest of the team all nodded their heads in agreement.

Against his better judgement, he took another handoff. His team didn't keep their word and he was again immediately tackled by the opposing team. Only this time, he wasn't let up straight away. Instead, the entire opposing team all piled on crushing him under a pile of bodies.

He was rightfully furious, when they finally did let him up. His fondness for the rules of the game caused him to shout, "That's a fifteen yard penalty for unnecessary roughness!"

"Okay, that's a fifteen yard penalty," the captain of the other team conceded. To his surprise, they let someone from his own team march off the penalty.

Thinking that the other team had learned their lesson, Marvin agreed to carry the ball again. He couldn't have been more wrong. Once again, he was tackled and then the entire other team piled on, some getting off the pile in order to jump on it again.

Now spitting venom, Marvin screamed, "I'm not playing with you!" He then picked up his ball and started walking back to his bike. Two boys followed him

"Aw, did we hurt you?" the taller boy asked patronisingly.

"You're not going to tell on us," the shorter rounder boy inquired.

"I just might!" Marvin screamed back through misty eyes.

"Oh, don't tell," the taller boy pretended to beg before shoving him in the back.

This infuriated Marvin to a point beyond recognition and in pure temper, he threw his glasses. His fury affecting his aim, the glasses struck the goal post causing one of the earpieces to break off.

"We didn't do that," the taller boy announced as Marvin picked up his glasses.

"You did, because you made me mad," he reacted.

"If you get us in trouble, we'll get the cops," the other boy warned.

As he got on his bike, Marvin retorted, "I might get

them myself."

"Oh we're scared," the taller boy came back.

Marvin ignored that comment as he rode his bike away from them. Once he was sure he was a safe distance, he flipped his middle finger at them. He could only just hear one of them shouting, "Come back here and do that, you won't have a middle finger."

He couldn't repel the tears as he rode his bike home. Marvin realised that those kids didn't want to play football; they were just out to hurt him. He relayed the story to his mother and grandfather who were sympathetic, but didn't respond to the pleas to call the police. That night, he found some consolation by playing out a fantasy in his mind where his old friends from Philadelphia would come down the next day and beat all those kids up in a gang fight. They would even hold the worst of kids so Marvin could take a baseball bat to them. But he knew in reality, this wasn't going to happen and the other thing he definitely knew was that he hated living in Ramsgate.

Chapter 3

The Box and New Name

Things seemed to level off for Marvin following the stadium incident, thus saving his sanity. While he was no longer confronted by crowds who sought to humiliate him for their own amusement, he was still subject to low-level harassment. Younger children would constantly call him "Marvin the Monster" after a popular cartoon. Todd LeMatt went through a phase where every morning, he would ask Marvin, "Are you going to slide in today?" His biggest nemesis remained David Fitzpatrick, who constantly made fun of everything Marvin did, said or owned, like referring to his bike as a "piece of shit." One day, David kicked his books in the playground scattering all of the loose papers in the playground. The funny thing was that David only harassed Marvin when he had the likes of Andrew Blumenthaw or Danny Hamer nearby.

However, some positives appeared for him as well. First, Judy Reese moved out of Ramsgate removing the threat of any more hassle from her and Liz Clover. Two boys offered the hand of friendship inviting him to their houses after school. The first was a boy named Peter Stratinsky, who was in Mrs Neil's class. However, that friendship only lasted two weeks because Peter's domineering younger sister, Martha, deemed that Marvin was not worthy to hang around with them. Though he never knew why, he suspected that it was the glasses incident, something the fourth graders would still sometimes give him grief about. The second friendship was more lasting. A boy in his own class named Gene Lancaster began inviting Marvin to his house after school where they would spend the afternoons playing football or basketball at the schoolyard.

He was even invited to play football with the other boys in the fifth grade, although Andrew Blumenthaw wasn't happy about it at first. However, for some reason, Marvin never had a pass thrown to him, but did make several good tackles. The problem was that Andrew seemed to take more notice of the tackles he missed. At least, he never was required to carry the football without blocking.

Things might have improved for Marvin on the social front, but school was still the same and Miss Erichetti let him know it. Parent-teacher conferences took place over the first week of December Miss Erichetti required all pupils to attend. With a fixed smile, the teacher told Mrs Leversee all about the time Marvin only managed to complete half the assigned work during one reading lesson. She expressed her concern over how he didn't pay attention and always seemed to be looking out the window. The teacher ended her little speech by saying, "Marvin, you have a good imagination, but you let your imagination run away with you."

It was now Mrs Leversee's turn to speak. "Marvin has always had a great imagination and sometimes he can't control it," she stated plainly. "He has displayed this trait all his life and they were investigating it at his last school. It was suggested that he has Asperger's Syndrome."

Miss Erichetti's smile rapidly degenerated into that all too familiar scowl. Her face puffed into a ball and began to go purple. Her tightly buttoned top looked as if it was the barrel of a gun that was going to project her head into the air. "Yes, I know, Asperger's Syndrome, ADD or whatever else is the condition of the moment," she spouted condescendingly. "These conditions are just excuses used by parents who don't want to believe their child doesn't want to apply him or herself in school."

Seeing the mother's jaw practically hit the floor, the teacher rapidly attempted to cover her tracks. "I have an idea," she suggested. "In school, there is a large cardboard structure which children can sit in. It's usually used for children who are naughty, but if you think it will help Marvin's concentration, then we'll try it."

Thinking it would help her son's education, Mrs Leversee agreed to try it and convinced Marvin that it would be for the best. When the conference did end a few minutes later, his mother could barely conceal the disgust on her face. He guessed this was probably why the expected lecture about doing better at school never came, but was relieved nevertheless.

It wasn't until another two weeks before Miss Erichetti put forth her plan of putting Marvin into the box. That only came when she left the classroom for a few minutes and returned to find the class making too much noise for her liking. In her fury, she singled out Marvin grabbing him by the arm and forcefully leading him out of the room.

"You think you're such a good little boy, you're worse than all the others," she snarled at him in the hall.

Marvin's confusion accelerated his anxiety. He was sure that there were others in the class who were making more noise than he, so he couldn't understand why he was being singled out.

Leaving him outside, the teacher went back into the classroom and addressed the class. "You all laugh at the clown of the class and then he gets upset and wonders why you all laugh at him," she declared. "Well you won't be able to see him anymore."

While Marvin stood dumbfounded at her words, she dispatched two boys on an errand. Minutes later, they returned carrying a large cardboard structure. It looked like a cardboard phone booth three cardboard walls each standing at least five feet high slotted into the square base. A wooden beam supported the structure across its open front. Marvin watched it set down on the side of the classroom forward of the teacher's desk and then he was instructed to move his desk and chair into the box. Once he did, Miss Erichetti informed him that was where he was to sit from then on.

The full effect of being put into the box wasn't felt for the first few weeks, as Marvin wasn't actually put inside it until two days before school closed for the Christmas holiday. Then, on the final day, she let him come out of the box to join the Christmas party. However, things definitely changed after the Christmas break. Whenever Marvin poked his head out from inside the box, someone, usually Andrew Blumenthaw, would tattle on him to the teacher. A boy named Matt Osmond would constantly make comments about a gopher putting his head out of his hole. Andrew also seized an opportunity to humiliate Marvin. When the class changed for a PE lesson, Marvin hung his clothes over a wall of the box. Andrew told everybody how he was hanging his clothes up like a girl, heaping more torment on him. Marvin was able to find slight relief by flipping his middle finger at people, including Miss Erichetti, from the safety of inside the box.

Whether or not it was down to Marvin's time in the box, there seemed to be no end to individuals calling him "stupid" or "weird," or just plain humiliate him. First, there was the Safety from the glasses incident who took great delight in reminding him all about it. Then there was a girl in his class named Donna

Bassoni, who constantly told Marvin that he was the dumbest kid in the class because all he thought about was football. Danny Hamer openly stated that he was fed up with Marvin's weirdness and tried to get Marvin to fight him one day after school. He refused.

A girl named Renee Tye would call him a "moron" and always made funny faces and noises whenever she was in his presence. She also mercilessly attacked his lack of fine motor skills, especially when he couldn't help staring at her one Chinese looking eye. Many of the other children would join with her due to her popularity. She was almost equal to Kim Havers in athletic ability, but her biggest advantage was the fact that her grandfather had been mayor of Ramsgate and the junior high school was named after him. Therefore Tye was a big name in the town and this allowed Renee to pretty much do as she pleased with little consequence. Even Miss Erichetti went easy on her.

Of course, Miss Erichetti made the most of Marvin being in the box. She appeared to call on him more when she asked questions and would say things like, "Just because you're in there doesn't mean you can go to sleep." It wasn't long before her true motivation for putting him in the box became clear. One day, when she was telling off Keith Wenger for his behaviour, she explained while pointing to the box, "I put him in there so I couldn't see him, I can do the same to you."

Still, Marvin's biggest nemesis continued to be David Fitzpatrick and Andrew Blumenthaw. David would take his football and with another boy named David Mc Donnell, would pass it back and forth keeping it away from Marvin, only giving it back when they were fed up. Andrew would humiliate Marvin every chance he got. The worst incident came when Marvin brought a picture of himself in his football uniform to school. Andrew asked to see it and then ripped it up in front of him.

It would have seemed that everyone wanted to have a go at Marvin and that being in the box was just one reason. Tormentors would justify their actions on account of him being "so weird." One behaviour people picked up on was whenever Marvin heard a word or phrase that amused him, he would constantly repeat it. After having watched a lot of football over the Christmas holidays, he picked up the terms "fair catch" and "good pursuit." He would say these phrases at every opportunity like when he made a catch in bat ball; he would raise his right hand and say "fair catch." Other times it would simply just blurt it out. Although he couldn't help it, it quickly got old with the rest of his class and it wasn't long before Danny Hamer wanted to beat him up again. Kids liked Guy Rialto would encourage him to say these phrases only to laugh at him afterwards and would do it because they knew it annoyed the others.

On the positive side, his circle of friends grew. Todd LeMatt began to invite Marvin around on weekends. Todd had a large basement in his house to play hockey, which Marvin thought was great. It didn't matter to him that Todd was better at hockey and basketball as their one sided games always indicated. The other friend was a boy named Tim Folder who was from Texas. Tim had moved to Ramsgate at the very beginning of the school year and like Marvin, had been accosted by Judy Reese and Liz Clover in his first week. They shared a similar sense of humour and similar interests like playing war. They would go to the beach and climb on the jetty. These two new friends were a boost for Marvin as he was beginning to question the sincerity of Gene's friendship.

After a few weeks of highs and lows, nothing could prepare him for his biggest shock. During the

Christmas holiday, his mother asked him if he wanted to change his name, to which he replied he would want to change it to Mark. Marvin had always hated his name and the "Marvin the Monster" cartoon only made him hate it more. He even declared that when he grew up, he was going to go to court and change it. Mrs Leversee never liked the name either as did his father. However, his father wanted to name him after an uncle he had, whose name was Marvin, and was very fond of, so badly, that he insisted on it. Marvin's grandmother advised his mother that she should just go along with it and not rock the boat. But now free of her husband, she decided to do what she thought was best for her son.

Nothing more was said on the subject after the Christmas holidays and Marvin put it to the back of his mind. One Friday, after coming home from one of his high/low days, his mother greeted him with a huge smile. "You had mail, today," she informed.

He looked at the official looking brown envelope on the table, but before he picked it up, she called out, "Congratulations, Mark!" Slightly puzzled he took a white piece of paper out of the envelope and began to read. The heading "Commonwealth of Pennsylvania" confirmed the letter's authenticity, but it was the very first line that confirmed it all. He read with increasing joy, "From this point forward, the above mentioned name shall be legally changed to "Mark Joseph Leversee.""

This was one piece of information that didn't need a few minutes to be processed through his brain. Almost overcome by the pure excitement, the boy now called Mark celebrated by calling up Tim, Todd and even Gene to share his good news. This was a new turning point in his life.

Mark was met with mixed reactions from his friends over the new name that weekend. Gene seemed to accept it straight away and Tim would need some getting used to it. However, Todd said that he didn't like the name Mark and would want to keep calling him Marvin. The real test came on the Monday morning when the school would be informed. Mrs Leversee met with Mr Quartz and Miss Erichetti and showed them all the legal paperwork. As far as the school was concerned, Marvin's name was now Mark.

From inside his box, Mark waited in anxious anticipation for Miss Erichetti to make the expected announcement to the class. In her dictator like fashion, the teacher called the class to order for the big announcement. "I don't know how we're going to get used to this, but Marvin is now Mark." Observing all the puzzled faces in the classroom, she clarified, "Marvin has had his name legally changed to Mark."

Mark listened gleefully to Miss Erichetti explain his new name to the class. It seemed that most of the class accepted it. The only one to say anything was Keith Wenger who remarked, "I thought it was against the law to change your name."

"You can change your name as long as you do it through the proper legal channels, like Mark did," she explained. With no more comments from the class, Mark was sure that everyone was going to accept his new name. However, it didn't seem so obvious during the boys' toilet break that morning.

"Why did you change your name?" Andrew Blumenthaw demanded to know the second Mark walked into the bathroom.

"I didn't like the name," Mark replied simply.

"I would have kept the name Marvin," John Lodge stated matter of factly.

Mark simply looked at John blankly, but in his mind was thinking, "No, you wouldn't." Keith Wenger offered another explanation when he identified, "He just couldn't take people calling him Marvin the Monster."

In his mind, Mark knew that was partially true, he didn't like being called that, but he also knew that wasn't the main reason for the name change. But while he was processing the information in his mind to give an answer, Mark went silent for a few seconds. This silence provided Keith with enough evidence to think his reason was true.

"That is the reason!" Keith concluded from Mark's silence. He then stated, "People used to call me "Keith the Peeth," but you don't see me changing my name."

Mark didn't see the connection but now most of the other boys believed Keith to be right, that Mark only changed his name because he couldn't take people calling him "Marvin the Monster." That made Mark look like more of a wimp in their eyes. However, they kept silent about it giving him the false impression that everything was going to be okay.

Chapter 4

The Episode

It wasn't long before Mark realised that the other kids weren't going to accept his name change. Outside the classroom, most of the kids in the class continued to call him Marvin, although they were careful not to use it within earshot of Miss Erichetti. The biggest evidence came when David Fitzpatrick took his ball and along with David McDonnell and Andrew Blumenthaw, kept it away from him while taunting, "Come and get it, Marvin." Mark would cry out in reply, "My name's not Marvin anymore," but this only encouraged them more. They only stopped when a teacher intervened. After that, Mark never brought his football into school again.

Two weeks later came the trip to Valley Forge. Many parents, including Mark's mother, questioned the logic of going there in the middle of winter. Miss Erichetti justified it by saying that the class would experience it the same way that George Washington's army had experienced it. They wouldn't fully appreciate the suffering of the troops if they went in the warmer weather.

Mark heard his mother silently chuckle when they walked into the classroom on the morning of the trip. This was the first time Miss Erichetti wasn't wearing one of her 1920s style prudish dresses, opting for trousers and large heavy boots instead. She had a thick blue vest over what looked to be several sweatshirts, which caused Mrs Leversee to whisper in her son's ear, "I'm surprised she doesn't have any hand grenades hanging off her vest."

When it was time to go, the teacher used this military precision to get the class on the bus. The one and a half hour bus ride was uneventful and Mark had a comic book to read to pass the time. He also had Gene as a trip partner so he had someone he could talk to, which made the trip go faster. Upon arrival, the teacher used the same military precision to file the class off the bus.

While the rest of the class seemed to wander about the Reception Centre, Mark was content to stay in the main room and look at all the cannons. There was one that was captured at the Battle of Saratoga and that really enthralled him. A thought entered his mind prompting him to ask, "Anyone got a match?" Mark knew that nobody had one, but in his mind, he would use the pretend match to light the pretend fuse to fire off the cannon. Back on the bus, Miss Erichetti wasn't so amused. She asked, "Mark, why were you asking for a match?" Then she warned, "Watch your step."

Despite the teacher making a big fuss over his comment, he was determined to enjoy the trip. He loved walking through George Washington's house, seeing the soldiers' huts and the hill forts with more cannons and going up the observation tower. For Mark, the morning couldn't have been better.

Everything changed at lunchtime though. In Miss Erichetti's letter to the parents, she gave the instruction that the children were to bring a box lunch. Mrs Leversee took the instruction literally and packed Mark's lunch in a shoebox. It was his so-called friend Gene who first alerted everybody. "Mark has his lunch in a shoe box," he informed.

The children in the nearby seats immediately jumped on the wagon and began teasing Mark. Once again, David Fitzpatrick was the self-appointed ringleader. He led the procession of taunts of "box lunch."

"It did say to bring a box lunch," he tried to protest, but this was countered by someone who replied, "Yeah, but it didn't mean bring your lunch in a shoe box. If anything, it added fuel to the fire. David continued to lead the procession of taunts of "box lunch" and "shoe box." The taunts sent Mark over the edge. In his fury, he threw his yellow apple at David and a cupcake at John Lodge. Still very aggravated, he threw his glasses onto the floor, prompting Gene to say, "He throws his glasses and blames it on others, what a nut."

The teasing turned into a chant with most of the class now chanting, "Marvin on the war path, ooh, ooh." Someone at the back of the bus, probably Andrew Blumenthaw or Guy Rialto threw an apple at him, just missing his head. That along with the chant sent Mark into overload. He shouted, "Fuckers!" very loudly. However, the class didn't stop until Miss Erichetti got back on the bus.

Her very presence silenced the bus and seeing the apple on the floor, immediately wanted to know, "What's that doing on the floor?"

"Mark threw it," volunteered a short dark haired girl named Lisa Horner.

It's not mine, my apple was yellow," Mark immediately began to protest.

Miss Erichetti cut him short by snapping, "Don't try to be funny."

In the end, she made Mark pick up everything from off the floor of the bus, much to the amusement of David and many of the others.

Although he felt that he had been wronged, Mark did well not to let it ruin the rest of the trip. He enjoyed seeing the rest of the sites like the bake ovens and of course he got to see more cannons. Therefore, it was no surprise that he bought four toy cannons at the souvenir shop at the end. Like everybody else, he felt very tired, so it was a very quiet bus ride home.

"Your lenses are chipped, did you throw your glasses?" Mrs Leversee inquired when she saw Mark's glasses the next morning.

"Yes," Mark confessed, "They were all laughing at me."

"Well no wonder kids laugh at you when you do stupid things like this!" she yelled.

"They laughed at me because you put my lunch in a shoe box. They were all calling me "Box lunch," he replied accusingly.

"You shouldn't let things like that bother you," his mother huffed before making it clear she was ending the conversation. She seemed to refuse to acknowledge that it did bother him. Everything said to him got to him; he couldn't just block it out. Mark suddenly felt abandoned, that even his own mother was taking their side. What made it feel worse was that it was her mistake of putting his lunch in a shoebox that caused all the problems on the trip.

It wasn't until a few days later before Miss Erichetti had her go at Mark over the trip. "I still want to know why you were asking for a match at the Reception Centre," she growled.

"I was making a joke," he answered, still wondering what all the fuss was about.

Before he got a chance to explain further that the joke was about pretending to light the fuse on the cannon, the teacher interrupted with, "You don't make jokes about things like that." She then walked off leaving Mark still to ponder what the fuss was all about. After all, what was he going to do, burn down Valley Forge?

In the weeks following the trip, Mark gave the children in his class more ammunition to use against him. He sensed that most of the kids were fed up with him raising his right hand and saying "fair catch" whenever he caught the ball at bat ball during play period, so he ceased doing it. Although, he couldn't understand how it was hurting anyone. However, he took a step in what many considered to be in the wrong direction. During the football playoffs, he watched his hero, Selmo White, a wide receiver for Denver; celebrate making touchdowns by doing a crazy dance in the end zone. Naturally, Mark wanted to imitate his hero so when he made a catch in bat ball, he would do a similar dance.

Most of the class were hostile to Mark's celebrations. Danny Hamer and Keith Wenger threatened him with violence if he kept it up. However, others like Todd LeMatt, Andrew Blumenthaw and especially David Fitzpatrick encouraged him. Mark didn't see that they simply enjoyed watching him make a spectacle of himself and they knew it got on the nerves of others. The more they saw that Danny and others were annoyed by it, the more they encouraged Mark. Danny especially grew more hostile towards him.

Miss Erichetti must have seen it too, because she told Mark to stop his celebrations. But the teacher's intervention did not stop Danny's increasing hostility towards Mark. Things finally went off the boil in an event, which Miss Erichetti would forever refer to as "The Episode."

It started one morning, when the class was lined up in the gym. Miss Erichetti had left them for a second to see about some query. Naturally the class began to converse in small groups while they waited. Mark was behind Tim Folder so they struck up a conversation. They talked about a Harlem Globetrotters special that had been on television the night before. Caught up in the discussion, Mark acted out a scene from it imitating one of the Globetrotters doing an imaginary hook shot and rhyming, "A tisket and tasket, I throw it in the basket."

Whether he was louder than he intended or Danny was looking for an excuse, but he was on him straight away. With clenched fists raised in a boxer's stance, Danny threatened, "Shut up, or I'll beat the crap out of you."

Mark tried to say that he was only talking to his friend, but Danny wasn't in the mood to hear any explanations. The moment Mark opened his mouth, he was there to say "Shut up!" and threaten him more. Only Miss Erichetti's appearance prevented anything from getting physical, but not before Danny whispered, "I'm going to get you after school."

David Fitzpatrick spent Mark's entire lunch period taunting him about how Danny was getting to get him after school. He followed Mark around the playground saying, "Hamer's gonna kick your ass." When the taunting became too much, Mark turned around and pushed him. David reacted by shouting, "I'm going to beat you up too." This didn't frighten Mark, as he was more worried about the other threat.

Sure enough, Danny was waiting for Mark after school. As soon as Danny squared up to him, Mark stammered, "I don't want to fight you." Only this time, Danny wasn't going to let him get away that easily. He shoved Mark, forcing him to struggle to maintain his balance, but dropping his books in the process. As Danny moved in for the kill, Mark, in sheer self-preservation, lashed out hitting Danny in the chest. Now feeling completely justified, Danny threw Mark to the ground and jumped on him. Sitting astride Mark, he removed his glasses and repeatedly reigned blows upon Mark's face. The pounding lasted several minutes before George Lane finally used his powers as safety patrol captain and stopped Danny. But by then, the damage had been done and Mark was in floods of tears.

"I'm going to get my cousin on you, he's eighteen and in the army!" Mark yelled when the tears lessened.

Danny smiled, but said nothing. Instead, David took up the baton. "Oh, we're all scared," he teased. "Who else are you gonna get, the Denver Broncos?"

"No, I'll get the kids from Woodhaven Heights!" Mark screamed in reply.

This brought Danny, David and everyone else in attendance to hysterical laughter. David then sneered, "What are they going to do, come on a charter bus?"

Mark had no answer for this. He knew what he had said was illogical. He did have a cousin in the army, but he knew he wasn't going to school the next day, nor would the kids from Woodhaven Heights. However, he wasn't feeling very logical at the moment and after all, he desperately wished it would happen.

Still very upset, Mark ignored the taunts of the others and went about picking up his books. Meanwhile, David went over to Mark's bike and knocked it over. After Mark had picked up all of his books, he found David kicking the seat of the fallen bicycle.

"Leave my bike alone!" he screamed, but David just ignored him and continued kicking the seat. As he got closer, Danny stepped in front of him, blocking his way. He knew that if he tried to go past Danny, he would beat him up again and there was no one around who he could tell. Besides, Danny would also prevent him from telling a teacher. The situation sent a feeling of helplessness through Mark's brain as indecision led to overload. Therefore, he simply stood there watching David kick the seat off his bike and then kick the stick shift breaking that too.

Further destruction of Mark's bike was halted only when George Lane suddenly reappeared stating the Mark had to go to the office. Neither Danny nor David wanted any grief from the captain of the safety patrol so they stopped and quickly left. However, Danny did mutter something about beating George up as well under his breath.

Mark said nothing as he accompanied George to the school office. When the pair arrived, Mrs Webberman and Miss Erichetti, who demanded to know everything that had happened, met them. George told the teacher how Danny and David beat Mark up and wrecked his bike. Then from out of nowhere came a surprise ally. Keith Wenger walked into the office and corroborated everything George had said. Having heard everything, Miss Erichetti declared that she would deal with it and instructed Keith and George to make sure Mark got home all right.

The two boys complied with their teacher's instruction and assisted Mark with his bike. Keith stated that because he only lived a block from the school that he should take Mark to his house and have his mother pick him up from there. George instantly agreed to this and so as they were about to part, Mark thanked him for all his help and George was gracious in reply. However, it never occurred to Mark why it took George so long to come to his aid. When Mr Quartz questioned him about it the following day, George explained that he wanted to make it stick.

As Mark and Keith were leaving the school grounds, they were met by Gene. It then occurred to Mark that Gene had been around but did not come to his aid either. As he pondered this, Gene plainly stated, "I'm going to be their witness."

Fortunately, Mark had regained enough presence of mind to respond, "That's okay, I have plenty of those."

His answer stunned Gene for a second, but he came back with, "Then you don't need me to be yours," before walking off.

Once Gene was clear, Keith pointed out, "You see what kind of friend he is, he desserts you when you need help." Mark had to agree with Keith's assessment. Gene hadn't been a very good fiend that day leaving him to his fate at the hands of Danny and David. But he knew also that Gene tended to hang around like a bad smell.

During the one block walk, Keith elaborated on why it all happened. "It's because you go around saying things like "fair catch" and do the silly dance when you make a catch in bat ball," he explained.

Mark didn't say anything to this. All he knew was that he had been beaten up and his bike destroyed. Nothing he did warranted that type of treatment.

Keith and his mother turned out to be very hospitable when they arrived at his house. They got Mark to sit down and gave him cookies and juice while Mrs Wenger telephoned his mother. Mrs Leversee had already received a phone call from the school outlining what happened and was ready to head there before she got the call from Keith's mother. Instead she headed for the Wenger's place.

Mrs Leversee was less than impressed when she saw the state of her son's bicycle, but was relieved to see that he was all right. Keith told her everything that happened, which made her so furious that it took both mother and son to help her calm down. Nevertheless, she declared that she was determined to go into the school and make the two boys who hurt her son got what they deserved. When she had sufficiently calmed down, the two mothers carried on making small talk while the two sons went to Keith's room to watch television.

The Wengers lived in a large house, like a mansion. It was full of rooms, which Mark would have liked to explore if he had more time. It turned out that Keith was the youngest of three boys, which explained lots about Keith's attention seeking behaviour in school. However, at that moment, neither Mark nor his mother cared about that. They were both grateful of the help, which Keith and his family had given Mark. Even when they were set to leave, Keith's eldest brother, Scott, gave them advice on where not to get the bike repaired.

That evening, when all had calmed, Mark's mother asked, "Are kids picking on you more since you got put in that box?"

"Yes," Mark replied. "They didn't give me any candy at the Valentine's Day party until I said something to Miss Erichetti. I think they missed me out on purpose."

She nodded at her son's answer and then responded, "I'm having you taken out of that box."

Mrs Leversee was determined to see justice was done for her son when she went into the school the next day. Danny and David were hauled before Mr Quartz and with Miss Erichetti in attendance were threatened with suspension. Mrs Leversee added that if it were to happen again, she would seek to press charges. In the end, both boys were made to apologise to Mark and it was suggested they assist with repairs to his bike. She also saw to it that Mark was taken out of the box.

Danny and David took their punishments in totally different extremes. Danny showed true remorse and was sincere in his apology. He even lent Mark his bike until Mark's bike got fixed. David, on the other hand, couldn't have been more hostile. He was almost mystified of the fact he was in trouble and immediately tried to downplay his guilt. "All I did was kick your bike seat," he moaned, "It was Hamer who beat you up." When that didn't get the desired reaction, he resorted to telling everyone who would listen, "Marvin got his mommy in and now I'm in trouble."

His lack of remorse became clear the next morning. It started when Andy Millenberg was baiting Mark about the episode. "I hear Hamer beat you up and made you cry," he teased.

Mark was thinking of a response when David intervened with both guns blazing. "What a pussy!" he bellowed. Seeing he got Andy's attention carried on, "Hamer beat him up and I wrecked his bike. He said he was going to get his brother in the army on us. There was going to be machine guns and bazookas. He said he was going to get the Denver Broncos on us too. Then his mother got us before Quartz and said if we do it again were would be arrested for assault and battery. Also when he was born, he was brainwashed to think sports. It's a shame he's not good at them."

Andy's wide grin confirmed that he believed everything that David had just said. Mark began to protest; "I never said anything about bazookas." But Andy brushed him off with a quick, "Yeah, right."

It was soon clear that most people's sympathies weren't with Mark, David saw to that. He openly boasted about what he and Danny did to Mark and wore as a badge of honour, the fact that he could have been reported to the police. In the hall and on the playground, people would make comments like, "Hamer kicked your ass" and "Are you going to do me for assault and battery?" One occasion, when Mark tried to join in a game of basketball, Andy Millenberg was there to growl, "Get out of here, sweetie Leversee!" Another boy named Matt Macadam, who was in Mrs Neil's class, would say things like, "Nice bike" and "Where did you get that bike from?"

whenever he saw Mark riding on Danny's bike. For the most part, Mark ignored these things, as he knew that he had been the victim.

Then came the news that the bike shop wasn't able to fix Mark's bike. His mother stated that the people responsible for breaking the bike in the first place should buy Mark a new one. The problem was that Mark couldn't keep his mother's thoughts to himself and told several people that Danny and David were buying him a new bike. Naturally, the news reached the two boys. Danny, whose family was of modest means, seemed okay with that prospect. However, David, the rich kid, blew his top upon hearing it.

"I'm not buying you a new bike!" he ranted. "I'm going to tell my father and he'll get the police," he raged further. "You're trying to jip me!" At every opportunity, David would say it to Mark.

If Mark's mind hadn't been as it was, he would have noticed how stupid and hypocritical David was sounding. Furthermore, he would have also known that if he said such things, David would have been the first one to ridicule him over it and the other kids would have sided with David. Instead, he did his best to ignore David's rants. Unfortunately, it didn't stop Mark's mother from going ballistic when she heard that he had been telling everybody about the new bike. In her initial rage, she slapped Mark hard screaming, "You couldn't keep your goddamn mouth shut! You had to tell people." Mark, didn't remember his mother telling him not to say anything, but he knew he couldn't say that. However, from that time on, he didn't tell anyone anything.

David did tell his father about the bike because one day Mr Fitzpatrick showed up at the house stating he would take Mark's bike away and repair it. Several days later, he returned with the bike, now sporting a new seat and stick shift. To the adults, it was the end of the affair. However, it would haunt Mark for a long time while David would continue to wear it as a badge of honour.

Chapter 5

Fights and the End of 5th Grade

While the episode continued to play in Mark's mind, the pain did gradually ease. It was especially helpful when his mother announced a surprise trip to Florida. It never occurred to him where she got the money to afford such a trip, nor did he care. Four days of swimming in the warm Florida sunshine made him forget all about Ramsgate for a while. It was only natural that he didn't want that time to end.

Unfortunately, it did end and he had only been back for a few days before he was wishing he was back in Florida. While David kept his distance, he still made little snide comments at every opportunity. Like the time he refused to read out a story he had written because he feared ridicule from the other pupils, David immediately called him a "baby." Worse however, was the fact that most of the class, led by Andrew Blumenthaw, still called him Marvin, because they knew it got to him.

Another boy in his class named Jack Glaughlin, took over from Danny Hamer in being fed up with Mark's perceived weirdness and lying. It started when the boys in the class were allowed to play basketball one play period. Before they began playing, Mark blurted out that he had organised an undefeated basketball team. In reality, Mark wasn't lying. Back in Woodhaven Heights, he got some kids from his street and played two basketball games against kids from a street nearby, which his team won. As usual though, he never got the chance to explain that part and was immediately branded a liar and Jack went on about it more than the rest.

Jack was so fed up about it that he called Mark out to a fight. Having been beaten up barely a month earlier, he refused the fight. However, Jack didn't give up so easily and kept on all morning and throughout lunch break. Keith Wenger, who had been a good friend to Mark weeks earlier, showed his two-faced nature by trying to pressure Mark into accepting the fight.

"You accepted Hamer and Fitzpatrick, who not him?" Keith wondered.

"I didn't accept, Hamer just attacked me," Mark clarified in reply.

Keith gave a look that said he didn't believe it. He carried on goading Mark by taunting, "You're just a sweetie." Jack took the cue and parroted Keith in calling him a sweetie.

Mark tried to walk away from them, but he walked straight into Gene Lancaster. "What are they saying to you?" Gene asked, appearing as if was offering a helping hand.

"They're trying to get me to fight him," Mark identified, pointing to Jack.

Instead of helping, Gene suddenly sided with the Jack and Keith. Now there were three of them trying to goad Mark into a fight with Jack. However, he did find some help when Tim Folder saw what was going on and offered, "I'll protect you."

"No you won't!" Keith interjected. "This is between Glaughlin and Leversee."

Keith's threatening stance was enough to deter Tim from making any more offers of help. The three then returned to harass Mark into a fight, which carried on until it was time to go back into school. Fortunately, he remembered he had an optician's appointment after school that day so he was able to say, "I can't fight, I have to go to the eye doctor after school."

Mark's excuse only temporarily put the three off. Keith suggested, "What about tomorrow, or do you have an appointment to get your head examined?"

Mark said nothing to this, but now, not only had he had to endure the original three, Gene began broadcasting the news of a fight around the rest of the class. When David Fitzpatrick heard about this, he was the first to egg Jack on further.

"Even if he won't accept, beat him up anyway," David offered and then to reassure Jack he ventured, "If Folder tries to interfere, then I'll beat him up myself."

The truth was that Mark actually did have an optician's appointment that afternoon, so the fight everyone was so badly craving was delayed for a day. Gene was quick to remind him that he would be fighting Jack the next day. But when the next day came, any idea of a fight seemed to dissipate. Jack's hostility no longer seemed to be focused on Mark, but on David instead. He declared that he was fed up with David's big mouth and how he always hid behind his friends when opening it. Therefore, it was he whom Jack wanted to fight after school. However, the fight never happened, as, true to form, David made sure he had Andrew Blumenthaw and co. around after school to make sure Jack didn't start a fight. Mark was just glad that the focus was off him.

David might have been cheated out of seeing Mark beaten up in another fight and he soon forgot that he could have been beaten up himself, but he still took every opportunity to humiliate Mark. Humiliation ranged from small things such as the time the class was asked to draw a picture of a human struggle, Mark decided to draw a picture of the Battle of Little Big Horn, mainly because some automatically assumed that he would draw a picture of his hero Selmo White.

When David saw his picture, he openly announced to the class, "Marvin's playing cowboys and Indians."

Humiliation also went to larger things like when they went to Glanville Avenue School, the other elementary school in Ramsgate to see a play put on by the pupils there. While everybody huddled in small groups around the school, David suggested to Andrew, "Let's tell them all about Leversee."

Andrew needed no further prompting and he began to broadcast to the Glanville Avenue pupils nearby, "He thinks the Statue of Liberty is thirty feet tall. He says he broke the world running record and he thinks Jim Lebversea is his cousin."

When Andrew had finished, David gladly picked up the baton. "He said his grandfather was the world champion at miniature golf and he was in a movie on the Dr Fright Show."

Mark felt powerless to do anything and just wanted to disappear as he could see the bemused grins of some of the Glanville Avenue pupils. One boy asked him if he really thought the Statue of Liberty was thirty feet tall. Mark simply shook his head as it wasn't worth trying to explain. What he didn't realise was the implications it would all have when he went to middle school the following September.

At least Jack had gone from wanting to punch Mark's face in to being his friend a few weeks later. The same was true for Keith and Gene. They would go to Mark's house and then usually to the nearby playground to play basketball. Mark began to feel some sense of normality and was inwardly glad that David was denied the chance to see a fight involving him.

If David, or anyone else at Confederate Avenue School wanted to see a fight, they didn't have to go very far. It seemed there was at least one fight a week and sometimes as many as four at the school at the end of the day. Usually, it was the younger kids, third and fourth graders mainly, but other grades would feature as well. Nor was it limited strictly to the boys- the girls were almost just as likely to go at it. Often times, Mark would watch the fights and if he knew any of the combatants, cheered them on. He wasn't alone as fighting was the main source of entertainment for the kids at the school.

Fortunately, Mark was never involved in any of those fights, which occurred over the next few months. Unfortunately, he was at home sick and missed seeing David Fitzpatrick get his comeuppance when Tim beat him up in a fight. He would have loved to have seen that and he would have been very vocal in cheering Tim on. Tim's mistake was trying to have a rematch a few weeks later. This time, David had Andrew, Guy and David McDonnell with him and the four of them made sure it was Tim who went home crying.

The only real problem that Mark had in those few weeks was Andrew's immediate assumption that he would be no good at baseball. One morning he heard Andrew spouting, "Leversee, I bet he couldn't hit a ball over that fence," pointing to a fence that was very close by. "I mean look at him," Andrew carried on, "Blue pants and green sneakers." Mark said nothing as he was running through in his mind how the fact that his pants didn't match his footwear had anything to do with his ability at playing baseball.

He continued to hang around with Tim, Gene, Jack and Keith, which was branded the "Gay Patrol" by Guy Rialto. Guy told his entire group the new name and soon many people were using that for Mark and his friends. Therefore, he was glad when the school broke up for Easter holiday. However, the Easter break brought a worsening of things for Mark.

It all started when he was playing baseball at Todd

LeMatt's house. He was playing with Todd and a boy he didn't know called Adam. Later, three girls and a boy joined them. Two of the girls were in his class, Lisa Horner and Amy Lornstein. The third girl was in the other fifth grade class and Mark knew her as Dawn Weiskoff and the boy was Amy's younger brother, David.

At first, everything seemed to be going well until Mark made a bad throw. He heard Dawn mutter under her breath to Lisa, "He's real good" in a sarcastic tone. She made a similar comment when his lack of motor skills let him down again and he missed a catch. When he missed a second catch, Dawn sarcastically asked him, "What's wrong Marvin, can't you catch?"

The combined frustration of missing those balls and Dawn's taunting seemed to scramble Mark's mind. The other two girls were now laughing at him and Adam now calling him "Marvin the Monster" compounded this. Starting to lose control, he shouted at Dawn, "Leave me alone, bird turd!" He picked up the name from his cousin who lived in Pennsylvania when he visited there recently.

"Bird turd, what rough language," Todd commented.

Amy and Lisa found the term very amusing and began chanting "Bird turd" back at him. Amy's brother and Dawn joined in with it as well. Frustrated by the fact that the name had not only been unsuccessful, it had been turned around and used against him, his frustration mounted to near boiling point and his mind went into overload. Totally flustered, he flipped his middle finger at them and when that had no effect he thumbed his nose. When that didn't have the desired effect, he did both. Everyone only laughed at this increasing his frustration further. In now total temper, he threw a stick at the girls hitting all three across the legs.

"Jerk off!" yelped Dawn, her face turning scarlet underneath her curly brown hair, which Mark thought looked grey as she charged at him.

You couldn't have called it much of a fight. Dawn's first blow only knocked Mark's glasses off his face and he retaliated with two rights to her face. Realising that she wasn't going to win, Dawn threw one more punch, which was largely ineffectual and then ran away.

"Pussy, you're running away," Mark chided feeling victorious.

Dawn said nothing and the others simply looked on in amusement. Todd decided to call it a day and Mark decided he had enough and got on his bike to go home. However, before he went Lisa informed him, "I'm going to tell lies to Miss Erichetti. I'm going to say you broke a window and that you kicked a dog."

Although he outwardly ignored Lisa's threats, a small worry niggled at his mind while he rode home. Upon relaying the events of that afternoon to his mother, she assured him that even if Lisa did tell Miss Erichetti those lies, the teacher couldn't do anything about it because it didn't happen at school. However, a new worry entered his mind and bothered him for the rest of the break. Even though most fight judges would have given Mark the decision on points from his brief fisticuffs with Dawn Weiskoff, he worried that she would tell everyone that she kicked his ass. He knew that whatever he said to the contrary, the masses would believe her.

When school resumed the following week, Mark was relieved not to hear anyone mentioning his fight with Dawn. He concluded that she knew that it was a lie. Besides, he had a credible witness in Todd who could have said what actually happened, or at least he hoped so.

It was never known if Lisa told her proposed lies to Miss Erichetti, but the teacher did seem to be on Mark's case more than usual when school started back. On the second day back, she wrote a quote, "This is the first day of the rest of your life" on the blackboard. Mark stood by the coat hooks reading and rereading the quote, contemplating its meaning in case the teacher asked questions about it in class. Despite the fact that there was still plenty of time before the start of school and only three other children in the room, it didn't stop her from growling, "Hurry up, slowpoke!"

"I was reading that," he squeaked pointing to the board.

"It doesn't take that long to read it," she barked in rebuke.

This was only the beginning. The next day, Mark innocently forgot to take his spelling homework home with him and when he confessed it to the teacher, she immediately flew into a rage.

"You're not having play period for a week!" she bellowed at him. Then she inquired of the rest of the class, "Anyone else not do the homework like knucklehead here?" That question brought smirks to many faces around the classroom.

True enough, Miss Erichetti stuck to her word and kept Mark off play period that week. He had to sit on the ground and read a book while the rest of the class enjoyed the session. One day, when Miss Erichetti hadn't yet come out to the playground, an argument between the two teams started. When she did come out, she asked him if there had been any arguments and he confirmed there had. She gave the class a dressing down about it after play period and while no one openly blamed Mark, he was sure something must have been said. That was because the very next day at play period, she came up to him and said, "I don't want to hear about your mouth getting involved in the game."

The fact that he tended to perceive the world differently to others combined with his difficulty in explaining what was in his mind also made him the subject of ridicule in the classroom. It was during an English lesson where the class was given an end phrase to a sentence and they had to come up with a beginning to it. The obvious answers, "I saw rain falling on a pond" and "I heard" went quickly. However, the teacher was still digging for more answers from the class. Mark thought he had an answer and put his hand up. When acknowledged, he gave the answer, "At camp, we saw rain falling on a pond," but when he saw the look on the teacher's face, it was evident that she thought he didn't.

"What do you mean?" she asked in that condescending tone of hers.

Desperately, he tried to explain. "What I mean is that when we looked out of our tents, we saw rain falling on a pond," he stammered. But the teacher's look only led him to realise that he was only digging himself deeper into a hole. While she didn't say anything, her shaking of her head gave the rest of the class the cue to laugh hysterically, humiliating him.

It probably had no connection with what went on in the classroom, but Mark was seen by a woman from the Child Study Team and the school psychologist. In both cases, he was given a series of tests, which he came through with flying colours. Therefore, the "experts" concluded that Mark didn't have Asperger's Syndrome even though they failed to take into account that Mark thrived on one to one situations.

Even when the school psychologist came to the classroom, he didn't see anything out of the ordinary regarding Mark. It didn't help that Andrew Blumenthaw stole the limelight by telling everyone how awful his home life was. Like Keith, he was the youngest of three boys, but unlike Keith, his parents seemed to be harder on him. To most of the class, it explained Andrew's attention seeking behaviour in the classroom. Because he was the popular kid, he was given a lot more sympathy from the others, which Mark knew he would never have gotten. Instead, it would have been assumed that he was lying.

To Miss Erichetti, the findings of all the experts only went to show that Mark was just lazy and not working to the best of his ability. She seemed to intensify her onslaught on him even singling him out for things that weren't his fault. When he did a project with Gene and Jack on Death Valley, which turned out to be wrong, she seemed to hold him solely responsible for the entire thing. During the two weeks he and Tim were captains for play period, whenever there was an issue regarding it, she would look to him and him only as if it was all his fault. Mark felt that she was picking on him by singling him out all of the time and as always; the other children picked up on it and used it against him.

He thought the teacher would have shown some appreciation when he fulfilled her request to bring in a cowboy hat to be used in some school production. Instead, Miss Erichetti simply dismissed it with a gruff, "We don't need it now," not even thanking him for at least offering. Therefore, having to take the hat home at lunch made him the target of more ridicule. Even though he didn't wear the hat and those in his class knew why he had brought it, it didn't stop kids in other classes from taunting Mark about it.

"I'm an old cowhand," a fifth grader named Mark Rossman sang fairly badly. It sent his two friends into wild laughter.

There were similar taunts, especially from the

younger children. All the while, Mark tried to process in his mind why they couldn't understand that he only brought the cowboy hat into school at the request of his teacher. Then it happened, as soon as he put the hat in his bicycle basket, Guy Rialto's younger brother, Matt, snatched it out and ran off laughing. Mark ran after Matt and caught up with him straight away. Matt threw a punch at Mark who retaliated, although neither blow was really effective.

"Leave him alone!" hollered a voice nearby. Mark turned to see a boy he knew as Tommy Allen coming over to square up to him. Tommy was about the same size as Mark and had bright red hair and freckles to match. He also had a reputation for being a good fighter.

"He took my hat," Mark began to protest.

Tommy showed no emotion in response to what he said and simply reacted, "I don't care, if you touch him, I'm gonna beat the shit out of you."

Mark hesitated while a response formed in his head. Remembering the episode involving Danny Hamer and David Fitzpatrick, he came back with, "If you do that, I'll have you arrested for assault and battery."

A smirk crossed Tommy's face as he sneered, "Go ahead and arrest me. Your mother's a pussy and your father's a pussy." Then he muttered under his breath but loud enough for Mark to hear, "I'll salt your battery."

Frustration led to confusion as Mark saw that the threat of arrest wasn't going to deter Tommy. Meanwhile, Matt Rialto saw his chance and fled still holding the hat. Mark immediately got on his bike to pursue him and was glad that Tommy didn't try to stop him. However, he did yell, "If I hear that you beat him up, then you're dead" and to Matt, he simply instructed, "Ditch him!"

Mark chased the boy several blocks before he caught up with him. When he did, there was no confrontation; Matt simply gave back the hat. The reason why was never known. Maybe he got tired of playing games or that he didn't want to have to explain to his parents where he had gotten a cowboy hat from. In any case, Mark knew that it wasn't because Matt was fearful of a beating; he was just glad to get the hat back.

He thought the whole affair was over, but when he returned to school after lunch, he found that he couldn't have been more wrong. While out on the playground, he was confronted by David Fitzpatrick, Alan Fishman, Guy Rialto and some fourth grader who he knew only as Damico.

"As usual, David led the procession. "Are you going to have us arrested for assault and battery if we beat you up?" he asked menacingly.

Before Mark could answer, Alan intervened with, "You're a pussy."

"No, I'm not!" Mark began to protest.

"Yes, you are," David affirmed. "And we should beat you up because you pick on little kids."

No, I don't," Mark protested again.

"Oh yeah, I saw you picking on Guy's brother," David informed him.

"He started it," Mark barked in defence while at the same time looking anxiously at Guy.

"Yeah, yeah," came David's disbelieving response.

Then the round-faced Damico joined in. "My sister says she's being picked on by you."

"I don't even know your sister," Mark clarified.

Ignoring the response, the chubby Damico continued, "She says she is being picked on by Marvin Leversee and he has black hair and glasses just like you."

"Your sister's a liar!" Mark hit back.

Damico said nothing, but Alan rejoined the conversation by challenging, "I call you out."

Before he realised what he had said, Mark accepted the challenge. With a big grin on his face, David ended things and walked off, obviously delighted by the fact that he caused Mark to be in a fight after school.

Somehow, Mark managed to put the impeding fight to the back of his mind that afternoon. Nothing was said about it until the very end of the day when David asked, "Are you fighting him?" when the class was lining up to go home.

Upon hearing David, Matt Osmond's ears pricked up and turning around he asked, "Who you fightin'?"

"Alan Fishman," David answered for Mark.

"Alan Fishman," Matt repeated, with a grin.

Anxiety flooded through Mark's veins as he began to worry about what would happen once he left the building. At first, he was relieved there was no sign of Alan when he got outside. Having arranged to meet Jack and Gene after school, he walked with them to get his bike. When he got bicycle racks, Alan was sitting at there waiting. Upon seeing Mark, Alan simply said, "Oooh, right, let's go." In the meantime, David had broadcast the news of an impending fight; therefore the grass plot where fights took place was full of expectant spectators. Mark felt he had no choice but to oblige.

Alan was on the grass plot bouncing up and down in anticipation. "Come on Leversee," he baited as he shifted his weight from one foot to the other.

In a futile attempt to defuse, Gene pleaded, "Come on, you know you can take him," but Alan paid no attention.

Mark simply handed his glasses to Jack and entered the circle that was formed by all the fight fans. While Alan continued to dance around baiting Mark, something inside of Mark's brain snapped. Whether it was the events at lunch, being falsely accused of bullying little kids or events before that, he was now seeing red. To everyone's surprise, he charged Alan and made a well-executed tackle taking Alan to the ground.

He was like an animal, fists flailing away on Alan's head. Even when Alan managed to reverse things and straddle him, delivering a blow to Mark's mouth, Mark somehow found strength he didn't know he possessed and rolled back on top. Then spurred on by the surprise that he had a much bigger cheering section than he anticipated, Mark renewed his fury on Alan and when an adult finally broke them up, it was Mark who had to be pulled off Alan, who now sported a purple eye.

Andrew Blumenthaw was the first to congratulate Mark, as did so many others, on his victory. Even Tommy Allen said he was impressed. On the way home, Jack and Gene gave him celebrity status. Naturally, Mark soaked up the adulation because for the first time since arriving in Ramsgate more than six months earlier, he had a moment of glory.

Like all moments, Mark's moment of glory rapidly faded away. After a few weeks, kids like Todd coming up to him and saying, "You killed Fishman," dwindled away to nothing. While David Fitzpatrick now left him alone, he did try to escalate a minor playground disagreement between him and Gene into a fight. However, neither Mark nor Gene wanted a fight. Otherwise, things went on as normal.

Three weeks later, Mark's victory was a distant memory. This became clear one day when he was playing baseball in the playground one-lunch break. Andrew Blumenthaw had been right: Mark knew he wasn't good at baseball; his year playing little league at Woodhaven Heights told him that. So he shouldn't have been surprised when he struck out when he came

84

to bat. What made it bad was the fact the pitcher was a girl named Monique Purvis.

Suddenly a crowd of children who had been nearby surrounded him. "How come a girl struck you out?" teased Kim Havers.

"It's because he's so gay," Andy Millenberg answered sarcastically.

"He's gay because he wears black shoes with white socks," observed a boy named Damon Bates.

The resounding laughter resulting from Damon's statement and the crowd pressing upon him began to send Mark's mind into a panic. Not knowing what else to do, he flipped his middle finger at them. Most of the crowd simply laughed and some of them flipped their middle fingers back in response. However, Damon seemed to take offence at the gesture and shoved him.

"Start a fight with him, Bates," Andy encouraged.

"He thinks he can take anyone because he beat up Alan Fishman," Kim added.

Obediently, Damon rolled hands into fists and moved in on Mark. David was tall, an inch taller than Mark, but just as thin. His normally sad looking eyes narrowed sadistically as he spat, "I'm going to kill you, Leversee."

Mark braced himself for the expected barrage of punches from Damon's fists, but they never came. At the last moment, Damon's hands were stayed by the voice of George Lane commanding him not to do it. Immediately, eyes turned on George and there was a muffled "Goody two-shoes" comment from someone in the crowd. Feeling the need to explain, George whispered, "I got shit off Quartz for not stepping in when Hamer and Fitzpatrick beat him up."

Andy nodded and redirected his attention back onto Mark and started new verbal onslaught on him. Nasty comments came thick and fast; so fast that Mark couldn't recover before the next one came. Seeing that George wasn't going to step in, he retreated inwardly in a vain attempt to stop the nasty comments getting through. Illogically, he ran a fantasy through his mind of his toy soldiers coming to life and shooting all of his tormentors. Realistically, he knew that this wouldn't happen and paralysed by not knowing what to do, he endured the abuse until the crowd got tired of it. That didn't happen until five minutes before the end of lunch.

Fortunately, that was the last major humiliation Mark had to endure, although he had to bear lots of low level taunting. Matt Macadam, usually with Jimmy Brown in tow, took every opportunity to tell Mark he was an asshole. Renee Tye would constantly wave her hands in his face making silly noises and Andrew Blumenthaw was there to remind him how much he sucked at baseball. Then there was the introduction evening at Bernard A. Tye School, the junior high school he would be attending in September.

For Mark, the experience of moving to junior high school excited him and he felt grown up the moment he walked into the school's gymnasium and saw the electric scoreboard. The principal, Mr Tasker, was a tall, thin, bald, assertive-sounding man, but his words were very welcoming. When Mr Tasker opened up the floor to questions, Mark felt comfortable about asking anything. Unfortunately for him, what entered his mind that moment was the memory of Miss Erichetti forbidding the class from going to the local drug store during lunch because on one occasion, Liz Clover, Lisa Horner and two other girls had gone there for lunch and returned to school late. In his mind, he wanted to know where he was allowed and not allowed to go during lunch. However, as typical with his mind, he chose the wrong words when he asked, "Are we allowed to eat lunch at the drug store?"

While nobody laughed and Mr Tasker assured him that any acceptable place was fine for lunch, some kids had fun with it the next day. David Fitzpatrick broadcasted it to everyone in the class who hadn't been there, resulting in much laughter at Mark's expense and Steve McGuire calling him a "dumb ass." Then there were the likes of Mark Rossman and Jimmy Brown who constantly repeated, "Can we eat at the drugstore?" every time they saw Mark. Fortunately, those taunts only lasted the day.

Mark expected more grief after his mother broke up a fight one day. It was between Jack's brother George and Matt Rialto and was probably fought to decide who was the toughest kid in third grade. Mark was having great delight in watching Matt Rialto getting beat up at the hands of George Glaughlin, but his mother didn't want to wait for the fight to end. Therefore, she stepped in to break it up. However, many of the kids watching didn't want the fight broken up and threw their bodies in front of Mrs Leversee to bar her from getting to the combatants. Andrew Blumenthaw added his two cents by demanding, "Let'em fight."

Not about to let a bunch of punk kids dictate to her, Mrs Leversee barged through the wall of bodies and pulled George and Matt apart. Not content with that, once the fighters were separated, she turned to the crowd and hollered, "You disrespectful kids!" The shrill volume of her voice stunned the masses assembled. Disgusted, she beckoned to Mark to follow her to the car. He obeyed, but inwardly began to worry about what shit he was going to get the next day about his mother breaking up the fight.

Only one person said anything to Mark about it the next day. That person was Damico, who with the sister Mark was supposed to have picked on, teased, "Your mother came and broke up the fight." The sister thought it was funny, but Mark thought that Damico just sounded stupid. Therefore, he didn't respond and concluded that the reason no one else said anything to him about it was the fear of another tongue lashing off his mother.

The month of June couldn't go by fast enough for everyone. The only memorable events those last few weeks were Mark's birthday party, where he had Tim, Jack, Gene, Keith and Todd in attendance and Tim returning to Texas. Mark was sad to see his friend go. Whether it was the fact that school was about to end or fear of his mother, Mark was left alone those last few weeks. Still, when the last day came, no one was gladder than Mark to see school come to an end.

Chapter 6

The First Summer

The summer didn't start out too well for Mark. On the first day of summer vacation, he went to see Todd and while Todd wasn't openly hostile towards him, every time he missed a ball when they were playing baseball, Todd would yell, "You bite it raw, Leversee!" Later Todd did give some insight as to why he was distant towards Mark when he moaned, "I can't believe you invited Wenger to your party."

Mark later learned that Todd and Keith had a fight a long time before he had even moved to Ramsgate, but he wasn't to know that. However, that didn't seem to matter to Todd who was unforgiving about it. To make matters worse, David Fitzpatrick showed up and joined them. As a result, Mark got pushed to one side and felt isolated. When he left, he was certain that he had lost Todd's friendship.

It wasn't just Todd's friendship that Mark thought he had lost. A few days later, after having a good time on the beach with Jack, he went to his house afterwards and joined the kids in Jack's neighbourhood in playing kick the can. Some of the kids in the neighbourhood weren't too welcoming of Mark. The worst of these were two brothers named Jim and Danny Benjamin. Jim was in Mark's grade at school and was friends with Alan Fishman. He resented the fact that Mark had beaten up his friend and the same was true with younger brother Danny, who was also friends with Matt Rialto. Both brothers were therefore clued up on what a weirdo Mark was.

Things were okay at first; there was an uneasy peace

between Mark and the Benjamin brothers. The first instance of trouble started when Mark caught some other boy he didn't know blatantly cheating at the game. When he protested, the others sided with the cheater. Then when Danny beat him to the can one time, Danny taunted, "What's wrong sweetie, you too slow?"

Mounting frustration bulit up inside him and the block between his brain and mouth surfaced yet again. "I quit!" he shouted, not really meaning it.

This seemed to be the moment the brothers were waiting for. Immediately, they instigated a chorus of "Marvin is a sweetie," which everybody joined in with. Jack only stopped to correct them that his name was Mark. Whether it was gang mentality or the fear of losing face in front of his friends, Jack joined in with the "Mark is a sweetie" chant.

Starting to become wound up, Mark tried to ignore the taunts and went to get his bike to leave. However, Danny barred his way. When Mark tried to go around, Danny gave him a push. Naturally Mark pushed him back. Danny retaliated by punching Mark in the stomach who hit back with a blow to the head that sent Danny reeling backwards. That punch was all the excuse Jimmy needed to come to the aid of his little brother. No punches were thrown, but Jim did push Mark and slap him several times. When Mark complained, Jim responded, "You hit my brother" and Mark's justification, "He hit me first" made no difference.

Then seeing one of the other boys tip his bike over and Danny jumping on it infuriated Mark further. He rushed past Jim and got his bike before anyone had a chance to do anything else to it. After a quick examination, Mark yelled to the warned the crowd, "If it's broken, you'll all pay for it."

"I like to see you make me," Danny snapped.

"I'll get the police," Mark informed remembering events from a few months ago.

"Oh, I'm shaking," retorted the cheater sarcastically.

No more was said and Mark rode home feeling very upset. He relayed what happened to his mother who listened but made it clear she wasn't going to do any more and simply advised Mark not to play there. She seemed more bothered that her son was giving her more worry.

Naturally, he didn't contact Jack for several weeks and made no attempt to contact Gene. He did visit Keith one day and had a great time on Keith's sailboat. However, when Keith told Mark to grab the bowline, his problem with mental blocks causing him to forget small details came back to haunt him as he temporarily forgot what a bowline was. That was enough for Keith to conclude that Mark didn't know anything about boats and while they enjoyed the rest of the day, they didn't meet up for the rest of the summer.

It didn't bother Mark that he saw little of his school friends, he still enjoyed the summer. He had the beach to go to and because he was now eleven, he was allowed to go on his own as the beach was only two blocks away. When he wasn't on the beach, he was fishing with his grandfather on his grandfather's boat. Both grandfather and grandson showed a great sense of pride when Mark caught his first flounder. He made many temporary friendships since he lived in an area where there were a lot of summer rentals. Therefore, with the summer bringing its usual tirade of visitors to the Jersey shore, Mark would find a boy his own age who had come to visit for the week and make friends with him. Furthermore, his relatives from Pennsylvania would visit as they had a free place to stay when spending a week by the shore. Besides, many of the adults could go to the casinos at Atlantic City, which wasn't too far away. What was better for Mark was when his relatives came, they would go to the boardwalk at nearby Bay City. Mark was really enjoying the summer.

Ugly reminders of school would sometimes rear their heads while he enjoyed the summer. On the odd occasion, he would see Guy Rialto at the beach and while Guy didn't give him any grief, he would still refer to him as Marvin. Consequently, others on the beach automatically assumed that was his name. Another time at the beach, he ran into Damon Bates who was with some kid Mark didn't know. Damon identified Mark to his friend as "the fairy of our school." There was also the time when he was out fishing with his grandfather; they stopped into one of the docks so granddad could replenish his cigars. They were greeted by a gang of young people, one of them Steve McGuire. Nothing was said while the boat was docked, but as they were leaving, Mark could hear Steve saying "Goodbye Marvin" in a condescending tone.

Then there was the time he took his sister to the nearby playground one evening. After having a good time on the rides, Mark noticed a baseball game going on. Curious, he stopped to watch. The moment they got close, they saw a girl whom Mark knew as Susan Piltro who called out to no one in particular, "It's Marvin Leversee and his stupid sister."

Mark paid no attention to this and watched the game, but while he concentrated, he did not notice that Susan had alerted others of his presence. Soon eight children surrounded him, the leader being a girl from his old class named Carol Kray.

"What are you doing here, Marvin?" the slender Carol asked under her long, straight blonde hair.

"Just going to the playground," Mark muttered.

"Going to the playground," a pint sized, male version of Carol, obviously her brother, repeated in a funny voice.

A familiar anxiety began to take hold of his mind, giving him flashbacks of the school playground as the crowd pressed in on him. Then, out of nowhere, a rock bounced at his feet. He looked in the direction it came only to see Susan throw another stone at his feet. This time she ordered, "Dance Marvin."

Mark did not comply, but many of the others saw what was happening and decided to join in with Susan. A cascade of rocks began careening around his feet with repeated calls of "Dance Marvin." The stones were coming in too fast for Mark to reach down and throw any back and he worried about his sister getting hit. This gave him a moment of indecision until Susan instructed, "Be careful not to hit his sister."

Instinctively, he moved toward his sister, his intention being to get her and go home. As he tried to avoid the rocks bouncing at his feet, Carol's brother stated, "He's trying to use his sister as a shield."

"He's a pussy," some other boy remarked.

Mark got his sister, but not before a large stone struck him in the small of the back. He gave an involuntary yelp before turning and crying, "I'll get the police on you for that!" With that, he took Leslie by the hand and left, ignoring some of the comments like, "He's gonna put us in jail."

It was Leslie who told their mother about what happened at the park. Upon seeing the welt on his back where the last rock had hit him, Mrs Leversee grew angry and suddenly disappeared. She returned about half an hour later. He listened with great delight to his mother tell how she tore stripes off his tormentors and he was not surprised when she referred to Carol as a

93

"mouthy bitch." He was glad that Carol and the others involved got a tongue lashing from his mom.

After that, Mark had no more incidents with people from school, for which he was grateful. He continued to go to the beach and go fishing with his grandfather, which he really enjoyed. By sheer chance, he ran into Jack and both boys acted as if the incident at the beginning of the summer never happened.

The final few weeks of summer vacation saw Mark's evening taken up by football practice as he attempted to play for the Ramsgate Colts. Several boys he knew were surprised to see that he had gone out for football and most immediately predicted that he wouldn't make the team. Practices in Ramsgate were different to those at Woodhaven Heights and the unfamiliar took him out of this comfort zone as the first practice showed. He couldn't seem to do anything right. Fortunately, Mark was able to pick things up quick and practices immediately improved. At one point, he was selected as a possible starter at offensive tackle, but that didn't last. His grandfather, when he came to watch a practice, gave him great encouragement by telling him he was as good as half of the boys trying out. Even Danny Hamer said a few words of encouragement, though Guy Rialto insisted he sucked. But Mark had the last laugh after he survived the first cut.

Chapter 7

The 6th Grade

Only having seen Tye School at night, Mark admired the sprawling one storey building as the car drove up. He now felt more grown up as he was entering middle school. The first person he recognised was a tall boy named Glen Baxter, whom he knew from football. Glen acknowledged Mark's enthusiastic "hello" with a neutral "hi." Mark thought nothing more about that as he walked around the school and into the main playground.

Tye School's playground probably covered more of an area than Confederate Avenue School's playground, but it didn't always appear that way owing to the awkward shape of the school buildings. Once out in the open space, he scanned the area looking for anyone who might be a friendly face. He probably looked like a lost puppy as he wandered about desperately looking this way and that. His concentration was so intense, he almost didn't notice when he walked into a crowd of boys he knew.

"Hey Marvin!" called the familiar voice of Andrew Blumenthaw. He then asked, "Are you looking forward to school?"

Slightly surprised that there were no snide questions or comments, Mark meekly answered, "Yes." However, the presence of others in Andrew's group such as Andy Millenberg, Matt Macadam and Guy Rialto, to name a few, made him feel rather uncomfortable. But much to his relief, the group moved on allowing him to continue his search for friendlier faces.

The encounter sharpened his senses to the point where he was not only now looking for friendly faces, but looking to avoid hostile ones too. He found himself steering clear of a group of girls that included Carol Kray, Donna Bassoni and Amy Lornstein. He did cross the path of Steve McGuire and John Lodge, but walked past as Steve was saying, "I saw you in your dinky boat."

It wasn't until the children started clearing the playground that Mark found Jack. With no time to talk or look for reinforcements, the two followed the large procession of kids into the school gym, which was now packed with every kid in the school. The sheer number of children in the gym began to play upon Mark's anxieties until the soothing voice of Mr Tasker chased them away.

"Welcome to a new year," the principal proclaimed cheerfully. He paused for a second to allow the inevitable groans. He then continued, "To the new sixth graders, we hope you will enjoy your three years at Tye School and welcome back to the seventh and eighth graders. We will now assign you to your classes."

A taller man with thinning black hair stepped beside the principal who announced him as Mr Fluyt before proceeding to read the names of the pupils in his class. It most likely did Mark a world of good to have his name called to the very first class. Otherwise, his anxiety levels would have risen with each class where his name wasn't called and he would have begun to fear that he had been missed out and that might have had some bad repercussions for him.

His excitement about being in junior high school prevented the realisation that none of his friends were in his class until long after the first day formalities were concluded. Many of his new classmates were from Glanville Avenue School, which presented an unknown entity for him. Then there were the ones he did know like Steve McGuire, Matt Osmond, Mark Rossman, George Lane's sister Mary, but worst of all, Carol Kray, all in his class. He did try to look on the bright side and was glad he didn't have the likes of David Fitzpatrick, Andrew Blumenthaw or Andy Millenberg in his class. It was bad enough he had to see Andy every evening at football practice.

Mark found his comfort zone quite quickly in his new class. He found Mr Fluyt to be the anti Miss Erichetti, for which he was extremely glad. He also thought that having a male teacher was cool too. Therefore, he was able to ignore a remark made by a tall red haired girl named Nancy Greenwood who muttered, "You're real smart," after Mark answered a few questions correctly. The added bonus came when he found that Jack was in the partner class. No one could have blamed him for thinking that everything was going to be all right in the new school.

It didn't take long before Mark found that he had been totally wrong. Before school, the very next day, John Lodge and a shorter, stockier boy named David Seinberg, who everyone referred to as Chip, confronted him.

"I know Jim Lebversea isn't your cousin," John accused. Seizing upon Mark's silence, he continued, "I looked it up, he doesn't even spell his name the same way, so you're a liar and a phoney!" He then poked his tongue out at Mark blowing a raspberry, with Chip copying him. They then walked off together with precision before he could piece a reply together. What bothered Mark the most was that he hoped it had all gone away, but with John Lodge, it clearly hadn't. He knew that his joke had backfired and it would always be used against him.

In the days that followed, a new problem reared its

head for Mark. Now eleven, he was beginning a growth spurt and was now growing too fast for what his mother could afford to buy clothes for. As a result, many pairs of trousers didn't reach his shoes and he was now wearing what many called "flood pants." Therefore, everyday when he wore trousers that were deemed too short, many kids would call out, "Where's the flood?" Steve McGuire and a dark wiry boy named Anthony Salvatino were the worst. Matt Osmond began calling him "nylon stretch." Even when he did wear trousers of the acceptable length, Steve would say that he was wearing his father's pants. That was before the children moved the goal posts and determined that trousers now had to cover the shoelaces. Mark felt that he couldn't win and every morning he went to school with the worry over whether his trousers would be long enough.

His mother wasn't very sympathetic either. When Mark complained that he was getting stick over his trousers being too short, she remarked, "Don't let it get to you" or advised him to go along with it by saying "That's right, I'm ready for it" or even, "if you don't like the length of my pants, you buy them for me." He wanted to explain that if he said either of those things, he would get punched, but she wouldn't listen. As for not letting the taunts get to him, he knew that it wasn't possible because whatever was said got through to him.

Steve McGuire didn't just rib him over the length of his trousers. One day Steve, accompanied by Mark Rossman, Anthony Salvatino and a boy named Joe Pellegrini, who was a shorter version of Anthony, accosted him wanting to know his favourite rock group.

"Who is it?" Steve inquired in that patronising tone. "I bet it's the Jonas Brothers."

Mark hesitated for a moment, he did like the Jonas Brothers a little bit, but if he admitted it, he would be exposing himself for more ridicule. Therefore he gave a soft "no."

"He probably likes Justin Beiber," laughed Anthony.

"Lady Gaga," added Joe. Mark shook his head at both suggestions.

"I bet he's into Marilyn Manson, he's a weirdo just like him," Mark Rossman indicated.

Church teachings suddenly entered Mark's mind. He remembered his Sunday school teacher and the church minister both condemning Marilyn Manson. So he responded, "No, he's Satanic."

The other three boys showed no response to his statement, but Anthony's face turned ugly. Through slitted eyes he snarled, "You would think that." The four boys walked off after that and fortunately for Mark, the subject was never brought up again.

Trouser lengths and favourite pop groups weren't the worst things Mark had to contend with. He thought that with half the kids being unknown to him at the start of the school year, they would automatically assume his name to be Mark. However, the pupils who knew him from Confederate Avenue School were determined otherwise.

It first started on the first Friday when Mark's class was going to the morning assembly. His class passed Mrs Benton's class where he discovered that David Fitzpatrick and Tommy Allen to be in that class. On this occasion, they were lined up one behind the other. Tommy whispered to David, "It's Marvin Leversee or Marvin the Monster." Mark was only able to see David give his condescending grin before he passed and was out of sight.

Mark Rossman seemed to be at the forefront of the "Call him Marvin" campaign and had a lot of support from Steve McGuire and Matt Osmond. Not only did they openly call him Marvin, even in the classroom, they happily told everybody else that that was his name. It came as no surprise that by the end of the second week of school; his entire class was referring to him as Marvin. What sealed it for everyone was the lunchtime break when he tried to protest after Tommy Allen had called him Marvin. Tommy silenced him by threatening, "My fist says you're name is Marvin." After that, everyone just called him Marvin, unless they wanted something from him. That was the only time they called him Mark.

Hassle at school infiltrated to football practice as kids who knew him from school began to talk about him. The first instance was when a boy named Mike McComly, who was the starting flanker, said to him out of the blue, "You think you're Selmo White." When surrounding bodies asked for clarification, Mike explained, "McDonnell told me that every time he made a catch, he would do a dance like Selmo White." The explanation caused Mark to get several funny looks from some of the others. After that, some of the team began calling him "Selmo." Although Mark should have felt honoured at being called after his hero, the boys said it in a way which left Mark feeling patronised.

It wasn't just kids from school either. At the first practice, he recognised a boy who was one of those from the Catholic school who had intentionally hurt him playing football several months earlier. Several weeks of practice sessions later, the boy named Richard Bethan recognised him and said to him, "I know your name is Marvin Leversee. You were going to sue us for breaking your glasses. We didn't touch your glasses, you threw them against the pole."

While he couldn't disagree with what Richard had said, what puzzled Mark was why he was bringing it up nearly a year later. Besides, there never had been any lawsuit, nor did he see much of those kids because they all went to the Catholic school. Still, Mark was relieved that most of his teammates who were around to listen didn't seem to take any notice. In spite of these minor instances, Mark enjoyed football and had the last laugh when he learned at the final cut that he had made the team and Andy Millenberg's younger brother hadn't. Although he never heard him, Andy was reported to have said to his brother, "I can't believe they cut you and kept that faggot Leversee."

Nothing, however, was as bad as what he experienced in school. Every morning there was the anxiety of his trousers being long enough and he would be teased for wearing flood pants. Within a few weeks of being in sixth grade, it appeared the entire school now knew him as Marvin and wouldn't have it any other way. Kids would openly say, "His name is Mark, but everyone calls him Marvin." This signalled that it was okay to call him by his former name and Mark felt powerless to do anything about it. It didn't help when people who knew him from Confederate Avenue School told everyone that he had changed his name to Mark because everyone called him "Marvin the Monster." This only confirmed his weakness to everyone.

The name change wasn't the only thing Mark's former classmates from Confederate Avenue School conveyed about him to their counterparts from Glanville Avenue School. They also painted him out to be a terrible liar citing his joke of saying that Jim Lebversea was his cousin. Therefore, when he mentioned he was on the Ramsgate Colts JV team, no one believed him. Jimmy Brown even teased, "Why don't you tell us some of your other stories, like you were in a movie?" His so called other lies were also used against him, so it was no wonder that he was beginning to hate Tye School.

Several things kept him from hating it totally. Classes only lasting forty minutes suited his concentration span quite well as he wasn't forced to stay in the same room for half the day. However, there were times when his concentration didn't last the forty minutes. He liked most of his teachers. While many in his class didn't like Mr Fluyt, Mark liked him and he also liked the partner teacher, Mrs Dorbano, who he had for science and English. He found the specialist teachers to be a case of hit or miss. He liked the gym teacher, Mr Benjamin, despite the fact that he was the father of Jimmy and Danny who had given him grief at Jack's house back in the summer and he wasn't sure of Mr Williams, the shop teacher. But he wasn't too keen on either Mrs Hundle, the art teacher or Mr Povetti, the music teacher. However, none of the teachers were anything like Miss Erichetti and Mark was extremely glad of that.

Teachers at Tye School might have ranged from cool to slightly bearable, but that only took away some of the grief he was getting from other students. Whether it was flood trousers or being called Marvin or some other thing, there was nowhere Mark could escape it at school. It wasn't only his class or his grade; seventh and eighth graders seemed to be in on it too, although they didn't bother him as often.

David Fitzpatrick and Andrew Blumenthaw might not have been in his class, but that didn't stop them from harassing Mark on the playground at lunch. "Is Jim Lebversea still your cousin?" Andrew goaded. "How about Muhammad Ali, is he your uncle?"

Andrew's taunts shouldn't have bothered Mark, but he couldn't help it. It only happened a couple of times, but David still carried on. He still wore the incident involving him and Danny Hamer as a badge of honour and constantly boasted about it to everyone. "Marvin had me done for assault and battery. Me and Hamer messed him up and his mother said she was going to have us arrested." Naturally, no one asked Mark's version of the event and as normal, it gave people more ammunition to use against him. It was at this point Tommy Allen would ask him, "If I beat you up, are you going to press charges?" If Mark answered no, Tommy would respond, "That's what you did to Hamer." He also told anyone, especially all of his friends, "If you beat him up, he has you arrested for assault and battery."

Life continued in this vein for Mark in the first few months of sixth grade. Apart from being called Marvin by practically everybody in Tye School, he also had the daily worry of whether or not his trouser length would lead to him being teased mercilessly for flood pants. This worry soon became an obsession, as every morning he would religiously check to see if they were going to be long enough and he soon found himself trying to avoid wearing certain pairs of pants. His mother would constantly tell him not to let it get to him, but Mark knew that it wasn't possible.

If it wasn't either of these two things, something else was always present to add to his anxieties. For instance, he was never allowed to join in any games at lunchtime. Andy Millenberg saw to that, as he was still upset that Mark had made the Colts over his brother. Even when he tried to join in a boys vs. girls game of "keep away," Andy very sarcastically said, "Sure Leversee" before Dawn Weiskoff ordered, "Get the hell out of here, Marvin." This rubbed off on the other children as one day, the ball came bouncing toward him. Seeing his chance to join in, Mark picked the ball up and began running. He skilfully dodged two girls who tried to get the ball away from him and then threw it to one of the boys. Right away a boy in his class named Danny Berkowitz came up to him and said, "Thank you Marvin, now get the fuck out of here."

There still remained the assumption that he totally sucked at sports when in fact he was quite average. His problem was that he would make a superstar play one day and then make an embarrassingly bad one the next. Of course his classmates, like Steve McGuire and Guy Rialto who was in the partner class, seemed to ignore the good ones but yell at him for the bad ones. It was the same at football practice. One practice, while playing at nose tackle, he blew past the centre and stuffed the running back for a loss. All the coaches sang his praises with compliments like, "Well done, Leversee" and "Good play, Leversee." One coach even went on to say, "If you did that more, you'd start." The next practice, he showed why he didn't start. He badly missed a tackle, leaving the head coach to say, "Leversee, I don't even know what to call that."

Playing football for the Ramsgate Colts Junior Varsity was bittersweet for Mark. Out of the eight games, his team only managed to win one and tie one, losing the other six. However, he got to play in six out of the eight games. He always played on defence and the other team never seemed to run his way when he was in. The one time they did, he managed to hold the ball carrier long enough for the rest of his team to complete the tackle. His last hurrah came on the final practice when he blocked one of Andy Millenberg's punts. When football finished in the November, he had to admit that he did enjoy it, but was also glad he now had his evenings free.

Chapter 8

Rumblings and Retreat

He wasn't sure how it started, except as an argument between Gene and a boy in Gene's class named Stephen Winger, who Mark first mistook for being David Fitzpatrick. It ended up as a fight between Mark and Stephen's friend David Kriss. David Kriss looked a bit like Mark with the same colour hair and glasses but had a darker complexion. He was also teased for his trousers not being long enough, although probably not as mercilessly as Mark was. Therefore, as news of the impending fight spread around the sixth grade, it was billed as a fight between the biggest fag from Confederate Avenue School against the biggest fag from Glanville Avenue.

Mark assumed that the fight would take place on the plot of grass located across the street from the school. That was where the few fights he had witnessed had taken place. David, however, insisted that the fight take place right there in the schoolyard. The amassing crowd, now baying for blood seemed to go along with his idea. Therefore, Mark felt he had no other choice but to fight him there.

Fighting on tarmac meant that Mark couldn't grapple, which was how he took Alan Fishman. This immediately took him out of his comfort zone making him feel somewhat awkward, but it didn't stop him landing a series of blows around David's body. David only managed to land one blow to the side of Mark's face, which only served to anger him into throwing more punches. Many of Mark's blows were ineffectual but he was landing more than his opponent.

Furthermore, he had the backing of most of the kids watching. Unfortunately, an eighth grade teacher broke the fight up before Mark could do anything decisive.

Immediately, Mark and David pointed to one another and collectively accused, "He started it."

The teacher, who stood well over six feet tall, imposed his size on them and cut them short. "I don't care who started it," he boomed. "You don't fight on school property. You can go two or three blocks from here and beat lumps out of each other, but you don't fight here on school property."

Both boys nodded to show they understood, but the teacher wasn't quite finished. "Now, I want you both to go separate ways and I better not see you fighting on the grounds," he warned.

Neither David nor Mark wanted to get into trouble, so they obeyed the teacher's command and went opposite ways. Gene was the first to meet Mark as he was walking away. "You won on points, I scored it 60-2," Gene informed him.

Mark took a little comfort from Gene's words, but he still wasn't convinced he'd won. However, as he passed more people, he received encouraging words from many of the people he passed. "Good fight Marvin," called a thin boy with dark reddish hair named Mike Deacher, who was one of the grade's basketball stars. Feeling more uplifted, he passed more and more kids who were just as complimentary towards him. Glen Baxter seemed to make a really big thing about it and even Nancy Greenwood gave him the thumbs up after telling him, "Good fight." It was the only time he didn't mind being called Marvin and went home from school feeling that he was actually the winner.

Like his victory over Alan Fishman, his one over David Kriss was quickly forgotten. The compliments stopped by the next afternoon, although he did get a twinge of delight when the pretty Kim Beckard, whom he secretly liked, complimented him. Shortly after, things returned to the way they were before the fight. He still went to school every day with the anxiety over whether his trousers would be long enough and he was really beginning to resent being called Marvin. One day, when the entire class seemed to be calling him by his former name, he screamed, "My name isn't Marvin!" But this only encouraged them more and even kids who had called him Mark in the past now called him Marvin.

Naturally, he turned to his mother for support, but there was none coming. "They used to call me worse names like "horse" when I was in school," she explained. "Don't let it bother you, they say it because it does get to you. Besides, what do you want me to do, announce it in assembly?" She didn't seem to realise that he couldn't help letting it get to him and her refusal to help only left him feeling abandoned.

He did his best to ignore being called Marvin and tried hard to fit in. Some in his class realised this and used it to their advantage. They turned him into the class clown by getting him to make funny faces in class. Mark also did impressions of characters from Bugs Bunny and Sesame Street, so children got him to do them. Normally, they picked inappropriate times in class to bait Mark to do these things. Usually, it was done in Mrs Dorbano's lessons, as nobody wanted to upset Mr Fluyt, especially Mark because he liked him. Of course, this changed whenever there was a substitute.

Things eventually went too far and one day, after they got Mark to make a particularly funny face, Nancy Greenwood laughed at it very loudly. Mrs Dorbano scolded Nancy and moved her to another table. After the class, Nancy's friend, Laurie Swords, went to Mrs Dorbano to defend Nancy. "It was him," she stated pointing an accusing finger at Mark. "He was making faces." The teacher stopped Mark and warned him, "I better not have any trouble from you." Her words sent all sorts of thoughts through his mind. He even suspected that Miss Erichetti must have written something in his school records to make Mrs Dorbano say that.

After that, no one egged him on in the classroom. They did get him to do impressions outside the classroom whenever Nancy was around. Each time, she would disgustedly respond, "He got me in trouble with that." If it hadn't been for teacher's intervention, the children in Mark's class would have gotten bored with it eventually. Not long after, any attempt by Mark to pull a face or do an impression was now greeted with hostility. Instead of laughing at Mark's antics, they were now threatening to beat him up if he didn't stop. Some of those who were now most hostile were the very ones who, a few weeks earlier, were encouraging him the most. Mark became very confused by this, as he didn't realise that things lost their impact with others a lot faster than they did with him. The reverse was true as well as they failed to realise that the same things didn't get old with him as quickly. However, the other kids weren't tolerant of this fact.

In spite of all the teasing he was receiving, Mark had no unprovoked threats of violence directed against him, nor did he have to endure being surrounded by crowds of kids who were bent on humiliating him. That was until the last few weeks of autumn. The first instance came when he was riding home from school with Gene. They were making plans as to what to do after school and discussing whom to call and as often was the case with the two of them, they got a bit silly.

Mark was saying, "Yeah, I'll call Jim and then Jack and then I'll call Rodak and Schmodak and Fodak." The first name he got from a character in a science fiction film he had watched.

In the midst of their collective giggle, a voice boomed over them: "What are you talking about?"

Both boys turned to see five eighth graders surrounding them. The boy behind the voice was a tall lad with blonde hair and grey eyes. Obviously focusing on Mark, he again demanded, "What were you saying? What's all this Rodak shit?"

The menacing appearance of this boy and his four friends sent a rush of panic through Mark. He desperately looked for a chance to run but couldn't see any. In desperation, he tried to explain: "I wasn't saying anything about you."

However, the ringleader wasn't interested. "I don't care," he snarled. "I just want to know what you were saying."

"I was just mumbling," Mark tried to justify himself.

"Mumbling what?" the boy asked more aggressively.

Confusion clouded Mark's mind. He knew that he had been talking nonsense with Gene, but he feared further ridicule if he admitted it. If he didn't tell the boy what he wanted to know, he feared physical harm. In sheer panic and confusion, he ventured, "I wasn't saying anything bad about you and if you touch me, I'll have you arrested for assault and battery."

The eighth grader grinned a mischievous grin to his friends, some of whom laughed. Turning back to Mark, he informed, "I'm not going to hurt you, I just want to know what you said."

Feeling slightly less intimidated, Mark ventured, "I was making a joke with him," pointing to Gene who he just noticed was looking very amused by the whole affair. "I was just naming people to phone up and I thought it would be funny to say names like Rodak, Schmodak and Fodak."

The boy grinned nastily again, but he seemed to accept Mark's explanation. Suddenly, from out of the blue, he then asked, "Who's your teacher?"

Slightly confused as to why he was being asked this, Mark responded, "Fluyt, Mr Fluyt."

"What's your name?"

"Mark Leversee"

Pausing for a second, the boy returned, "I'm going to tell Mr Fluyt that you smoke marijuana."

Not knowing how to respond to that comment amidst the laughter of the five eighth graders and inwardly believing the boy might be serious, Mark simply stared blankly. However, his thoughts were interrupted by an older voice.

"Leave the kid alone!" called the voice. All turned their heads to see a much older man at the door of a house across the street.

"He's my brother, we're just messing with him," one of the other boys quickly interposed. He then gave Mark looks that warned him he had better not say anything to the contrary.

"Well do it somewhere else," the old man ordered.

Concluding that it wasn't worth the hassle, the eighth graders rode away leaving Mark and Gene on their own. Nothing was said about it as the two boys rode home, but Mark was convinced that Gene got a thrill out of seeing Mark picked on like that.

Mark felt like he might have dodged a bullet that time, but worse was to happen a few days later. When walking home from school, he crossed paths with Liz Clover. He tried to ignore her, but he couldn't help staring at her because he was amazed to see her smoking a cigarette.

"Oh look, it's Marvin Leversee," she informed the three girls with her. Without warning, Liz went over to Mark and pushed him so hard that he fell over. As he got to his feet, she jokingly asked, "Why can't I be as rough as you?" She lunged for him again, but this time, he sidestepped her and ran out of the way.

"Oh, he faked me out," she declared mockingly.

Mark stopped for a second; he didn't know whether to stand his ground or keep going. Two boys who were spectating made his mind up for him. The shorter of the two, whom Mark would later discover was Liz's older brother Joe, jeered, "You're gonna get your ass kicked by a girl." When his taller friend burst out laughing, he continued, "Because if you touch her, I'll kick your ass."

Knowing he was in a lose-lose situation, Mark resumed his pace and quickened it into a run. As he fled, the only resistance he met was hearing Liz shouting, "You better run you faggot!"

While he was able to escape the torment outside of school, inside it there was no escape. A boy in his class named Joe Gerberwitz instigated it. Joe was one of the class heroes and some of the girls were heard to say he was the cutest boy in the class with his curly black hair and perfect complexion. He was also one of the main protagonists who got Mark to perform in Mrs Dorbano's class. However, he now suddenly claimed that he was fed up with Mark's silliness.

It started with threats of violence each time Mark said anything and then it turned actual with constant punches in the arm and the ribs anytime Joe was near him. Next, Joe decided it was a good way to amuse his friends. Therefore, he would threaten or use violence on Mark even when Mark didn't say anything.

The worst instance came at the very first school

basketball game. Joe sat next to him at the game and whenever he tried to cheer when the school team made a basket, Joe would say "Shut up" and punch him in the side. When Mark tried to protest Joe only threatened to beat him up and when he told Joe that he would have him arrested, Joe simply responded, "My father has a lot of money so he'll get me a good lawyer." When that failed, Mark simply left the game. After that, Joe could and did brag about how he made Mark leave the game.

It didn't take long before others in and out of Mark's class began to follow Joe's example. A tall boy with red hair named Mike Sigfried would grab his hand and squeeze it until Mark said "uncle." Then there was a girl named April Aiken who would slap him or pull his hair. In the hall, he experienced the odd occasion where Tommy Allen would punch him in the arm and say, "Sorry, my hand slipped."

The violence and threats of it didn't happen every day or even most days, but the merciless teasing did. Steve McGuire, Mark Rossman, Anthony Salvatino, Joe Pellegrini and Nancy Greenwood along with Laurie Swords led the procession of taunts against him. If it wasn't kids in the class, there were ones outside the class who would gladly oblige in teasing Mark. Jimmy Brown was one and a tall blonde boy named Joe Kellerman carried things on. These were the main protagonists, but others were known to join in as well.

It all started to get to Mark and he felt there was no place to hide or no one he could turn to. His only two real friends were Jack and Gene and while he could confide in Jack a little, he would quickly get fed up if Mark went on too much. Besides, he would go for long periods without seeing Jack or then see him quite a bit.

Gene, on the other hand, was proving to be very unreliable. If Mark told him anything, Gene would use it to make fun of him. Not only that, Gene would tell others so they could make fun of Mark as well. The worst was when Mark told Gene he liked Kim Beckard. Gene wasted no time in telling the whole sixth grade and even Kim herself who wasn't amused. Even though little was said about it, Mark felt humiliated, especially when he denied it when Kim confronted him over it. As a result, Mark tried to avoid Gene, but he always seemed to find him.

Worst of all for Mark was that he no longer felt he could rely on his family for help. His mother's favourite line seemed to be, "You're eleven year old now, it's time to stand on your own two feet. Besides, I have to look after your brother and sister who are younger than you." If that wasn't enough to make him feel rejected, his mother also repeatedly stressed that the things being said to him weren't that bad and urged him not to let it get to him. As for the physical aggression, she just told him to fight back. She didn't want to know that it wasn't in his nature and that he believed he wasn't a good fighter. Likewise, his grandfather only repeated what his mother said.

Mark found himself resenting his little sister. She seemed to have been accepted by her peers in Ramsgate while his didn't accept him. He had few friends and one of those was proving to be unreliable. Leslie, on the other hand, always seemed to have friends at home or be visiting their houses while Mark was either by himself or stuck with Gene. Therefore, one day while he was playing alone in the back yard, she asked if she could play with him and he roughly told her "No!"

"Play with me, I'm so lonesome," she whimpered.

Showing no mercy, he barked, "How can you be lonesome, you have lots of friends. You don't know what it's like to be lonesome."

Without hesitation, Leslie opened up the waterworks and ran back into the house. He took some sinister delight in the fact that he had made someone feel as bad as how others made him feel, even if it was his own sister. Unfortunately, that good feeling was interrupted by the voice of his mother demanding, "You play with your sister and be nice." The good feeling dashed, Mark obeyed his mother, but inside he was feeling that life wasn't treating him fairly.

Feeling totally alone and ganged up on from all sides, he rapidly began to retreat within himself. His invisible shell offered some protection from the outside world. He kept away from people at school and they seemed to leave him alone more. To fill the void, he created a fantasy world where he played hockey for the Philadelphia Junior Flyers. Like his fantasy football games, this was real in his mind as he played the games in the back yard. One game, he scored seven goals as his team won 12-7! As his imagination grew, fantasy team mates began to spring up as well as imaginary teams, which formed an imaginary league. No doubt, his team was one of the best in the league and he was the league's star player. For Mark, it provided a great escape.

Hockey wasn't his only escape. Learning about the Greeks and Romans in Mr Fluyt's social studies lessons reawakened his love for learning about war. He would have pretend battles in the back yard and much to his mother's dismay, began playing with his toy soldiers again. Only this time, he was much more imaginative in the way he played with the soldiers. He built fortifications and used rubber bands as bullets and small rocks as bombs. Mrs Leversee constantly told him that she thought he was too old to be playing with army men, but she never stopped him from doing so.

School also gave an opportunity for Mark to indulge his liking for war. Mr Fluyt allowed the class to play Age of Empires on the computer, as he believed that it

114

aided in learning about ancient history. It also helped them with math as well. Each child was given half an hour a week on the computer to play the game. Mark proved to be very good at it as he was able to build up his civilisation quickly and employ the tactic of using cavalry to outflank the enemy. The teacher was so impressed, he told his mother so at his parent- teacher conference. Mrs Leversee was glad to hear this and decided she would put the game on his Christmas list.

Mr Fluyt also expressed some concerns about Mark. "He's no trouble," he began, "And his work is at least average. But his concentration levels aren't good at all.

Mrs Leversee nodded in agreement. "His concentration has always been a problem as has his short term memory."

It was now Mr Fluyt's turn to nod. He thought for a moment and then offered, "I know they tested Mark for Asperger's Syndrome at Confederate Avenue School, but I am convinced he may have it to some degree and so does the other teacher, Mrs Dorbano. She has said there is something not quite right with Mark and not in an awful way. In fact, I think he may have something called DAMP."

He paused to let Mrs Leversee to ask for further details about DAMP and why Mark might have it. "DAMP," Mr Fluyt continued, "Means deficiencies in attention, motor skills and perception. I've seen these things in Mark. As you know, his concentration span is either very short or he gets so engrossed in an activity that all his focus goes onto that and he is oblivious to anything else. He can get easily distracted by outside influences or even his own thoughts. I know from his handwriting and practical work that his motor skills are lacking. As for his perception, I've seen him miss the main point of an exercise but be able to pick out some little morsel of information that even I didn't notice.

It's kind of amazing at times and there is a link between DAMP and Asperger's Syndrome."

Again the teacher paused a moment to let mother take all he said in. He then continued further, "He seems to have a one track mind. He has an obsession with hockey to the point where others in the class get annoyed with him."

Mr Fluyt failed to mention, however, how the other kids treated Mark as a result. Either he didn't notice anything or just shut his eyes to it. Mrs Leversee took on board everything Mr Fluyt told her. However, when she spoke to Mark about it that evening, she seemed to dwell more on the negative. "Your teacher says you think too much about hockey and it annoys the other kids," she lectured.

"I can't help it," Mark tried to explain. "Besides, the other kids all talk about things like that and nothing is said to them."

"Maybe they know when to stop," his mother returned before going on to say, "You used to do the same thing about war and I'm not going through that again."

Mark now felt that his mother and teacher were siding with the other kids. Therefore, it was little comfort when she mentioned the positive things the teacher had told her and when she mentioned him being tested for DAMP, she said it as if it was going to be a burden on her. He was now feeling more and more isolated and alone.

Chapter 9

Conversion

Mark's grandparents had always been deeply religious and went to church every Sunday. Their example did rub off on his mother, but she wasn't as conscientious about going to church. As a result, Mark didn't go to church as often as his grandparents. However, ever since his football ended, his mother insisted they go every week. He assumed it was simply due to the fact that Christmas was coming and his Sunday school class would be participating in the Christmas programme.

Whatever mother's reasons for going to church, Mark didn't mind very much. Admittedly, he wasn't keen on getting up early on Sunday, but it was only for an hour or so. Furthermore, the church his family went to was in the neighbouring town of Vincent. Therefore, he didn't have to see anyone he knew from Ramsgate. Better still, the kids in his Sunday school class seemed more accepting of him. Besides, he did like listening to the bible stories. In the recent weeks, those stories seemed to be about accepting Jesus as Saviour. The story booklets, which he liked to read, also seemed to be about it as well. However, those messages didn't seem to sink into his mind, he just liked the stories.

The final week before Christmas, something opened up in Mark's mind and the theme of accepting Jesus finally sank in. It was at the church's Christmas programme where he had a small speaking part, which doubled when his teacher asked him to speak another part meant for a boy who didn't show up on the night. He thought he had memorised the new part and he said his original part quite well. However, while he was saying his new part, he suddenly got stuck on the second line. Normally, with all the eyes of the church upon him, his mind would have gone into overload and a sense of panic and humiliation would have set in. Instead, a calm fell upon him and he simply reached into his pocket and took out the words to read. But as he was going to open it, he realised he didn't need it. The words miraculously returned to his mind and he was able to say the piece unassisted.

Any worry over his near disaster with the new lines never entered his mind. Mark found himself totally absorbed in the rest of the Christmas programme. One of the leading families of the church was on stage giving a small production. The six-year-old son was saying that he wanted to give his heart to Jesus.

Immediately, something hit Mark like an epiphany. All the Sunday school teachings and booklets finally sank in and he knew what he had to do. Silently, without drawing attention to himself, Mark slightly bowed his head and inwardly prayed, "Dear Jesus, I accept you as my saviour. I give my heart to you, amen." With the satisfaction of knowing that his place in heaven was now assured, he enjoyed the rest of the evening.

Both of his Sunday school teachers were quick to tell him how well he had done when the programme was over. While no one else complimented him, no one said anything negative, to Mark's relief. He kept thinking that had it happened at Tye School, somebody, if not everybody, would have wiped the floor with him over it. Mark concluded that it was because he now had Jesus in his life.

Reality set in almost the very next day when Mark was out of the protective environment of St James' Church. The normal experiences of school sometimes made him feel that Jesus wasn't always with him. The last week before Christmas break, Joe Gerberwitz seemed more hostile, even trying to get Mark to fight him after school. One afternoon, when he was late leaving gym class, he ran into the next class in the locker room. Unfortunately, it was Mrs Benton's class and even worse, Tommy Allen was the first one into the room.

"Get the fuck out of my way, Leversee," Tommy snarled, shoving Mark into the door.

Following Tommy was his pint-sized friend Don McCoy who also gave Mark a less forceful shove into the door. A few boys down the line was David Fitzpatrick, who couldn't resist the chance to get at Mark. He also shoved Mark into the door but not as hard as Tommy or Don. Mark was able to get through the door after David, but he had to run a gauntlet of boys who made comments like "Who's that gay kid?" As he neared the end of the line of Mrs Benton's boys, one more boy gave Mark a push. Only this time, Mark pushed back before walking off. The last thing he heard was Andy Millenberg, who was at the end of the line; say "Hit' em back."

Fortunately, school was let out for the Christmas holidays at the end of that week, so Mark's faith wasn't badly tested. He was certainly glad to be away from Tye School and all of those kids he disliked for twelve days. Besides, he got some great gifts for Christmas such as a new computer and the Age of Empires and NHL games to go with it. With those games, he could conquer nations and live out his hockey fantasy when the weather prevented him from using his new hockey stick outside. He never had to leave his house for the entire vacation.

The one time he did venture out of the house he regretted it. He went roller-skating with Jack at the roller rink in Vincent. He sensed trouble the moment he got out of the car. Jim Friend, who had been quarterback of the football team, recognised him straight away and alerted others by shouting, "It's Mark Leversee!" Eyes turned on him and he wished he could disappear, especially when Jim's friend, John Maple, whispered, "Marvin" as he walked past. It was Jim's audience that worried Mark. There were three girls, two of whom he knew, Nancy Greenwood and Laurie Swords and with them was their friend Janice Ricardo. As he waited in line to go in, Laurie turned around and said, "Leversee, I'm going to deck you."

Inside the rink, Laurie's words became true. Anywhere he tried to skate, somebody like Laurie or Jim was there to either try to trip him up or push him over. Worse still, Liz Clover and three of her friends turned up and joined in the hunt for Mark. He wasn't even safe on the other side of the rail as Laurie or Liz would skate behind him and push him or knee him in the back of the leg. But his staying off the rink floor began to annoy Jack who reminded him, "We're here to have fun, not stay on the other side of the rail;" and Mark's explanation, "Everybody from Ramsgate is out to get me" didn't sway him.

Mark did go back out onto the floor and Liz and her friends were waiting for him. As he went around, one of them was there to either push him or try to trip him. It wasn't long before he had had enough and cried, "I'm telling!" to a bemused Liz. He told the rink guard who simply shrugged, "They're just stupid girls, skate away from them."

Insult added to injury, as no sooner after skating away from the guard, a female guard came over to him and ordered, "These girls say you're tripping them, you're off for fifteen minutes."

"I didn't do anything," Mark tried to protest.

"You either stay off for fifteen minutes or you can

120

leave," the guard informed him, ignoring his plea of innocence.

Like a condemned man, Mark complied with the guard's instructions. Tearfully, he sat down on a bench to do his time. He hadn't been sitting there five minutes when the guard came over to him again and sternly warned, "Watch your language" before skating away as Mark was claiming, "I didn't say anything."

Shortly after that, Liz and her friends skated over to the tearful Mark to twist the knife. "Look, he's crying!" laughed one of the girls.

"Can't you take it?" Liz asked smugly and then sneered, "That's what you get for calling us fuckin' bitches."

"I didn't call you anything," Mark responded curtly.

"Yes you did," the blonde of the group countered.

"No, I didn't, because I don't curse," Mark asserted, remembering the promise he had made to himself after taking Jesus as his saviour.

The girls all giggled to each other before skating off and leaving Mark to finish his sentence in silence. When he did venture back onto the floor, he had no more trouble from Liz and her pals. However, this didn't stop Laurie from trying to get him down. She eventually succeeded in tripping him over and making him fall. When she did, she boasted about it to Nancy, Janice Ricardo, Jim Friend and anyone else who would listen. As for Mark, when the skating session finally ended, he was glad to be out and vowed never to go to the roller rink again.

Mrs Leversee didn't agree with her son's decision when he and Jack got into the car to go home. "Don't let a bunch of silly punks keep you from doing what you want," she said before lecturing him, "I wouldn't have sat out, I would have complained to the manager."

Mark suddenly felt that he was in the wrong. The

options his mother gave him never occurred to him- although it never occurred to her that the manager would have probably sided with the guard. There was also the fact that it was four witnesses against one or two if Jack spoke on Mark's behalf. Instead, he felt that once again, he had gotten it wrong.

The only thing she said about the false accusation of cursing was to ask, "Are you sure you didn't say it under your breath?" She seemed satisfied when he gave an emphatic "No," and left it at that. In spite of what his mother thought, Mark was still determined not to go to the roller rink ever again. He figured it was God's way of telling him that he shouldn't go where the heathen dwell.

Chapter 10

Further Rumblings and Retreat

A few weeks following the Christmas holiday, it became clear to Mark that his newly found faith wasn't going to save him from his tormentors. If anything, it seemed that things were getting worse. It seemed that the entire town was still out to humiliate him in some way. If not humiliation, there was still violence or the threat of it from the likes of kids like Tommy Allen, Joe Gerberwitz or Steve McGuire. Mark tried his best to ignore it by coming to the conclusion that his new faith was being tested.

Things only got worse when his entire class decided that he and a girl named Jody Molstein were now a couple. Jody Molstein was considered the "ugly" girl of the class. The fact that she wore cat's eyes type glasses did her no favours and when she didn't wear them, she bore a striking resemblance to a turtle. Like the rest of the class, Mark also considered Jody to be unattractive.

While he wasn't hostile to Jody, unlike some of the other boys, this changed when everybody started saying he and Jody were an item. Joe Gerberwitz, Nancy Greenwood or someone else would get Mark to say something horrible to Jody. If he refused, they would then say that it was because he liked her and started teasing him mercilessly about it. When he did, it only encouraged them more. Whenever anybody wanted to have some fun at his and Jody's expense, they would say something like, "Go and call her a fat slut." If he said no, they would begin to chant, "You like Jody Molstein" until he got so wound up denying it. "Prove it then," the tormentor would command. Therefore, in order to prove he didn't like her, he would go and say something horrible to Jody and it brought much amusement to the faces of everyone.

His conversion to Christianity did nothing to stifle his wild imagination. If anything, his imagination grew as it provided him with an escape from the realities of school life, but it still continued to cause him problems.

One day, Tony Salvatino, who made a habit of asking Mark strange questions in order to make fun of him, asked, "Do you believe in the sandman?"

Mark sensed that it was another attempt by Anthony to patronise him and Mark decided to open his imagination. "I saw the sandman and I killed him," he answered with a grin.

Unfortunately, things backfired as it only encouraged Anthony to probe further. Not seeing the trap, Mark obliged further, "The sandman came into my room, so I chopped his arm off with a big sword," he told him.

To Anthony, this was gold dust. He immediately went and told Joe Gerberwitz, Matt Osmond and anyone else who would listen. "Leversee says he killed the sandman," Tony declared. Immediately, both Matt and Joe insisted Mark tell them the story. Oblivious to any attempts at humiliation and enjoying temporarily being in the spotlight, Mark elaborated, "The sandman came into my room, so I took my sword and chopped his arm off. Then I watched him bleed to death." It wasn't long before more kids in the class came to Mark to hear his tale. He didn't care that anyone might be making fun of him, he just enjoyed the spotlight.

Those who listened found the whole story amusing and made comments. "I bet you killed the candy man too," jested Matt Osmond. Jim Friend and Damon Bates also made fun by saying, "Oh you killed the sandman, you bad boy."

Others like Joe Pellegrini made more barbed comments like, "He's mentally retarded or emotionally disturbed." Mark Rossman immediately jumped on that train and at every opportunity would say, "Marvin, you're mentally disturbed."

Mark ignored the negative comments and allowed himself to believe that everyone who didn't make negative comments thought he was amusing. For him, it was an opportunity to let his imagination run wild. If he or anyone else had thought about it, what he was saying could have been recorded, as it would have made a good story. Instead, in the weeks that followed, it was used to heap further ridicule upon him.

Anthony or Joe Pellegrini would come up to him with one person or another to get him to tell that person about how he killed the sandman. It wasn't long before Mark grew tired of it, especially when one of the kids Joe brought with him one day was Tommy Allen.

"Tell him about how you killed the sandman," Joe begged sarcastically. Tommy just sniggered, probably relishing the fact that he had something more to use against Mark. Mark simply shook his head, ignoring the condescending pleas from Joe. He was slightly surprised and relieved that his refusal didn't result in Tommy threatening to put his fist down Mark's throat for not telling the story.

Happenings at school enriched his imagination at home as Mark retreated further into himself. After losing two games and drawing two, he began to master the NHL game on his computer and started winning games and scoring goals. To him, the losses and ties made his fantasy more believable. He was playing for the Junior Flyers and was the leading scorer. However, the fantasy began to cross the borders of reality as he would sometimes not be available to meet someone, usually Gene, because he had a hockey game that day.

Lines between fantasy and reality became even murkier when Mark confessed to Gene that he played for the Junior Flyers. He recounted a game in which his team recently won 3-2. He had scored the first goal and assisted on the third goal. Furthermore, he added a slice of believability to his story when he mentioned that he had received a ten-minute misconduct penalty for arguing with the ref when he disallowed a goal. Gene seemed to believe him but he also started telling others that Mark was on the Junior Flyers.

"Yeah, right, tell us another one," Steve McGuire chuckled in disbelief when he heard it.

"He'll say that he plays for the real Flyers next," teased Matt Osmond in amusement.

Of course, the story made its way to the ears of Andrew Blumenthaw and when he heard it he really tore into Mark. "Let me guess, Bobby Carlson is now your cousin," he sneered.

Mark would have loved to have been related to the star player of his favourite hockey team, but he knew better than to say so. Besides, his favourite player on the Flyers was Kip McClary, who was a new rising star, scoring lots of goals and had several hat tricks. The funny thing was that some people seemed to actually believe that he played for the Junior Flyers. This further obliterated the line between fantasy and reality. As for those who didn't believe him, he expected that and concluded that no matter what he said, no one was going to believe him anyway, so he might as well have some fun by telling a whopper.

While his hockey fantasy was good for forgetting about school and horrible kids, Mark wasn't a total recluse. He joined the sixth grade basketball league. The fact that he was the very last pick in the league and forced onto the team captained by John Lodge, who wasn't happy about it, didn't bother him. When the league games began, his tendency to make a great play followed by a really bad one manifested itself once again and as usual, everyone remembered the bad play more. In one game, he stole the ball off Tom Lamaina, one of the best players in the sixth grade, and dribbled to the basket. However, the thrill of a chance to score got too much for him, his anxieties caused the ball to slip as he was shooting and he missed the basket badly.

The next week, his team-mates, John Lodge, Jim Friend, Mike Sigfried and a boy he knew from football named Curt Cadell all ribbed Mark about missing the lay up. When he tried to explain that it was because the ball slipped, the response he got was, "That's because you suck!" When Mark did eventually make a basket some weeks later, those teammates simply dismissed it with, "That was luck." Therefore it was no surprise that when the league finished, it only cemented people's feeling towards him.

As winter warmed into spring, everything stayed the same for Mark. He was either ignored, which he preferred, or set upon. One day, while watching the jocks of the year play baseball in the playground one lunchtime, David McDonnell came by and started throwing small stones at his head. He didn't watch any more playground baseball after that, especially as three girls in his class who had witnessed it found it amusing. Anthony Salvatino found another thing to pick on Mark for as he wore a baseball jacket in the warmer weather.

"That's why nobody likes you," Anthony pontificated, "You wear babyish things." While Mark processed through his mind how wearing a jacket would cause people not to like him, Anthony explained, "Baseball jackets are out of style, they're not for sixth graders. They're for little kids." In spite of Anthony's words, Mark felt adamant that he wasn't doing anything wrong.

For all the bad experiences he was having at school, there was one activity where he enjoyed and excelled at, Age of Empires. Mr Fluyt allowed the class to play Age of Empires II when they were learning about the Middle Ages in social studies and then III when they went to the next chapter, which was the Age of Discovery. He was so good at these games, that when the teacher paired the class off in boy-girl partnerships, none of the girls really minded being partnered with him. The first time, Laurie Swords ended up as his partner and the fact that she openly stated her dislike for Mark didn't stop her from basking in the glory of the pair being class champions at Age of Empires II. While she tried to take some of the credit, she knew it was Mark's use of flanking manoeuvres that won it for them. The same thing happened when he was paired with Mary Lane for Age of Empires III. Again, he was crowned class champion, although this time, Mary gave more credit to her partner. Furthermore, both times, he went on to defeat the champion in Mrs Dorbano's class, making himself the overall champion of the circuit. He was glad there was something he was good at and it contributed to the A he got in social studies.

Like all his brief moments of glory, his Age of Empires victories soon faded and things went back to normal. When he signed up to play in the one-on-one basketball tournament, his opponent Harry Walker came over to him and informed him, "I talked to kids in your class about you, they all say you're a faggot."

Mark desperately wanted to come back with, "They're the faggots," but he knew if he did, someone would tell them and kids like Joe Gerberwitz, Mike Sigfried and Steve McGuire would rain blows down on him. Therefore he simply shrugged.

Losing to Harry 5-2 in the one-on-one brought renewed attacks on him. "Ah, Walker beat you," Steve

McGuire chided. Curt Cadell gave the knife a further twist by following Mark around the school and saying, "You were bragging about how you were going to beat Walker and he beat you." Mark knew this was another major exaggeration.

In his mind, Mark deflected the taunts through his fantasy. "I don't care," he would respond. "I had a hockey game anyway and as soon as I got on the ice, I scored and then I scored the winning goal in overtime." He knew that people like Steve and Curt didn't believe him like most of the grade, but it did give him a buffer against the comments.

His hockey fantasy did little to stem the tide of physical attacks. It provided no protection when one day after school, he was waiting for his mother to pick him up when Joe Kellerman, Jim Friend and a boy he knew as Ken Packer started slamming him against the fence. A chunky boy with thick black hair named Mark Ruth joined in, making it four. This caused Jim to stop slamming him; instead he began clouting Mark over the head with his book. After a few minutes of taking it, he managed to get away. Ken and Jim decided they had had enough, but Joe and Mark Ruth went after him and collectively grabbed Mark and threw him to the ground. When he got on his feet, Mark lashed out with flailing fists and by pure luck, caught Mark Ruth with a blow to the side of the head. That was enough to make them stop, although Mark Ruth vowed to get revenge.

Mark discovered two things after the event that made him feel worse. Like the episode with Danny Hamer and David Fitzpatrick, Gene watched and did nothing to help. At least he didn't say that he was going to be a witness for Mark's attackers. Second, when he told his mother about it, she told Mark that she wouldn't intervene. "I can't go into the school each time somebody gives you trouble," she explained.

"You're nearly twelve now, you have to stand on your own two feet." Mark now felt suddenly alone and helpless.

Feelings of helplessness increased when Mark Ruth extracted his revenge a few days later. It happened the night of the student-faculty basketball game. After the game, Mark and his grandfather were walking back to the car when he felt a hard blow to the middle of his back. The blow momentarily winded him, but it was enough for the assailant to escape under cover of darkness.

"What happened?" his grandfather queried. "Did someone hit you?"

"It was Mark Ruth," a short stocky boy with brown hair named Josh Bonnet, who was standing nearby indicated. "He punched him because Marvin hit him in the mouth."

"Is this true?" Grandfather asked Mark

Mark nodded in the affirmative and quickly explained, "It was because he was one of the ones who were throwing me against the fence the other day."

Grandfather gave a look that said he believed Mark and that he might have been justified in punching Mark Ruth in the first place. However, when the event was relayed to his mother, she seemed unsympathetic.

"You should have found that kid and socked him back," she barked. The fact that the boy had disappeared didn't seemed to matter to her. What mattered to Mark was that he felt even more helpless.

Back at school, the few who knew about the punch were decidedly sympathetic to Mark Ruth. Josh Bonnet was the worst. "You deserved it," he said, ignoring the fact that Mark was simply lashing out in self-defence. It seemed that everyone was against him and there was no hiding from it.

Chapter 11

Champions and the End of 6th Grade

The goalie had saved his penalty shot in game four and the other team went on to win the game in overtime and stay alive in the final. Now in the final minute of game five, behind 4-3, it looked as if the Junior Flyers were going to lose again. In a mad rush to try and tie the game, Curly Kramer, the right-winger, carried the puck over the blue line. Meanwhile, the Junior Flyers' goalie made a mad dash for the bench and a sixth skater rushed onto the ice in a last ditch bid for the tying goal.

In desperation, the Junior Flyers stormed the net, but each time the Dover Cougars' goalie denied them. Then, with a half-minute to play, Mark pounced on a bad-clearing pass and skated ferociously past both opposing defensemen. As he closed in on the goal, he made a feint with his left shoulder sending the goalie that way. However, he suddenly changed direction and, remembering the goalie's quick reflexes, fired a wrist shot about eighteen inches off the ice. The goalie tried to stretch out his leg to stop the puck, but it was too late. The puck flew into the back of the net and the red light went on signalling that Mark had sent the game into overtime.

At the start of the overtime period, the Junior Flyers had to survive an attack from the Cougars' forwards. Now it was their turn to counter attack. Curly again speedily brought the puck into enemy territory and fired a vicious slap shot at the goal. Luckily for the goalie, the shot was just high and wide of its target. Left-winger Gene Shamrock zeroed in on the careening puck and swatted it at the goal. The shot hit the goalie's pads and stopped dead, but with Mark ferociously rushing in for the puck, the goalie fell on it killing the play.

Mark won the ensuing face off getting the puck back to the point where a defenseman slapped it at goal. Again, the goalie stopped the shot, deflecting it towards the corner. An opposing defenseman picked up the puck and passed it to a forward who was breaking at the blue line. However, Gene managed to get his stick on it and redirected the puck across the ice. Mark homed in on the wobbly puck and fired a hard shot towards goal. Only this time, the goalie wasn't equal to the task and for the second time in less than two minutes of play, his shot found the back of the net.

Leaping out of his seat in his bedroom, Mark punched the air in triumph. With great delight, he celebrated as "Flyers win 5-4" flashed across the computer screen. A warm feeling flowed through his body. It may not have been real, but the Junior Flyers had become league champions and he had scored the winning goal. In his mind and computer, he was a hockey hero.

Nothing at school could remove the warm feeling he had over the next few days. He even signalled number one when he met Gene in the schoolyard the next morning. Even the total disbelief by many of his classmates did nothing to remove that good feeling. It didn't matter if it happened on pixel, he just enjoyed the fact that for once, he was on a championship team and he was the star player.

Fantasy hockey turned to fantasy baseball as the warm weather took hold. The favourable weather allowed him to play his games outside, making the need for playing on the computer less necessary. A fantasy league sprang up in his mind. To avoid detection, the league was located in Philadelphia so no one could physically disprove the league's existence. Furthermore, the Naval dispensary that sponsored his team actually existed. He started at second base and was the lead off batter. After a few games in the back yard or by fielding balls against the front of the house, his batting average was .600, had hit a couple of home runs and the team was undefeated.

Fantasy baseball was far better than the reality for him. In his first gym class baseball game, he struck out three times and made several errors in the field. After the game, he had to endure the familiar calls of "You suck!" from the likes of Mike Sigfried, Joe Gerberwitz and Steve McGuire. Not even when he rapidly improved throughout the spring and even hit a home run, did the opinion alter much. Therefore, whenever he made a great hit or fielding play in his fantasy league, he had the satisfaction of no one devaluing it or saying it was luck. It provided him with some escape from the harsh realities of school life.

As far as the classroom went, things weren't too bad for him. One day, when all the class seemed to collectively call him "Marvin," he finally snapped. "My name's not God damn Marvin!" he wailed. Some kids hummed "Oooh" taking delight in the thought that he was in trouble from Mr Fluyt, others were only encouraged to call him "Marvin" more. There may have been some anticipating smiles at the first sound of Mr Fluyt's voice, but these turned to frowns when his words rang out, "How would you all like to write his name a hundred times?" The class went immediately silent and the teacher asked them menacingly, "What's his name?"

"Mark," the class reluctantly replied in meek unison. After that, no one dared to call him Marvin in the class. Even when John Lodge heard about it from the moaning Steve McGuire and responded with bravado, "I wouldn't pay attention to that. I'd still call him Marvin and if I had to write Mark a hundred times, I'd give Leversee a hundred punches," nothing changed. The only challenge came when Mark Rossman tried to say, "Your name is still Marvin, Mark is actually like a middle name."

Mark was prepared for this eventuality. "I have an official letter from the State of Pennsylvania saying my name is Mark," he retorted. Then feeling he had the upper hand declared, "I also have a new birth certificate that says my name is Mark. If you want, we can go to court about it and then I'll be the new owner of Chessington." Chessington was a furniture store Mark Rossman's father owned.

Whether that was the cause, Mark Rossman never called him Marvin in class after that. However, he did use Mark's words as a source of amusement. "Leversee is going to sue me because I said his name was Marvin," he would say to his friends and it resulted in a lot of laughs. Furthermore, Joe Pellegrini, who loved spreading exaggerated stories about Mark, took it further afield and blew it more out of proportion. He said things like, "Leversee will take you to the Supreme Court if you say his name is Marvin." Therefore, for a few days, he had to endure comments from the likes of kids like Jimmy Brown such as, "If I call you Marvin, are you going to sue me?"

Things took an unexpected turn in the playground. It started when Gene would call out to a boy named Andy Stowe, "Kid with the funny glasses," every time Andy was near. However, instead of saying anything to Gene, Andy approached Mark. "Leversee, what's this kid with the funny glasses shit?" he demanded to know.

"It's not me, it's him saying it," Mark replied innocently while pointing to Gene.

"You better not say it again," Andy warned, acting

as if Gene wasn't there. Of course this only encouraged Gene more. He repeated the funny glasses taunt on several occasions, but fortunately for Mark, Andy said nothing more to him.

He wasn't so lucky in the final weeks of school. One lunchtime Curt Cadell was saying something to Gene, which Mark couldn't quite make out, but Curt's tone made it appear the two were arguing. Thinking he was helping his friend, he advised Gene, "Tell him to blow himself."

Gene took the advice in his stride and relayed to Curt, "Mark says to go blow yourself," after which he turned back to him and said, "He's gonna get you for that."

Out in the playground, Gene's prophetic words were fulfilled. Mark was suddenly grabbed from both sides by Joe Kellerman and Keith Wenger and hurled up against the fence. With his captive securely in place, Curt confronted him. "What did you say about me in the lunchroom?" he asked angrily.

"I said to tell you to blow yourself," he whimpered in reply. "I thought you were fighting," he added before Curt could ask why.

"We weren't fighting," Curt huffed. "If you say it again, I'll beat the crap out of you!" He slapped Mark hard across the face for good measure and before they let go, Joe and Keith collectively gave him a kick to both of his hips.

After he let go, Joe warned him, "If you tell, I'll break your jaw."

"We'll work him over after school if he does," Keith added.

Mark ignored the comments and got away in a hurry. He was met by Gene, who had carried out his normal tactic of running away immediately, watching from a safe distance and not offering any help. "Tell Mr

Tasker," he advised, but Mark just shook his head. He knew that nothing good would come out of it.

No more major incidents befell Mark for the rest of sixth grade. The only backlash from the Curt Cadell incident was the next day when a different boy warned him, " You better stop pushing around my friends Curt Cadell, Joe Kellerman and Keith Wenger." However, he then laughed and said, "I'm only kidding," before Mark respond, "They were pushing me around."

He did have a minor confrontation with Keith a week later. Keith began telling another boy, "He thinks he can take Fishman, he thinks he can take Glaughlin." Then turning to Mark, he sputtered, "You're weak man, you're weak!"

Anxiety and doubt vied in Mark's mind. Surely Keith remembered he had beaten up Alan Fishman last year, all of Confederate Avenue School saw it and he never said that he could take Jack Glaughlin.

Mark's silence spurred Keith on further. "Now he's gonna put up his hand and say, "Foul!"" This was something Mark had done during basketball season because the referee's signal for personal foul amused him. "You're weird and you're weak!" Keith barked at him.

"Fuck you," was all Mark could think to say before walking off. He ignored Keith as he returned, "Fuck you too." He bumped into Gene almost straight after the confrontation with Keith and asked Gene if he had ever said that he could take Glaughlin. He was relieved and assured when Gene answered "No."

The rest of the school year ended without further fuss. He was glad to have passed the grade and had a decent report card of B's and C's. Most of all, he was glad to be out of school and not have to see anybody he hated.

Chapter 12

A Week in Paradise

Summer couldn't have had a better start. The baseball team was 11-1 and Mark's batting average was over .500. The one loss, where he went 0 for 6 at bat, made his fantasy seem more believable. However, the very next game, he went 3 for 4 and hit a three run home run and his team won that game 9-1. The weather allowed him to have his games outside. He would play them either by hitting a ball in the back yard or throwing a ball against the porch and fielding it in front of the house. Either way suited his needs just fine.

In the final weeks of school, he had gotten a paper route, which made him feel grown up as he was making money. Like with a lot of things with Mark, he had some problems initially. There was some confusion about two residences at the same house number when he took the route over. It wasn't his fault, but it didn't stop the district manager telling the likes of Joe Pellegrini that he got twenty complaints a week. He knew this was a major untruth, but the end of school ended worries about Joe. By the time school had ended, the complaints had all stopped and the district manager was happy with his performance.

In the second week of summer vacation, his mother enrolled him and his sister in bible school at their church. While his conversion to Jesus six months earlier did little to help him at school, it was a blessing at bible school. He felt really comfortable there and enjoyed learning about the bible. His class was studying the Apostle Paul and as a result, Mark was sure he was going to be a missionary when he grew up.

Furthermore, he became friendly with a boy name Arthur Wilton whom he knew from Sunday school. Free from the grief given him by kids at his school, he found bible school far more enjoyable.

Bible school yielded another blessing for Mark. During the entire three-week period, the pastor and bible schoolteachers were plugging a summer camp in Pennsylvania. He desperately wanted to go, but he was worried that his mother would give her favourite response, "We can't afford it." He figured that if he offered to pay for some of it with his paper route money, she might go for the idea.

Once evening, he plucked up the courage to ask. "There's this summer bible camp in Pennsylvania and I want to go. I can pay for some of it with my paper route money."

Mrs Leversee looked at her son and immediately Mark braced himself for the inevitable "No." However, a small smile appeared at the corners of her mouth. "I want you to go to the camp too. I've spoken to Pastor Bachman and the church is going to pay some towards it. Also your Aunt sent $20 for your birthday and we'll use that too. So you are going."

The response somewhat shocked him. Inwardly, he wanted to jump up and cheer, but he suppressed it. Instead, he gave an enthusiastic "Great," but the joy filling up inside him was bubbling over. Although he tried, he couldn't think of anything else. When he tried to take his mind off of it by having a baseball game out front, which consisted of throwing a ball against a low wall and fielding it, he made so many errors, that it was a very high scoring game. Still, his team won 17-14 and he went five for six at the bat, but his excitement overrode everything.

The few short weeks leading up to when he went to camp couldn't go by fast enough. When it was time to go in mid July, he was brimming with excitement. Fortunately, the Sunday school lesson that morning consisted of singing and a talk by one of the deacons because Mark couldn't concentrate one bit. After Sunday school, he was pleased that his mother decided to head up to the camp early and even more pleased when Pastor Bachman said it was a good idea.

Normally, three hours in a car would have been an extremely boring experience for Mark, but this was different. He was excited about the fact that once they got through Philadelphia, the car would take him to places he had never been to before. He loved exploring new places and stopping for lunch at Burger King was an added bonus. Furthermore, he was given the role of navigator; so he had to keep a sharp eye out for places so his mother could get him to his destination.

His navigational skills were spot on perfect as he found all the landmarks given in the directions. Thus he was easily able to guide his mother to Three Streams Bible Camp. The camp was situated in a very large open area at the foot of some very high hills. The scenery was simply breathtaking. It got its name from the fact that there were actually three streams running through it. When the car pulled up, Mark wasn't sure whether he should be disappointed by the lack of buildings or excited about beginning a new adventure.

Arriving an hour and half before registration gave Mark and his mother the chance to have a good look around the grounds. Any feelings of disappointment rapidly withered away while they walked around the spacious camp. They identified some buildings straight away, the snack bar, the dining hall and the office as well as the dormitories and eventually, at the top of the hill, the swimming pool. Purposely, taking their time, they had a good look around before the other campers began arriving and it was time to register.

In the midst of their wandering, they met two other early arrivals, a girl and a boy, both a few years younger than Mark. The boy was named Harry and had very short brown hair and loads of freckles. The girl, named Bonnie, had long blonde hair and glasses, which were very similar to those worn by Jody Molstein. Both were from suburbs outside of Philadelphia. Harry was very outgoing and because he had attended the camp the previous summer, was able to impart lots of information to Mark and his mother. Bonnie was more introverted. However, for all of Harry's genuine friendliness, Mark still wanted to meet kids closer to his own age.

That chance came not long after. Cars began pulling up and parents and children disembarked from them. Old friendships were reforged as those who had been to Three Streams in previous summers reunited with one another. For Mark, there were no reunions, he didn't know anyone; but he didn't think about that as he stood by his mother's side as she registered her son. Fortunately, she had the sense to beat the crowds and be the first in line.

"Mark Leversee," uttered the woman sitting behind the desk. She was a broad woman with premature grey hair worn in a bob. He would later learn that she was called "Sergeant" because of her bossy nature, although her real name was Barbara North. In a military manner, she informed him, "You'll be in room ten in the boys' dorm and your counsellor is Gerhard Bauer."

Mrs Leversee took a load of papers from Barbara and after sifting through them, passed two cards to Mark. "This one is your registration card and the other is your snack card," she pointed out.

He took the cards and examined both of them. From the registration card, he reaffirmed he was in room ten and he learned that he was on the Joshua team. The snack card allowed him to order food and drink from the snack bar and he had a dollar a day to spend on snacks. Putting the cards safely in his pocket, he followed his mother back to the car to get his suitcase. Once they had gotten it, they walked together up the hill stopping short of the boys' dormitory.

"I'll let you go from here," she said to her son. "Remember everything I told you. If you have a problem, talk to a counsellor and call me collect on Wednesday." When Mark nodded that he understood, she gave him a kiss on the cheek and watched him walk the remaining few yards. Once he disappeared through the door, she walked back to the car with mixed feelings- proud her son was becoming independent and worried for him only as a mother could, especially with her son's needs.

Without ceremony, Mark entered Buck Lodge and walked down the corridor looking for his room. Odd and even numbers were on opposite sides making the task of locating his room even easier. Voices of boys rang out from every direction. He paid little notice to them as he focused on his task. When he found room ten, he simply went inside and began unpacking.

The rooms could have been like an army barracks. Every room had two bunk beds on each side and bureau full of drawers between the bunks at the back wall. At the foot of the beds were places for hanging clothes and more drawers underneath. He had a brief glance around what would be his home for the week and then took out his sleeping bag and officially claimed the top bunk on the left. Finally and as quickly as he could, he put his clothes in the top three drawers in the middle before officially deciding he was settled in.

Not long after, a boy his age entered the room and said, "Hi," which Mark reciprocated. The new arrival's name was Tony and he came from a suburb of Philly whose name Mark could never remember. Tony was about the same height and build as Mark except Tony's hair was lighter and he had noticeable freckles on his face. They talked about all the basic get to know you stuff while he watched Tony claim the opposite top bunk and stash his things away.

Just when Tony finished moving in, a man entered their room. He was tall and thin with a pointy nose, which was de-emphasised by a reddish brown, curly beard. "Are you Mark and Tony?" he asked the boys in a very strong German accent. When they both confirmed their identity, he continued, "I am your counsellor, my name is Gerhard. Is there anything you wish to ask me?"

Tony shook his head and it occurred to Mark to ask, "Is it just us in the room?"

Gerhard nodded vigorously while saying, "Yes, it's just you two." With that he disappeared and when gone, Tony mocked, "Are you Mark and Tony?" in a very bad attempt at a German accent. It still got Mark laughing hysterically and Tony couldn't help laughing hysterically too.

Not long after, the pair ventured out and began meeting the other campers. In the room opposite were four eight-year-old boys, three of them triplets. Mark and Tony paid them no further attention. In the next room, number eleven, were three African American lads. The stockier of the three was named Henry Williams, who had lived in London when he was younger. The two thinner boys were brothers named Daryl and Nick Webber. Nick was very tall, well over six feet while Daryl was much shorter. In room twelve, next to Tony and Mark were four boys. Two were brothers named John and Mike McCeaver; the thinner of the other two was Jeff while the spectacled, heavier boy was named Craig. It was discovered that all of them were under Gerhard's counsellorship.

After the normal introductions and informal chat that included an impression of Curly from the Three Stooges by Henry, which Mark found hilarious. Nick came up with an idea to sneak out at night and go to the girls' dorm. Everyone thought it was a cool idea, especially Tony, who had noted that there were some good looking girls at the camp, joked, "Maybe if we get caught, they'll make us sleep with the girl of our choice." This brought hysterical laughter and Mark especially liked the idea, so that night, the plan would be set in motion.

All the new friends were in good spirits when they went down for dinner. Each of them was excited about the plan to sneak out that night. Tony continued to make the others laugh by making constant sexual innuendoes. Mark suddenly felt comfortable in his new surroundings and began looking forward to the rest of the week.

While the entire camp waited outside the dining hall, Mark observed that Tony was right, there were some pretty girls at the camp, quite a few his own age. Although an idea of a girlfriend flashed in his mind, he discounted it as he believed it wouldn't happen in reality. Things like that just didn't happen to him.

Dinner consisted of chicken, mashed potatoes and vegetables. The taste of the food reminded him of his father's stories about the food in the navy. The bad food gave them something else to joke about. No one could hold back their laughter when Tony referred to the gravy as "goose shit." Even at a Christian camp, none of the other campers seemed to be too bothered at Tony's choice of words. After dinner, the pastor's wife, who was a short plump woman with short grey hair and the recreational director, made announcements. The announcements consisted of the evening fun activity and the evening meeting. Mark was looking forward to both.

Evening fun started almost immediately after dinner. The campers were divided into their teams for the week. Mark was a little disappointed that none of his new friends were on his team. Tony, Henry, Nick and Daryl were all on the David team, while three of the four boys from room twelve were on the Solomon team. Jeff, being the exception, was on the Samson team. Joshua team's counsellor was named Roger, who was tall and thin with greasy looking black hair. He had a larger nose than Gerhard that supported wire frame glasses and on his head was a straw trilby hat.

"We probably won't beat the other teams by saying our bible verses," Roger began when the team was fully assembled. "So, we'll have to beat them on the ball field." While he listened to Roger, Mark surveyed his team. There were a couple of boys near his own age and one just younger. There were also three girls his age, none of which he found attractive. After the team sorting, there was a "Get to know you" game where you had to match campers by a list of statements. Tony took immediate advantage of this, as he already knew Mark fitted the "Boy from New Jersey" statement. It was all amusing fun.

The evening meeting started with singing and progressed to an introduction of camp leaders, counsellors and the week's speakers. Then each camper in turn was expected to stand up and introduce themselves. At first, Mark was dreading the exercise as he hated being in the spotlight. He even had flashbacks of Miss Erichetti and worried that this was an attempt to humiliate him in front of the camp. However, seeing younger children do it with little problem helped to chase the anxieties away. Therefore, when his turn finally came, he stood up and announced, "My name is

Mark Leversee and my home church is St. James by the Sea Church in Vincent, New Jersey." He sat down feeling very relieved. Following the introductions, there was a talk given by a Reverend McCeaver who was John and Mike's grandfather. He spoke about the bible acting as a light that shows you the way and Mark seemed to glean every word.

Any ideas about sneaking into the girls' dorm were quickly thwarted that night. All of the counsellors in the boys' dorm patrolled the corridor like prison guards. Any noise was met with the threat of losing pool time and in Gerhard's case, the offending boy was made to come out and do push ups. This happened to Mark. When Tony stated he couldn't sleep, Mark suggested he count sheep. Tony sarcastically replied, "I'll count teddy bears, they're my hero." Mark couldn't help but to burst out in laughter.

Gerhard stormed in like a Gestapo officer. "Who was laughing?" he demanded. Mark confessed, went out to the corridor and took his punishment of twenty-five push-ups. Tony apologised for getting him in trouble when he returned, but Mark lightly shrugged it off as it was no problem. Eventually, the excitement of the first night of camp wore off and everybody got to sleep.

Excitement returned to Three Streams that first morning as over half of the boys were up before Barbara North's voice crackled over the intercom, "Rise and shine, rise and shine for a wonderful day at Three Streams." Mark and his friends were among the early risers. They walked up to the pool area and then down near the girls' dormitory venturing close to the area nearby which was forbidden to boys called "No man's land." The main topic of conversation was the frustration of not being able to sneak out the previous night. Tony sarcastically sobbed, "I wanted to sleep with the girl of my choice" and then made a few more innuendos afterward. Henry kept repeating his catchphrase, "Fun, fun, fun, hey, hey, hey!"

Jokes about the quality of the food at the previous night's dinner were recycled at breakfast. This time, the over crisp bacon and the hard as rock oatmeal were the main targets. Nothing memorable happened in the early part of the morning, despite Gerhard's attempt to inject a little excitement into the morning devotions. That changed dramatically at the morning meeting. As Mark was walking into the small chapel, sitting there with the Solomon team was an angel. He couldn't stop staring at her. The long shiny black hair seemed to sparkle ebony in the lighting of the chapel and proved the perfect contrast pretty, round, white face that was in no means too chubby. Her loose fitting t-shirt might have hid the true shape of her body, but that didn't matter. Because extending from her pink shorts were the most beautifully formed pair of thighs he had ever seen. They were in no way thin, but had just the right amount of baby fat on them for his liking. He couldn't take his eyes away.

She may or may not have realised that Mark was staring at her, but she suddenly turned her head and met his gaze. The angel flashed him a smile and he nervously smiled back and inwardly began beating himself for making it look too obvious. Mounting anxieties made him quickly turn his head away; however, he did have one more look at the angel as he sat down with his team. She was whispering something to the girl sitting next to her and the two girls appeared to be giggling, while the whole time she was looking his way.

An air of nervous confidence came over him and he became a man on a mission. He was now determined to impress the young lady sitting on the other side of the chapel. That chance came almost immediately. After the first song, there was a bible quiz between the teams. Both times, when it was the Joshua team's turn to answer the question, it was he who answered them correctly scoring twenty points for his team. The only reason his team didn't win was because the man leading the quiz asked the final question to the Solomon team when it was meant to be a first team to answer question. Not winning meant little for Mark though, he just hoped he impressed the angel with his biblical knowledge.

These thoughts stayed with him throughout the morning. He managed to push them to one side of his mind during the morning softball game against the David team. He really didn't mind that his team didn't win because he had played very well, getting hits both times he batted. The highlight of the game was when Harry got a hit for the other team, but ran to second base instead of first.

Lunch and the early part of the afternoon went by in a blur. Roger's theory that the team would score points on the ball field proved to be wishful thinking as the Joshua team was soundly thumped by the David team at volleyball. Although Mark was his team's best player, the rest of the team wasn't very good. So he acknowledged the fact that he was going to be on another losing team.

Pool time was when he finally got to see the angel in her full splendour. She wore a purple and white one-piece swimsuit that fitted snugly around her body. It highlighted the small, unripe peaches on her chest, which would one day grow to full fruition. That didn't bother Mark much. Even at twelve, he already knew he was a leg man from the days of seeing Kim Beckard in a short skirt at school. But even her legs were nothing compared to the ones he was viewing at that particular moment. It was no surprise that when they were finally given permission to enter the pool, he was glad the water was a little on the cold side.

After about half an hour of swimming and diving off the board, he joined a keep away game in the shallow end in which his angel was playing. Even better was that the teams consisted of boys against the girls. Naturally, he joined in. As the game progressed, he moved closer and closer to her and when at one point the girls were in possession of the ball, he assigned himself the task of guarding her. From her smile, she didn't seem to mind.

The ball landed with a splash near the both of them. Mark and the angel in the purple and white swimsuit battled the friction of the water to get to it. He got there first but she was right behind and wasn't going to give up easily. As he grabbed the ball, she jumped on his back wrapping those gorgeous legs around him. With an air of bravado, he gave her a piggyback ride while looking for someone to throw to. Part of him didn't want to get rid of the ball as it meant that she would release her grip on him, which he was enjoying. Even the cool water couldn't prevent the reaction now taking place inside his bathing suit. When he did throw the ball, she took a little time to actually climb off his back.

After that, both players closely guarded one another. There were more instances where those legs would encircle him and he loved every minute of it. Obviously, he didn't want pool time to ever end, but it eventually had to. Free from fears of taunts by Gene or anyone else from Ramsgate, he summoned the courage to walk with her as everyone was walking down the hill. To his surprise, she stopped talking to her friends and walked with him.

Her name was Lisa and she was from Estminston, a suburb northeast of Philadelphia. It seemed she was part of the perfect Christian family as her parents were still together. She had an older sister who was coming to the camp at "Teen Week" and a younger brother the same age as his sister. From the things she was telling him, it sounded like Estminston was a great place. However, she only said, "It's okay," when he mentioned it. She expressed genuine sympathy at the fact that his parents were divorced and he hadn't seen his father in two years and she also thought it was great that he lived so close to the shore and had the beach to go to everyday when he wanted. He agreed with this, but made sure he did not mention how awful the kids actually were in Ramsgate. That week, that part of his life didn't exist and so he steered the conversation away from it and although he didn't notice, she didn't speak any more of home. Instead, they talked about things like music and she was amused at his lack of knowledge of it. She opened his eyes to the existence of Christian rock and he made mental notes of some of the acts she mentioned. The more they talked, the more he liked her.

Tony had also found love at the same pool session. While Mark was having fun with Lisa in the pool, he was doing the same with a girl named Joyce. Joyce had long black hair and was taller and slimmer than Lisa. Mark agreed Joyce was pretty, but he still believed that he had gotten the better deal.

The four of them sat together at dinner and again at the evening meeting. After that, they all occupied a booth in the snack bar where they talked over sodas and Popsicles. It was where they made plans to sneak out and meet each other after lights out.

The planned liaison never happened that night. While Tony and Mark managed to sneak out of the dorm, the girls weren't so lucky. Therefore, the two boys waited in vain for nearly two hours. The next morning, Joyce explained that the counsellors were still patrolling the dorm like prison guards making escape impossible. Still, they didn't let it spoil the day times as they spent as much time as possible together.

Day two at Three Streams was even better than the first day. Practically, the only times he wasn't with Lisa were the morning meeting where he had to sit with his team and the afternoon activity where they played the Samson team at softball. Both of these came as a blessing for him as, once again, he answered all the bible questions, scoring points for his team and went two for two at the softball game and even though his team lost again 4-2, it didn't matter. Furthermore, he was making more friends with boys on his team and counselling group. Mark felt that for once God was making things all right for him.

Pool time on the second day was even better than the first. Of course there was the keep away game between the genders in which Mark and Lisa assigned themselves the task of guarding one another. Late in the pool session, chicken fights were suggested, with girls getting on the boys' shoulders. Lisa climbed onto Mark's without hesitation and together, they charged into the fray. Having her thighs so close to his head was plenty of incentive for him not to allow her to fall off and it felt like the same for her. Immediately, she pulled one girl off of the boy carrying her and minutes later separated another girl from her boy. However, the team of Joyce and Tony proved to be just as formidable and when they were the only two pairs left in the competition, it was the fact that Joyce was able to use Lisa's momentum against her that separated her from Mark. Not even Mark's incentive was enough to cancel out physics and as a result, Lisa came off his shoulders. There could be no rematch as the lifeguard immediately banned chicken fights after that.

Fun on the second evening consisted of roller-skating at the local rink. Mark was excited about this for two reasons. He was confident that his newfound friends wouldn't try to make him fall over, putting worries about what happened at the rink in Vincent out of his mind. However, he was looking forward more to the couple's skates and going around the rink hand in hand with Lisa. For once in his life, the reality matched the fantasy. No one at the rink made things difficult for anyone else. Craig Stevens amused everyone by making fun of the organ music played as background. It didn't matter that the camp would allow commercial music to be played, nor did it matter when the session was halted in the middle to have the evening meeting. Mark was on cloud nine as he skated with Lisa for all three couples skates on the night. As the pair skated round and round, he thought there was nothing better in the world.

Once again, clandestine plans for sneaking out and meeting that night were made during the evening. It was the main topic of talk between Mark and Lisa while they skated together. The four of them were all buzzing with excitement on the bus ride home that evening in anticipation of the night's events. When they got back to camp, they managed to slip under the counsellors' radar long enough to say a proper good night to each other.

"I'll see you tonight," he whispered with a grin. Lisa nodded with a similar grin and leaned forward towards him. Sensing what she was going to do, he bent forward a little too. Their lips met for an awkward second before pulling back with a nervous smile. They prepared to go for another less awkward attempt but a counsellor's voice ordering all campers to their dorms laid waste to it.

"We better go," Joyce stated urgently. The two girls

each gave their men pecks on the cheek before disappearing to their dorm. When they were gone, the two boys high fived each other and returned to their own dorm in anticipation of the night ahead. However, the planned liaison was once again thwarted. The counsellors in the boy's dorm were patrolling the corridors in Gestapo like fashion making escape impossible. They would learn the next day that the girls had experienced the same difficulty. Although it was speculated, they would never know for sure if the counsellors had found out that two boys had gotten out the night before and therefore were on their guard.

Things continued in the same vein for the third day. Mark's constant prayer, "Dear Lord, please don't let me say anything dumb, especially around Lisa," seemed to be answered that week. He made no oral gaffs, for which he was glad. Being one of the "stars" of the camp not only gave him a wide circle of friends; it greatly improved his self-esteem and confidence. Of course, being with Lisa did a lot to help this too.

In spite of all his best efforts, Mark's Joshua team was in dead last place and falling farther behind. Mark contributed all he could, learning his bible verses each day, on the ball field and answering questions in the morning bible quiz. He even won his team ten points when the song he suggested was voted the best one at the skit night. Furthermore, the song would be a hit with the rest of the camp for the week.

That evening, after the meeting, Mark, Lisa, Tony and Joyce all slipped away under the cover of darkness. Campers and counsellors were busy with evening free time and going to the snack bar so no one missed them. Quietly, they walked as a group towards the canoe pond and separated when they got there. Each couple went to a different bench by the pond. Had there been a full moon, it would have provided a romantic setting.

The two couples on the benches paid no attention to details like that anyway. They were too busy concentrating on the person next to them. This time, there was no clumsy lunge between Mark and Lisa. With a unified purpose, their lips met. Only this time, there was no shy pulling away as their mouths remained connected. All awkwardness vacated his mind each second he kissed the angel on the bench. He grew more and more confident. Without realising it, his hands began to slide along her body, stopping momentarily over the small, unripe peaches on her chest, which would one day grow to full fruition. She made no attempt to remove his hand. Meanwhile, thoughts of laying her back across the bench and getting on top of her like in the movies formulated in his mind. He shifted his weight for the attempt.

"This is not how you behave at a Christian camp!" a mysterious voice rang out. Both couples immediately stopped and looked to the direction of the voice. Standing there were Barbara North and a female counsellor.

"Get to your dorms now," Barbara ordered in the same voice.

"You two girls, come with me," the counsellor ordered less forcefully.

Sheepishly, the lovers got off the benches and went their separate ways. The girls followed the counsellor, while Barbara made sure the two boys headed off in the right direction. However, when they were out of sight of Barbara, Mark and Tony high fived and laughed the rest of the way to the dorm.

Feelings from his intimate moments with Lisa lingered in his mind as he was preparing for bed. It was all he could do to conceal the tent that was trying to erect itself inside his pants. He locked himself in a toilet stall in the hopes that it would eventually die down. However, the thoughts of the evening wouldn't leave his mind. Instead, they took him to a scenario where he and Lisa didn't get caught. Overcome by his fantasy, Mark decided right there in the toilet stall of a religious camp to officially enter puberty.

Steps were taken by counsellors to ensure the two couples were kept apart as much as possible. Thursday's activities, the Olympics and team canoeing in the afternoon made it difficult for the couples to meet. That didn't stop them from stealing brief moments or being together in the pool. While they couldn't be separated in the pool, the counsellors did watch them like hawks. Still, Lisa did get to jump on his back during the keep away game. However, that evening, they made sure that the couples didn't leave their sight.

Friday was the last full day of camp and Mark was determined to enjoy every minute of it. He took everything in that day, from Tony's constant jokes about sex to Henry's now famous quote, "Fun, fun, fun, hey, hey, hey!" Of course it was the last day he had with Lisa and nothing was going to spoil that.

At breakfast that morning, it was announced that voting for camper of the week would take place. A boy named Steve, who was on his team and sitting at the table suggested that Mark should be given that honour and he was surprised to hear the responses from around the table.

I'll vote for you," Tony declared.

"Me too," remarked Henry.

Then Joyce added, "I'll vote for you, you probably won't win, but why not."

"Well, I'll definitely vote for you," Lisa added with a smile and giving him a quick cuddle.

A warm feeling filled in him. Nobody had ever thought of him that way before and in his mind, he wasn't sure how to handle it. Bible verses about pride humbled him, but these were soon countered by the fact that he had never been this popular in his life before and he recalled bible verses about false modesty. It all threatened to send his mind into overload; however, the soft, gentle touch from Lisa made him feel that everything was all right.

Steve took on the role as Mark's campaign manager. He went around the camp urging everyone to vote for Mark. Most of his team was going to do that anyway since he had gotten a lot of points for the team. But it appeared others were going to vote for him as well. Several campers informed him, "I'm voting for you" and one kid whom he barely knew declared, "I put down the kid in the glasses on my vote." In spite of all that, he was still sceptical about actually winning.

Thoughts about camper of the week were shelved to another part of his mind that afternoon as his team met Lisa's team at softball. He and Lisa were both had been ribbing the other how their team was going to win, although in the back of his mind, he knew that his team would probably lose. The Solomon team had been in first place all week while Mark's Joshua team was in dead last.

For the first inning, there was the possibility of an upset on the cards as the Joshua team drew first blood. Mark hit a double when he batted and then scored on Roger's hit, but that was the only scoring they would do in the game. After that, it was all Solomon. They scored eight runs in the first inning and nine in the second to win 17-1. Mark wasn't really surprised at the result and was felt upbeat after the game.

"I thought you said you were gonna beat us," Lisa chided immediately after the game.

"You were lucky," Mark responded with a grin.

Lisa returned with, "We could beat your team at

anything."

A sly thought crossed his mind. He let the thought fully process before he offered, "You couldn't beat us in wrestling."

A glint briefly flickered in her eye as Lisa seemed to get the subtlety of his words. In a single motion, she said, "Oh yeah," before putting a tackle on him that would have impressed his old coach from the Ramsgate Colts JV. Mark went down like a felled redwood tree and Lisa landed on top of him, pressing her body onto his. For a moment, he thought about wrestling her off of him, but as the fruit on her chest pressed against his and the flesh of her thighs contacted the flesh on his, he decided not to. This contact resulted in the scientific reaction of a banana magically appearing in his pants. From the grin on her face, he guessed that she felt the banana too.

If there ever was a moment in his life he could have forever frozen in time, it would be this one; lying there, acting as a human mattress for Lisa. He didn't know how long the freeze frame lasted, but it ended when a counsellor bellowed, "Get off of him, this is a Christian camp!"

The last pool time of the week gave one more final time to see her amazing developing body. They joined in the final keep away game but only for a while. For the last hour, they stayed in a secluded corner of the pool in the deeper end. Using the water for support, he held her afloat with one arm while they other supported her legs. There they just talked.

"I need your address so I can write to you," Mark started.

"I'll give it to you," she assured him. "but we can send messages on email and Facebook. Do you have an account?"

Mark had to say no and explained that his mother

wouldn't allow him on Internet sites like that because there were too many weirdoes. This didn't deter her one bit though. "There's nothing wrong with Facebook," she explained. "Besides, the camp has a page on it where everyone can keep in touch with each other." This was welcome news because he was sure he could, with the help of Lisa, persuade his mother to change her views.

The thoughts and feelings from the afternoon overwhelmed Mark's mind. Therefore, as he was cleaning up for dinner, he once again sought sanctuary in a toilet stall and reaffirmed his entry into puberty. That brought temporary relief because the anxieties again returned to haunt his mind at dinner. He managed to keep a lid on these during the meal, but it came increasingly difficult to do so when the pastor's wife began the evening announcements. First, she spoke about the evening campfire service and scoring points would end at seven o'clock.

"Now, for the camper of the week," she began as if she was feeling his anxieties too. Mark held his breath while she continued, "It wasn't even close! One fellow, and I do mean fellow, ran away with it. That fellow is Mark Leversee."

Shocked, but delighted, Mark got up to collect his reward, punching the air in triumph. At a nearby table, he saw Steve was celebrating the win even more than he was. He stood by the pastor's wife as she announced, "For being camper of the week, he gets the big cheese." He laughed along with the others as she handed him a pin of a mouse eating a piece of cheese. The prize was inconsequential; this was the greatest moment of his life. He had never been so popular and never again would be.

An hour and a half later, the entire camp walked up a hill and across a large field. A mysterious opening suddenly appeared in the tree line, which led to a spacious open area. Square planks of wood were arranged in rows, which everyone sat down on in their teams. A large fire was lit at the front. The whole scene would have provided a romantic atmosphere if Mark and Lisa had been allowed to sit together.

The scene did provide the perfect atmosphere for the campfire service. Songs were sung collectively and one by each team. Teams also shared a bible verse that was followed by an inspiring talk from Reverend McCeaver. After that came the chance for all to share their testimonies. One by one, campers, counsellors and the staff stood up and declared how great it was to have Jesus in their lives. Even Tony stood up and told how he became saved and how he wished his father would come to know the Saviour.

Suddenly, a feeling inside of him told Mark to stand up. He felt the eyes of the camp were on him, however, he also felt that no one was going to judge him. There were no serious anxieties, just a few butterflies as he felt confident that nothing he said would be turned into a reason to ridicule him. Feeling as calm as he could have been, he began to speak.

"I became saved at my church's Christmas show last year. I accepted Jesus because I didn't want to go to hell and wanted Jesus in my life. But I didn't really know what it was like to be a Christian until I came here. Here, I found true Christian friends." In another part of his mind, he fought off the urge to say, "Unlike all the jerks in Ramsgate." "Now, I can say I can serve my Saviour with all my heart and I will read my bible and pray every day."

Not knowing what else to say, he sat down. The speaker acknowledged, "Thank you and I'm glad you got to find true Christian friends here." He then handed over to the next testimony giver. Testimonies lasted for another quarter of an hour before the final song was sung. The service concluded with a final prayer and the dousing of the campfire before everyone marched in the dark back to camp, all inspired by the evening's festivities.

"I really liked your testimony," Joyce complimented Mark when they all returned. Lisa simply gave him a big hug, burying her face in his shoulder. The hug was only stopped when counsellors began ordering campers to their dorms. When they separated, he knew for sure he was going to miss Three Streams.

Saturday was the final day of camp and Mark, with many others, greeted it with dismay. The idea of leaving Three Streams and returning to Ramsgate lingered like a black cloud in the back of his mind. He sombrely packed his things and with Tony, took them down to the front of the camp to be stored for when their parents arrived to take them home. After that, there was a final meeting and a case of waiting around before lunch.

He spent the entire time with his angel. He sat on the grass with her on his lap facing him, her legs wrapped around his waist. Surprisingly, no one told them to break. They talked about how they were going to miss each other and she gave him assurances that she would help convince his mother to let him message her on Facebook.

Lunch was like a condemned man's last meal. The only announcement was the obvious fact that the Solomon team had won the week, while the Joshua team finished last. He did clap for Lisa when her name was called to collect her prize of a candy bar. After lunch, parents began arriving to take their children home. The two brothers on his team left first and then Steve. All gave assurances they would keep in touch. Then Joyce's parents came and after Mark and Lisa said good-bye, they left Tony and Joyce to say good-bye to each other properly.

Ten minutes following Joyce's departure, mother's car pulled into the lot. Mrs Leversee was pleasantly surprised to see a large group of people coming to see her son off. She was more intrigued by the young lady holding onto his arm as they came closer. Dutifully, Mark introduced Tony, Henry and Daryl, saving Lisa to last. While she acknowledged the boys, she was more interested in the girl. This proved to be an advantage as Lisa got to explain about how the camp has a page on Facebook and how all the campers kept in touch on the Internet. When the car was packed, Mark shook the boys' hands with promises to keep in touch and then accepted Lisa as she threw herself into his arms. They had a long kiss, all the while mother waiting for the big love scene to end. When it did, he got into the car waving to everyone as they drove off. He did not see the tears now rolling down Lisa's cheeks.

He was prepared for the barrage of questions him mother fired at him about his week. She wanted to know all about Lisa saying, "If I'm going to let you onto Facebook, I need to know everything about her.." Mark provided all the information he knew and she seemed to be glad, especially at the fact he had been voted camper of the week. The further the car drove away from the camp, the more he wanted to go back. However, he knew this wasn't possible, so he settled himself in the knowledge it would be a full year before he could return. Another year of living in Ramsgate.

Chapter 13

Paradise Lost

Great feelings from his week at Three Streams lasted over the weekend, long enough for his mother to boast about her son being voted camper of the week to everyone at St. James church. Harsh realities of Ramsgate set in on the following Monday. Before he went away, Mark signed up for a baseball and basketball clinic at Ramsgate Field. He wasn't overly enthusiastic about it and joined mainly because Gene nagged him into it. So, while he liked the idea of playing baseball and basketball, he also worried about who else had signed up for it.

Some of his worries were justified when he showed up on the first day. While there were none of the likes of Andrew Blumenthaw type jocks present, David Fitzpatrick and Joe Pellegrini were. Fears about what those two might say about him filled Mark's head with anxiety. However, David didn't say anything about him. He guessed that it was because they were on the same team for the basketball-dribbling race and it was Mark who actually had won the race for his team. Joe, on the other hand, was a different story.

"There would be bases loaded and he strikes out one batter. Then he says, "I got a no-hitter going,"" Mark overheard Joe telling some unknown boy.

"What, did he walk them all?" the boy inquired.

"No, they all got hits," Joe clarified.

While Joe didn't say his name, Mark he that he was talking about him. Furthermore, he remembered things happening differently. True, he did say he had a no-hitter going, but only because he had gotten the first three batters out in the first inning. The scenario Joe had described to the boy was true as well; he did strike out a batter with the bases loaded. Only he said, "At least I still have my shut out." Therefore, he concluded that Joe was up to his old tricks of spreading lies about him.

The first week at clinic wasn't too bad for him. David Fitzpatrick never came after the first day and Joe Pellegrini lasted the first week. He even hit well at baseball and threw out a runner at third base from centre field. In the first basketball game, he made a basket and got many rebounds. That all changed in the second week. Mark's athletic inconsistency began to show itself. In one basketball game, he missed several easy shots and made a bad pass, which was stolen away by the other team. This resulted in his team captain as well as some precocious 5th graders chanting, "You stink, Leversee" for the rest of that day. Baseball progressed to fast pitch in the second week with more disastrous results. His eyes were unaccustomed to the speed of the ball and this led to several strikeouts. Inevitably, more kids joined the "You stink, Leversee" club.

Clinic was just a two hour blip on the day and he was secure in the knowledge that if he didn't want to go on a particular day, he didn't have to. There were a few days where he simply rode his bike on the boardwalk in Vincent instead of going to the clinic. No one would check up on him. Furthermore, he had the rest of the day to spend at the beach or go fishing with his grandfather.

The fishing wasn't as good as the experience of the previous year. Coming back each time without catching any fish began to frustrate Mark. There was one time when several of his relatives were down; he was the only one who didn't catch anything. One day, after he had a bite and nearly reeled it all the way up, the fish got away. The frustration sent him into a temper and he began kicking the boat.

"Stop that now!" his grandfather ordered. "When you go out fishing, you need to have the patience of Job. Catching fish is only a minor part of it."

His grandfather's stern tone was enough to make him stop. However, confusion ensued in his mind as mixed messages grappled for supremacy. On previous trips, grandfather had encouraged him to catch fish, so telling him that it was only a minor part was too much. The confusion caused him to retreat further into himself the rest of that day. He would only go out fishing one more time that summer.

Things didn't seem much better at home. His mother seemed to be telling all and sundry about his girlfriend. This led his sister to constantly tease him about it. "Mark's got a girlfriend," she would say to anyone who would listen. After a while her teasing began to get old to the point where it began to grind on him. When she said it to Gene, that was all that he could take. Gene was the last person whom he wanted to know about his summer romance. Totally frustrated, Mark punched his sister.

Naturally, Lesley went crying to their mother and she immediately came down hard on Mark. It wasn't the punishment of being banned from the computer that night that bothered him; it was her lecture that got to him. "This is not how a boy who's been to bible camp is supposed to act," she reprimanded.

"But she was teasing me about Lisa," he protested.

"That's no reason for hitting a seven year old," she retorted. "Besides, why don't you punch those kids who pick on you?"

Her words struck Mark like a large blunt instrument. He would have loved to punch out all the kids who made his life a misery, but what he couldn't tell his mother was that if he did, he would be the one who was worse off. The few times he did fight back, he was always made out to be the troublemaker. Also in his mind, he had taken enough crap off these kids; he wasn't about to take it off his seven-year-old sister.

His mother began to use Three Streams and his commitment to Jesus as a stick to beat him with. When any doubt of wrongdoing arose, she would remind him, "You committed your life to Christ, so you better not be lying" This always had the desired effect as he was afraid of disappointing his mother by her thinking he was a bad Christian.

In the days that followed, a worse event occurred. In the second week after camp, a family from Philadelphia rented a summer home nearby. Mark became friendly with a boy near his own age named Dominic. One evening Dominic's family invited him to go to the boardwalk in Bay City with them. He wanted to go, but it was on an evening when he had to collect for his paper route.

His grandmother was quick to remind him of this. "You have to do your collecting first."

"I can go when I'm done," he replied.

"What time will that be?" inquired Dominic.

"Seven-thirty," he informed.

"That might be too late," Dominic stated.

In desperation, Mark devised a plan in his head. "I'll do most of my collecting tonight and then finish it off tomorrow," he offered with a satisfied smile.

Unfortunately, his grandmother threw a wrench in his plan. "You might not have the money ready for when the district manager comes," she warned.

Everything began to rush around in his head as he struggled to come up with a plausible solution. He thought about going collecting on the following afternoon, before the district manager came, but the thought of his grandmother shooting the idea down stopped him. His mind began to go into overload and the anxiety made him twitch. While he vainly thrashed about to formulate a plan, his sister's voice sounded in another part of his brain. "Mom wants you to go collecting," she said.

A volcano suddenly erupted inside his head. Seeing Lesley standing near them, he turned to her and screamed, "Shut your fuckin' face!" before he even realised he had said it.

The second she heard about it, his mother had a field day with him. "I see that bible camp didn't do you any good," she sneered.

"I'm sorry," he apologised, then tried to explain, "I had Grandma nagging me, Dominic talking to me and then she comes up with her big fat mouth."

"That's no reason for cursing at your sister," mother cut short. She then banned him from going out with Dominic's family and going on the computer that night. "I suggest you spend the night reading the bible," she told her son. This was exactly what he did that night as a sign of repentance.

Knowing that Liz Clover lived on one of the streets where he had his paper route didn't faze Mark. He saw her a couple of times and each time she would shout, "Marvin!" but nothing more happened. However, one evening, when he was out collecting, Liz was there with a large group of friends. When she saw him, she shouted, "Hey Marvin," which the rest of the group copied. He did his best to ignore the taunts and continued his rounds, making his way through the assembly of kids. Sensing that her taunts weren't having the desired effect, Liz took the ice cream cone she was holding in her hand and stuck it in his face. Mark, feeling outnumbered, wiped the ice cream from his face and continued on. Seeing she was getting to him, she threw the cone at him, narrowly missing. This brought a chorus of "ooohs" from the crowd. However, all he could think about was how she had just wasted a perfectly good ice cream cone and simply went on finishing his collections on the street.

That wasn't the end of it. Two weeks later, while he was collecting on that street, he spotted an even larger group of kids. He did his best to ignore them but an unfamiliar voice called out, "If I kick your head in, are you going to get me arrested for salt and battery?" Mark took a closer look at the group. Standing next to the boy who asked the question was Tommy Allen.

Before he knew it, Tommy and his gang had completely surrounded Mark. Instinctively, he protected the pockets where he kept his money, but it wasn't that they were after. "We're gonna put air in your tyres," Tommy informed him.

Another boy in the group produced a long nail. Mark gulped in fear that the boy was going to stab his bike tyre. However, the boy put the nail in the valve of the tyre and let out all the air.

"Stop that!" Mark protested.

"Shut up and let us put air in your tyre," growled the boy who had spoken earlier menacingly, with Tommy standing beside him looking just as threatening. He knew fighting back was useless, there were too many of them. Feeling helpless, he stood there and watched the boys drain the air from both of his tyres. Once done, Tommy smirked, "You better get some air in your tyres."

Totally humiliated, Mark walked with his bike away from the laughing crowd. As he finished the rest of his collections for that street, he had to endure taunts like, "Why don't you come and kick our asses, you pussy?" Worse, when he got home, he was met with the predictable, "Why didn't you go and sock one of them?" Naturally, she didn't want to hear his, "There were too many of them, I couldn't fight'em all" response. However, after that, his mother did accompany him when he collected on that street, so at least he didn't have any problems after that.

Great memories of Three Streams faded in his mind in a few short weeks after that one glorious week. Those memories might have faded even more if it hadn't been for the Internet. Daily, he would send and receive emails from Lisa and the other friends he had made there. Nearly every day, sometimes for two hours at a time, he and Lisa would converse through instant messaging. That kept the memories fresh and made the notion of living in Ramsgate for a year bearable and gave him something to look forward to for the next summer.

In the meantime, he still had to survive another year in Ramsgate. The summer wasn't too bad, as he didn't see too many people from school. When he did, there would always be some comment made or at least they would call him Marvin. In fact, every one called him Marvin so much; even Dominic began calling him it. When his mother asked, "Why is he calling you Marvin?" he spat, "It's because all the jerks here call me it." Although she wasn't happy with her son's tone, she must have said something to Dominic, because he never called him Marvin after that.

Inconsistent play once again reared its head at the baseball and basketball clinic. It seemed that he would never hit well and field well on the same day. One day he went five for five at bat, but made three errors in the field. The very next day, he made three great catches in the outfield, but went 0 for 3 at bat with a strikeout. It was the same in basketball. One game he blocked two shots and grabbed a number of rebounds but missed two easy shots. The next, he made two baskets but committed two fouls. Naturally, everybody remembered the mistakes and paid little attention to the good plays he made. As a result, the chant "You suck Leversee," became a number one hit with the boys at the clinic. To make matters worse, thanks to some mouthy former fifth graders, everyone called him Marvin and even put that name in the scorebook.

Failures at the clinic stuck in his mind more than he wanted. When he was at Three Streams, he told himself he wasn't going to continue with his fantasy baseball when he returned, but as things worsened, he started it up again to escape. He concluded that even though it only existed in his mind, it wasn't a real lie if he didn't tell people about it, so he didn't. After determining his team had won and lost one game each while he was at camp, he recommenced games in the back yard or in front of the house. His team won all their remaining league games and after losing the first game, swept the opposing team three straight games to advance into the championship series. Of course, Mark was the star player with a .600 batting average.

Fantasy baseball compensated for clinic and his mother went with him to collect on Washington Avenue. So he had no more grief from the likes of Liz Clover or Tommy Allen. But what really saved his summer were the visits from his relatives from Pennsylvania. It meant that he didn't go to the beach alone or with his annoying sister every day and his cousins were all near enough his own age. They were all excited about him showing them the ocean and teaching them how to body surf. They would go out on his grandfather's boat together and at least once during the week's stay, the adults would go the short distance to Atlantic City. When they went, they would leave money for Mark and his cousins to play miniature golf and have ice creams afterwards. Other evenings, they would go to the boardwalk in Bay City and ride on the amusements. This happened each time any of the relatives visited and seemed to come in rapid succession. It was no wonder he enjoyed that summer.

He always had a good time with his cousins, no matter if they visited him or he visited them. Most of the ones who came that summer he already knew, but there were some he had never met before. One of those was his cousin Tom who was his age and like Mark, had a younger sister and brother. He was also about the same size and wore similar glasses, but had lighter coloured hair. Like all of his cousins, Mark showed Tom how to body surf, took bike rides to the bay, went out on the boat and went to the boardwalk. They had a good time the week Tom's family came to stay. However, there was something in Tom, which Mrs Leversee saw. To her, he seemed like some sort of "golden boy." He got good grades and helped look after his siblings and didn't seem to be targeted by bullies. In Mrs Leversee's mind, Tom was the sort of boy she wanted her own son to be.

Fortunately, his mother's views on Tom hadn't yet manifested themselves onto Mark. He simply enjoyed the visits of all his cousins and lamented when they had to leave at the end of the week. He would have loved to go with them and live in Pennsylvania because it was so much better than Ramsgate. Besides, he would be closer to Lisa. Instead, he had to stay in a town he hated and while the relatives' visits made him temporarily forget his problems, it didn't make them go away. Therefore, despite all of his good experiences in the late summer, things were no better or maybe worse for him since that heavenly week he had at Three Streams.

Chapter 14

Baseball to Football

Just like in his ice hockey season a few months earlier, the team Mark was playing against for the championship managed to avoid the clean sweep in game four. In that game, his team was leading 13-10 in the final inning before an opposing batter hit a home run with runners on all the bases. The grand slam made the game a 14-13 win for the other team and brought the series to three games to one.

Game five was shaping into more of a pitcher's duel. At the bottom of the fifth inning, with his team leading 1-0, Mark stepped up to bat. So far in the game, he flied out to centre field and hit a single. Once in the batter's box, the pitcher wasted no time and immediately wound up and hurled the ball towards him. With a pinch of anxiety, he watched it speed at him, only to veer off target at the last moment.

"Ball!" the umpire called out.

Mark relaxed for a second and then braced himself for the next pitch. This pitch came close to hitting him, forcing him to step back. He didn't need to hear the ump call, "Ball two!" Now up two balls on the pitcher, he decided he wasn't going to swing at the next pitch unless it was perfect. It wasn't perfect, but it was good enough for the umpire to call, "Strike!"

The call forced him to refocus, so with renewed determination he settled in for the next pitch. He watched it come towards him and as it did, he determined it was perfect. With all his focus, Mark stepped forward and swung; the result was a resounding prang from the bat striking the ball.

Without hesitation, he dropped the bat and sprinted to first base. It was when he followed the first base coach's direction to go to second base; he saw that his hit had sent the ball way out into the outfield, the outfielders madly chasing after it. He rounded second and gave an extra burst of speed towards third base. The third base coach's instruction to go for home said it all. Mark sprinted the rest of the way, touching home plate to the cheers of his teammates and spectators.

Mark's home run was the last score of the game. When the final out of the game was made, his team were winners 2-0. Furthermore, his team were champions winning the series four games to one. A glib feeling engulfed him as he put his glove and ball back into the shed and went into the house. His baseball team were champions and his home run helped to win it, at least in his own mind.

He had four days of feeling good about being champions at baseball before time came to sign up for football. Age-wise, he was supposed to sign up for varsity that season, but his grandfather constantly advised him that he should play another year of jayvee. What he knew the rules to be and following what his grandfather advised him became a conflict in his mind. That conflict was still there when he and Gene got to the field.

"You'll make it a lot, Lancaster," greeted the voice of Steven Winger when they arrived at the clubhouse. Seeing Mark with him, Steven further commented, "You too, Leversee."

"I made it last year," Mark retorted, getting looks from some of the other boys in the line.

Those words were enough to silence Steven and the faces surrounding him. Nothing more was said as he and Gene took their places in the back of the line. However, while he waited, his mind still wrestled with

171

the conflict of going out for varsity or trying to play another year of jayvee. He still hadn't resolved the conflict by the time he got to the front of the line. Inwardly, he hoped he could play another year of jayvee.

The varsity head coach's voice snapped Mark out of his mental battle. "Jayvee or varsity?" the coach's voice asked impatiently.

"Uh, I was hoping to go out for jayvee," Mark responded nervously.

The jayvee coach, who had been standing unnoticed in the background, came over. "Leversee, I know that you're of varsity age," he identified.

"I remember you," stated the varsity coach, "Why would you want to go out for the jayvees?"

Before Mark could answer, the jayvee coach piped in with, "He doesn't have any sense." Both men looked at him as if they expected him to say something.

Normally, his mind would have gone into overload, but his grandfather had given him a good answer, or so at least he thought. "My grandfather said I should play another year of jayvee, I told him I wasn't allowed to but he wouldn't listen," he wailed.

The two coaches looked at each other for a second and then the varsity coach responded, "You should have just said ok to your grandfather and done what you knew was right."

Once again, he felt that whatever he said in response would be wrong, so he said nothing more. He collected his uniform and left the clubhouse as quickly as he could, doing his best to ignore some of the potential jayvee players, some of whom he recognised from the clinic, who were lining up say, "Oh, you're real smart." If he hadn't promised Gene he would wait for him, he would have left immediately. When Gene came out with his uniform, they left saying very little on the ride home. When he got home and told his grandfather that he had to go out for varsity, grandfather's only response was, "So, you're gonna get slaughtered this year."

In the first weeks of practice, grandfather's words became prophetic. Mark always seemed to go up against eighth graders who were forty pounds heavier than he was and always came the worse off. It didn't matter what the drill was- whether it was tackling, nutcrackers, fumble recovery or scrimmages, he always seemed to get battered around. The fact that Gene wasn't doing any better, if not worse, brought little consolation. In the third week of practice, while standing on the sidelines during a scrimmage, they both agreed they weren't going to make the team.

As the final week before cuts loomed, their theory seemed to be becoming more of a reality. It was little comfort when Steve Winger and many others who were in line that first day had cut themselves over the past few weeks. It only meant they got battered around more in practice. His hope of getting sent back to the jayvees was dashed the first week when the head coach warned him, "You either make this team or get cut, I'm not sending you back to the jayvees."

When the day of cuts arrived, Mark went to practice feeling like a condemned man going for execution. He merely shrugged and muttered, "I don't know" when those whose places on the team were already assured asked him if he thought he was going to make it. When Gene didn't show up for practice that evening, Mark simply assumed that he was already cut or didn't show up because he knew he was going to be.

It turned out that Mark's first assumption was the one, which proved to be correct and that Gene and another boy were cut before practice started. However, no one knew this until the end of the night. Practice

173

went pretty much the same way for Mark, although he did try a little harder to impress. At the end, the team lined up at the clubhouse where he learned that he had actually made the team. He had so been so sure he was going to be cut that he didn't know how to react when he learned that he had actually made the team. His mind was still processing this when he collected his game uniform.

The very next practice, the assistant coach was quick to inform him why he made the team. "Do you know why you made the team?" he snarled at Mark after he didn't do a block drill satisfactorily. When he shook his head, the coach answered for him, "Because you're a seventh grader!" He then went on, "You might have made the team, but you're not getting into any games until you show me you want to play football. And I don't care if we're winning 100-0."

It seemed clear to him that the assistant coach resented him for making that team. At least once every practice the coach would ask him, "Are you sure you want to play football?" It seemed that it was going to be a long football season, even if the team fulfilled the head coach's prophecy of winning the championship.

Chapter 15

Bad Seed Bear Fruit

Just like every year, Mark was definitely not looking forward to the start of the new school year. He dreaded seeing all those kids who made his life miserable. Even the new sixth graders were kids he knew from the summer clinic and he felt there wasn't going to be anywhere to hide. He did have one tiny piece of reassurance from his online chat with Lisa the night before. Like him, she was also not looking forward to going to school, but she gave him words that soothed him. "I know you're smart because you got all those bible questions right at camp," she reassured him. When he read that on his computer screen, he knew why he loved her.

Reality immediately took its grip on him when he walked through the gates of Tye School that first morning. Although he tried his best to hide in the shadows, he was spotted by the likes of Andrew Blumenthaw, John Lodge and others.

"Hey Marvin," Andrew greeted him sarcastically.

"Where's your homo friend, Lancaster?" John asked in the same sarcastic tone.

Mark just shrugged, but his mind was processing John's insinuation about his sexuality. Back in the summer, he had probably been farther with a girl then any of them ever had, so there was no way he was homosexual. Fortunately, the group let him alone, but he wasn't free for two minutes before he was accosted again, this time by Steve McGuire and the blonde Adrian Adler, who had been in his class in sixth grade.

"Marvin," Steve barked, "Do you still think you're

Kip McClary of the Flyers?"

Mark gave a soft "No," but inside his head, he was thinking about the fact that Steve had a similar hero, Rob Knorr, who played for the Boston Bruins. Therefore, Steve was being a hypocrite, but before he totally processed it, Adrian sarcastically added, "Why don't you tell us about some of your adventures on the Ramsgate Colts?" Then, in a strange voice, he continued, "I was standing here like this," making a stance like a football player, "And this big halfback came and I tackled him."

Steve erupted in hysterical laughter, while Mark was left to process in his mind the fact he knew it didn't happen like that. All he ever said was that he had made his first tackle of the season. His silence while trying to process things made Steve and Adrian laugh more.

Once they had stopped laughing, Steve turned serious. "You better not be in my class this year," he warned. All Mark could think of was that it wouldn't be his fault if he was in the same class as Steve. This was still filtering through his mind when Steve threatened, "If you are in my class, you better not say shit like "Two minutes in the penalty box" or "The foul's on McGuire" or I am gonna beat the shit out of you."

Adrian and Steve were long gone by the time his mind fully processed the fact that Steve had originally started that and it was only after he was fed up with it that he complained about it. Mark's only crime was not to get fed up with it as fast; because those phrases continued to amuse him. However, it didn't stop Steve complaining about him to Mrs Dorbano over his constant repetitions of them. Adrian and Steve were no longer there to hear any explanation from him, not that they would have accepted it anyway. Worse, they probably would have turned hostile.

No one else approached him for the remaining

minutes he was out in the playground. However, his hope of getting to the gym without more occurrences was dashed when he passed Joe Gerberwitz and another boy in the hall.

"There's a real faggot," Joe remarked as Mark walked past.

Not being able to stop himself, he gave Joe a disdainful look. This only made him laugh and then inquire, "Who's your victim tonight? The Sandman? Jack Frost?"

Mark would have desperately loved to have said, "You are," but he knew where that would have led. Joe Gerberwitz, like most kids in Ramsgate, loved to dish it out but couldn't take it himself. Any witty comeback would be countered by physical aggression. Therefore, he just quickened his pace and headed straight for the gym.

"What, you made the team?" Gene asked in surprise when he met Mark in the gym.

"They said it was because I was a seventh grader," Mark clarified.

Gene opened his mouth to state, "I'm a seventh grader too," but he realised that because he was already thirteen, he was of eighth grade age as far as the football team was concerned. After that, the two boys went silent and waited for class assignments. That silence lasted only a few minutes when a gruff voice barked, "Get the fuck out of here, Leversee!" Mark turned to see several eighth grade team mates from the football team all looking angrily at him. Since they were at least thirty pounds larger and were starting players, he decided to follow their order. However, he did conclude that they weren't being very good teammates.

Mr Tasker made his usual welcome speech and the sixth graders were all assigned to their classes. Mark

177

and Gene waited patiently as pupils in the seventh grade were assigned to theirs. This time, Mark wasn't called to the first class, nor the second. Gene was assigned to the third class Mr Tasker called, Mr Danko's class, while he still waited. Fears that he was going to be missed out altogether began stoking the flames of anxiety after he wasn't called to the fourth class. Those fears rapidly went away when he was called to the fifth and final class, Mrs Hinton's who was a short but authoritative looking middle aged woman.

Not being called to the last class of the seventh grade had its advantages. He had the satisfaction of knowing that he wouldn't have boys like Tommy Allen, David Fitzpatrick, Steve McGuire, Joe Gerberwitz or Andrew Blumenthaw in his class. Nor would he have any girls like Liz Clover or Nancy Greenwood. As he surveyed his new class, he saw the only kids he may have a problem with were Mike Sigfried, Damon Bates and possibly Jim Friend. However, Damon had hardly acknowledged him in the past year and Jim was only a problem when there were others around. As for Mike, he always blew hot or cold. Keith Wenger was also in his class, but Mark decided to wait until he found out which of his two faces Keith had decided to wear for that year.

As for the girls, the only problem he could see was Renee Tye. Laurie Swords was also in his class but he knew she wouldn't say much without Nancy or any of her other friends around. Kim Beckard was in his class too, but those feelings he had for her had long since dissolved. Seeing Kim reinforced in his mind that she didn't hold a candle to Lisa.

Mark's first day of seventh grade went by with no further heartache. At least not from any of the kids, although he was befuddled when his new Social

Studies teacher, Mrs Bromberg, set them a task to write what they knew about the scandal involving a US Senator from New Jersey who was caught taking backhanders from an anti- environmental group. He had heard about the scandal but paid little attention to the news over the summer, so he knew very little. He wrote what he could. Fortunately, Mr Lejeune the Math teacher and Mr Danko the Science teacher were more merciful. On the whole, he left school that first day feeling a little optimistic and hoped that his continual prayer that God wouldn't let him say anything stupid would continue to be answered.

For the first two weeks, things seemed to go his way. He even won a number game in French class, receiving accolades from Damon Bates and Mike Sigfried for winning it for the boys. Things soon changed after that, everyone, even kids he hardly knew were calling him Marvin; Renee Tye helped see to that. A girl named Diane Boreman from his class picked up on that very quickly. Once again, he had to withstand being called by a name that wasn't his and he couldn't do anything to change it.

Being called Marvin wasn't the worst of his problems. For the second straight summer, he had another growth spurt. Once again, his trousers weren't long enough, which resulted in more taunts about wearing flood pants. Even the new sixth graders joined in. Worse still, when he did wear trousers that were long enough, kids simply changed the rules. When he tried to argue back, "These aren't floods, they touch my shoes," the response would be, "They have to cover your shoe laces." When there was a group of kids involved, they would simply shout him down and in the case of Joe Gerberwitz who said, "My fist says they're flood pants."

Naturally, his mother gave him no sympathy. She

repeated previous statements like "Don't let it get to you" or "At least, I'll be ready for it." Only this time she added, "I bet your cousin Tom wouldn't let it bother him." This made Mark feel worse, that he couldn't measure up to his golden boy cousin. Furthermore, if he said anything to his tormentors, they would only respond with violence.

It wasn't just his name or his trouser length that contributed to the grief he suffered. In spite of God seeming to answer his prayers about not saying anything stupid, his reputation for being a "weirdo" was strongly ingrained in the minds of the children of Ramsgate. So was the belief that he was a liar. A day didn't pass where somebody didn't make some sort of comment. It might have been Joe Gerberwitz asking him if he was going to kill the sandman, Steve McGuire calling him gay or David Fitzpatrick telling all about Mark getting him done for assault and battery. Girls would tell him that Jody Molstein wanted to go out with him, even though he knew it wasn't true. It wasn't long before he was dreading going to school and his only escape was talking to Lisa on line most evenings.

Chapter 16

End of a Career

Mark wasn't surprised that he didn't get into either of the first two games his football team played. The first game was a 0-0 tie even though Ramsgate was the better team. They just couldn't get in the end zone that evening. The second game they lost 8-6 to the team whom the head coach said they would be playing again in the championship.

It was the third game that the assistant coach's earlier warning came to pass. In that game, Ramsgate blasted the opposition 24-0 and the head coach began putting many of the back-up players into the game. However, Mark was one of the few players who didn't get in. While he was happy his team won, he was still upset that he didn't get to play.

"I feel like quitting," he wailed on the drive home.

"Then go ahead and quit," his grandfather assured him. "They should have been putting people in when it was 16-0," he added.

When he got home, Mark's mother agreed with her father. "You sweated it out to make the team, you should get a chance to play," she supported. Content that he had the backing of both his mother and grandfather, Mark decided he was going to quit the football team.

"So, you're quittin'," the head coach remarked when Mark showed up to turn in his equipment that Monday evening. Mark simply nodded and the coach further pontificated, "I cut a kid to keep you, I thought you had potential for next year." Again, he said nothing and handed everything over. When the coach checked

181

everything, he concluded with, "Don't try coming out next year, I won't even give you a uniform." Those words had no effect on him as Mark had no intention of playing the next year anyway. That night, he felt a calm he hadn't felt since he was at Three Streams.

As usual, his feelings of calm were shattered when he went to school the next day. He was barely through the school gate when the tall, curly haired starting centre Dave Roseman asked, "Why'd you quit?"

Mark simply responded, "I didn't want to play anymore."

Minutes later, the bespectacled Bobby Rossini, who caught the last touchdown in the game inquired, "Why did you hang up your spikes?"

Again, he was prepared and gave the same answer. He continued to give that answer throughout the day as former teammates kept asking him why he had quit. Most seemed to accept his answer, but others wanted further clarification or rejected it. Some even turned hostile.

"We need thirty six guys," reasoned the tall brown haired Mark Wolfe, a linebacker. "We don't need you really, but we need to have thirty six guys on the team."

"Somebody else could have made the team," argued Alan Fishman.

"You just couldn't take it," concluded Chris Ferguson, a wide defensive tackle.

Fervour over him quitting the team didn't subside after a few days, it carried on. A few weeks later, people where still asking him why he had quit, even boys who weren't on the team. Others made snide comments like "You quit football, you pussy!" That was a favourite with Mitch Waterman, a seventh grader and second-string defensive lineman. Glen Baxter would call out, "It was too tough for him," whenever he came into view. The anxiety of it all began to overwhelm him and he began to retreat further into himself, especially as no one at school seemed to show him sympathy. Even Gene criticised him for quitting football. The only thing keeping him from completely going under was the support he had at home and online.

Lisa's words on the computer screen gave him great comfort when they instant messaged each other in the evenings. When he told her he quit the football team, she responded with, "At least it gives us more time to talk online." When he stated that some of the kids in school were giving him grief about it, she answered back, "They're not you and don't see things from your side, just ignore them." It seemed she had an answer for everything and that made him feel good. That's why every night, he thanked God for sending him such a great girl.

Whatever comforting words Lisa said to him in the evening, they rapidly diminished when he went to school the next morning. Every day, someone would say something, if not about quitting football, something else, like the length of his trousers. If not by taunts or intimidation, they would get him in trouble with teachers. One occasion, he was given permission by Mrs Hinton to go to the office and get his jacket because he had left it behind at lunch. However, Marge Heller, a girl in his class who the teacher appointed as secretary, still marked him late in spite of his explanation. Even though she would often let her friends and others in the class slide when they had been late without cause.

Another time a boy threw a spitball at him. When he threw it back, he tattled to Mr Lejeune, "Mark Leversee threw a spitball at me." When Mark tried to argue that the other boy had thrown it first, the boy's friends all backed his subsequent denial. As a result, he was given detention that evening. It seemed that the entire town had it in for him, partly because he had quit football, although another boy had quit and gotten no grief, but mainly because they could. It seemed all of Ramsgate was against him and no one was on his side, especially not Gene.

Chapter 17

Wrecked Again, It Gets Physical

"Sorry, my hand slipped," smirked Tommy Allen as he thumped Mark hard in the gut, amusing all of his friends.

Not long after that, Tommy took another opportunity to amuse his friends at Mark's expense. Nobody ever paid attention to the rule whereby cyclists had to walk their bike once they came through the school gate. When Tommy saw that Mark wasn't doing this, he decided to have some fun.

"Why didn't you walk your bike?" Tommy asked menacingly, not that he had any regard for school rules.

"No one else is doing it," came Mark's reply.

"Well, I'm telling you to do it," Tommy barked in the same tone before punching him in the arm and laughing about it with all of his friends. After that, a ripple of anxiety flowed through his body each day when he rode his bike through the gates. He found himself looking around to see if Tommy was in the area and would breathe a sigh of relief when he wasn't.

If Tommy Allen had been the only one to take things to a physical level, Mark could have coped, but he wasn't. Joe Kellerman was the next one to join in. It started as soon as he learned that Mark said he played for the Junior Flyers.

"Yeah, right, you play for the Junior Flyers. If that's true, then I play for the Montreal Canadians," Joe said in a disbelieving tone.

"He does," Gene reaffirmed and Mark simply nodded.

Still looking unconvinced, Joe suddenly threw his

hip into Mark, slamming him up against the wall, a well executed body check. Mark let out a squelch but recovered quickly. So Joe checked him into the wall again.

"You can't be on the Junior Flyers," Joe chided, "You can't take a check."

He body-checked Mark into the wall again and followed it up with a few punches to his upper arm. Only the appearance of a teacher prevented any more harm. But that wasn't the end of it. From then on, any time Joe saw him in the hall, he would give him a check into the wall. If he was standing in line waiting to go into a class, Joe would punch him in the arm or chest as he was walking past and there was nothing Mark could do about it.

The eighth graders from the football team and a few who weren't soon got into the act. Whenever he was walking in front of any of them, they would step on the back of his shoes in an attempt to make his foot come out of it. If they weren't successful, then they would try to trip him or kick the soles of his feet. One boy, a tall heavy lad named Jim Nickerson would just punch him in the back. Another named Joe Callazone, who was wide receiver, would poke him in the lenses of his glasses. He did it more when Danny Hamer informed him, "He might try to have you done for assault and battery like he did me."

Mid October brought basketball tryouts and it was the dream of most of the boys at Tye School to play for the Tornadoes. Mark joined the rest of the hopefuls of the seventh and sixth grades hoping to make the jayvee squad. He saw as soon as he went through the drills and fundamentals that he wasn't as gifted as some of the other boys, but he didn't let that spoil his determination.

The eighth graders hoping to make the varsity team

practiced at the other end of the gym. This didn't stop some of them from coming down to watch the jayvee hopefuls. As he took his place to do suicide drills, he saw the likes of Joe Callazone, David Roseman and Jim Nickerson, all of whom were likely to make the team, all looking at him.

"Go Marvin!" David sarcastically called out as he ran past.

"Get the lead out of your rear!" Joe chided.

When he ran back the other way, a tall thin lad named Vince Czenko made a move as if he was going to trip him. Mark sidestepped this would be attempt, but nearly stumbled in the process. This sent the eighth graders into hysterics. However, when he turned back to run up court again, Jim looked as if he was going to repeat Vince's trip attempt. Thinking it was another joke, Mark ignored it and ran with an extra burst of speed in an attempt to go past. Only this time it wasn't a joke. At the very last second, Jim extended his leg and sent Mark crashing face first to the floor.

"What's wrong Leversee, can't you stay on your feet?" Mr Danko queried as Mark picked himself up with the eighth graders cackling behind him.

All he could think was "Didn't he see them trip me?" as he got up and continued to run the drill. However, the eighth graders weren't quite finished with him. As he ran the final leg, Joe Callazone stepped in front of him to block his path. He tried to sidestep Joe but he pushed him into the arms of the waiting group who collectively pushed him into the wall.

As he tried to get away, Jim grabbed his shirt and putting his face near Mark's breathed, "If you tell Danko I tripped you, you're dead."

Seeing the upset look on his face, Mr Danko asked him what was wrong. "The eighth graders pushed me up against the wall," Mark explained.

Mr Danko gave them a brief look and then said to Mark, "Don't worry about it." Nothing more was said or done.

For the next two weeks, he had no further trouble at basketball practice. The jayvee and varsity held their practices at opposite ends of the gym and whenever the practice for either went full court, the others were ordered to sit and watch. This steadied Mark a little, but it wasn't enough to help him make the team. At the end of the two weeks, he was cut along with Gene and many others.

They might have been cut from the team, but that didn't stop Mark and Gene from staying behind to watch basketball practice after school on some days. For them, it was something to do and they stayed out of the players' way so they didn't get hassled. That was until one evening when after watching practice, he went to retrieve his bike.

As he turned the corner outside the school building, he saw four boys standing around a fallen bicycle. All of them he knew to be eighth graders and one of them was Mark Wolfe, who he knew from football. One boy was beating one of the tyres with a huge metal chain. Taking a few steps closer, he became horrified to see that it was his bike that was being smashed to bits.

"Is this your bike?" Mark Wolfe asked in a condescending tone. "Well, you'll have trouble getting it home tonight."

"We didn't do this," another boy pleaded innocently. "We saw some other kids doing it."

"But I just saw you beating the tyre," Mark pointed out.

"That's all we did, we didn't do the rest," Mark Wolfe declared.

With that, the four boys all walked off, giving Mark a combination of cold stares and slimy grins as they went past. He was left to survey the damage to his bike. The spokes on both wheels had been completely smashed in, the seat was ripped to shreds and the handlebars were dislodged. All he could think about was what his mother would say.

Mrs Leversee was upset when she picked Mark up that evening, but not with him. After they had put what was left of the bike into the trunk of the car, she wondered out loud, "Why is it always your bike?"

"It's because I quit football," he offered in response.

Mother gave a look of disbelief at her son's last statement. But she asked, "Are kids picking on you because you quit the football team?"

He gave a nod and she further ranted, "It wasn't like you were the star player! This shouldn't be happening to you just because of that."

Her words gave him some comfort as they drove off. To his surprise, she headed straight for the police station. The police officer at the desk had them fill out a statement based on what he knew and he indicated Mark Wolfe by name. He watched as the officer collected the statement and followed them out to view the destroyed bike. He assured Mrs Leversee that the case would be looked into and action taken. Therefore, when he got home that night, Mark felt certain that justice would be done.

Everything seemed fine the next day. He didn't see Mark Wolfe or any of the other boys who were involved with the wrecking of his bike, so he believed justice had truly been done. It was only after he arrived home from school that he learned otherwise.

"It was terrible," Mrs Leversee moaned when he got in. "The detective had all four boys in together and questioned them as a group. The one boy did all the talking and the other three just went 'Yeah, yeah' at whatever he said. They claimed all they were trying to do was take off the back tyre and that other kids had done the rest, although they couldn't describe those other kids. I bet if that detective had questioned them separately, it would have been different."

Mark wasn't completely surprised at the news and went to school the next day anxiously worried about retribution. Nothing happened at school for the next two weeks, except for the usual teasing, Tommy Allen's hand slipping a couple of times and body checks from Joe Kellerman, so his worries began to ease a little. That was until the last day of school before the Thanksgiving weekend.

As he was getting on his bike to leave school, Mark Wolfe and his chain-wielding friend stepped in front of him. "I see you got your bike fixed," sneered Wolfe with an evil smile. As he was speaking, he reached into the basket on Mark's bike and took one of his books and threw it.

"What you gonna do about that?" he asked menacingly. "Are you gonna get the cops on me?" With the second question, he kicked the larger sprocket on the bike.

"We don't like liars, or quitters," he spat further and then gave the front tyre two kicks. "We didn't wreck your bike, we told you that."

"He was probably trying to get you to buy him a new bike like he did me," a fresh voice intervened. Mark knew that voice straight away, it was David Fitzpatrick. He stood not far away delighting in another spectacle of Mark being humiliated.

"You better not say I was involved in this," he warned.

"Me neither," Wolfe breathed, sticking his fist up to Mark's face. "If you do, we'll just tell the cops you're making up more lies."

"And if you try to get him arrested for assault and

battery, my father says to let him know and he'll defend them in court," David added.

He wasn't sure whether or not to believe David. This caused so much anxiety and confusion, that all he was able to do was to squeak, "I won't." Wolfe punched him in the arm and gave one last kick to his bike before walking off. David too rode off looking very bemused. Mark was left to retrieve his notebook and ride home feeling humiliated yet again. He now knew that justice certainly hadn't been done.

Chapter 18

Bad Grades, Admission

Mark always got a little nervous when parent- teacher conferences came around, but this time it was more than just a little. Seventh grade was going the same way fifth grade had gone for him, in spite of the fact there were no teachers as bad as Miss Erichetti. Mr Danko always seemed to be on him any time he went even slightly off task and like Miss Erichetti, always seemed to single him out. In math, Mr Lejeune had a sixth sense that told him to only ask Mark questions when he didn't know the answer. The previous week, Mrs Bromberg informed him that he had an "F" on the last social studies module because he hadn't turn any work in. What actually happened was that he had lost is assignment sheet but experiences of Miss Erichetti made him fearful of asking for another.

His fears were justified. That evening, his mother sat him down for a big talk and it was clear from her face that she wasn't happy.

"Your teachers tell me that you aren't doing very well in school," she began. "Mrs Hinton was ok, she says you have a lovely smile and that in English you're doing okay, a "C" average or better. The other teachers weren't so positive. Your social studies teacher, Mrs Bromberg, says that you didn't turn in a single thing on the last module. In math, you're working at a "C" or "D" borderline and your science teacher says you're lazy. I know you can do better, so what's the problem?"

A series of possible answers all raced through his brain and competed to be the one that came out of his mouth. However, he dismissed each one on the grounds that they would all be wrong. In the end, he simply shrugged and muttered, "I don't know."

"Well you better know," she snapped. "What do you want to do, work at a gas station your whole life? Because that's what's going to happen if you don't do well in school."

"I can't help it," he replied. "I pray to Jesus to help me in school but he doesn't answer."

"You can help it and God has more things to worry about than your school work!" she barked back. "It's like what all your teachers say, you don't pay attention in class. Mrs Hinton also says you're out the classroom door the moment Gene appears. I also think it's because you spend too much time on the computer talking to that girl."

Those words made his blood start to boil. Without even realising he was saying it, he snapped back, "You wanna see good grades, move out of Ramsgate. I hate it here!"

Mrs Leversee's face softened a little. "Mrs Hinton did say that some kids were teasing you and she was sympathetic when I told her about your bike being wrecked," she offered in consolation. "But that's still no excuse for not doing well in school. If kids are teasing you, ignore them. If someone hits you, hit them back. I know that's what your cousin Tom would do and he does well in school."

A feeling of hopelessness fell over him. He desperately wanted to tell his mother about the eighth graders and Joe Kellerman and Tommy Allen, but he believed that anything he said would have been wrong. Therefore, he agreed to his mother's rule that he only go on the Internet at the weekends and promised to do better at school. She also made him give up his paper route because she believed that getting up at 5:30 every morning might be having an effect on his schoolwork as well.

Something weird and wonderful happened to him in the weeks that followed the parent- teacher conference. His mother took him to a psychologist who explained that she thought Mark had Asperger's Syndrome or DAMP. At Mrs Hinton's suggestion, he also saw Mr Gaynor, the school psychologist. In both instances, he was subjected to a barrage of tests and questions, which he tried his best to answer. Of the two, it was the questions by Mr Gaynor he dreaded the most.

Mr Gaynor, who looked like an ageing hippie, had a session in which, Mark was given a phrase and had to give one to complete the sentence. Most of them he coped with, but ones like "When it comes to going with girls," he hated. The last thing he wanted was to tell a stranger about his summer with Lisa, so he said nothing. But that was not what got Mr Gaynor's attention. That came when the psychologist read out the phrase, "Sometimes he wishes," to which Mark responded, "He wasn't in Ramsgate."

Dr Walton, who looked like a character out of a TV medical drama, took a different approach. They just had normal conversations. Soon, he felt comfortable enough to open up about things, perhaps too comfortable. He told Dr Walton about Lisa and his week in paradise and how he couldn't wait for next summer so he could go back to Three Streams again. He also told about how he hated living in Ramsgate because of how everyone treated him. But he went too far when he told the doctor about how he used to play hockey for the Junior Flyers and now he played for the Woodhaven Blue Blazers.

When Dr Walton relayed his fantasy to his mother, she was livid. "You don't tell lies like that to a psychologist!" she screamed. Her words were followed by slaps to the back of the head. Mark had to endure the screaming and slapping the entire car journey home and when they got there, she told his grandparents about his lie. She rejected his excuse that he couldn't control it and ended the rant with, "That's not someone who's committed themselves to Christ is supposed to do."

Mark was full of apologies on his next visit, but the doctor didn't scold him. Instead, he asked Mark to tell him more about his hockey fantasy.

Once he was assured that it wouldn't be used against him by his mother, he opened up. "Last year, I played for the Junior Flyers and we won the cup. But this year, I play for the Woodhaven Blue Blazers because Woodhaven was closer than Philadelphia. Besides, they're a weaker team and needed me more. So far, we're 4-0-2 and I'm one of the leading scorers with four goals and seven assists."

The doctor listened very intently as Mark went into details about his hockey. An entire league of twenty teams from New York City to Baltimore and going as far west as Hershey, Pennsylvania had sprung up in his mind. He even drew up a table of the current standings for the doctor. Obviously, the doctor made many notes and when the hockey fantasy was exhausted, Mark told of his baseball fantasy from the previous summer, although he didn't give as much detail. However, he did recount his homerun in the final game of the championship. However, he was totally truthful about his abilities for computer strategy games "Age of Empires." He was in the computer games club at school, run by Mr Fluyt and was dominating the club at it. Even the top eighth graders were no match for his flanking manoeuvres. By the time he was done, Dr Walton could have written a book on Mark.

"Your son definitely shows traits of Asperger's Syndrome and DAMP," Dr Walton revealed to his mother. "He has created the hockey and baseball fantasies because he doesn't get to play them much and it helps him to cope with the difficulties he is facing in school. I'm not saying you should indulge his fantasies, just help him manage them so he doesn't say the wrong thing to the wrong person. His apparent talking to himself is simply him acting out what he's thinking in his mind. Most of the time, he's unaware that he's doing it. I will say one thing in confidence though, he really hates Ramsgate and I know it might not be practical now, but it might help him if you moved out."

Donna Leversee wasn't unaware to her son's hatred of Ramsgate. Ideally, she would have loved to move out of Ramsgate that day, but she knew it wasn't practical at the moment. She now regretted telling him that his hockey fantasy was the reason why he was getting picked on so much. At least now, she knew what was wrong with her son and that it could be dealt with and was glad about that.

In the end, a big meeting took place with his mother, Dr Walton, Mr Gaynor, his teachers, Mr Tasker and other officials all in attendance to see what could be done for Mark. After initial resistance by the teachers, who all shared Mrs Hinton's response that Mark looked too normal to have Asperger's Syndrome, it was unanimously agreed that he indeed had traits of Asperger's Syndrome and DAMP. They further agreed it was serious enough to warrant special provisions being made for him. How to address that would be discussed at a future date. What was also brought up was Mark's desire to move out of Ramsgate.

"He said that he hates Ramsgate and wants to move out," Mr Gaynor began.

"He is finding things difficult here," Mrs Leversee stated.

"Well there are children teasing him," Mrs Hinton contributed with Mr Danko nodding in the background.

"Off the record, it would be better for Mark if he wasn't in Ramsgate, but I know that might not be possible at this time," Dr Walton stated with a smile towards Mrs Leversee.

"I don't think that would be good for him at all," Mr Lejeune declared in an authoritative voice. His tall stature emphasised his point. "Who's to say that if you moved out of Ramsgate, things would be better for him? Even if he did move out and things were better for him, it would teach him the wrong lesson for life. He would believe that you can solve your problems by running away from them."

Dr Walton thought that this interjection was of little help. He opened his mouth to voice his opposition, but seeing all the surrounding heads, including Mark's mother, all nodding in agreement to it, he felt outnumbered and remained silent; a decision he would later deeply regret.

Donna Leversee left the meeting worn out but feeling relieved. She was overjoyed that there was in which something she could identify with her son. It confirmed beliefs she had been too fearful to express. Still, she wanted to reach over and slap Mrs Bromberg who still insisted that her son was just lazy. Mr Danko was originally of this mindset, but he changed his tune when he remembered Mark pointing out a little known fact about the orbit of Pluto cutting in front of that of Neptune. Mrs Hinton too, at first, found it difficult to accept anything was wrong with Mark, but the evidence provided by both psychologists helped her see the light. Donna was still thinking about all of this when she picked up Mark's new prescription for Respiradone.

That evening, she explained to her son the importance of the meeting. "The school and teachers will do everything they can to help you and you'll see Mr Gaynor once a week. If you find anything difficult, you are to ask for help and you are to keep your hockey fantasy to yourself." When she was done speaking to him, she hoped that everything would now be all right.

As always, Mark's hopes that things would be better for him were quickly dashed. When faced with the usual brandings of "weird" and "freak," his attempted explanations about his conditions of Asperger's Syndrome and DAMP were used as ammunition against him.

"Your brain is damp," Renee Tye teased.

"It means deficiencies in attention, motor skills and perception," Mark vainly attempted to explain.

"Uh, um, uh, what?" Damon Bates sarcastically rebuffed in a silly voice. Obviously Mark's explanation was too much of a mouthful for him, but it still sent the others howling with laughter.

Worse still was the information Jim Friend revealed. "My father says that your family gets a lot of money from the government because of your condition." Jim emphasised his last two words by making quotes with his fingers. Mark began to deny this, but Jim continued condescendingly, "So you're just living off our taxes, living off welfare just like the niggers."

"He's a nigger anyway," Damon added, inciting more laughter from everyone.

As always, he took this on board and began wondering if his mother was getting money for him. He asked her if this was the case, but upon hearing the question, her mood suddenly darkened. "Tell those kids it's none of their goddamn business!" she snapped.

"But they're saying we're living off welfare like the n, n, black people," he justified.

"Well, those kids are ignorant!" she growled.

He knew not to press the matter any further. If his mother was getting any money from the government on his behalf, it would have to remain a mystery. As for

198

the kids at school, he knew if he told them it was none of their business, it would be disaster for him. He simply hoped that the subject would never come up again.

His teachers now made allowances for him, but made it quite clear they would only bend so far. Mrs Hinton seemed to pay the most attention to his needs and when the next unit of social studies was handed out, Mrs Bromberg made sure he fully understood what was expected of him. Mr Danko and Mr Lejeune, on the other hand, weren't so flexible. Mr Danko seemed to always repeat, "Come on Leversee, I know you have difficulty concentrating, but you will still have to complete the assignments."

Mr Lejeune went straight for the jugular. Your mother isn't going to move out of Ramsgate, so you better get with the programme," he sternly advised one day. That statement prompted a lot of talk from kids afterwards.

"What, you want to move out of Ramsgate?" Keith Wenger questioned.

"We don't want you here anyway," Jim Friend contributed.

"I don't want to be here," Mark stated. Then a thought appeared in his head. "I don't want to live in Ramsgate and you don't want me here. Why don't you start a petition to get me to move out?" he suggested.

"That's a good idea," Damon Bates stated with Renee Tye adding, "If it gets him out of here, yes."

However, Mrs Hinton put an end to any thoughts of a petition. "It wouldn't be accepted on account of your ages," she declared to the class. "You can't force someone to move just because you don't like them."

"But he wants us to," Damon said with Mark nodding.

"No matter, it wouldn't hold up," she responded in a

voice that stifled the thought of further debate. For Mark, it meant that while everyone knew what his problems were, nothing was really going to change for him. The only option he felt he had was to pray to God to cure him of his infliction the way Jesus healed the sick. Therefore, he hoped and prayed nightly.

Chapter 19

Father and Ted

Since his parents had split up over two years earlier, Mark only had one phone call from his father. That was at the first Christmas following the separation. Unbeknown to him, for the past Christmas and birthday, his mother had actually bought the presents for Mark, Lesley and Douglas on their father's behalf. Now after more than two years, his father had faded into a distant memory.

Out of the blue, one day, a few weeks before Christmas, Mark picked up the phone to a strangely familiar voice who identified himself as his father. It took him several seconds to reconnect the voice to his father, but when he did, they spoke on the phone for twenty minutes. Mark told his father about school and playing in the seventh grade basketball league. When his father asked about football, he gave vague details leaving out the fact that he quit the team and he didn't mention what he was suffering in Ramsgate.

Mark also learned that his father was now living in Florida, had remarried and his wife had just had a baby girl. He was a little excited about the prospect of having a half sister. At the end of the conversation, Rusty Leversee made promises to his son that he could come to Florida for a few weeks in the summer. As a result, when the conversation ended, Mark felt really glad that he had spoken to his dad.

To further add to his surprise and his mother's, he opened a card from his father on Christmas Day. Inside the card was twenty dollars. Mark was exceedingly glad about this and Donna was so impressed that she let him phone his father up and thank him. He had another nice conversation with his father who made renewed promises about Mark visiting in the summer. He had more positive feeling as he handed the phone for his sister to speak. What he didn't notice was that her conversation with their dad wasn't as long as his had been.

No one special had appeared in Donna Leversee's life since she had split up with her husband two years earlier. She had been on a few dates in that time and even brought one man home to meet her children, but that relationship didn't lead to anything. However, she didn't seem to mind as she focused most of her attention on her kids, especially on Mark after he had been diagnosed.

That was all before she introduced Ted to the family during the Christmas holiday. Ted Zimminsky stood about six foot two with light brown hair, which he kept in a cropped military style. At first glance, he appeared thin, but when he took his coat off, it was obvious that he was well conditioned.

The entire family took an immediate liking to Ted, Mark and his grandfather especially. His grandfather liked him because of his knowledge of sports, especially basketball, while Mark was more impressed with the fact that he had been in the marines during the Gulf War. He had served in an elite marine recon unit that carried out missions behind enemy lines. Mark learned that Ted had been awarded a bronze star for bravery and a purple heart when a hidden bomb wounded him. However, Ted was very reluctant to say any more about his wartime experiences.

By the time the holidays were over, Ted was pretty much seen as part of the family. He spent more and more time at the house and Mark hadn't seen his mother that happy in a long time. Mark too had formed a bond with him. When the weather permitted, they would go to the playground to play basketball. Ted would give him coaching tips and as a result, his skills began to improve. It was Ted's skills, however, that were the most impressive. One day, he and Ted played two on two against two teenage boys; he demonstrated his dribbling skills running rings around the opposition. He also had a deceptive move where he stuck the ball between his legs and pretended to shoot, which he did so fast, no one could see it. But his best move was when he passed the ball under his legs and under his opponent's legs to Mark who shot it in the basket leaving the other boy to comment, "I didn't see that." Therefore, Mark was exceedingly glad when he agreed to help out with his seventh grade basketball league.

On the Saturday, after the second week after school had resumed, Ted had a bigger surprise for Mark. The two of them were riding in Ted's car when he pulled up to Ned's Shooting and Gun Club less than ten miles from Ramsgate. An unexpected surge of excitement circulated through him as they walked through the door as this was going to be a new and exciting experience for him.

At first, he was content to watch Ted fire rounds down range with his nine-millimetre pistol as he thought that was all he would be doing. He silently rejoiced as the shooter put each round in the bull's eye of the target, a standard police target, which was the silhouette of a man. After fifty shots and three targets, Ted suddenly turned to Mark and asked, "Would you like to shoot?"

His excitement knew no bounds and quickly overcame anxieties about his mother not being pleased to hear he was firing real guns. "Yeah, please!" he answered with great enthusiasm.

Ted must have been reading his mind. "I had to

convince your mother it would be all right to let you shoot," he began. "She wasn't too crazy about it at first, but I explained to her about all the safety precautions at the range and that I would look after you."

Before he was allowed to even touch the gun, he was given a fifteen-minute lecture on how the 9mm worked and how to use it safely. He listened carefully to every word. When he finally did get to hold it, it was without the magazine inserted. The pistol felt heavy at first in his hand but he soon get comfortable holding it. Ted also showed him how to stand with his body aligned to the target and how to breathe properly. It was only when Ted felt he was ready that Mark was allowed to shoot.

Anxiety, nerves and a natural unsteady hand consumed him all at once while he took aim. He could hear Ted whispering, "Relax and breathe," as he centred the sight on the bull's eye. Before he knew it, he fired. A second later, Ted informed him that his shot had completely missed the silhouetted man but had at least hit the paper.

"See, that wasn't too bad," Ted reassured. "Now just focus on the target, it's just you and your enemy."

The word "enemy" sent impulses to Mark's brain. While he was aiming for the second shot, Tommy Allen's face suddenly appeared on the target. An eerie calm fell over him as he squeezed the next shot off.

Mark's shot hit inside the silhouette of the man just to the left of the bull's eye. Ted told him that if had been an actual human, his shot would have wounded him, passing through his lower right abdomen. He didn't think about the details as he aimed for his next shot at the now wounded Tommy Allen. When he pulled the trigger, Tommy wasn't wounded anymore.

The complimentary words, "Great shot!" made Mark feel really good inside. With new confidence, he aimed again. Now the target turned into Joe Kellerman. Joe was dead with one shot. The faces of various eighth graders from the football team now appeared on the target, most of whom were dead on Mark's first shot, definitely on the second. After his final shot, Ted asked him, "Were you aiming for the head?" Mark couldn't answer that for sure, all he could see when he shot was the face of David Fitzpatrick.

He sat rejoicing and looking at his target seeing where his shots had hit while Ted pulled out an Uzi sub machine gun. While three to five round bursts of automatic fire rang in the back of his mind, Mark admired the results of his first time shooting a real gun. He then watched Ted fire into the target's centre keeping his shots in nice little groups. When he finally finished, he declared to the impressed looking Mark, "Maybe one day, I'll let you shoot this," showing him the now empty weapon.

When he got home, Mark proudly showed everybody how well he had done shooting the pistol. His grandfather looked very pleased, but his mother wasn't so impressed. She still wasn't completely sure about her son shooting guns, but was very glad that her son and her new man were getting along so well. The contradictory thoughts still wrestled for control of her mind as she watched Mark hang up the target on his bedroom wall. Seeing the genuine contentment on his face, she concluded that it wouldn't be right to take this away from him. Besides, she trusted that Ted would not let anything happen to her son.

Chapter 20

Safe Havens Overrun

Being taught how to shoot definitely raised Mark's self esteem the first few weeks after the Christmas holidays. Other factors too had kept his spirits high despite the constant teasing and physical aggression from the likes of Tommy Allen, Joe Kellerman and the eighth graders from the football team. For one, his anxiety at the beginning of the school year about which face Keith Wenger would was relieved when it became clear Keith had chosen his friendlier face.

He made other friends from some of the boys in his class as well. The most surprising was Jim Benjamin, who seemed to have forgotten the occurrences from the summer before last. Another boy named Chris Rawlings, who he knew as one of Jack's friends from sixth grade, joined the group. But the boy he liked most was Alan Green. Alan was shorter than the others, with curly black hair and silver rimmed glasses. A joke went around that he looked like a typical Jewish accountant, which wouldn't have been too far from the truth. Alan was in the top groups for both math and English. It seemed that he saw something in Mark, which no one else did.

One place where Mark remained unassailable at school was the computer games club, which happened every Monday afternoon, final period. He was the champion of all three Age of Empires games as well as their expansion packs. No one in the club could counter his use of flanking manoeuvres nor could they penetrate his defences. Whatever any of his opponents tried, it seemed that Mark was always one step ahead of them. One eighth grader, after being defeated by Mark on Age of Empires 3, referred to him as a "Little Napoleon," a comment, which he took as a great compliment.

Meeting Ted also gave him further advantages at computer club. They would watch war movies together in which Ted would point out everything they were doing wrong from a military standpoint. Mark listened carefully as he explained fields of fire, avenues of approach and the combined arms theory of using infantry, tanks, artillery and air support. These all soon became ingrained in his mind and he soon put them into practice when playing the computer game he got for Christmas, "Empire Earth." So, when Mr Fluyt introduced the game to his computer games club, again, no one was any match for Mark.

Church was another place where he could escape from the hassles of Tye School. The kids in his Sunday school class were friendly, although with the exception of Arthur, he couldn't count them as friends. At least none of them gave him any bother and he enjoyed learning about the Bible. He was even looking forward to the start of Confirmation Classes starting in March.

He still had his hockey fantasy, which continued to grow in his mind. In one of his recent games, his new team, the Woodhaven Blue Blazers beat his former team, the Junior Flyers in a goal fest that ended 9-8. He scored two goals including the game winner and he even had a fight in the game. His mind reasoned that it was because a former team-mate resented him for switching teams. By the end of the first half of the season, he had scored 14 goals with 18 assists and made the all-star team, where for the second straight season, he scored a hat trick in the All Star Game.

But of all the things that kept his spirits raised, the main one was Lisa. She had been very accepting when he explained how his mother was limiting his time online on account of his grades. She said that her parents were on her case about spending too much time on the net as well. For Mark, the reduced time only made their online chats even more enjoyable. It was even better over the holidays when the restrictions were relaxed and as part of his Christmas present, he was allowed to call her up and talk on the phone for twenty minutes. What they chatted about was inconsequential to him; he just loved hearing the sound of her voice again. Therefore, it was a real downer when school resumed and the restrictions were back on again. Still, in his mind, Lisa was the girl God had chosen for him and that was worth going through all the things he was going through at school.

Nevertheless, school was still an anxious experience for him. He still had to endure body checks from Joe Kellerman and slipping hands from Tommy Allen. He did his best to avoid the eighth graders, although that wasn't always possible. When they saw him, Joe Callazone would always try to heel him to chants of "Faggot" by David Roseman. Furthermore, there were still altercations with other kids. For instance, one day after nearly bumping into Mark Ruth in the hall and saying, "Excuse me," Mark Ruth growled, "Watch it, Marvin!" Nerves led him to simply reply, "Ruth," to which he received several punches in the back with Mark Ruth chanting, "Don't say my name," to the rhythm of each blow.

It was the same in his own class. He might have been the class miracle worker when his actions won a game of bombardment for them, but that didn't stop Jim Friend hiding his math book for a day causing him to get into trouble with Mr Lejeune. Another time, in social studies, when Mrs Bromberg was talking about the defeat of General Braddock in the French and

208

Indian War, he pointed out, "He made his men stand shoulder to shoulder because in that time, they used smooth bore muskets that weren't very accurate. So they all stood close together in a group in the hopes they would hit something."

Mrs Bromberg was astonished at his explanation, but could only say, "That's probably true." When he turned his head, he saw Alan give him a thumbs up and Keith nod and smile. However, after the class, others weren't so impressed.

"You think you're so smart," one girl spat.

"They used smooth bore muskets," chimed Mike Sigfried in a squeaky voice. His friends Damon and Jim joined in with the taunts. It was clear that no one else was impressed with Mark's display of knowledge.

Then came the time in shop class when Damon Bates snatched the compass from his table barking, "What are you doing, Leversee, stealing my compass?" His response, "I didn't steal it," brought no response from anyone including Mr Williams who it occurred right in front of. This was probably due to the shop teacher being an assistant coach on the basketball team on which Damon played.

The playground at lunchtime provided no safe haven for him either. He always had to be on the look out for marauding gangs of eighth graders or Joe Kellerman and Tommy Allen. If any of these saw him, there would always be several punches or him being pushed into the wall of the school building. If he tried to run away, there always seemed to be kids willing to help his pursuers. Once, it looked like half the school was chasing him. Then there were the verbal onslaughts from the likes of David Fitzpatrick, Anthony Salvatino and Joe Gerberwitz. He felt he had no escape.

Whenever any of these things occurred, Gene was nowhere to be seen. He had never been a good friend to

Mark, but now it seemed it was becoming worse. At every opportunity, he would cut Mark down or humiliate him in front of someone. Recently, while staying behind to watch basketball practice, Mr Williams gave him some change and asked him to get a soda for him. When Mark enquired from where, the teacher replied in a huff, "From the teachers' room."

"Where did you think he meant?" Gene asked sarcastically.

"From the Glanville store," came Mark's reply.

"What all the way to the Glanville store for a soda," Gene teased. As he accompanied Mark to the teachers' room, Gene proceeded to tell every kid they passed about it. "Mr Williams asked him to get a soda," he explained pointing to Mark, "And he thought he had to go to all the way to Glanville store for a little soda."

By the time, Gene told the third person, a boy in Mark's class named Bobby Blit; Mark could no longer contain his anger. He gave Gene a forceful shove and bellowed, "I didn't know there was a soda machine in the Goddamn teachers' room!"

Immediately, Gene went silent, his face forming a hurt, victim look. "Jesus Christ, Marvin, lighten up, he's only kidding," Bobby chastised.

Mark gave Bobby a disdainful look. In his mind he thought, "You don't know the whole story," but those words never made it to his mouth.

Another incident occurred in the weeks that followed. It happened while he and Gene were playing football at Jim Benjamin's house with Jim's brother Danny, Jack and three girls, Kim Havers, Renee Tye and a short, frizzy haired girl named Robin West. When making a play in the huddle, Jim instructed Mark to go out for a pass and he would fake a pass to him. Unfortunately, it didn't totally filter through to his brain and he thought he was supposed to go in the backfield for a handoff. The miscommunication caused the play to fail miserably and resulted in expressions of disappointment.

"I thought you meant to come around for a fake handoff," Mark explained. Jim accepted this and his apology for the miscommunication, but Gene wasn't going to leave it alone.

"You suck," he snarled. When Mark tried to re-explain the communication breakdown, he snapped back, "That's because you're deaf."

That, combined with other factors, bottled up inside Mark. Suddenly, he lunged at Gene flailing a wild punch that missed badly. However, in his attempt to get away, Gene stumbled and fell, cutting his knee. Immediately, people stepped in front of Mark, blocking his way and allowing Gene to scamper off to a safe distance with that familiar hurt victim look on his face.

"What are you doing?" asked Robin who was flanked by her two girl friends. Kim was silent, but Renee repeated, "What are you doing, Mark?" It was the first time she ever called him by his right name.

"He made me mad," was all Mark could respond with.

"I get mad too, but I don't go after people," Robin stated.

That remark sent Mark's memory back to the time when Robin beat up Andy Stowe back in sixth grade because he spat on her. The fact that she was now being hypocritical confused him slightly. He also felt suddenly outnumbered. Even Jack, Jim or Danny said nothing while Robin continued her rant. All he could think about was how Robin didn't know the whole story, but as usual, the words came out all wrong. "I got into trouble a lot of times because of him!" he answered back.

"So what!" Robin stated, it was obvious she was

going to ignore anything he said.

Then out of the blue, Renee piped in with, "He's going to use him having DAMP or whatever it is as an excuse."

Mark felt no other option than to go. He felt eyes burning into his back as he did. The next day, he braced himself for an onslaught from the three girls at least, but the only comment made was "It's Joe Maniac," by Robin when she passed him in the hall. That event wouldn't be the last one concerning Gene.

Gene Lancaster had a reputation for being mouthy. He would make comments at someone and then immediately run away at the first sign of confrontation. The persons Gene mouthed at never involved Mark until one day, when he was being his usual mouthy self to a boy named Martin Tobias, who was in Gene's class. As usual, Gene ran away, but this time it was a different result for Mark.

"Grab him," Martin directed to his friend standing nearby looking puzzled. "We'll take him as a hostage," he further explained.

Mitch Waterman got the message and immediately grabbed Mark. The events still hadn't processed fully through his mind, so he didn't struggle when the former defensive lineman who was forty-five pounds heavier first enveloped him. Mitch manhandled Mark over to the disabled ramp that started on the ground at the end of the new wing and led up to a fire door where it rose to about two and a half feet off of the ground, as directed by Martin. He then forced Mark to sit on the edge of the ramp while holding his legs.

"Lay down," Martin commanded trying to sound menacing. Seeing Mitch's evil grin and a boy named Max Friend, who looked nothing like his cousin Jim, appear and say, "If he moves, I'll punch him," Mark felt he had no other choice than to comply.

Satisfied his captive was secure, Martin instructed Mitch, "Every time he lies, pull him closer to the edge." He then leaned over Mark and asked, "Are you in league with Lancaster?"

"No," came the reply.

Martin gestured to Mitch who pulled Mark's legs bringing him closer to the edge. He then asked, "Why are you and Lancaster in league against me?"

"I'm not against no one," Mark answered in desperation. "It's his big mouth that got me into all this."

This time, Mitch needed no further prompting. With one heave, he pulled Mark off the ramp causing him to drop the thirty inches to the tarmac below. He landed awkwardly, falling on his arm. He tried in vain to stifle a small cry from the pain. The three captors all laughed at his misfortune and two girls looked on in amusement. The distraction was enough for him to get up and run away. As he fled, he noticed Keith go over to the three and inform them, "He'll probably go and tell his mommy and you'll all be in trouble."

Mark did tell his mother about what happened, but she didn't go charging into the school as Keith had predicted. She did, however, mention it to Mrs Hinton at the next PTA meeting.

"Martin Tobias, he's such a good boy," the teacher responded in disbelief when Mrs Leversee mentioned the name. When further details were given, she conceded, "Yes, I know Gene and he can be very mouthy." Mrs Hinton did, in the end; promise to speak to the boys involved.

When she did question Martin and Mitch, Martin made Mark out to be just as guilty as Gene. Furthermore, he stated that the two of them took his hat and played "keep away" with it. Mrs Hinton pointed this out when she mentioned this to Mark and Gene and looked sceptical when the pair denied it. She did inform them that Martin would stay away and that was good enough for Mark.

He might have learned from the experience, but Gene hadn't. He continued to mouth off to other boys and run away if they even looked like they were going to confront him. Only now, Mark didn't wait to see if anyone would come after him instead, he ran away with Gene. This at least safeguarded him from anyone who might go after him because they couldn't catch Gene.

Gene seemed to be further encouraged by this, probably because he now wasn't running away alone. He became even bolder with his mouth and then came the day he decided to steal Chris Rawlings' hat. Each time Chris would try to get his hat back, Gene would do what came naturally and run. He further taunted Chris by offering to give the hat back, but then run off when Chris came near.

Suddenly, he threw the hat to Mark who had been watching uninvolved. Anxiety and indecision suddenly filled within him. If he gave the hat back, Gene would start calling him "Chicken" or other taunts and then play the victim if Mark retaliated. Acting against his better judgement, he threw the hat back to Gene. Unfortunately, the wind made it a bad throw and the hat went right into a puddle.

Nobody stopped Chris from picking up his hat nor did they stop him from going into the classroom. Gene began the teasing chant of "You're in trouble" to Mark the moment Chris disappeared into the classroom.

"You're the one who took it," Mark argued. The sounding of the bell signifying the end of lunch ended any further discussion on the matter.

Mrs Hinton waited until the end of the day before she cornered Mark about Chris's hat. "A few weeks ago, you were having problems with Martin Tobias and

Mitch Waterman picking on you, now I hear you're taking people's hats and throwing them in puddles."

"It was an accident," was all Mark could say. His mind was filling with anxieties about being blamed for something someone else did.

"You took someone's hat by accident," she responded in a questioning tone, which he mistook for patronising.

"I didn't take it," he came back desperately.

The teacher regarded him for a moment but said nothing more. Maybe she knew that he was caught in the middle of something that Gene actually did, but he would never know. He did apologise to Chris for the hat going into the water and when he met Gene, he had to endure his taunts of "You got in trouble." However, he still felt that it was wrong that he had.

Chris and Mrs Hinton might have forgiven him for the hat, but Chris's younger brother Doug didn't. The next day, he was cornered by Doug, who was shorter and stockier than his brother, and four of his friends from sixth grade. "You took my brother's hat and threw it in the water," he reminded aggressively.

"I didn't take it, it was Lancaster and I apologised to your brother for it going into the water. That was an accident," he justified.

Doug's face remained unchanged. "I'm telling you, if you take my brother's hat again, you're dead," he warned. "I look after my brother."

A thought popped into Mark's brain. Throughout most of the school year, Keith had been constantly picking on and teasing Chris. "You look after your brother, huh? Keith Wenger has been making his life hell, why aren't you going after him?" he ventured.

"Because I'm comin' after you," Doug retorted.

From somewhere within him, Mark found the courage to come back with, "Maybe it's because he can

215

kick your ass."

Momentarily Doug's expression changed to the defensive, as did his reply of "I'm not afraid of him." As Mark's face changed to a sceptical look, he added, "Just stay away from him, Marvin."

"My name's not Marvin," Mark snapped, still feeling bold.

Doug looked as if he was going to contradict the last statement, but a boy from his gang piped up, "His name used to be Marvin, but he changed it to Mark because he's a faggot."

Mark identified the speaker as Mike Gabriel, who he remembered from Confederate Avenue School. He didn't like him then and it was clear to Mark that Gabriel hadn't changed, so he wasn't going to like him now. A second reason why after the gang walked away, he felt he was being unfairly singled out.

His usual tormentors continued to single him out anyhow; the eighth graders were becoming even worse. David Roseman continuously called him "faggot" and while that wasn't bad in itself, David found ways to make it worse. "I bet you and that Lancaster kid are gay together," he would say. "You two homos probably suck each other off."

"No we don't," Mark would deny.

"Yes you do," David would retort. "I bet you two love to corn hole each other."

Throwing insults as they passed each other must have gotten boring for David as he took things even further. It happened one rainy lunchtime when Mark was sitting on his own in the gym. David sat beside him and when his group of friends were all seated around them announced, "This is my old homo buddy, Marvin. We used to be gay together."

After the expected laughter, one of his friends inquired, "How many kids did you have?"

"Well, we couldn't quite make that out," David chortled.

After soaking up more laughter, he turned back to Mark and suggested, "Why don't we try again, Marvin? I loved it when you sucked on my dick and I fucked your tight ass."

Mark gave him a disgusted look and uttered, "You're sick."

"You're the sick one!" David bellowed. "You're the one who acts like a faggot."

"We could have an orgy," Joe Callazone suggested mockingly. Seeing Mark's puzzled face, he explained, "An orgy is when we all get together and jerk off. The best part is that there's no girls."

Confusing thoughts began to race rapidly through Mark's mind. "No girls," he thought triggering memories back to that wonderful week from the previous summer. "I like girls," he declared.

"Oh really, like who?" Joe quizzed.

"I have a girlfriend in Pennsylvania," he admitted and as soon as the words left his mouth, he began to regret saying it. Inwardly, he braced himself for a barrage of questions that never came. Instead came comments like "Yeah, right," from the eighth graders and for once, he was glad people didn't believe him. Only Gene knew what he was talking about but the eighth graders pressed him for more. He managed to dismiss it by explaining that it was just some girl he met at the camp he went to last summer. That deflected things away from him for the moment.

David Roseman's display in the gym only seemed to intensify Mark's torment. It seemed everybody from seventh and eighth grade made insinuations that he and Gene were gay lovers. Some even began to confuse the two of them, calling Mark "Lancaster" and vice versa. He felt the one place where he was safe was computer games club on Monday afternoons. There, he was respected, even revered for his dominance of strategy games like Age of Empires and Empire Earth. That safety net disintegrated the moment he walked out of Mr Fluyt's classroom to the lobby where two corridors joined. The sports films club met in the lobby and it was made up of half the male population of Tye School.

He first became aware of them when he suddenly stepped out of his shoe, compliments of Joe Callazone. Then Brian Cullen came up from behind and after shoving him into the wall, demanded to know, "Why didn't you pick me up? You saw I was thumbin' for a lift."

His mind flashed back to the previous Sunday when he was riding in the car with Ted after a trip to the shooting range. He had seen Brian and another boy hitch hiking but Ted flew by too fast to be able to stop. In order to prevent further calamity he quickly explained, "I told the driver to stop but he didn't."

He knew it was a lie and so did Brian who returned, "No, you didn't." Any attempt to form an answer was thwarted by a fist to his back from Jim Nickerson. The blow sent him reeling forward, almost causing him to fall. It provided a lot of laughter from those who were nearby to witness it.

After that, every Monday at the end of the day became a nightmare for Mark. The eighth graders seemed to lay in wait for him to come down the corridor and then start on him. Each time it was the same, Brian Cullen would get in his face and ask why he didn't pick him up or say, "Next time you don't pick me up, I will punch your head in." Joe Callazone would always try to either heel him or poke the lenses of his glasses with his fingers and Jim Nickerson would punch him in the back. If he tried to hide, seventh graders like Jim Friend or Martin Tobias or even sixth graders would be more than happy to point his location out to them. Watching Mark get picked on by eighth graders became a Monday afternoon spectacle and the fact they had an audience only encouraged the eighth graders more.

Worries about the impeding Monday afternoon abuse began affecting him in computer games club. He began making errors in his strategy, which he wouldn't have normally made. In one game of Empire Earth, he came close to total annihilation had not his opponent gotten too overconfident. He was able to force a stalemate, but it did show that he wasn't invincible at strategy games. To avoid the beatings, he began staying after the bell, offering to do jobs for Mr Fluyt at the end of the day. Fortunately, the desire to get out of school was enough to make the eighth graders not want to wait around for him.

As usual for Mark, when he thought he found one safe haven from the bullying, another one would be overrun. Normally, he felt somewhat safe outside of school, but that too changed. Around the corner from his house was an alleyway next to a pizza parlour. Sometimes, he would go there to play his fantasy hockey games and no one bothered him. One day, he was hitting a ball back and forth with a boy named Kenny who was Ted's nephew and several years younger than Mark.

A mysterious voice suddenly called out from inside the pizza place, "Get the fuck out of the alley!" Before Mark and Kenny could react, Tommy Allen, a blonde, skinny girl named Linda Boston, who he knew to be a trouble maker in school, and three other boys came out of the pizza place and surrounded them.

Linda shrieked "Faggot" at Mark while punching him in the arm.

219

"What are you doing here, Leversee?" Tommy asked abruptly.

"I always play here," Mark responded sheepishly, quickly wishing he had chosen better words.

"Well I say you don't," Tommy stated with that threatening look Mark knew so well.

Then one of the others boys, a shorter boy with a large nose named Mario Vickerino, pointed to Kenny and blurted, "This kid owes us a dollar."

It suddenly looked as if Linda was struck by an epiphany. "That's right, he owes us a dollar!" she exclaimed.

She walked over to Kenny whose flustered red face now nearly matched his hair and covered up most of his freckles. "You're gonna pay us our money," she snarled.

As Kenny pleaded, "I don't have it," Tommy and the other boys grabbed the hockey sticks off Mark and Kenny and began hitting the ball to each other. Meanwhile, Linda continued to rant, "We're keeping these until you pay us and if you don't, he gets it," she spouted pointing to Mark.

Mark followed Kenny back to his house cursing the fact that he had once again been dragged into something that was really nothing to do with him. He did though agree with Kenny's assessment that Tommy, Linda and the rest of them were a bunch of drugged up freaks. He was left in a quandary about what to do when they got to Kenny's house. "Do they tell their mothers and risk a backlash sometime in the future or does Kenny simply get a dollar and pay them off?" This debate was still going on in his mind by the time they arrived at the house.

Kenny made that decision for him. The moment they were through the doors, Kenny relayed what had happened to both mothers. He told them how they wanted him to pay them money and how they would beat Mark up if he didn't. The two mothers reacted differently to what they heard.

"I know about those kids and they're nothing but trouble. I should get the police on them," remarked Kenny's mother Josie who was also Ted's sister. The serious tone of her voice blended in well with her stony face, complemented by her dark blonde hair and slightly larger frame.

Mark's mother was more condemning of her son. "Why didn't you try to get your sticks back?" she wondered.

"There were too many of them," Mark offered in explanation.

"A few punches wouldn't hurt you for very long, I hit you hard enough. It's a lot better than letting someone take your things," she countered.

"I would have tried to get my stuff back, even if they did beat me up," another voice chimed in. The voice belonged to Josie's eldest son, Jimmy, who was two years older than Kenny and two years younger than Mark.

"See, he would have fought for his things and he's only ten," Mrs Leversee affirmed. Those words only made Mark feel worse. He realised that in his mother's eyes, Jimmy was another Mr Perfect like his cousin Tom and she would now use both of them to make him feel like a failure.

Both mothers put their sons into the car and headed off for a confrontation. When they pulled up to the pizza parlour, no one was outside and the hockey sticks were on the ground out front. Obviously the kids had gone back inside. Mark breathed a sigh of relief and retrieved his hockey sticks. However, the whole episode left him feeling inadequate.

He thought he might have dodged a bullet as no one

said anything to him about the incident. He saw Linda at school, but she said nothing to him the only time Tommy said anything was after a chance meeting in the street where he asked, "Why didn't that kid pay us our money?" and seemed satisfied with Mark's answer of "You'll have to ask him."

A couple of Saturdays later, he discovered his hope was in vain. When walking home from Gene's house one late afternoon, he met Linda and a gang of five kids. Any chance of flight was quickly stifled when the gang quickly surrounded him. Empowered by her numerical advantage she accused, "You brought your mother back that day."

He had been subconsciously preparing himself for something like this so he was able to confidently respond, "No, he brought his mother back." After all, he was telling half the truth.

It was hard to tell from the look on Linda's face whether or not she believed him. However, she did decide on another approach. "I want to see if you have any money," she demanded. When Mark stated that he didn't, she ordered, "Let me see, empty your pockets."

Outnumbered and knowing he had nothing to lose, he willingly complied. When Linda saw the empty pockets, she huffed and beckoned to her friends to follow her. However, as he was breathing a sigh of relief, she called back over her shoulder with a parting shot, "You tell that kid he better have our money."

After that, there was nowhere in Ramsgate where he felt safe. Wherever he walked, he began using shortcuts through motel complexes and down alleyways to avoid possible hostile detection. He thought it proved to be a good idea one time after cutting through an apartment complex; he spied Terry Cratt, a kid from his class who was friends with Tommy Allen, walking along with Ron O'Malley. He was able to retrace his steps and get away unnoticed. Whenever he saw someone in the distance, he would quickly turn down the next street or cut into an alleyway to avoid them. He now avoided the pizza parlour altogether now he knew the likes of Tommy and Liz Clover hung out there. He no longer felt safe and there was little respite except for when he went shooting with Ted. It was a skill he was rapidly becoming proficient at.

Chapter 21

Allegations, Championships and Partings

His new glasses weren't the only reason for him to feel good as spring approached. The Woodhaven Blue Blazers had finished the season undefeated, twenty-six wins and four ties from thirty games. He was the team's top scorer and joint top in the league with twenty-nine goals and twenty-seven assists. His skills on the computer and with the hockey stick in the backyard saw to that. Therefore, in his mind, he was getting excited about the upcoming playoffs.

Sports in the real world were going just as well for him. Ted coached his seventh grade basketball team and proved to be quite good. It also helped that Tom Lamaina and Mike Deacher, who were two of the best basketball players in the seventh grade, were also on the team. Furthermore, Ted's coaching helped Mark to improve his game, for he tripled his point tally to six for the season and made fewer mistakes on the court, although it didn't stop the likes of Todd LeMatt from saying "That was luck," whenever he made a basket. The best part of all came when the team went on to win the league championship. For Mark, he was ecstatic about actually being on a real winning team and the idea of getting a trophy in June gave him a glimmer of delight.

With all of his sporting success, both real and imagined, it was no wonder his new glasses had taken a back seat. He liked them very much though. The frames were of a thinner metallic make and the lenses were smaller and more rounded. He didn't look or feel so much like a fool in them and early feedback from his friends, even Gene was positive. The best news came when he emailed a photo of himself wearing them to Lisa who said he looked a lot better in them.

Her words immediately erased all the fears he was having about the relationship for the past few weeks. She wasn't online much and when she was, she usually cut the conversation short. Therefore, he breathed a sigh of relief when the online chat they were having went on as long as the old ones used to. However, memories of the old times quickly became clouded when Lisa asked him about kids from Ramsgate posting messages to her on Facebook asking if she was his girlfriend.

Thoughts immediately drifted back to events at school, which he believed triggered her queries. It was one of those typical days when the likes of Jim Friend, Damon Bates and Mike Sigfried were saying that he and Gene were homo buddies. When Mark took the bait and denied it, Mike countered with, "Yes you are, you don't like girls."

"I like girls," Mark replied, when the three and their spectating friends looked disbelieving, he qualified, "I have a girlfriend in Pennsylvania." He regretted saying it the second the words had passed his lips.

Instantly, the most of the class wanted to more about the mystery girl in Pennsylvania and pressed him for details. Not wanting to give too much away, he gave the basics like her name, being from Estminston, PA and that they met at a camp back in the summer. Otherwise, he gave little detail and even the girls chastised Mike when he asked, "Did you put your dick in her?" Nevertheless, the enquiries began to overload him and had not it been for his medication, probably would have gone into meltdown. In fact, he was sort of glad when it appeared that most of the class didn't believe him.

"This is one of his fake stories like his cousin being on the Mets," indicated Renee Tye.

While he was processing everything that was wrong with her comment, others joined in with branding him a liar. The anxiety and fear of being called such forced him to state, "She's on Facebook," against his better judgement. That might have temporarily ended the verbal inquisition, but it re-emerged when Keith went on Facebook and found her and confirmed that she did know Mark. Of course, over time, others went on to Facebook to see her as well and some of them asked her if she knew Mark.

More than a minute elapsed while he replayed that scenario in his head. It did give him an answer for Lisa. "They're just a bunch of unsaved kids trying to say that I made you up," he typed in his message to her. She simply typed back, "Oh" and changed the topic of conversation, much to his relief. They spent nearly another hour instant messaging each other, thus chasing away his fears that there was anything wrong between them.

Any hopes about things improving because of the new glasses were obliterated on the first day he wore them to school. Attitudes toward him remained the same; the constant teasing continued and Joe Kellerman still body checked him into the wall when they passed in the hallway. The new lenses gave Joe Callazone new incentive to poke them with his fingers and constantly did so. The obvious sign came when he was walking down the hall talking to Alan Green, whom he now counted as a friend. Talking as he walked past Tommy Allen, Tommy growled, "Shut the hell up Leversee or I'll ram those glasses down your throat." Joe Gerberwitz, who was nearby, advised, "Don't be so cruel, stick'em up his nose instead." Events like this made him follow the usual precautions while walking alone in Ramsgate.

One thing that his new glasses didn't do was improve his hand-eye coordination. It became quite obvious while he was playing basketball in gym class. He happened to be playing four on four with the substitute gym teacher, whom everybody called Smiley playing on the opposing team. Smiley was a large man with a heavy brown curly beard who coached the football and wrestling teams at nearby Downbeach High School. After two passes went off Mark's fingertips and missing a fairly easy shot, Smiley branded him "Coordination Plus."

It wasn't the name that bothered him, he had been called much worse, but being constantly called it throughout began to raise his anxiety levels. When he did make a basket, Smiley congratulated him by saying, "Nice shot, Coordination." Later in the game, he positioned himself nearby Smiley to receive a pass. He stood there a second too long as all of sudden; Smiley came behind him and in one swift motion, pulled his shorts down to his ankles. He quickly pulled them up amid the laughter of Smiley and some of the other boys on the court. As the game resumed, he hoped beyond hope that news of the incident wouldn't spread.

"He pulled your pants down," Gene laughed to Mark as they walked from gym class.

"Don't remind me," Mark whispered.

Then with a hint of seriousness, Gene suggested, "You should tell on him." Mark's silence as he pondered this spurred him on further. "I'll be your witness," Gene volunteered.

Mark pondered the suggestion further as he made his way to his next class. The main problem was that given Gene's history, Mark wasn't too sure he would be a good witness. When he got to his next class, he wasn't too surprised that news of the de-pantsing had begun to spread.

"Smiley pulled your pants down," Jim Friend teased the second he walked through the classroom door. Damon Bates and Mike Sigfried stood behind Jim laughing loudly. Soon most of the class, including many of the girls had joined in the laughter.

"What colour underwear did he have?" Diane Boreman asked.

"I didn't see," chuckled Jim.

"I bet it's boxer shorts with little choo choo trains," added another boy.

"No, the homo probably wears pink underwear," Damon offered.

He had to endure an onslaught of taunts through the rest of the day, especially as the story spread to other classes. Lunchtime was particularly unbearable with the eighth graders being extremely cruel to him. "I bet you were hoping he was going to corn hole you," David Roseman sneered. The others all laughed and were in further agreement with Joe Callazone who shouted, "The homo probably loved it!"

Surprisingly, there were some who were actually sympathetic to him. Nadine Salvatino, a pretty blonde cheerleader and Anthony's sister, said what happened was terrible and several times asked if he was all right. Then there was Sarah Levine and Hope Anderton, who put together could almost make Lisa. Sarah had the round face and Hope, the ebony black hair. "He shouldn't have done that to you," Sarah sympathised, with Hope nodding in agreement. His own circle was also with him, both Jimmy Benjamin and Alan agreeing it was wrong, as did Keith. Still, he was in two minds as whether or not to follow Gene's advice.

A chance meeting in the hall where Smiley bellowed, "Hey Coordination!" to the amusement of several pupils in the vicinity helped him decide. So did another meeting after school where Smiley again yelled, "Coordination Plus!" However, when Gene smirked "Coordination Plus," Mark concluded that he would be an unreliable witness and therefore decided against going to Mr Tasker right then and there.

Mother's intuition told Donna Leversee that there was something wrong with her son the moment he came in through the door. She wasted no time and inquiring and Mark, still traumatised by the day's events immediately relayed what had happened.

"The substitute teacher, his name is Smiley, keeps calling me "Coordination Plus," he blubbered. Mother began to breathe a sigh of relief that it was nothing serious and her mind began to form the words to reassure him that. But Mark carried on, "He pulled my pants down."

Her jaw could have hit the floor and it took several long seconds for her to regain her composure. "He did what?" she demanded to know, not intending to be as loud as she was. Before he could repeat himself, she asked, "Why didn't you tell the principal?" in the same demanding tone.

"I was afraid I'd get beat up," he answered, glad that he prepared a response in his mind. "He's a coach at Downbeach High School and all the football players know him."

She began to counter that response but her son's needs came to mind. Besides, yelling at him wouldn't solve anything. Naturally, she sought advice from her father.

"He's committed indecent assault!" his grandfather boomed upon hearing what happened. Without further argument, he ordered Mark and his mother into the car and drove straight to the police station.

The Ramsgate Police were very cooperative and understanding towards Mark owing to the fact that it was an indecent assault of an adult on a child. They took him into a room with a supervising adult where he wrote out a statement about what happened. It didn't seem a big deal when he could only name his assailant as Smiley. When it was finished, the police assured mother and grandfather that the matter would be fully investigated.

They were true to their word. A shocked Smiley, real name Jeremiah Barrownoski, was taken in for questioning that evening. He admitted pulling Mark's pants down and his defence that it was only a joke, met with no sympathy from the police. Even though he couldn't believe it and openly stated that it was bullshit, Smiley was charged with indecently assaulting a minor.

It also turned out that Jim Benjamin told his gym teacher father what had transpired in his absence that day. Mr Benjamin immediately telephoned Mr Tasker who informed him that he had already been informed of Smiley's arrest and that the school was working closely with the police on the matter.

The next morning, his mother had given him strict instructions not to say anything about the case to anyone at school. Therefore he didn't and was relieved when no one at school mentioned it. In the middle of the morning, the boys in the class were suddenly taken out and asked to go into an empty classroom, except for Mark who was told to sit in the school office. All Mr Tasker said was "They're going to write out statements about what they saw yesterday," but said nothing more to him. He was glad that he wasn't interrogated further. However, when all the boys returned to class, nothing was said although there were some whispers and Mark was sure that Jim Friend was looking directly at him, making his anxiety levels rise.

At lunchtime, the moment Mark was outside of the classroom, Jim Friend and four other boys immediately surrounded him. "You got Smiley in trouble!" Jim accused. "It was only a fuckin' joke."

Remembering further instructions from his mother that morning, Mark came up with a quick response. "Smiley got himself in trouble," he replied.

His answer only served to fuel Jim's rage further. He got into Mark's face and screamed, "If Smiley gets banned from the school, you're dead!"

His mind wrestled with his mother's advice and the desire to tell Jim and the others that the police were going to put Smiley in jail. The silence only encouraged the others to laugh at him until it was broken by a voice from behind. "What's this all about?" enquired Joe Callazone.

"This fuckin' little pussy told his mommy about Smiley and got him in trouble," Jim informed pointing to Mark.

Further anxiety began to fill in Mark as he prepared for a comment from Joe, but it never came. He simply shook his head and walked on. The non-involvement of Joe prompted the crowd to disperse but not before Jim gave one final warning, "Remember what I said."

Having had time to think of a response, Mark warned, "You touch me and I'll have you arrested for assault and battery."

Jim grinned an evil grin and turned his head to his friends and laughed, "He's going to have me arrested," causing small amounts of laughter. Turning back to Mark, he countered, "Try it; my uncle's Chief Gregory."

Gene proudly recounted how he wrote out his statement against Smiley while they ate their lunch together. The boys in Mr Danko's class were also taken out to write statements on what they saw and Gene was very proud of his. It was as if his statement alone was going to send Smiley to jail for a long time. Mark began to think that maybe in this case Gene would be a reliable witness.

Doubts about Gene's reliability came back later on that lunchtime. The regular crew of eighth graders gathered around him, pushing him back and forth among them. It was Jim Nickerson who revealed the group's feelings. "You got Smiley arrested," he snarled.

"Yeah, you fuckin' little faggot," Brian Cullen chimed in.

Both boys gave him a punch inciting the rest of the gang to join in with kicks and punches. "We don't like faggots here," Dave Roseman spat as he delivered a blow to Mark's arm. They decided they were finished and left after that leaving Gene who had watched the entire affair with a bemused face.

"Did any kids give you grief about what happened?" his mother asked when Mark came home from school. Mark wasted no time in recounting the incidents with Jim Friend and the eighth graders.

"Did they?" she asked already knowing the answer. "The police have said to write down anything anyone says or does to you and show it to them," she explained. Her words were all he needed to write down the events of the day. He hoped that it would get people to leave him alone.

He was partially correct this time around. The next day at school Jim declared, "My uncle says we got to leave you alone or it will hurt Smiley's case but I told him about what a lying troublemaker you are."

At lunchtime, he guessed that Jim must have said something to the eighth graders. His anxiety levels shot up momentarily as they surrounded him again in the playground. They went back down after Brian Cullen announced, "We're not gonna touch you or it might hurt Smiley's defence but all of us are gonna testify in court against you."

That only bothered Mark a little and then Jim Nickerson added, "You better not go to Downbeach High School. They all know about you so if you do, your life won't be worth living."

Jim's threat had no real impact on Mark. He had over a year to go before he worried about high school and he inwardly clung to the hope that he would have moved away by then. He was left alone at school after that although he still exercised the same caution when travelling alone through Ramsgate.

His mother told Pastor Bachman about the assault who was very supportive of Mark. The pastor advised, "While he should still pay for his crime through the justice system, you must forgive him." He instructed Mark to read Luke 17:3, which said: "If your brother transgress, rebuke him. If he repent, forgive him." He took some comfort in this passage. Besides it was easy to forgive someone who was going to jail for his crime.

Playing for the Woodhaven Blue Blazers in the first round of the playoffs helped to take his mind off things as well. They easily brushed aside the defending conference champions, the Dover Cougars, sweeping them in four straight games and outscoring them 19-4. In the final game, when it was clear the Cougars were going to be eliminated, Mark went at it with his old rival from the Cougars, Jim Hornsby. After rolling on the ground for a minute and delivering a few punches to his imaginary foe, the linesman pulled Mark off of Hornsby. He grinned all the way to the penalty box. Since the Blue Blazers were the only team to sweep in the first round, he didn't have any backyard or computer hockey games for a few days.

He intended to use the free time to talk to Lisa online. However, what he saw on his Facebook wall completely shocked him. Someone, who went by the name "Xyxatil," had posted "LIAR!" on his wall. Another unknown person, using the name Frank N. Stein, had written "HOMO!" A further person, going by Wee Willie Webber put "FAGGOT!" Naturally, he reported the abuse realising that the only thing that would happen is that those profiles would be shut down. The actual culprits would get away with it.

Lisa wasn't online so he decided to post a message on her wall. Opening her profile, he saw that Jim Friend already had. He had written, "Mark Leversee is a liar." He retaliated by clicking "Comment" and writing, "He's the liar" in response. He then scanned further comments on Lisa's wall and was relieved not to fine anything else. Instinctively, he also had a look on the Three Streams Page and was relieved that no one from Ramsgate had written anything there.

The Facebook postings were still on his mind when he went to the range with Ted. Ted had been very supportive of Mark and even told him that he would have gladly put a round through Smiley's head. That made Mark feel better. Still, Smiley's face still appeared on the target and Ted didn't have to ask if Mark was aiming for the head when he put three rounds there. Afterwards, he sat there feeling smug while he watched Ted fire the Uzi down range. Ted emptied three magazines but instead of putting the Uzi away, he turned to Mark and asked, "Would you like to learn how to shoot this?"

"Yes," Mark replied barely able to conceal his excitement. As with the pistol, he listened very carefully to Ted's instructions while he explained how to fire the weapon. When he was finished, he handed the Uzi to Mark. Assuming the stance that Ted had instructed to use, he aimed at the target and taking the safety off, fired a five round burst. All five round hit paper, four of them inside the silhouetted man, two of those in the bull's eye.

"Not bad," Ted remarked. "Just remember to keep your groups tighter.

He took those words on board and the next five rounds produced a tighter group. Jim Friend was dead immediately and his friends were dead with the next few bursts. After that, the eighth graders and then Tommy Allen and Joe Kellerman all met the same end.

"That was some fine shooting," Ted complimented after Mark had emptied two magazines. He felt really good about his latest accomplishment.

Shooting experiences carried over to hockey when the second round of the playoffs, the conference final began. This time, Woodhaven were facing the conference powerhouses, the Hershey Cubs. Woodhaven won the first two games, both by a 4-2 score. But those games were at home and travelling to Hershey for the next two games was going to be different. The Cubs were invincible at home having won all their regular season and playoff games there. Therefore, they knew it was going to be tough.

Game three proved to be a cracker. The lead changed hands three times in the game, neither team gaining the upper hand for very long. It was only fitting that it was tied 4-4 at the end of regulation time. For Woodhaven, that was a major feat in itself as no team had done that this season. But this was the playoffs, so a tie meant sudden death overtime.

Mark could almost hear his coach speaking in the locker room during the intermission. "You've done something no other team has done all season. You played them to a tie at the end of three periods. Now one goal stands between us going 3-0 up or slipping to 2-1. We either end their undefeated home record or they end our undefeated season."

The coach's words injected a new determination

235

into the Blue Blazers when they came out for the start of the overtime period. The Cubs were just as determined not to lose and pressed hard for the winning goal forcing goalie Bill Jackson to make several great saves. Then Phil Robins, the right-winger on Mark's line, gave a Hershey player a devastating body check into the boards, winning the puck. A Hershey defenseman skated towards Phil with the same intention. Keeping calm, he banked the puck off the boards before absorbing the hit from the Hershey player. Seeing its trajectory, Mark skated towards the puck, collected the pass and dashed towards the Hershey goal on a breakaway. With the other defenseman in hot pursuit, he crossed the blue line and gave an extra burst of speed. Seeing that his teammate wasn't going to catch Mark in time, the Cubs goalie skated forward to cut down the angle. That was what Mark was waiting for. When the goalie started forward, he fired a low wrist shot past the goalie and into the back of the net. The red light flashing, Woodhaven were the winners of game three.

"They're not going to want to lose two straight games on their home ice, so they'll be out for revenge tonight," Mark imagined his coach saying before game four. "And they think they're too good for us to sweep them four straight." He played the coach's words in his mind as he set up the goals in the backyard for the game.

On the opening face off, Mark got the puck to his left-winger, Jim Barsome, who carried over the red line and shot it into the Hershey zone. Right-winger Phil Robins raced into the zone chasing down the opposing defenseman who was collecting the puck. Phil gave him a huge but legal body check before getting the puck and making a perfect pass to Mark who was skating towards the goal. Hershey's goalie and two other *players prepared themselves for a shot from Woodhaven's leading scorer. Mark eyed the goal for a second as if he was going to shoot, and then at the last second, swatted the puck to his left. Jim, who was unmarked and in the perfect position chipped it at the goal once the puck came to him. With the goalie out of position, the puck found the back of the net and after just thirty two seconds, Woodhaven were 1-0 ahead.*

A defenseman from the second line scored soon after to put the Blue Blazers 2-0 ahead with just two minutes played. Things settled down for the next few minutes, but Woodhaven scored again, so by the end of the first period, they were ahead 3-0.

Hershey made a valiant attempt to battle back and with a minute left, the score was 4-2 to Woodhaven. Their season about to end, the Cubs pulled their goalie for a sixth skater in a desperate attempt to tie the game. However, the Blue Blazer's defence held tight and got the puck out to Mark who showed why he led the league in empty net goals. Skating just over the red line, he fired the puck past two defenders and into the open net. The Woodhaven Blue Blazers were 5-2 winners of the game, had swept the mighty Hershey Cubs in four straight games and were conference champions. Mark was now looking forward to the league final against his former team, the Junior Flyers.

Hockey glory got him through another week at school. It also helped that no one gave him any real trouble that week. Mark concluded it was because of the Smiley incident. The fact that it was the last week before the Easter break might have had something to do with it too. Facebook was another story. He still got postings of "Faggot" and "Homo" from fictitious people calling themselves things like Dracula. One posting, purportedly from his hero Kip McClary, who wrote, "I don't want a faggot like you as my fan." He

237

knew it wasn't really his hero and ran a range of suspects through his mind, Mike Sigfried and Steve McGuire at the top of the list. He simply reported it like he did all the others.

There had been no contact with Lisa for nearly two weeks, so decided to post on her wall. The comments he discovered shouldn't have surprised him but what he found managed to do so nevertheless. More postings of "Mark Leversee is a liar" were written on it. Mike Sigfried had posted, "Do you know his real name is Marvin?" while Damon Bates had written, "He tells everybody he's some great hockey player when he's not." All of those postings prompted Mark to send a message to Lisa.

He wrote:

Dear Lisa,

Don't believe anything they say about me, they're all liars. They're just mad because I told the police about a substitute teacher who pulled down my shorts. All of the jocks are friends with him so they say this stuff about me. It's true, my name used to be Marvin, but my mother changed it when I was ten because I hated the name. This is all the truth.

Love,

Mark xx

The following day, she messaged back:

Mark,

I never believed any of those things. OMG! What that teacher did to you was horrible! I hope he goes to prison for it.

Lisa x

p.s. It wouldn't have bothered me if your name was Marvin, but I do like Mark more.

He took great comfort from that, however, he saw something else on her wall that bothered him. It wasn't anything about him. Someone calling themselves "Barbie" and with the doll's face as the photo, posted "Lisa Farmer is a whore" on her wall. This got Mark thinking, was she going through the same thing he was?

Mark pondered this on the last day of school before Easter holiday. All was well until just a few minutes before the final bell. Copies of the school newspaper, The Tye Times, ware given to everyone who all began instinctively to read it. While Mark was still reading the second page, Mike Sigfried blurted out, "It says here you're gay, Leversee!"

Laughter erupted from many of the children sitting around him.

Renee Tye affirmed Mike's finding, "It does say that he's gay.

"We don't need the paper to tell us that," laughed Damon Bates.

Dutifully, Mark looked at the last page of the Times. At the bottom of the page was the headline, "Gay Kids at Tye School." He didn't have to look far down the list for his name; it was at the very top. Not even the fact that he wasn't at least put down as Marvin didn't make it any better.

Being branded "Gay" in the school newspaper weighed more on his mind than the "F" he had gotten in math on his report card. Unfortunately, his mother saw it the other way around. "You got an "F" in math!"

she yelled, stating the obvious. "You used to be so good at math."

"I don't get percentages," he wailed.

This was true, no matter how hard he applied himself, he just couldn't get percentages to sink in. He would do the proper method, but the answer would almost always come out wrong. His struggle became another source of amusement for his classmates. When he asked for help from Mr Lejeune, a girl in the class called out, "Pay attention, dummy," although it did make him feel better when Renee Tye, for the one and only time, came to his defence by chastising the girl with, "He can't help it, he has DAMP." It didn't help that kids would hide his books causing him to get miss assignments and get in trouble with the teacher.

Mrs Leversee seemed to accept this explanation, but then announced, "In that case, you're going to summer school. Even though you have those conditions, you still have to get an education to get a decent job. This isn't Europe where you get loads of money from the government because you have something wrong with you."

"I'm going in the marines, like Ted," Mark returned.

"You think they'll take you with Asperger's Syndrome and DAMP?" she countered.

Having no sensible answer, he changed the subject. "If I have to go to summer school, what about camp?" he enquired.

"You'll still go to camp, if we can afford it," she assured. "You will just miss one week of summer school."

He accepted his mother's conditions consoled by the fact that he was going to Three Streams in the summer. Therefore, his report card didn't deter him from declaring, "They said I'm gay in the school newspaper," showing her the back page.

Mother looked at the paper for a second and turning away she asked, "What do you want me to do about it?" Seeing the disappointed look on his face she added, "You got to stop letting little things like this get to you."

Remembering something he learned in social studies, he offered, "But it's libel, we could sue and get thousands of dollars."

"I don't think the courts will take something like that seriously, we'd be lucky if we got any money after the costs of the lawyers," she returned. "Besides, you'll be thirteen in two months, a teenager. I can't still be going around fighting your battles for you."

Being the Easter break, Mark didn't have to worry about the newspaper or anything else to do with school for ten days. Therefore, since the Junior Flyers also swept their opponents four games straight to win their conference, the league championship round began.

The first game set the stage for what would be an exciting series. After a hard fought game, the score was tied 2-2 at the end of regulation time and the first overtime period brought forth no goals. Mark led his team out for the second overtime period. Just a minute in, he carried the puck into the Flyers' zone on a three-on-two break. Looking out the corner of his eye, he saw his left-winger, Jim Barsome, breaking down the wing. He attempted a pass to Jim, but the puck hit the Flyers' defenseman's skate deflecting behind him. The defenseman tried a quick turn to go after the puck, but the awkwardness of the move combined with Jim's speed proved no match. Jim blew past him, got to the puck and simply shot it past the surprised goalie.

Mark smiled as "Blue Blazers win 3-2" flashed across his computer screen. He simply saved and exited the game content of his team's victory. With the improving spring weather, that would be the last official game he would ever play on the computer.

Only one period of overtime was needed to beat the Junior Flyers in game two, again it was by a 3-2 score. That game was played on a piece of paper at his uncle's house during the three glorious days he spent with his cousins in Pennsylvania. Game three happened when he returned and unfortunately, the Flyers were out for vengeance after having lost two games in overtime. From the first drop of the puck, they skated all over the Blue Blazers handing them their first loss, 4-2. Again, in his mind, the loss gave his fantasy an air of plausibility.

Neither imaginary talks about losing from the coach nor the branding of gay in the school newspaper were on his mind when he returned to school after the Easter break. Those were replaced by Smiley's upcoming court date. The day before the court appearance, Mark, his mother and grandfather were asked to meet with the district attorney handling the case. All three entered his office with the expectant news that Smiley was going to jail.

Joshua Goldstein was a young ambitious lawyer. Not yet thirty, he was already making a name for himself in the legal world. However, he was still the most junior member of the district attorney's team and the reason why he had been handed the case. When the three entered the room, he was seated behind a desk with an older, heavier balding man, who they knew was the Ramsgate Chief of Police, standing next to him.

Without any ceremony, Mr Goldstein announced, "Mr Barrownoski will be pleading guilty to the charge of "Lesser Degree Indecent Assault.""

The two adults sitting across from the young lawyer nodded together, while Mark blurted out, "He's going to prison then."

Mr Goldstein looked thoughtfully at him for a

second before looking back at mother and grandfather and declaring, "No, we've come to a plea bargain with Mr Barrownoski's attorney. "For his guilty plea, he will receive one year's probation, be put on the sex offender's list for two years and banned from working with minors for five years."

Mrs Leversee stated what was on all of their minds, "So he's not going to jail then."

The district attorney was prepared for this response. "I know it sounds like justice hasn't been done, but this is the best for all. If we go to trial, there is a chance he could get a lighter sentence and even a small chance of him being acquitted," he explained. Pausing a second to let them digest what he had said, he then continued, "I have been reading about Mark's conditions of Asperger's Syndrome and DAMP. The defence could use this against him and make things really bad for Mark on the stand. Would you want him to go through all that?"

"Then there's the fact that he's not very popular in school," the police chief suddenly chimed in. Seeing that he had grabbed everyone's attention, he continued, "We have signed statements from kids at Tye School on Mr Barrownoski's behalf. All of them pretty much say that Mark's a liar and a troublemaker. My nephew is in his class and he says the same thing; he makes up lies and starts trouble."

"He's the liar!" Mark suddenly interjected. "And it's them who start all the trouble."

The chief threw Mark a disbelieving look, which seemed to say, "I'm going to believe what my nephew says over you," before directing attention back to the DA. The district attorney explained, "This is a good deal. He won't be allowed near any minors for five years and even then, it's not automatic that he will be allowed to work with them after that."

243

Mrs Leversee and her father had to concede that the DA was right. Deep down, neither of them wanted to see Mark humiliated on the stand by some hot shot defence lawyer. Therefore, they felt they had no other option than to accept the plea bargain; consoled in the belief that Mark would be safe.

Mark might have been safe from Smiley, but he definitely wasn't safe in the school playground at lunchtime. It had been bad enough he had to endure the taunts of Jim Friend and his pals over Smiley not going to prison, but it was worse when the eighth graders accosted him in the playground.

"Smiley's not allowed to coach anymore because of you," Brian Cullen growled in his face and then thumping him on the arm.

David Roseman followed with, "You just couldn't take a joke."

The rest of the gang of eighth graders all waded in with punches and knees to Mark's head and body. The ordeal lasted for several minutes before the aggressors grew tired and left him alone but not before issuing the stern warning, "If you tell on us, we'll do it again." His physical pain was bad enough, what was worse was the humiliation of seeing the bemused faces of the crowd that had gathered around to watch the spectacle and hearing comments like, "Marvin got his ass beat" from some sixth grader. Only Nadine Salvatino looked on him with any sympathy.

Whether it was escape or unspent aggression for not being able to retaliate, the beating received by the eighth graders spurred Mark on that evening. Furthermore, suffering their first loss of the season seemed to catapult him and the rest of the Blue Blazers to a new level. The determination of the Junior Flyers wasn't quite a match for the Blue Blazers who led 2-1 in the second period in a bruising game four.

Furious tension from the game erupted near the end of the second period. A player from each team crashed into the boards together. Without any hint of a prelude, both players had dropped their sticks and removed their gloves before they railed into one another in full fisticuffs. The remaining eight players on the ice, barring the goalies, all followed suit in dropping sticks and gloves before grabbing handfuls of opposition jersey. Probably influenced from a similar incident during a recent Philadelphia Flyers game, the Junior Flyers' bench emptied, the entire team rushing out onto the ice and prompting the Woodhaven coach to command his troops, "Get out there!"

Without a second's hesitation, Mark and the rest of the team were on the ice and skating viciously towards the fray. As he drew very near, a Junior Flyer met him and in some sort of choreographed display each took handfuls of the other's jersey. Mark and his opponent gave each other death stares while neither was willing to let go of the other. The Junior Flyer then whispered, "Let's go" to Mark and together they released their right hand's grip and balling them into fists, which they brought up to the other's face. Mark felt the adrenaline rush through him as he delivered blows to his invisible opponent's face while ignoring imaginary blows to his own. When the two combatants went to ground, Mark knelt there in his backyard for a second and felt a lot calmer after.

The rest of the game finished without further excitement, as he could no longer match the pre-brawl intensity. But it was his goal in the third period that put the game out of reach. The Blue Blazers had won 3-1 and took a similar lead in games in the final round. They were now one win away from being league champions.

Feeling triumphant, he went on line to find Lisa but

as usual, she wasn't there. Looking at her Facebook wall, he found that this Barbie and others with obvious made up names had done more postings on her wall. There were the similar ones like "Slut," "Bitch" and "Whore" and even "Skank." Someone else had written, "Mark Leversee is a homo, he likes boys" as well. Clicking on his own wall, any abuse Lisa was suffering was pushed to the back of his mind as he read the usual, "Homo" and "Fag." One person asked, "How did you like your ass being kicked today?" However, a post from the same Barbie who had posted on Lisa's wall caught his eye. She had written, "You don't need that whore."

He sat there for what seemed a long time staring at his Facebook wall. It was plane to him that his angel was going through some of the same things he was. He also wondered if the abuse she was suffering was physical like his but he couldn't think of any words that might make things better. Therefore, he shut his computer down.

At lunchtime the following day, Mark was again surrounded and grabbed by the eighth graders. Only this time, they held him in place while a short dark haired boy named Matt Barber, who he remembered as the punt returner for the Colts, stood in front of him.

"I didn't tell anyone about yesterday!" he cried.

"It's not that," Matt replied. He then screamed in Mark's face, "You got me fired as editor of the Tye Times!" before slapping it.

Mark recovered quickly and pleaded, "No, I didn't."

Matt slapped him again, "Bullshit! Your parents got a lawyer and said they were going to sue the school for saying you were gay in the paper, which you are."

"That wasn't me," he protested weakly.

"Yeah, right," Matt sputtered before kicking him in the shin. He then stepped back and allowed his fellow eighth graders to rain punches and kicks to Mark's body like they did on the previous day. And just like the previous day, there was a crowd on hand to watch and taunt him when the beating was finished about getting his ass kicked.

This time he did tell his mother and grandfather what had happened. "They're saying we got a lawyer and are suing the school because they said I was gay in the school newspaper, he told them.

"We should involve the police," grandfather stated adamantly.

Mrs Leversee shook her head, "No, but I will be speaking to the principal tomorrow," she declared.

Relieved at the prospect that all would be resolved, he again went in search of Lisa online. Not only wasn't she online, her Facebook account had been disabled. He concluded that she closed it down due to all the nasty things those girls were saying to her on it. So he thought he'd send her an email and after struggling to find the right words for a long time, he managed to write something he thought was suitable.

Dear Lisa,

I'm sorry those girls are being nasty to you. The posted things on my wall about you but I'm not paying any attention to it. That man isn't going to jail for what he did to me and I've been beaten up by kids at school because of it. I know things are bad for both of us, but I also know that with our love and the love of Jesus, we can overcome them.

Love,

Mark x

Pressing "Send" left him full of optimism, which carried over to the next day. Mrs Hinton, who was the teacher in charge of the school newspaper and had gotten a ticking off from Mr Tasker for not spotting the "Gay Article" summoned him and Matt to her room at lunchtime. She was the one who had actually fired Matt as editor. In front of Mark, she explained to Matt that he wasn't the one whose parents had gotten the lawyer in and sternly warned Matt, "You and your friends are to leave him alone."

"Who was it then?" Matt asked.

"Never mind," the teacher answered, "But rest assured, it wasn't Mark."

The eighth graders left him alone at lunchtime after that although Mark still spent his lunchtimes in a remote part of the playground, just in case.

Game five was always going to be a tense one. The Blue Blazers were determined to win the championship on their home ice, while the Junior Flyers were equally determined to avoid elimination and bring the series back to Philadelphia for game six. The game started exactly in that vein, but midway through the first period, with the puck in the Flyers' zone, a Junior Flyer attempted to clear the puck out. However, Mark stopped the puck with his stick and with one smooth motion, fired a backhand shot that beat the unprepared goalie and found the back of the net, putting Woodhaven ahead 1-0.

The Junior Flyers equalised in the second period paving the way for a thrilling third period. For nearly half the period, both teams went up and down ice in fast and furious action but neither team wanted to concede a goal. Then with just over seven minutes left, Phil Robins, the right-winger on Mark's line and who assisted on many of his goals, pounced on an unsure defenseman, stole the puck and skated swiftly towards the opposing goalie. The goalie stood firm but Phil made a feint sending him one way and then sliding the puck under the goalie's pad. The red light behind the goal flashed signifying the Blue Blazers were ahead 2-1.

To avoid defeat in the game and the series, the Flyers threw everything they had at their opponents. Several times, they managed to penetrate the defence only for Bill Jackson to show why he was an all-star goalie. In the final minute, the Junior Flyers pulled their goalie in place of a sixth skater in the hopes of a last minute goal and sending the game into overtime.

Defending, Mark wasn't worried about getting another empty net goal; instead he wanted to keep the puck out of his own team's net. Passes and shots from the desperate Flyers poured in from everywhere, but none of them found their final mark. Mark did get one shot at the empty net from deep inside his own end but the shot wasn't even close. With ten seconds to play, a Flyers' shot was miraculously batted down by the glove of a Woodhaven defenseman who shot the puck across the blue line. The Flyers had to leave the Blue Blazers' zone to avoid the offside and the time it took to regroup, it was too late. The final buzzer sounded meaning the Woodhaven Blue Blazers had won the game and were league champions.

Before putting the goals away, which were upturned lawn chairs, he imagined the scenario of being awarded the trophy and inwardly smiled as he envisioned team captain, Jim Barsome, carrying the trophy around the rink. Having played on two championship teams in two years, it was a good feeling that lasted beyond clearing the backyard away.

After completing his homework, Mark checked to see if Lisa had answered his email, she had. He read:

Dear Mark,

I'm sorry to hear that kids are beating you up in school because of that teacher. I have too many problems of my own right now and I don't think we should speak to each other anymore. Besides, you wouldn't want me anyway and I know that one day you'll find someone better. So don't email me or IM me as I am closing my internet down and if you write, I won't even open the letter. I won't be going back to Three Streams this summer either. I'm sorry if this hurts you but it's for the best. You'll thank me one day

Lisa

p.s. I'll never forget what we had last summer

He read the email fifty times or more in the hope that somehow, the words on the screen would change. While, he didn't cry out, he let the tears flow for several minutes all the time remembering Pastor Bachman's words: "One night stands and short meaningless romances are against the Lord's will." The fact that his angel was sinning made it hurt worse. He stayed in his room the rest of the night sobbing quietly into his pillow.

Chapter 22

Closer

Ted was also supportive of Mark and his siblings and even more so to his mother, especially during the Smiley affair. He was now a regular feature around the Leversee household, even staying over on the occasional nights. His mother hadn't been so happy in a long time especially as Ted was so good with her children. He always seemed to know what to say, especially when Lisa ended things. The explanation that the summer wasn't just a meaningless romance because it meant so much but was just a relationship that ran its course. His words gave Mark a tiny bit of consolation but did nothing to take away the pain.

What Mark liked most about having Ted around more often was that it meant more trips to the shooting range. The warmer weather meant that Ted could deliver on his promise to take him on the combat course in an isolated part of the range's property. He realised now that this was the reason why he was encouraging Mark to fire the pistol faster. Again he grasped this concept quite well and was really looking forward to doing the course.

Keeping a safe distance behind, Mark followed Ted through a sparsely wooded area. He tried to imitate Ted who, with his Uzi at the ready, kept an eye out for enemy targets. They had gone about one hundred yards when suddenly, a Muslim terrorist clad with explosives popped up on the right. With a quick four or five round burst from Ted's Uzi, the terrorist was eliminated. One hundred feet later, a second terrorist popped up in front of them. He was quickly eliminated too. Three more enemies met a similar fate by the time they came to an open area with four raggedy looking wooden huts. When they got near to them, Ted suddenly turned and fired two five round bursts at a window in one of the huts. Mark turned just in time to see a Russian sniper go down. Right after the Russian, another target popped out from the side of the hut. However Ted didn't shoot at this one, for it was a mother pushing a baby carriage. The pair walked past the huts and Ted took out two more targets before walking a few yards more. There they stopped and Ted turned to Mark and said, "Your turn."

"Now, I have to tell you, the targets won't be in the same places, so you'll have to be on your guard," Ted explained while they walked back to the starting point. "See, I designed the course and the targets are all program to pop out at random. It's all computer operated and because I designed and installed it, Sonny the owner, lets me use it for free."

The awe in which he held Ted in grew even more after he had told him that. Mark wished he had the computer know how to do such things. Those thoughts disappeared when they got back to the start. Ted handed him the pistol and a full magazine, which Mark accepted. Keeping the pistol pointed in the direction they were about to head, he fed the magazine into the pistol and set off.

He walked stealthily through the woods scanning right to left and back for enemy targets. He knew enough about flanking manouvers not to let it happen to him. Only fifty yards along, an AK47 wielding Muslim terrorist popped out on the left. Full of excitement and adrenaline, he fired at his adversary. The first shot was way off and the second missed as well. But having acquired his target, the third shot wounded the target and the fourth finished him off.

"Relax," Ted soothingly assured. "The target's not shooting back, so there's no need to rush the shot. Concentrate on hitting the target, speed will come later."

Taking Ted's words on board, Mark breathed and relaxed. Keeping the same vigilance as before, he continued on. He must have walked for several hundred yards without encountering any targets. Then out of the corner of his eye, an enemy appeared, almost behind him. Quickly turning and relaxing and aiming, He put a shot right on target. "Much better," Ted complimented.

Another target was liquidated before the huts came into view. As he drew near, a target jumped up on his right. The image of a hot looking young woman made him hesitate at first. However, upon closer examination, she was dressed in camouflage and holding a rifle. Instinctively, he shot, the round hitting the ground just below the target. He fired again and scored another kill.

"Ah, you almost fell into the trap," Ted laughed. Then with a more serious voice he added, "That was a good first shot. You didn't hit but you kicked dirt up in her face. That would have made her hesitate in returning fire, good job."

Ted's compliment filled him with more confidence. Still remaining vigilant, he neared the huts. He was not surprised when another enemy appeared at one of the windows; it was quickly taken out. A terrorist bomber appeared around the corner of another hut and was dead in one shot. He wasn't fooled when an old lady popped out behind the last hut. Mark made his way out of the built up area and soon finished the course but not before neutralising one last target.

"You're a natural," Ted commented sounding impressed. Mark felt very proud of himself.

Confidence gained at the shooting range was

slightly dampened when the Blue Blazers took the ice against the Junior Bruins from Boston in the first round of the National Championships. At the opening face off, Mark got the puck back to his defenseman, Jerry Jacobs, who shot the puck on goal. The Bruins goalie must have been just as nervous because he misread the bouncing puck letting it go into the back of the net. With Woodhaven up 1-0 in just ten seconds, Mark decided to put more obstacles in front of the goals in the back yard so it wasn't so easy to score.

The improved goals did not allow any more easy goals but both teams scored two more times in the first period. Twice the Bruins equalised and twice the Blue Blazers went back ahead and therefore led 3-2 after the first period. The second period produced plenty of action but produced no further scoring and the third period was looking to do the same.

In the final minute, with the score still 3-2; the Junior Bruins pulled their goalie for a sixth skater. Two shots were fired at the Woodhaven goal, one went wide and Jackson saved the other. A Woodhaven player got the puck to Mark who carried it down the ice. He passed it to Phil who slapped a shot just missing the open net. A Boston player tried to clear the puck but Jerry managed to stop it. He fired a shot toward the goal. It looked as if a defenseman was going to stop the shot but at the last second, Mark got his stick on the puck and redirected it into the empty net. Woodhaven won 4-2 and was heading into the next round.

Nothing happened to him that week that week at school. He guessed the eighth graders left him alone because the true identity of the boy whose parents threatened to sue the school was learned. His name was John Bettis and his name was just below Mark's on the list of "Gay Kids" in the school paper. He was a skinny sixth grader and his blonde hair made him look like a character named Harold from an old sit com and was often called by that name. He came to Mark's attention when Carol Kray's younger brother pointed out to him, "He's even goofier than you." In spite of all that, no action was taken against John when it was discovered that his father threatened to sue and Mark knew it would have been different if it really had been him.

That Saturday, Woodhaven met the Bangor Lobsters from Maine in the second round of the National Championships. The team from Bangor were formidable opponents and tried to intimidate the Blue Blazers with physical play. The Lobsters did score first only for the Blue Blazers to equalise less than a minute later.

There was no scoring in the second period, just a lot of physical action. In the third period, a Bangor player gave Mark a vicious cross check from behind sending him sprawling face first onto the ice. As he was getting up, he watched as defenseman Jerry Jacobs discarded his gloves and stick and began pummelling the Bangor player who had cheap shotted Mark. When the linesmen pulled Jerry/Mark off the invisible opponent, he headed for the dressing room after being given a game misconduct from the referee. Mark stopped assuming Jerry's identity; secretly wishing he had such an enforcer with him at Tye School.

Neither team scored in the third period either sending the game into sudden death overtime. The overtime period continued with the same physical up and down ice action. However, one Bangor player became too physical committing a hooking penalty and giving the Blue Blazers a power play.

Woodhaven made the most of their one player advantage on the ice. Keeping the puck in the Bangor end, they fired shots at the goal but the keeper saved all of them. Then, with thirty seconds remaining in the power play, the goalie stopped another shot but the puck careened out in front of the goal. Jim Barsome and a Lobster defenseman both went for the loose puck and both hitting it at the same time, forced it to bounce to one side. A scramble for the loose puck ensued but Mark got to it first and fired a backhand shot that trickled past the goalie. The flashing red light behind the goal signified that he had sent the Woodhaven Blue Blazers to round three of the national championships.

Not surprising to Mark, things didn't last and any good feeling from the weekend was quickly chased away the following Monday. It started that morning in gym class. Standing out in centre field, he let his concentration slip and let the ball get by him resulting in a home run for the other team. A chorus of "You suck!" came his way from his teammates and worse came when his team went into bat.

"You weren't paying attention and let the ball go by, "Chris Rawlings accused.

"I lost it in the sun," Mark tried to justify.

"Bull!" Mike Sigfried emphasised. "And if you let the ball get by you like that again, I'm going to beat the crap out of you."

He was able to keep his concentration although no more balls were hit out his way. Therefore nothing further was said until the last inning. He was due to bat second that inning but because his team was losing, Mike Sigfried tried to change the order so that the best batters could bat first. When Mark tried to protest about this unfairness, Mike simply growled, "Shut the hell up."

Two kids on the other team somehow remembered the batting order and one of them complained, "They're trying to cheat! It's not Keech's bat, Bloom is supposed to be up." The rest of the other team soon joined in making such a fuss that Mike had no other choice than to follow the correct batting order. He took his frustration out on Mark.

"It's your fault, he moaned angrily. He then punched Mark twice in the shoulder. Mark took a step back and then swung wildly in retaliation but his punch was way off. "Yeah, try to hit me, Mike threatened. Feeling in danger, Mark picked up a bat that was lying nearby and raised it to swing at Mike. "Go on, I dare you," he baited.

Mark didn't, not because he was afraid to but because Mr Benjamin had walked into view. Mike saw the gym teacher as well so he let things go as well but not before muttering, "Homosexual" at Mark.

The incident at gym class seemed to instigate a whole new torrent against him. Tommy Allen's hand "slipped" several times when they passed each other in the hall and Joe Kellerman checked him into the wall a couple of times. There was also the usual taunting from the eighth graders such as Joe Callazone asking him, "When are we going to have that orgy?" It didn't help that he had another growth spurt and renewed the problem with flood trousers. The sixth graders were worst for this. Every time he passed a group of them, one of them would ask, "Where's the flood?" And of course, everyone continued to call him Marvin.

Two rays of sunshine did emerge through those gloomy clouds. The first was in math class where Mr Lejeune was teaching negative numbers. Unlike percentages, Mark understood it straight away; it just seemed to click in his mind. For the first time in seventh grade, he was actually enjoying math.

The second ray of light came from playing baseball in gym class and was a pleasant surprise for him. Despite the not paying attention in the field incident, his batting had dramatically improved from a year ago. He wasn't simply hitting ground balls to the third baseman any longer but getting lots of distance hits in the outfield. He even hit three home runs. Furthermore, the one game he played where Andrew Blumenthaw was on his team, even he was astounded at Mark's improved hitting when he commented, "Oh wow!" at his good hit that went for a ground rule double. Inspired by this improvement in his batting, Mark got the idea to try out for little league baseball.

A small voice in his mind told him he was making a mistake when he went to sign up for little league. The voice spoke louder when the man handling the sign ups informed him that because he was turning thirteen in June, he had to go out for senior league. However, he ignored the voice and signed up anyway.

David Roseman's voice on the phone should have been a further warning about going out for baseball but again he ignored it. David told him that the first practice was on the Sunday and that he was on the Bennett's team. Mark knew that Bennett's was a local car dealership and was obviously sponsoring the team but that didn't matter. He was just exciting about playing.

More good feelings came on the Saturday before when the Blue Blazers advanced to the semi finals of the national championships. In an uneventful game, they beat a team from Raleigh, North Carolina 3-1 and although he didn't score any goals, he did have one assist. Still his mind was glad that his team would be going to Columbus, Ohio on the following Saturday.

Gloomy clouds returned when he arrived for practice that Sunday afternoon. David was there along with some of the eighth graders who were his audience when he made his homo jokes about him. While there were none of the likes of Joe Callazone, Brian Cullen or Jim Nickerson, there wasn't any faces he could call friendly nor did it help that Jim Friend was on his team as well.

Those clouds darkened more not long after practice began. The first part of the practice was a batting practice and he was the fifth one to bat. All the good batting he had accomplished playing slow pitch baseball in gym class went for nought when he faced the fast pitching of Jim's older brother Tom. He missed the majority of Tom's pitches although he did have one good hit that went far out into left field. Other than that, most of his other few hits were just groundballs.

Fielding was just as bad. He declared that he wanted to play the outfield but he only managed to catch just two of the nine balls the coach hit out to him. The others either sailed over his head or he dropped them. As a result, he was very doubtful about making the team.

Mark pondered this on his way home while still being vigilant over being spotted by Tommy Allen or his crew. What went through his mind the most was the fact that he really liked the coach. Bob Fields was in his early thirties and had unusually long hair for a man his age. But it was Bob's playing career that interested Mark. He had played professionally in the Chicago White Sox organisation but never made it to the major league and was now coaching the county college baseball team. A very soft-spoken man, he did not chastise Mark once for the many errors he made and from how he spoke, Bob definitely knew his baseball. In his mind, Bob was a great coach.

After practice, he called on Gene and they spent most of the day playing baseball in the backyard. As the day began to draw late, they spied Terry Cratt walking past. "There's two faggots, " Terry called out.

Mark simply ignored it but Gene suddenly piped up, "It's poopy Cratt! Which way's the ocean? That way," he teased pointing his thumb in the opposite direction of the ocean.

He couldn't help but to laugh at all of Gene's antics. Terry just gave them both an angry look and kept going. Gene only stopped his taunts once Terry was out of hearing distance.

"Are you gonna quit baseball like you did football?" David Roseman asked snidely when he saw Mark in school the next morning.

As Mark was shaking his head, one of David's friends standing nearby chimed in, "He's not going to make the team anyway."

"Yeah, that's true," David agreed watching him walk past.

Things continued to go downhill at lunchtime when he and Gene decided to go to the Glanville shop. Brian Cullen and a friend happened to be inside the shop and started on them as soon as they walked in. "Look at the two homos," he chortled with his friend sniggering in the background.

Mark said nothing but Gene answered back, "You and him are the homos."

Brian waited for the two boys to make their purchases and then followed them outside. Grabbing them by their arms, he roared, "Who the fuck are you calling homos?"

He appeared to be looking directly at Mark while he was asking the question so he managed to force out, "I didn't say anything."

His protest of innocence seemed to only enrage Brian more. "I don't care who said it," he growled. "I ought to kick the shit out of both of you."

"Yeah, beat'em up," encouraged a sixth grader who was among an increasing group of onlookers. The look in Brian's face gave both of his victims the dreaded feeling that he might follow through on the advice. Instead, he pulled Gene closer to him and putting his face near Gene's demanded, "Say you're sorry."

"Sorry!" Gene cried out.

Brian turned to Mark and asked, "What about you?"

In his mind, he knew he was innocent, but he knew better than to protest. "S S Sorry," he stammered.

Brian let his captives go and while they were walking away, justified to the crowd, "Those two aren't worth it."

As normal practice for Mark on a Monday afternoon, he stayed behind after computer games club to do jobs for Mr Fluyt. However, on this particular Monday, the teacher didn't need any jobs doing. Therefore, he left earlier than he wanted and as he went past the sports films club, he hoped that either the eighth graders wouldn't see him or because it had been a couple of months, would leave him alone. He was wrong on both counts.

Without warning, the usual crowd of eighth graders came up behind him. Joe Callazone wasted no time in heeling him and Jim Nickerson repeatedly punched him in the back as they walked down the hall. Mark absorbed the blows the entire way until he got close to his classroom.

Fed up with the constant punches to the back and hopeful that he could get to his classroom in time, he turned around, punched Jim back and took off running. Unfortunately, Jim's friends all chased after him and it was hard for Mark to run with his foot about to come out of his shoe. Just as he got to the classroom door, Mark Wolfe and Joe Callazone grabbed him and held him for Jim who came by and punched him in the head. Somehow, he slipped from his captor's grasp and dashed into his classroom giving them the finger as he did so.

Inside the safety of his classroom, he did his best to conceal his upset but Nadine Salvatino must have sensed it and asked if he was all right. Her pretty face was sincere under her straight blonde hair.

Mark nodded and nothing more was said about it. Nevertheless, he couldn't put the incident out of his mind to the point where his mother sensed something was wrong when he got home. He told her everything that happened in the hall that afternoon.

"Why didn't you sock him one?" she asked when he'd finished.

Frustrated at the notion that she didn't hear him say he had retaliated, he yelped, "I did, then all his friends jumped me."

Mrs Leversee gave a look that said, "So what," but didn't say anymore about it. That was until later on that evening when Ted, his sister Josie and her children paid a visit. When eight year old Kenny, who was the same age as his sister Lesley, was in the living room the same time as Mark, Mrs Leversee asked him, "What would you do if some fifth grader was punching you in the hall?"

"I'd punch him back," Kenny answered.

"I did punch him back!" Mark interjected from a distance.

Ignoring her son, she then asked Kenny, "And what if his friends jumped in?"

"I'd punch as many of them as I could," he returned.

She then focused her attention back on Mark. "See, he would have fought back," she indicated.

Her words cut through Mark like a samurai sword. It was obvious that she thought that even a little kid like Kenny was better than him and that he was a failure and a disappointment. He waited for her to start going on about what his cousin Tom would have done, but she didn't. He left the room without further word struggling to keep a lid on his feelings.

It wasn't Jim Nickerson and the other eighth graders

he had to contend with at the school gate the next morning. There to meet him was Tommy Allen, Terry Cratt and the rest of that gang. He braced himself for some sort of onslaught from Tommy but he was caught off guard for it was Terry who spoke. "What's all this shit you and Lancaster were saying about me last week," he asked aggressively.

"It wasn't me, it was Lancaster," Mark pointed out.

His protest was momentarily ignored as Terry was distracted by Tommy's question, "What's this all about?"

"On Sunday, I saw him and Lancaster," Terry began, "And I said, "Look, there's two faggots." Then Lancaster starts going "Which way's the ocean?" and shit like that."

While Tommy was nodding his understanding, Mark seized his chance to protest his innocence further. "See, I didn't say anything," he affirmed.

"You were laughing," Terry spat back.

Mark began to process the thought that he couldn't see that there was anything wrong with that but Tommy and his friends began to aggravate the situation.

"Just hit him," suggested Tommy.

"Yeah, kick his ass," encouraged Joe Clover.

"I should hit him, but he'll probably go and tell Mr Tasker," Terry reasoned.

Then Tommy came up with a solution. He turned to Mark and suggested, "Why don't you fight him after school?"

"It's not my fight, it's Lancaster's," he justified.

"It's not my fight," Tommy repeated in a silly voice.

Terry then declared to the others, "If I see him anywhere around the bay where I work, I'll throw him in." After that, the crowd dispersed letting him go but not before Tommy's hand slipped again landing with full force on his arm. Mark got out of there quickly. He was thankful to be alive but still mad about the prospect of getting another beating for something Gene had done.

Avoiding Terry and his friends at the end of the day was no major feat. However, another old problem reappeared when Mark was waiting for Gene at the end of the day. He heard the voice of Jim Nickerson commanding someone to get him. He immediately fled before the two eighth graders came after him, but he ran immediately into a third eighth grader who held him long enough for the other two to come and secure him fast for Jim.

The ordeal didn't last very long, time wise. While the others held him bound, Jim bombarded him with a flurry of punches to his head and body. Feeling fulfilled, Jim simply walked off and his captors let him go. Still, in spite of the briefness of the beating, the after effects took their toll on him.

"You should tell," Gene advised when the eighth graders were at a safe distance. Inwardly, Mark weighed the pros and cons of following Gene's advice. Seeing his silence, Gene repeated his advice, this time his voice sounded more reassuring. Then Jack, who hadn't seen much of for the past few months, appeared and asked what happened. Gene divulged the incident to Jack who took the same stance. "I'd tell Mr Tasker," he simply said. That was enough to convince Mark to do so.

Mr Tasker was his usual understanding self as he listened to Mark's complaint. "He belted you around," the principal stated in confirmation. When Mark reconfirmed, he said that he would deal with the matter and that was good enough for Mark.

He thought he had survived the Wednesday. Nothing was said or done to him throughout the entire day. That was until the end of school when a menacing

Brian Cullen faced him. "You got one of my friends in trouble," he barked. "If I see you outside of school, you're I'm gonna kill you."

Brian's threat unnerved him a little but it was nothing like when Jim Nickerson saw him a few minutes later. "You told on me," he declared. "You're dead!"

Those words filled Mark with dread. On the way home from school, not only did he have to worry about coming across Tommy Allen and his gang, he now had to be on the look out for Jim Nickerson or Brian Cullen. He now travelled the streets of Ramsgate terrified that he would run into any of them. Fortunately, he did not see any of them, only a brief glimpse of Terry where he did a quick u-turn on his bike and rode the other way, hoping Terry didn't see him.

Similar fears haunted the back of his mind when he went to baseball practice that evening. While standing in the outfield, he kept a constant vigilance for Jim Nickerson, but he never appeared. The strange thing was that his worries did not effect his playing. There was an improvement in his fielding and even more in his batting. When practice ended, he thought his chances of making the team improved.

Thursday was a little better. The only direct confrontation he had was Terry asking why he had ridden from him the previous day. Obviously, Terry had seen him. Mark responded that he had to get home fast although he wanted to say that he didn't want to get into something that wasn't his doing. Friday, on the other hand, was a different story.

The day had started well for him. He surprised his class and even himself when he got 98% on the negative numbers test in math. Even Mr Lejeune looked impressed and after the class, Jim Benjamin,

Chris Rawlings, Alan Green and even Keith Wenger were quick to compliment him on his good fortune. However, the rest of the class wasn't so complimentary.

"I can't believe Leversee got a 98!" Diane Boreman exclaimed, not caring if he heard her or not.

"He probably cheated," Renee Tye concluded.

When the class entered the room for the next period, three girls proceeded to interrogate him about his result. "Did you have some sheet to copy from?" asked one of the girls.

Mark shook his head prompting a second girl to ask, "How did you get a 98 on the test? Don't say it's because you're smart, I know that isn't true."

Knowing it to be partially true, he responded, "It was just luck," which the three girls all seemed to accept. Besides, even if he could have explained properly how that for some reason, most likely owing to his condition, negative numbers just seemed to make sense for him, they wouldn't have believed him. Furthermore, they definitely would not have understood that God had actually answered his prayers about doing well on a test.

Things continued to slide downhill at lunchtime. Too afraid to go himself, Gene got Mark to go to the Glanville shop for him with the promise of sharing some of what he bought. Something in his mind was telling him it was a mistake. Even before he got to the shop, he was met by Mark Wolfe and Joe Callazone walking the other way. As they passed, Mark Wolfe spat his drink in Mark's face then joking, "In you eye," before walking on with Joe who was in hysterical laughter.

Inside the shop, things were worse. The shop had none of the things Gene had asked for but that wasn't the real problem. As he was turning to leave, Brian

Cullen barred his way.

"Hey Leversee, I hear you've been saying things about me," he said aggressively.

Knowing this to be untrue, but still feeling intimidated, Mark responded, "I haven't said anything about you."

His face unchanged, Brian warned in a threatening voice, "You better not be." He then gave Mark a violent shove, which forced all the loose change he was holding to spill out over the floor. Brian picked up a coin and gave Mark a look daring him to say something about it.

Joe Kellerman picked up a couple of rolling coins saying, "You don't need these," before stuffing them in his pocket.

"I do need them, it's not my money, it's Lancaster's," he pleaded with Joe.

"Too bad," Joe dismissed before adding, "If you're butt buddy Lancaster wants his money, tell him to see me about it."

All the bemused faces now looking on sent his head into a spin. Looking around, he spied the owner behind the counter and looked pleadingly at him for assistance. However, that assistance never came. The owner, who was in his mid thirties, regarded him for a second and then asked, "You know you're gonna get picked on, so why bother to come?"

The response totally defeated him. Feeling helpless like usual, Mark left the shop, avoiding a trip attempt by Joe's friend. Outside provided no sanctuary either as Matt Osmond and some non football playing eighth graders accosted him, pushing him over. When he got up, he was hit on the head by a paper cup hurled at him before he was able to get away.

Gene showed no sympathy when Mark relayed the events of the shop upon his return. Mark vetoed Gene's idea of telling Mr Tasker because he knew very well where that led. The amount missing added to less than a dollar so Mark simply agreed to pay Gene back. Nevertheless, when the bell rang at the end of the day, he was certainly glad that the week was over. It had been a particularly bad week for him, even by Ramsgate standards.

All that torment he had received that dreadful week was pushed to the recesses of his mind on the Saturday. Mark was very much looking forward to going shooting with Ted because Ted was going to let him use the Uzi on the combat course. It was no wonder he was shivering with excitement when they arrived at the range.

"It will be no different from when you used the nine mil," Ted explained. "You're just using a more powerful weapon. Remember, squeeze off three to five round bursts and you don't have to hit the target on the first shot. Just kick dust up in his face."

Mark absorbed the instructions but he had to admit he was still feeling a little giddy when he inserted the magazine into the Uzi and set off. The giddiness rapidly subsided as he moved further along the course. Two hundred yards in, the first target popped up to his left. However, Mark didn't see the Muslim terrorist, he saw Jim Nickerson. He squeezed off a four round burst, three of those rounds blew the target away.

"Outstanding," Ted complimented.

Keeping on the alert, he continued down the course. After fifty yards, Brian Cullen was eliminated with two rounds in his torso and a third in his head. One hundred yards later, Joe Kellerman bit the dust with little effort. Joe Callazone was taken out just before he reached the wooden huts. He braced himself for an ambush as he walked past the huts but no enemies appeared. Only a little girl holding a dolly appeared at the door.

Just before he reached the last hut, Ted motioned for him to move to the left by the last hut. "Don't be so eager to move out into the open," he instructed.

Mark obeyed and stopped at the edge of the hut. A target that quickly became Tommy Allen popped up in the open about twenty yards away. He wasted no time in taking Tommy out. The second Tommy went down, Terry Cratt popped up just a few yards away from the fallen Tommy. Terry hadn't even gone down from the hits scored from Mark's shots before Joe Clover appeared more to his front. But Mark was able to position himself and take the target out without too much strain. Two more targets appeared and died there in the open before Ted leaned over his shoulder and whispered, "I think you got'em all."

Ted was right, no more targets appeared in Mark's killing field and only one more dared to show itself and die before they finished the course. As they walked back to Ted's car, he complimented Mark on how well he had done. He also explained, "You see, staying by the huts like that opened up a kill zone for you. All that open space gave you superb fields of fire on your enemy and you dealt very well with it."

Like many new words and phrases when he first learned them, the words "kill zone" greatly amused Mark. He ran the words repeatedly through his mind and couldn't help vocalising them a couple of times. Ted just smiled at him when he said it and Mark couldn't help thinking, "At least he's proud of me." The good feeling stayed with him the entire ride to Ted's place.

The apartment Ted lived in was large enough to suit his needs. A large grey collie with black and white streaks jumped up onto Ted when he went through the door. He gave the dog several long minutes of attention before introducing Mitzi to Mark. After an uncertain few seconds, he reached out and gave the collie a couple of strokes. Mitzi responded to his affection so he rapidly grew more confident. A few minutes passed with Mark getting to know the dog before Ted motioned for her to go to her bed and gave Mark a grand tour of the apartment.

There wasn't much to Ted's place. A decent sized living room with a very comfortable sofa was the highlight. Next to the living room was a small kitchen with all the basic necessities, refrigerator, stove, microwave and a small round table with two chairs. Mark followed him down the small corridor. Halfway, he stopped at a pad locked closet door. Ted opened this door and stepped inside. From what Mark could see, this was where Ted kept his guns. He watched as Ted put the nine-millimetre pistol in one drawer and the Uzi in another. Ammunition was likewise separated out and put into different drawers. When he finished, he put the pad lock back on and led Mark back into the living room and told him to have a seat. Without a second's hesitation, he plopped himself down on the sofa and settled himself to watch the Cubs and the Astros who just appeared on the large TV screen while Ted placed a cold soda in his hand.

Half an hour later, the soda long since drunk, he almost didn't want to get off the sofa when Ted beckoned. Still, he followed him and Mitzi out of the apartment. Together, man, boy and dog walked the three blocks to the beach and when they got there, Ted let Mitzi off the leash. Mitzi took full advantage of her freedom, darting wildly back and forth across the sand. At first Mark feared she might run away but each time she came running back to them as fast as she had ran from them. They spent an hour watching Mitzi wear herself out before Ted decided to head back. The dog obediently let her master put the leash back on her and when he did, Ted turned to Mark and offered, "Would you like to walk her?"

Mark eagerly accepted the leash and they began walking back. Just like when he was shooting, he listened carefully to Ted's instructions but it also helped that Mitzi was so obedient. He soon became very relaxed walking the dog. The only anxiety he felt was when Liz Clover and some other girl crossed their path. Fortunately, Liz just gave him a look and continued on. When they returned to the apartment, Ted stated, "I have to go away overnight on Monday. Could you come and feed and walk the dog on Monday night and Tuesday morning? You can stay for a bit and watch the television or go on my laptop. And yes, I have already Okayed it with your mother."

"Yes, of course," Mark accepted with great enthusiasm. He was over the moon with the fact that Ted was giving him this responsibility. Saturday had definitely made up for the rest of that week.

The fantastic Saturday served to spur him on more when he stepped out onto the ice in Columbus, Ohio that evening. His good feeling spurred on both teams as the Blue Blazers and Columbus Explorers skated up and down the ice in a fast paced, exciting hockey game. The puck found its way into both nets twice in the first period making it 2-2 at the intermission.

In the second period, behind 3-2, Mark carried the puck into the Columbus zone. Faking a pass to Phil Robins on his right, he sent the opposing defenseman that way. He then made a quick pass to Jim Barsome on his left. Jim took the puck and immediately passed it back to Mark who was streaking toward the net. The give and go play worked perfectly. The other defenseman was unable to stop Mark who skated in and fired a shot that whizzed by just under the goalie's glove. He momentarily celebrated with his imaginary teammates as he tied the game.

The second period ended tied at three but just two minutes into the third period, the Explorers retook the lead 4-3. However, Woodhaven quickly equalised and then with just under seven minutes left, scored again to go ahead 5-4. However, Columbus wasn't finished. With four and a half minutes to play in the game, they made sure the game would go into overtime.

Overtime was a blur. Both teams stormed their opposing goals in search of that game-winning goal, but it didn't come. Then the centre on Woodhaven's third line won a face off in the Columbus end and got the puck back to a defenseman at the point. He wound up for a slap shot but instead pulled up short on his shot and passed to right-winger Joe Findley, who was all alone. Taking advantage of being unguarded, he took a couple of strides forward and then slapped the puck that sailed through the air and unheeded into the back of the Columbus net.

Instantly, Mark stopped assuming Joe's identity, still amazed at the shot he had just made. He stood there a few more seconds as the ice rink in Columbus turned back into his own backyard in Ramsgate. Before reality fully returned, he raised his stick high in the air in triumph. The Woodhaven Blue Blazers were now one win away from becoming national champions.

In shouldn't have been any surprise that his fantastic Saturday would fade away the next day. On the Sunday afternoon, he had baseball practice, which consisted of a practice game against the Chessington Team. The wait for the game to begin seemed to go on for an unusually long time and players from both teams were starting to get impatient.

Jim Nickerson didn't play for either team but he was there anyway. He made a bee line straight for Mark the instant he saw him. Thumping him in the chest, Jim demanded to know, "Why did you tell?" Before Mark could formulate an answer, Jim explained to the onlookers, "He told Mr Tasker on me."

"Kick his ass," clamoured a boy on Mark's team. Others, especially Jim Friend, encouraged Jim to follow that advice.

He gave Mark another punch and asked again, "Why did you tell on me?"

"You were punching me on the hall for no reason," Mark replied in a near wail.

"Those weren't punches, they were taps," Jim retorted. Turning to the audience, he demonstrated, "He thinks this is a punch," landing a lazy blow on Mark's arm.

Mark braced himself for a harder blow but it never came. The coaches from both teams arrived ready to start the game forcing Jim to stop his display. He left him alone but not before Jim Friend whispered, "Get him after practice," to the other Jim.

"I will," he grinned before walking off.

It was probably a good thing that Mark didn't start in the practice game. His mind was still in a whirlpool following the confrontation with Jim. However, as he watched Joe Callazone, who was pitching for Chessington, get his teammates out one by one, he began to focus more on the game. While he sat watching, Bob informed him and the others not yet playing that they would all get in the game soon.

In the final inning of the game, Mark finally got his chance to play. He felt a little nervous stepping up to the batter's box to face Joe. What added to his fears was the fact that Jim Nickerson had been drafted in as umpire. Mark was sure he would call him out on strikes to get revenge.

Joe's first two pitches were unhitable and Jim rightfully called them as balls. When the third pitch was called a strike, he only braced himself for the next one but that one missed its target as well. The fifth pitch came right at him, so he had to back away from it. Hearing Jim call, "Ball four, take your base," he slid his bat toward his team's dugout and jogged down to first base.

Standing on first base, Bob gave him the signal to steal second. However, Joe kept a watchful eye on him from the mound so he didn't venture far from the base. Joe did try one attempt to pick him off at first, but Mark dived back to the base in plenty of time. With the next pitch, he seized his chance and made a mad dash for second base. Unfortunately, George Lane was the Chessington catcher and he made a good hard accurate throw. Mark was out by a mile.

Playing out in centre field that final inning, Mark only had one ball hit to him, which he fielded on one bounce and threw back to the infield. The final out of the game was made shortly after that so Mark came in to see when Bob was going to call the next practice. The small senior league stadium seemed suddenly deserted when Bob called Mark over to him.

"I'm afraid I have to cut you," Bob apologetically announced.

Mark simply nodded his acknowledgement and Bob asked him, "How old are you anyway?"

He confirmed he was twelve, which prompted Bob to ask him, "Why didn't you go out for little league?"

Mark clarified, "It's because of that rule that says because I'm thirteen in June, I had to go out for senior league."

Bob nodded his understanding but his face said that he didn't completely agree with the rule. "Well don't feel bad, you still have three more years so you can try out again next year," he consoled.

Mark again nodded his understanding and he and

Bob parted company. The funny thing was that he didn't feel particularly bad about being cut; he was sort of expecting it. Besides, he could have the summer evenings to himself. Seeing his grandfather's car in the distance, he put the thought out of his head. Unfortunately, he didn't notice Jim Nickerson coming up behind him.

Giving him a forceful shove from behind, Jim bared his teeth and growled, "I'm gonna kick your ass, Markie."

Thinking of a fast deterrent, Mark hopefully stated, "My grandfather's over there," pointing in the direction of his car.

"I don't care," Jim snarled making it clear that it wasn't going to deter the inevitable.

He tried to run, but Jim stuck his foot out and tripped him. Mark struggled to stay on his feet but Jim grabbed him and wrestled him to the ground like a rodeo steer. He tried his best to cover up from the blows that Jim was now raining down on him but most were still getting through. Not even his grandfather's commanding voice demanding Jim get off of him made Jim stop his assault. It felt like a great weight at been removed from him. Mark turned to see that his grandfather had pulled Jim off of him and Jim didn't look to pleased about it.

"Get the hell off me, old man!" he shouted at Mark's grandfather. "You can't touch me."

"I can touch you if you're hurting my grandson," Grandfather came back.

"He started it," Jim accused.

"He's the one that was punching me in the hall," Mark identified.

Grandfather said nothing to Jim but called Mark to follow him. As they walked away, Jim shouted from behind, "I'm going to the cops and having you arrested!" When they were well out of Jim's hearing range, Grandfather said, "We'll go to the police ourselves, he's committed assault on you."

That was exactly what they did. Once again, Mark went to the police station and he and his grandfather filled out a statement. The sergeant behind the desk promised that the matter would be looked into. For some reason, however, a voice inside Mark's head was telling him that the sergeant was also thinking, "Not you again."

Mother was glad when she heard that the police were going to handle it and said no more about it. No one was in the least bit bothered when Mark finally got to announce he hadn't made the baseball team. All his mother said was, "They shouldn't have made you go out for senior league." Her attitude changed later on that evening when the police knocked at the door.

"We're hear to see Mr Johnston," the young patrolman declared.

When Mark's grandfather presented himself the officer continued, "We received a complaint that you assaulted a minor at the Ramsgate Sports Field this afternoon and need you to come down to the station."

Grandfather swiftly silenced any intended outbursts from his wife and daughter and dutifully surrendered himself to the officer. He wasn't handcuffed and willingly sat in the back of the patrol car. The entire family watched the car drive off and after it was out of sight; Mrs Leversee turned to her son and shouted, "Because of you, your grandfather could go to jail! Why can't you fight back? And don't blame your having Asperger's or DAMP, I know of people with the condition and they don't let themselves be bullied."

His response came from something he learned in confirmation class. "The bible says to turn the other cheek."

The answer only served to pour oil on the flames. "That doesn't mean you have to let people use you as a punching bag!" she exploded.

Mother's comment sent him into total confusion. Upset over the prospect that he caused his grandfather to get into trouble vied with the idea that his mother was contradicting the word of God. Only the soothing voice of his grandmother broke the tension. "Shouting like this won't do anybody any good," she explained. Mother immediately took herself to the kitchen to calm down while Mark bolted directly upstairs to his room hiding the tears that were now forming in his eyes.

Inside his room, he instantly turned on his computer and went onto his email account. He saw he had numerous Facebook messages, which he knew to be more insults so he deleted them without evening opening them. He then focused on the intended task. Entering his father's email address, he proceeded to type:

Dear Dad,

I hate it here, can I please come live with you in Florida? I promise I won't be any trouble. Please let me come, I can't stand it here any more.

Love,

Mark

He clicked "send" and felt relieved. However, he did not venture from his room for the rest of the night. All he knew was that he couldn't stand it in Ramsgate for one minute longer.

"The police didn't charge your grandfather last night," his mother informed him the next morning. He was exceedingly glad at the news, the worry over his grandfather being arrested had kept him awake half the night. He was a little disappointed she didn't apologise for her previous night's outburst at him but he knew better than to say anything about it.

Riding to school that morning was extremely stressful, fuelled by fears of seeing Jim Nickerson. Those fears were proven right when he arrived. After locking up his bike, Jim was standing there with David Roseman, Joe Callazone, Mark Wolfe, Brian Cullen and some of the other usual suspects. "You're grandfather is going to prison," Jim called out to him as he passed.

"The cops didn't charge him," Mark executed in quick reply.

"They will," Jim retorted as Mark walked away.

He continued walking shutting out comments from David Roseman about getting cut from baseball. Inwardly he was more relieved that Jim didn't try anything physical. Mark guessed that it would have landed him in trouble with the police if he had.

That evening, he carried out the duties that Ted had assigned him with ease and enthusiasm. Walking Mitzi to the beach and back and letting her run off the leash was a joy. Back at Ted's apartment, he went on the laptop and saw that his father hadn't answered his email. He assumed it was because his father was seeing if it was okay with his new wife.

Two hours later, feeling bored, he found himself fiddling with Ted's set of keys. One key grabbed his attention. Knowing it was the key to the closet where Ted kept his guns; he gave into the temptation and tried the padlock. To his surprise, the lock opened with considerable ease. He went straight for the drawers where he believed held the Uzi and nine millimetre. Opening both, he gazed at both weapons but didn't touch them. He must have stared at them for half an hour before closing up the drawers and relocking the closet and going back to the comfy sofa to watch television for a half an hour before going home.

Things seemed to go Mark's way for a couple of days after that. The police decided there was no real evidence to charge his grandfather and there was the added bonus that they obtained a restraining order on Jim Nickerson. Ted told him he had done a great job in looking after Mitzi. Still, none of these things were enough to completely lift the gloom from his shoulders.

Three days on and he still had not received an email from his father. Optimistically, he hoped the delay was simply down to his father making provisions for his arrival. Pessimistically, he worried that his father was simply not going to answer his email. It was his mother who broke the news.

"I got an email from your father saying that you want to live with him!" she announced in a scream. "What's this all about?" He's done nothing for you in the last three years, it's all been me!"

He was semi prepared for this response. He calmly tried to reason, "It's nothing against you, I just don't want to be in Ramsgate anymore. I hate it here and would rather live with him than live in Ramsgate."

Her features softened for a moment and then hardened again. "You think kids pick on you here," she spouted. "It will be worse in Florida with all the Blacks and Hispanics and your father won't fight your battles for you."

He wasn't prepared for that response. Rumblings in his mind centred on the thought that Florida wasn't that bad and the fact that he had made black friends at Three Streams. It all sent him into near overload. What he did know was that his mother wasn't going to let him move to Florida. So he conceded and took himself to his room and turned the computer on. This time there was an email from his father.

Dear Mark,

I'm very sorry but it's not possible for you to come and stay right now. We just don't have the room with the new baby. I know you think things are bad for you right now but they will get better for you. You're better off staying with you mother.

Love

Dad

Once again he felt rejected. His father didn't want him just like Lisa and his mother thought he was a disappointment. In order to stop the tears, he went outside and beat lumps out of a hockey puck. It relieved some of the frustration and in his mind; he was practicing for the national championship game that Saturday.

Feeling defeated, he put the fact that he would probably stay in Ramsgate until he left school to the back of his mind when he went to school that day. Taking over was the amusing phrase "kill zone," which he learned when he went shooting with Ted on the previous Saturday. The phrase ping ponged in head and brought a smile to his face, which he quickly removed in case someone saw it and ridiculed him for it. As he rounded the corner of the newly built wing of the school, the phrase lit another thought up. The new wing had formed a u-shaped space in between the school buildings creating a perfect kill zone. If he had the Uzi, all the kids in front of him that moment would be dead meat. He could just squeeze off three to five round bursts and watch the bodies fall, it was that easy. The only escape would be past him or if the teachers opened the back doors to their classrooms. The thought brought him amusement and stayed with him even after school began.

Chapter 23

National Champions

The station identification flashed in Mark's brain. "You're watching ESPN Jr, America's best channel in youth sports." On the screen, the station logo changed to two men holding microphones. Both were aged between 35- 50 and wore the standard three-piece suits of all sports commentators.

The older of the two greeted, "We're here at the Carson Arena in Kansas City for the junior national hockey championship game between the Woodhaven Blue Blazers from New Jersey and the Seattle Red Sharks from Washington. I'm your commentator, Jim Bowers and with today is former New York Islanders star, Eric Van Buke."

The other commentator seized his chance at the pause. "This promises to be a fabulous game. Both teams come in here having dominated their respective leagues and winning the four games needed to get here."

At Eric's pause, Jim took back the initiative. "Right you are Eric. Let's go down to the ice for the introductions."

Both teams were lined up on their respective goal lines. One at a time and in numerical order, the Seattle Red Sharks were introduced, having their moment on national television. Immediately following the introduction of the Seattle team, it was the Woodhaven's team's turn to have their moment in the spotlight. Starting with the goalie, number one Bill Jackson, each of the Blue Blazers were introduced in turn skating from their goal line to the blue line. Mark prepared himself as number eighteen Phil Robins was introduced to be called next. Then it came, without missing a beat, the rink announcer introduced, "Number nineteen, Mark Leversee."

He skated forward oblivious to the fact that the television commentators were talking about him. "Mark Leversee," Jim Bowers began, "He's the leading scorer and definitely a player to watch on this Woodhaven team."

Mark wasn't thinking about the commentators as he lined up for the opening face off. The puck dropped and he was able to beat his opposing centre to it and get it over to Jim Barsome who crossed the red line and shot it into the Seattle zone. However, a Seattle defenseman quickly recovered the puck and began the Red Sharks' attack. Seattle brought the puck across the Woodhaven blue line and managed a shot that was easily saved by Jackson. After a minute of play in the Woodhaven end, Jim Bowers' voice took over again.

"Nagle has the puck, he passes to Robins. Robins has Leversee breaking down ice, what a pass! Leversee has a partial breakaway, Swanson is right behind though. He skates in on the goalie, he shoots, saved! No, Leversee can't get to the rebound."

On the ice, Mark turned his body as the Seattle defenseman tried to run him into the boards. Therefore, it was only a glancing blow when he hit them and was able to spin and get away from the opposing player.

"Meanwhile Jim Bowers' continued, "The puck goes into the corner. Haywood gets it for Seattle, but he's flattened by a vicious check from Robins. Robins has the puck looking to pass. He sees Leversee skating to the front of the goal. Another perfect pass by Robins to Leversee! Leversee has a man behind him. Leversee turns quickly, a backhander, score! Mark Leversee has scored the first goal of this National Championship

game in less than two minutes of play!"

Those inside the arena didn't have the colourful commentary from the two men on ESPN Jr. They had to wait for the rink announcer. Dutifully, thirty seconds after Mark's goal, the announcer put the crowd out of their misery. "Woodhaven Blue Blazers' goal scored by number nineteen Mark Leversee. Assisted by number eighteen Phil Robins. Time of the goal, one minute and thirty eight seconds in the first period." The announcement sent a small ripple of cheers to the tiny crowd who made the trip from Woodhaven.

Seattle didn't let the early goal deter them and after four minutes of pressing for the equaliser, it finally came. Seattle didn't stop there; they continued to play hard and got a well-deserved go-ahead goal at the eight-minute mark. Suddenly finding themselves behind, Woodhaven decided they weren't going to give up either. With just under five minutes to play in the first period, Jim Bowers again livened the television audience.

"Barsome keeps the puck in the zone. He passes to Leversee who skates around the Red Sharks' defence looking for an opening. None there, he passes to Nagle at the point. Nagle fires a slap shot and the Blue Blazers have equalised! Earl Nagle has tied the game 2-2 with assists from Leversee and Barsome."

"Mark Leversee shows why he's the best player on this Woodhaven team," Eric Van Buke cut in. "We're only in the first period and he already has a goal and an assist to his credit."

The rest of the opening period was scoreless and at the siren to end the period, Jim Bowers declared, "This has been a whale of a first period. Some great action with the lead changing hands. It's only fitting that as we head to commercial, the score is Woodhaven Blue Blazers two and the Seattle Red Sharks two.

Jim Bowers and Eric Van Buke carried on their exciting coverage of the second period as the fast action went up and down the ice. Still sounding fresh at the midway point, Jim commentated, "Barsome skating down the left wing looking to pass. He centres it to Leversee, he shoots, score! Leversee has scored his second goal of the game and the Blue Blazers retake the lead 3-2."

"At this rate, Leversee could get a hat trick in this game," Eric pointed out.

Mark stood for a second as the announcer in his mind announced, "Woodhaven goal scored by number nineteen, Mark Leversee. Assisted by number sixteen Jim Barsome. Time of the goal is seven minutes and two seconds in the second period."

His goal was the only goal that period, which turned out to be a very important one because it gave his team the lead heading into the final period. However, just two minutes into the third period, a desperate Seattle scored to tie it 3-3. About three minutes later, Woodhaven proved they weren't a one-player team. With Mark on the bench, Ed Josephson, the second line centre, scored to put Woodhaven ahead again. The Blue Blazers went into a defensive mode to protect their lead. As expected, the Red Sharks went on the offensive and the Woodhaven defence held for five minutes. Then the inevitable happened, the Red Sharks scored and tied the game 4-4. In the final minutes, both teams went for the game winner and Mark thought he had it along with his hat trick but the goalie made a spectacular save. With no more scoring, the final buzzer sounded sending the game into overtime.

Just two minutes into the overtime, Mark and a Seattle player collided as they went for the puck. Mark was sure he could feel the wood of the opponent's stick against his helmet and the referee's whistle seemed to confirm it. Jim Bowers, still full of enthusiasm, commentated, "There's going to be a penalty against the Red Sharks. It looks like Don McCorkle will receive two minutes for high sticking. This power play for Woodhaven will give them a golden opportunity to win the game."

The commentator paused for a moment to let those watching on television see the teams line up for the face off. He carried on, "Woodhaven are out to score and win the game here, they are putting their big guns out for the power play. There's Leversee, Barsome, Josephson and their top scoring defensemen, Tatum and Nagle. The linesman drops the puck. Leversee wins the draw and gets it back to Nagle. He shoots; it's blocked by the defence. The rebound comes out to Josephson, he shoots, and it's saved. The puck careens out in front, Leversee has it, is he going to shoot? No, he passes to his left, to Barsome who is alone in front and slams it into the net! The game is over, Jim Barsome has scored and the Woodhaven Blue Blazers are national champions by a score of 5-4!"

Eric Van Buke put in his final two cents, "Jim Barsome may be the hero for scoring the winning goal but he wouldn't have done it without my vote for star of the game, Mark Leversee. He was the player of the game with two goals and two assists."

After the obligatory handshake between the teams and the presentation of the National Championship Trophy to the Woodhaven Blue Blazers, Mark and Jim took each side of the trophy and skated around the rink soaking up the applause from the appreciative fans. The small contingent from Woodhaven seemed to roar the most. Soaking up the adulation for several minutes, Mark realised that he must have looked somewhat silly carrying a trashcan around his back yard. So, he put the can back and waited for the Carson Arena to completely disappear from his mind but it didn't completely. Instead his mind took him to his team's dressing room.

A pretty young woman who had light brown hair with highlights stood next to him with a microphone in her hand. She spoke to the television camera that was pointed at them nearby, "I'm here with Mark Leversee of the national champion Woodhaven Blue Blazers." Then turning to him she asked, "How does it feel to be national champions?"

"It feels great," Mark admitted trying to sound humble.

"Well you must be proud of your contribution, two goals and two assists," she pointed out for him.

"I'm glad I got those goals," he returned with the same attempt at humility. "But it was a team win, besides, it was Jim who scored the winning goal."

"It was your pass that helped him score that goal," the reporter reminded.

"Yeah, that's true but the whole team played a part in winning the game," he reiterated.

She smiled at him and turned back to the camera. "Mark Leversee of the national champion Woodhaven Blue Blazers, this is Carol Griffin for ESPN Jr."

The second that television camera cut off, the locker room faded away completely in his mind. He tried to put the feeling of being on a national championship team to the back of his mind but the thought of it all was too much for him. That good feeling remained the next day when he went out shooting with Ted. With Uzi in hand, the targets didn't stand a chance. He only hoped it would get him through school the next week.

Chapter 24

Forced to Plan

At first, he thought his hopes were right for once as no major attention was paid to him for the first two days. Naturally, that all changed the third day. In the playground before school, Brian Cullen, Joe Callazone, David Roseman and some of the other eighth graders and Jim Nickerson standing in the background came up to him. "I'm going to kick your head in so you can get a restraining order on me," Brian sneered.

"I want a restraining order too," laughed Joe.

"Yeah, put one on all of us," David mocked. The others all joined in chanting, "We want a restraining order." They kept on at Mark for several minutes before he was saved by the imminent start of school.

Jim Nickerson wore the restraining order taken out on him by Mark and his family like a badge of honour. He even brought it to school to show all his friends and anyone else who might be interested in seeing it. Eventually, news of the restraining order spread to Mark's class. Late that Wednesday afternoon, while waiting to go into Mrs Bromberg's class, Joe Kellerman walked past him, giving a punch in the arm as he went.

"Don't do that, he might get a restraining order on you," Jim Friend said mockingly as Joe walked towards him. When Joe and some of the other surrounding faces looked for clarification, Jim explained, "He got a restraining order on Jim Nickerson. If he goes within one hundred feet of Leversee, he can have him arrested."

"Typical pussy," Damon Bates was heard to grunt.

Soon news of the restraining order had spread all around Tye School. It seemed everybody, even sixth graders, was coming up to Mark and asking, "If I beat you up, will you get a restraining order on me?" It encouraged both Joe Kellerman and Tommy Allen to abuse him more. With each punch or body-check into the wall, they would say, "I want you to get a restraining order on me."

Things came to a head when one day, Mike Sigfried was pounding repeatedly on his back while they were walking out of Mrs Hinton's classroom. "Get a restraining order on me," he chided in rhythm with each blow.

Fed up, Mark turned around and threatened, "Maybe I will get a restraining order on you or maybe I will send you to prison where you can get corn holed in the shower by a bunch of niggers." He didn't mean to use the n- word; it simply came out in his anger.

Ferocious laughter erupted between Mike and his friends and Mark learned that he had played right into his tormentors' hands. Jim Friend then informed him, "They wouldn't send him to jail, the cops will just say, "Leave the kid alone." Besides, my uncle says that the cops are sick and tired of having to handle all your problems. You do nothing but cause them trouble."

Mark wasn't sure whether or not to believe Jim or not. His words brought back recent memories of similar words from his mother who told him, "The police say that they can't put a guard on you or fight your battles for you. That's something you'll have to do for yourself." Therefore, he thought perhaps Jim was right; the cops weren't going to get involved anymore.

When David Fitzpatrick heard about the restraining order, he couldn't resist adding his two cents. He told Mark that he wanted a restraining order too and once, when he had a good crowd with him, declared, "My father says that we should all beat you up and then everybody could use his law firm to defend them in court. They could even give discounts." Those around him thought it was a good idea.

Of course, that wasn't the worst of it. One morning, Jim Nickerson along with the usual suspects surrounded him one morning before school. "Feeling threatened, Mark immediately blurted out, "You're violating your restraining order."

"I don't care," Jim shrugged.

"We don't see him anywhere near you," Joe Callazone stated. "If you say anything to the cops, we'll just tell them you're making things up to get Jim in trouble."

Mark believed they would do it, even if it was a lie. That and the imminent fear of an attack caused overload in his mind. Playing off the obvious fear, Jim made a threatening lunge at Mark but stopped short. He simply punched him in the shoulder before going off with his friends in giggles leaving Mark feeling totally helpless.

Believing that the police would no longer come to his aid, Mark felt that his only option was to beg the Lord for help. He had been going to Confirmation Class at his church and was learning a lot about the bible. He was shown that through God, all things were possible. Therefore, he increased the intensity of his prayers for God to deliver him from his tormentors and to cure him of his DAMP and Asperger's Syndrome but so far, neither seemed to be happening. Jesus also talked about forgiveness, which was something he was finding harder and harder to do.

It certainly didn't feel like God was with him in school when he had the usual troubles with Tommy Allen, Joe Kellerman and others as well as more intimidation from Jim Nickerson. He felt it even less

290

when some unknown sixth grader blatantly spat in his face. The only escapes he had was when he went shooting with Ted and the fantasy farm baseball league that now sprung up in his mind.

He was playing in the Woodhaven Heights Stan Musial League where he played for the Phillies, which was one of four teams. The Phillies had their first game and were simply thrashed 11-3 by the Giants. He only played in right field for the last three innings and had one hit out of two bats. Even so, at least he was playing some kind of baseball and that helped a little.

That weekend, when he went on the course with Ted, it suddenly began to resemble the playground of Tye School. The area around the huts became the school building. The usual people appeared as the targets came up only to be gunned down by Mark's Uzi. The trip to the range that Saturday fitted nicely around Keith's Bar Mitzvah. Although he was completely bored by the ceremony mainly because most of it was in Hebrew, he was still impressed with the fact that Keith had to recite large parts of the Torah from memory in another language. As he listened, he secretly wondered if he would be able to do it.

The evening's festivities were much more to his liking. A huge Bar Mitzvah reception was held at the Wenger's mansion. While the adults stayed on the ground floor in the spacious living rooms, the youth were confined to a larger room on the upper floor where they had everything they needed. Mark never drank so much soda than he did that evening.

As the evening progressed, the party got wilder in Mark's eyes. Marge Heller got some boy who Mark didn't know to dance with her. Within a few minutes, others began pairing off and copying. He was hesitant about doing the same. He was still smarting from Lisa ending their relationship and now had a mistrust of girls. Furthermore, he was more worried about Gene finding out he danced with girls because if he did, he would torture him about it for a long time.

"Why don't you ask a girl to dance?" a boy named Derek Thackerman asked him some time later.

Mark simply shrugged and said, "I don't know," as he thought his reasons would make it worse for him.

"Are you afraid?" Derek speculated in a sarcastic manner.

"No," Mark replied trying to sound convincing, at least to himself. Fortunately, Derek pressed him no more and went off to find a girl to dance with him.

Another half hour elapsed before Mark finally decided to go for it. He concluded that he didn't want to be the only one not having fun. He spotted a pretty blonde girl in a blue dress named Connie; he knew was in sixth grade. She seemed to be ignored by the other boys; so he asked her. He was pleased and surprised at her acceptance, especially as she had the nicest legs he had seen since Lisa. Therefore, he had already convinced himself she was going to say "no." He was glad he was proved wrong when without a word she got up and began dancing with him. While they danced, Derek, who was dancing nearby commented, "See, that wasn't so bad." Derek was right and his confidence grew to a new level it hadn't been since Three Streams.

Mark proceeded to dance the final few hours of the party away. He didn't get to dance with Connie again but a tall black haired girl named Carol Cumberweiss kept wanting to dance with him, which did wonders for his self-esteem. When he left the party that night, Mark felt happier than he had in a long time and he was very much looking forward to Alan Green's Bar Mitzvah the following Saturday. First, he had to survive another week at Tye School.

Surviving that week was the hard part, even if it was

a short week thanks to the Memorial Day Weekend. When he returned to school on the Tuesday, Jim Nickerson and his eighth grade cohorts were on him that morning. They only pushed him around the group chanting, "I want a restraining order" for a few minutes before getting bored and leaving him but for Mark, that was the final straw. When he got home that evening, he informed his mother about what was going on. Naturally, Mrs Leversee phoned the police and they paid the Nickersons a visit. However, when the police reported back, they confirmed the eighth graders' threats were true.

"The Nickerson boy claims he hasn't gone anywhere near your son and he says he has witnesses to corroborate this," the officer explained to mother and grandfather. "He also says that your son has said that he was going to lie to the police to get him in trouble."

"He's the one who's lying!" Mark cried out when the heard the officer's words.

The officer disregarded the outburst and tried to reassure mother, grandfather and son by saying, "I've reminded the Nickersons that there is a restraining on their son and he is to stay away from Mark. But we can't put a patrol car at the school, besides it wouldn't catch him breaking the restraining order.

"Why can't you use an undercover car so you can catch him?" Mark suggested.

"I think you've been watching too many cop shows on TV," the officer smiled. When he left, mother, grandfather and son all had the impression that the police simply weren't that interested. Mark now truly felt that no one was going to help him.

In spite of all his many prayers the night before, the Lord didn't keep Jim Nickerson away from him the next morning. "I said you can't prove I was anywhere near you," he boasted as he grabbed Mark's arm. Mark braced himself for the impending blow but it never came. Instead, Jim flung him to the ground. Again, he curled up in preparation for blows that never came. The eighth graders just stood there laughing at him. He got up without interference and feeling totally humiliated, got away as quickly as he could. However, he still heard Jim's parting shot, "We can get you anytime and you can't do anything about it."

He tried to put all feeling of helplessness out of his mind and he succeeded when he came around the corner of the new wing. Thoughts of eighth graders were replaced by thoughts of the kill zone. It was easy, he concluded. All he had to do was come around the corner and simply open fire. He would hit some of them and direct his fire so they had to run into the open area between the buildings. There he could have his pick of targets or just mow down people at random. The eighth graders did bring one thought to mind. They were every bit the enemy and they would be needed to be eliminated first. He would have to modify his planning.

Locking up his bike in the racks provided on the following morning, he observed that he had great fields of fire from them. The racks were in a corner of the playground with the eighth grade classrooms nearby. He could shoot in two directions thus taking out many people including his enemies who like to sit on the steps at one of the entrances into the building. However, two problems emerged as he thought it through. First, there was the angle he was at. He probably wouldn't get all the intended people with his first shots allowing at least one to duck inside the building and raise the alarm. The second problem would be getting the guns out. There were too many people nearby and someone could easily get to him before he fired a shot. He realised he needed somewhere less crowded.

Even though no one gave him any serious grief on the Thursday or Friday, he still searched for a place where he could get his guns out without being noticed too much and still be able to wipe out the eighth graders before moving to the next kill zone. He found it on the Friday morning. Walking past the eighth graders sitting on the steps and along side of the new wing, he noted that the majority of kids stayed closer to the building, while closer to the fence, it was less populated. He stopped and stood in an open space for a few minutes observing his surroundings. No one seemed to pay any attention to him in spite of the fact he was less than one hundred feet from his main target. It would be very easy to get his weapons out and move towards the first kill zone; it would be a complete blood bath. That thought got him to the weekend.

For the second Saturday in a row, Mark found himself attending a Bar Mitzvah. This time it was Alan Green's. Like Keith's ceremony, Alan's was just as boring and mostly in Hebrew, so he didn't understand much of it. Still he was just as impressed with Alan's ability to recite from memory in the language. After the ceremony, there was food laid on but the spread wasn't as palatial as Keith's not that he really minded. What really balanced things was the reception that evening.

Mr and Mrs Green totally splashed out on their son's Bar Mitzvah reception. They rented a function room in a large hotel called The Empire in Atlantic City. The Empire was right on the boardwalk and not terribly far from the casinos. Mark wasn't the only one who was impressed when he walked in with Keith, Jim Benjamin and Derek Thackerman. All four boys concluded that someone would have to be very rich to stay at this hotel.

Further confirmation of their theory came as they

walked into the enormous function room. It was a large rectangular room with many tables and chairs. On the left, there was the drinks bar and beyond the tables was the dance floor. Musical instruments were stacked around a drum set in the right hand corner. Obviously, there was going to be a live band that night. Not far from the instruments stood two long tables, one higher than the other. That was where Alan and all his friends, including Mark would be dining.

Immediately, Mark and the others began to mingle in the immense room. He found Alan dressed on a smart tuxedo consisting of a cream coloured jacket and smart black trousers. Alan was definitely enjoying his time in the spotlight, as he was busy greeting and talking to the many guests. Mark helped himself to one of the many glasses of coke that was laid out on a table and observed the festivities. Sarah Levine and Hope Anderton passed by and said "hello" to him and he was surprised when Marge Heller had done the same. After all, she had spent the entire school year teasing him about his flood pants and anything else that she could find. Others from his past and present were in attendance at the reception. Most of them he viewed as hostile. However, none of them said anything to him as no one wanted to be the one who caused trouble that night.

The evening went smoothly. Dinner was delicious although Mark thought all food was better than what he had at Three Streams. Like his peers, he managed to sneak and drink a whiskey sour but he didn't like it and so only drank half of it. After dinner dancing was kicked off by a slow dance between Alan and Marge and when the band decided to speed up the music, some young men and women began to get on the dance floor two by two. When that happened, he was overcome by an anxious fear that people would try to encourage or even force him to dance with Jody Molstein who was also in attendance but that never happened.

He wanted to ask Sarah to dance but Chip Seinberg got to her first. Instead he set his sights on a girl named Barbara Newman. Her long black hair reminded him a little of Lisa but that was the only similarity. Barbara had more of a triangular face and obvious nose and she was noticeably thinner. However, as Mark was summoning the courage to ask her for a dance, his mother and Ted suddenly appeared to take him home, thus missing his chance.

There was a lot of talk about Alan's Bar Mitzvah reception when the friends met on the Monday morning. Chris made a big deal over Jimmy dancing with Jody Molstein even though it was just one dance. What mattered most was that Alan had a magnificent night and Mark had to admit so did he. He was now looking forward to his on birthday the next Saturday. He wasn't going to have a huge Bar Mitzvah and reception because he wasn't Jewish but he, his friends who were assembled at that moment plus Gene and Jack were going to a pizza place. All Mark had to do was to survive another week.

Chances of surviving the week diminished rapidly the Monday lunchtime when he was assaulted by a sixth grader named Nick Higbee. He wasn't in Nick's way but that didn't stop him from giving him a forceful shove and spitting, "Get out of my way or I'll make you into a hamburger."

"Kill him, Higbee," encouraged a shorter stout friend of Nick's known as Fritz.

Grabbing Mark's shirt with both hands, Nick chortled, "Maybe I should kick your ass.

Initial fear was quickly brushed aside as a self defence move that Ted had taught him entered Mark's mind. Instinctively, he reached out behind Nick's head and grabbed a handful of strawberry blonde hair. Then with one fluid motion, he gave a quick jerk snapping Nick's head to his left and then in the same motion forcefully brought his palm to Nick's chin. Nick went straight to the blacktop with Mark ready to press forward his advantage but he was thwarted by two thick arms that encircled his waste pulling him away. Mark struggled free to see that the interloper had been Fritz.

"What's going on here?" queried Andrew Blumenthaw who appointed himself spokesman of the small crowd that was now gathering around in the hope of seeing a fight.

He jumped in because he couldn't take it his friend was losing," Mark sputtered pointing the finger of accusation at Fritz.

"You pulled his hair like a girl," Fritz justified with a self-righteous grin.

"It's a legal self defence move," Mark returned in hope of silencing the impending laughter from the crowd. However, right away he knew that his words probably sounded stupid to those listening.

"It's a legal self defence move," Mike Gabriel repeated in a funny voice.

"Maybe he knows karate," an unknown voice in the crowd added followed by a few "Hi ya's" from others.

"Is there an illegal one?" Damon Bates asked him before the assembly.

Seizing an opportunity, Mark quickly got in, "No there isn't, because there are no rules to fighting."

A few people nodded in agreement to Mark's statement but Fritz took an object that looked very much like a knife out of his pocket and holding it towards Mark declared, "I'll stab you with this, I mean there are no rules to fighting."

Before he had even realised he had said it, Mark snapped back, "I'll get a gun."

A roar of laughter went up through the crowd and some made "Bang, bang" noises. Meanwhile, Mark's mind was processing the fact that he could actually get not one, but two guns and use them. His thoughts and the entire altercation was broken up by the sound of the bell and the appearance of teachers.

Several of his classmates, namely Jim Friend, Damon Bates and Mike Sigfried kept the occurrence at lunchtime alive that afternoon. A couple of boys asked for a demonstration of the move Mark had used while Damon and Mike dared, "I'd like to see him try that on me." More humiliation was heaped upon him when Joe Kellerman passed by in the hall and delivered the traditional punch in the arm as he past. From behind, Jim Friend encouraged, "Pull his hair." The comment brought lots of laughter but left Mark feeling helpless.

Helpless feelings were temporarily chased away that evening when he took Mitzi out for her walk. However, they didn't go away completely and allowing the dog an extra ten minutes of running on the beach didn't do the trick. Back at Ted's apartment, the lack of entertainment on television and the laptop did nothing to remove the thoughts that were now going through his head. Obeying the thoughts, Mark found himself unlocking the door and entering Ted's gun closet. It was all there, the Uzi, the nine millimetre, all of the ammo and the magazines and bandoliers in which to load and transport them. All he had to do was to load it and take it with him. The only obstacle was concealing it, otherwise it was that easy.

Watching Mitzi run around on the beach early the next morning, his thoughts still focused on how easy it would be to collect Ted's guns and take them to school. He also thought about the main obstacle of hiding them until they were ready to use. The he realised that if he got the army ruck sack he asked for on his birthday, that would no longer be an obstacle.

When he arrived at school the next morning, he played through the intentioned plan in his head. As he stood not far away from the eighth graders sitting on the steps, he mentally practiced getting his guns out of the ruck sack he was getting for his birthday and shooting the eighth graders. Another variable entered the equation. Tommy Allen and his friends walked through the gate as he played through the scenario. Instinctively, Mark made haste away as fast as he could but when he was at a safe distance, he realised he had an opportunity. If he timed it right, he could get Tommy and his friends as they entered the school grounds and then redirect his fire at the eighth graders, two birds with one stone.

Turning the corner of the new wing, he came upon his second kill zone. He realised that he would have plenty of time for both if he ran from the first kill zone to the second. It was all there in front of him. He could open fire at will and force his enemy into the open space, the kill zone. There he could blast away making sure he got the ones he really wanted to shoot and others would be collateral. Besides, they were all guilty of crimes against him anyway. It would be total annihilation. He already knew that Ted was going away over the last two days of school and he wanted Mark to look after Mitzi for him, so the last day of school would be perfect for his extravaganza. All he needed now was the encouragement to go through with it.

That encouragement began to come once he was inside school. "Why do you let him do that to you?" Hope Anderton asked as Joe Kellerman thumped him when he walked past.

Mark simply shrugged and responded, "What's the point?" He knew he was right. He tried everything else, fighting back, going to the principal and even the police but none of it did any good. As far as prayers, he was beginning to think that he was talking to a wall. Consequently, he thought he had no other choice than to just take it. Whether it was Nick Higbee giving him a shove, Mike Sigfried punching him in the back, the eighth graders, Tommy Allen's hand slipping, Joe Kellerman's punches or body checks or anyone else for that matter, he felt defenceless against it. Even just normal teasing, if he said anything back even teasing the teaser, he would come off worse. It was just no use.

Those thoughts were with him every morning. Almost involuntarily, he found himself at the spot where he planned to take out his weapons for the massacre and then gunning down Tommy Allen and friends at the school gates and then the eighth graders on the steps. All the while, he would constantly check his flanks and rear to make sure he wasn't taken by surprise. Then after inflicting casualties in the initial bursts, he would make sure those he wanted dead were by putting a round in their heads with the nine millimetre before high tailing it to the next point of carnage. Anyone unfortunate enough to be present between his travels between the kill zones would be immediately neutralised. He had to hope that the alarm hadn't yet been raised and the children in the second zone would still be there, still sitting ducks. This way he could move in and kill as many as he wanted to. When it was all done, he would just self terminate.

That last thought remained with him constantly. He realised that the last thing he wanted to do was to be taken alive; there was no way he could handle life behind bars and he knew it. He was already convinced that no jury in the country would acquit him in spite of what he was suffering. This prompted him to research school shootings on the Internet one evening. He didn't look at the Columbine shooting as that was too obvious

301

but two others definitely interested him. One happened in Maine, the other in Maryland. Both were high schools but more importantly, in both cases the shooter was captured alive, tried and sentenced to life without parole. He could not and would not let that happen to him.

As a result, he read how both shooters were taken alive. The police arrested the Maine shooter. It was obvious that he had gotten too carried away with the shooting and let his spree go on for too long giving the police ample time to capture him. Mark knew speed was important. Ted's words "Get in, do your damage and get out" when he was talking about conducting a raid entered his mind. Those words now made good sense.

The Maryland shooter was tackled from behind by a have-a-go hero and held there until the police arrived. In Mark's eyes, the shooter allowed himself to be flanked and that was the one thing he was determined not to let happen to him. Another mistake that both shooters made was that they entered the school building to do their work. While there were some advantages to that, there were some definite disadvantages. He had no intention of entering the building when the playground provided the perfect killing fields.

Mark's birthday part that Saturday sidelined any plans for destruction for that weekend. His mother piled him, Keith, Jack, Alan and Jim Benjamin into the car and took them to Giorgio's Pizza in Vincent. Keith had fallen off his bike the day before and had broken his leg, but his mother still made allowances for him. They all had a great time devouring two pizzas, garlic bread and large pitchers of coke and seven up. After Giorgio's they went to the only arcade on the Vincent boardwalk. Keith proved to be very good at the trap shooting game and while Mark was tempted to have a go himself, he was too afraid of giving anything away.

His thirteenth birthday party had been a good one. He had gotten some really nice presents: an expensive looking wallet from Keith, a book about the solar system from Alan and some money in a card from Jack and Jim. However, his best gifts were from Ted. He got the army backpack he was hoping for but he had a bigger surprise inside Ted's birthday card. When he opened the card, he saw a wallet sized card stating that he had junior membership in the NRA. It truly had been the best birthday in all his thirteen years.

All the euphoria from Saturday created a dilemma for him on the Sunday. He realised that he had some good friends after all and didn't want to see any of them get hurt. He wrestled with these thoughts straining his brain on how to prevent it that day. Owing to his injury, Keith would be allowed to use the main entrance, so he would be safe. Jim always came to school with his father and Jack usually came with him. They usually stayed near Mr Benjamin's office until school time so that wasn't too much of a problem. His big worry was Alan. He needed to find some way to get him out of the kill zone.

Thoughts over Alan played in his mind as he rehearsed on the Monday morning. He found one positive when he was at the starting point and no one seemed to notice him taking things out of his pack. That gave him confidence that he could get his weapons out unnoticed. When the rehearsal took him to the second kill zone, he noted that Alan was standing by the door to Mrs Hinton's classroom. There was a good chance that Alan could escape unhurt unless someone he really wanted to shoot got too close to him. Mark decided that it was too risky and needed to get Alan out of danger.

Doubts also began to creep into his mind when the

expected tirade of abuse didn't come. He was certain that Mike Sigfried would say something to him about the class coming in second in the sit ups race on Play Day the previous Friday. Mike had blamed him solely for not winning the race, which was rather hypocritical. Mike had gotten the class disqualified in the hurdles race after he failed to pick up a hurdle he had knocked over. However, nothing was said to Mike about it by anyone.

It seemed all attention was turned towards Keith and his broken leg. Most of the class seemed to be convinced that Keith was faking his injury. Mark couldn't understand why Keith would do something like that although Damon Bates speculated that Keith was looking for sympathy. The argument didn't convince him and his sympathies were with his friend. After all, Mark knew what it was like to be branded a liar. However, the focus on Keith kept people off his back. Except for a few teasing comments, Mark experienced no abuse between Monday and Thursday that week. Maybe things were going to get better after all.

By Friday, he was in the mind to abandon his plan. When he walked past the eighth graders and David Roseman called out, "Nice back pack Marvin," he simply replied, "Thank you." It didn't bother him when Matt Barber tried to turn everyone's attention onto Mark's socks although no one seemed to follow the lead. When a seventh grader named Lee Fedico openly criticised him because his green socks didn't match his maroon sneakers, he knew in his mind that it wasn't his fault that he didn't have a pair of sneakers in every colour to match his clothes. Those should have all been wake up calls for him but they weren't. Besides, he was particularly excited about this Friday because he was going to be recognised for playing on the team that had won the seventh grade basketball league. The fact that the shipment of trophies hadn't yet arrived made no difference.

At the awards assembly, he waited patiently with bubbling excitement as students and groups were called up to the stage to receive their recognition and prize. Mark gave a thumbs up to Jimmy Benjamin received an award for improved reading. Somehow, he managed to keep a lid on his excitement as he waited for his turn in the spotlight. Finally, Mr Benjamin ascended the stage and first read out the players on the winning team of the sixth grade league.

"Now the winners of the seventh grade league," he announced. Predictably, the stars of the team were called first: Tom Lamaina, Mike Deacher, Lee Fedico and Jim Friend's cousin Max. Without missing a beat, Mr Benjamin then called out, "Gene Lancaster."

Mark couldn't conceal his upset. Once he again, he had been confused with Gene. Mrs Hinton must have seen his expression because she was at his side in a flash asking what was wrong.

"They called Gene up there and it should have been me," Mark declared between breaths.

"We'll straighten it out," the teacher reassured before going back to her seat. When she did, Mark heard the patronising voice of Terry Cratt saying, "Don't cry Mark." It was clear that Mrs Hinton wasn't the only person to see how upset he was.

For Mark, the assembly had been ruined in spite of the fact that Mr Benjamin announced from the stage, "We'll straighten this out afterwards, Mark and Gene." Gene had at least done the right thing and pointed out the error to Mr Benjamin. The school would say that it was a tiny mistake but Mark knew that if he had made such a tiny mistake, everyone would have crucified him for it. However, he was glad about Gene's honesty and began to think that maybe he didn't deserve to die.

Straight after the assembly, Mr Benjamin came to Mark and admitted there had been a mistake and told him not to be upset over it. Back in the classroom, with Mrs Hinton not there yet, his classmates immediately pounced on the chance to humiliate him further. "Why were you crying?" Renee Tye asked in a condescending tone.

"Because he didn't get a trophy," Damon Bates answered in Mark's place.

"What, he didn't get a trophy," Renee repeated in mock disbelief.

"No!" Mark interjected. "It's because they called up Lancaster instead of me." He immediately saw that his words had fallen upon deaf ears.

Sarah Levine took up the case on his side, "He was just upset," she told them. "I mean if you can't show your feelings, then something's wrong."

Most of the class simply ignored her speech and kept on at Mark. Mike Sigfried began making crying motions with his hands at him. This totally wound Mark up and he stuck his middle finger up at Mike for all to see. Mike wasted no time in going over and raining blows down upon Mark. As he covered himself up, most of the blows landed on his back. "You don't put your finger up at me," he growled as he continued his assault. Only a warning that Mrs Hinton was coming ended it.

For the rest of the day, he had to endure Mike's boasting about how he beat Mark up. Comments like "I wish I could have seen it," from Diane Boreman didn't help. Nor did Jim Friend's warning, "You better not go to the cops. My uncle says that won't do anything about it and they know that you start trouble."

Worse came that afternoon when Joe Kellerman checked him into the wall leading Damon Bates to say to Joe, "Don't do that, he might cry." Even after school while riding home on his bike, he passed Tommy Allen, Terry Cratt and others. Terry made the same crying motions Mike Sigfried had made earlier that day and said, "I'm still pissed off at you." Tommy threw an apple at him that skidded along the road under his bike. The rest of the ride home was uneventful but one thing was certainly clear; nothing was going to change.

"It's for safety reasons why we can't have targets pop up behind you," Ted explained when they were on the course that Saturday. "Still, I like your thinking, it's good to check behind to make sure no enemies are there."

With renewed purpose and bloodlust, he followed the course his Uzi mowing down any targets that came up. The two targets that met him by the huts were gunned down with the same finesse. When multiple targets began to spring up beyond the huts, they too were taken out in rapid succession. At the completion of the course, all Ted could say was "You have one hell of a killer's instinct." That made Mark smile widely.

Monday morning, the day before the last day of school, he was totally numb to everything around him. His mind was only clear to his rehearsal for the big event the next day. Therefore he was able to shut out the fact that when he got to his classroom door, Mike Sigfried was there to meet him. Mike grabbed his arm bending it behind his back and trying to bring it up to his head in a chicken wing.

"I want you to take back every fucking thing you did to me," he demanded applying more pressure.

Mark's mind was thinking, "Why don't you take back all the things you did to me," but his mouth submitted, "I take it back."

Knowing he had control, he forced Mark to say it again. Before releasing him, Mike gave a stern warning, "You better not do any of that shit to me again."

His mind was too numb to say anything else and he had to watch Mike high five his friends in celebration. When school began, he suffered no further acts of physical aggression but many verbal reminders in the class and hall. Joe Kellerman only threatened to punch him when he walked past and when Mark winced, he laughed at the fact he had intimidated him, although an actual punch would have had little effect. He just went through the motions that day.

Mrs Bromberg had brought in a guest speak to talk to the entire seventh grade. He was a lawyer named Howard Bernstein who worked for the law firm of Silverman and Pizzano. Most of what the speaker said went through one of Mark's ears then out of the other. However, there was something he said that grabbed his attention.

"A dying declaration is one statement that may not be considered a lie," the lawyer explained. "See, if you are truly believe you are going to die, then it is believed that you have no reason to lie."

Andrew Blumenthaw asked the question that was on Mark's mind. "What if the person is a known liar?"

"It's still regarded as the truth," Mr Bernstein answered. "Even a known liar will tell the truth if he believes he's going to die."

The rest of the talk affected him as before but Mark stored what was said about dying declarations into a compartment in his brain. There were no further developments to the day but when the end came, he made it a point to see Alan Green and Sarah Levine before he left.

"Can I talk to you both before school tomorrow?" he requested. "There's something I need to give you both." Seeing Hope Anderton standing next to Sarah, he told her, "You can come too."

All three classmates had puzzled looks on their faces but they agreed to meet him. He felt relieved as he went out of the door as if he had accomplished something. Even when Nick Higbee tripped him from behind and then ran off, it didn't phase him. It affirmed his thought that tomorrow would be his day and he took that thought with him when he went to Ted's apartment that evening.

Chapter 25

Pop Star For a Day

Leversee's Last Stand

How is one supposed to feel when they know they're going to die? Mark couldn't answer this; all he knew was that he had to see his plan through this day. After he had walked Mitzi the previous evening, he spent the rest of the time loading magazines and putting them into holders or bandoliers and fastening the pistol ones onto a cartridge belt. At that moment, he had 300 rounds of Uzi ammo and another 100 rounds of pistol ammo. He could have been ready for a war.

That morning after leaving a note under his pillow for his mother, he arrived at Ted's apartment earlier than usual. Mitzi's walk was a little shorter than normal so he could get back and carry out the final details of his plan. First, he carefully packed the guns and ammo in the rucksack and then briefly went on Ted's laptop to make an entry on Facebook. Seeing all of the nasty comments posted by people onto his wall only served to strengthen his resolve. When all was done, he locked the door and headed for school.

His mind was filled with great conflict as he rode. He wondered if he was doing the right thing and several times he thought about turning back and putting the guns and all the ammunition away. Maybe it will get better, maybe his family would move out of Ramsgate- but those thoughts were quickly drowned out by the other side of his mind.

Since he moved to Ramsgate nearly three years earlier, he had known nothing but heartache. The bullying, humiliation and failure were all too much for him now. He was a failure to his peers and teachers in both school and sport, a failure to his mother for not being like his cousin Tom or Ted's nephew Kenny and a failure to Lisa. This was the one thing he was going to do right.

It wasn't all his fault though. Others had let him down too, the school, teachers, the police and even God. Nobody was on his side; so while he didn't particularly want to die, he couldn't see any point in living either. He knew that the inhabitants of Ramsgate were the ones responsible for all of his grief and torment, so if he was going to die, it was only right that he take as many as possible with him.

As for God, Mark had been a dutiful Christian for a year and a half and had done his best to serve Him. However, God showed no acknowledgement of this and while Mark thought he had suffered as much as Job, there were no blessings for him. God didn't stop the abuse he was getting in spite of all his prayers. He thought that it was because he was failing God. He had read many stories of how bad criminals had found Jesus and suddenly turned their life around; but it didn't seem to be the case for him, despite how hard he tried. It all left him feeling very confused.

Recently it occurred to him that perhaps God was showing him a different way. For the past few weeks, he had been reading from the Old Testament and the same verse, Deuteronomy, Chapter 20- verses 16 and 17 kept coming back to him:

"But of the cities of these people, which the Lord thy God doth give thee for an inheritance, thou shalt save none alive that breatheth. But thou shalt destroy them."

It did seem to him that his recent prayers of having the courage to go through with what he was about to do were being answered.

A few blocks from the school, he slowed up, as he didn't want to get there too soon. That gave one last opportunity for the one part of his mind to talk him out of it. It reasoned that the eighth graders were leaving and wouldn't be there to harass him. He might get some good kids in his class; but the other side of his mind quickly countered, "He might get a worse class. He might get Tommy Allen or Joe Kellerman in his class or worse, both of them. Even if neither of them were in his class, there would be someone in it to carry on the abuse." That final statement ended all doubts.

It was that doubtless determination, which overrode his pounding heart when he came through the school gate. No one seemed to pay any attention to him as he parked and locked his bike; that was the first obstacle overcome. His heart skipped every other beat as he walked past the eighth graders sitting on the steps. He threw a quick glance at them- just to make sure his intended targets were among them, David Roseman and Jim Nickerson were. He already knew that Joe Callazone wasn't going to be there as he was in Puerto Rico on some basketball exchange. The second obstacle had been cleared.

Moving quickly to his chosen spot, he made a quick reconnaissance of the area; no one was near him. Keeping vigilant, he took out the bandolier filled with Uzi magazines and put it over his left shoulder. Still no one noticed it or when he put on his cartridge belt with six magazines of nine-millimetre ammo. He took a look behind him and quickly inserted the pistol into the holster. With his hand ready for a quick draw, he checked again. All of the students were too caught up in their own conversations to take notice of him. He put his hand inside his rucksack feeling the cold steel of the Uzi. Glancing at his watch, he saw Tommy Allen and his friends crossing the road towards the gate. Taking the Uzi from out of the pack, he proceeded to remove the top magazine from the bandolier and insert it into the weapon. Tommy and Co were entering the school gate, it was go time!

"What the fuck are you doing, Leversee?" Tommy asked in his normal aggressive manner as Mark approached.

"Hey Allen!" Mark called out, making sure he had Tommy's attention. "My finger slipped."

Just like he had practiced on the course, he brought the Uzi up and in one fluid motion, aimed and squeezed off four rounds. All of them hit the intended target square in the chest and Tommy went down like one of those same targets on the course. Before Joe Clover, Ron O'Malley or Terry Cratt knew what was going on, they too were struck by bullets and went down the same way, except for Terry who pirouetted like a ballerina from the two rounds that hit his shoulder.

Before he had a chance to celebrate, David Roseman yelled out, "What the fuck!" but as he was saying "Marvin," he was hit by three rounds as Mark redirected his fire without hesitation at the steps. Remembering Ted's instruction, he concentrated his fire on the door, hitting a couple more as they tried to get inside the building. He made sure Jim Nickerson was hit as others fled to his right. Mark ignored them; instead he focused on Mark Wolfe who had escaped the initial burst and was fleeing to Mark's left. Mark cut him down seconds later by the final rounds of the first magazine. "So far, so good," he thought to himself as he felt the elation begin to build.

With a quick change of magazines, he prepared to strike at more targets. From his brief surveillance, he smiled at the bleeding bodies of David and Jim Nickerson on the ground. A feminine voice shouting,

"Jesus Christ!" from outside the school gate directed his attention there. "Excellent," he thought, the voice belonged to Liz Clover and with her was Linda Boston. He grinned sadistically at the thought he was about to get revenge on the girl who had tormented him in fifth and sixth grades and the girl who tried to extort money from him for something not of his doing. Before Liz knew it, she was filled with lead and went down after a second's hesitation. Linda tried to turn and run but Mark sent her sprawling face first onto the street.

"What are you doing, Mark?" a sweeter sounding voice asked from seemingly out of nowhere. Snapping his mind out of further celebrations, Mark turned to see Nadine Salvatino, white as a ghost, looking at him and then the fallen girls with utter horror.

He regarded her for a half a second and then assured her, "Don't worry Nadine, I'm not gonna shoot you. You were one of the few who was good to me." He turned and left her to attend to the fallen Liz and Linda.

"What about me, Leversee? I was good to you," Brian Cullen sarcastically inquired from a safe distance, as Mark prepared to continue the mission. The answer came swiftly as Brian's head collapsed like a watermelon thanks to three well-aimed rounds from the Uzi.

Quickly checking his flanks and relieved that those around the bike racks had already retreated, he moved just beyond the corner of the building, giving himself two kill zones. His left had been cleared of people but those now in front of him began to run in blind panic down the long side of the school building. Mark hastened their getaway by firing into the crowd. Except for the blonde eighth grade cheerleader who fell about ten yards in front of him, the identities of the other casualties he was inflicting would always remain anonymous to him. In the ten seconds it took to empty his second magazine, kill zone one was secure, some of the main targets were annihilated and he could briefly delight in seeing the bodies on the ground.

He knew he had to make haste to number two before the alarm was completely raised. Otherwise, he would have paused a further second to listen to the screams of some of the wounded. Changing magazines of the Uzi, he held it at his side and reached for the pistol as he neared Tommy Allen's lifeless looking body. He was glad he had watched DVDs of "Saving Private Ryan" and "A Bridge Too Far," otherwise the ocean of red now created by the bleeding bodies of Tommy, Joe, Ron and Terry might have made him sick. He had no time to think of that now. Standing over Tommy, he took the nine-millimetre pistol out of the holster and pointing it at Tommy said, "My finger slipped again," before squeezing off one round into the middle of his forehead.

Jogging on a few steps, he stopped at the steps that were strewn with the bodies of dead or dying eighth graders. Not wanting to get too close, he took the Uzi and pumped a four round burst into the body of Jimmy Nickerson before saying, "Here's a restraining order for you." He did likewise with David Roseman but this time he asked, "Who's the faggot now?"

In order not to be sick from the sight of blood all around the steps, he went into a full run as he made his way along the new wing towards kill zone two, only stopping to gleefully pump another burst into the body of Mark Wolfe and keeping himself positioned dead centre of the fence and building. Going about half way, he saw some kids who watched him coming towards them. Immediately, they tried to run away but Mark got his Uzi ready and hit three of them before they made it to the end of the new wing. A fourth fled, not to the school, but made haste to get out of the school gate along with some other kids who saw him coming. When Mark reached the end of the new wing, Joe Kellerman was walking towards him.

"Oh shit, he really does have a gun. Are you going to shoot me?" he teased. The answer came in the form of three rounds that pierced his body and Mark's reply of "Yes you mother fucker."

He kept firing as he moved towards the kill zone. Andrew Blumenthaw was spotted and gunned down immediately with four shots to his body. Bullets bouncing around the feet of Mike Deacher told him to get out of there but others, like John Lodge, weren't so lucky. A group of girls that included Nancy Greenwood, Laurie Swords and Janice Ricardo also a met similar fate.

The third magazine was emptied by the time he got to where Joe Kellerman lay. He stopped for a moment and took out the pistol, putting a round in his forehead just like Tommy. Only this time, Mark said sadistically, "I can't take a check, you can't take a bullet." Moving on again, he was surprised to see that he had actually hit Joe Gerberwitz who lay on his side but still conscious. He must have seen what Mark had done to Kellerman and the look of sheer terror in his eyes gave away the fact that he was expecting the same fate. He wasn't wrong; Mark simply went near him and informed him, "You're my victim today," before placing a pistol round into Joe's skull.

He now hastened to the second kill zone. However he stopped for the briefest of seconds to let his mind digest one fascinating site. Nancy Greenwood had fallen onto her back with Janice Ricardo falling on top of her; both girls were wearing short skirts. This would be the last erotic thing he would ever see. Still, he had no remorse for the girls who had constantly teased him.

Mark arrived at the kill zone in the nick of time. Just

seconds after he began letting loose with automatic fire across the playground, teachers began to fling open doors desperately screaming for children to get inside. The hysteria started a crush, more people would be injured from bumps, cuts and bruises in trying to get away than by Mark's bullets. Still, he continued firing; Jim Friend, Damon Bates and Mike Sigfried all went down. He would never know that he scored a head shot on Jim or on Renee Tye. David Fitzpatrick and Steve McGuire were two others who were unfortunate enough to enter his line of sight. Both fell before they had a chance to move.

Loading his fifth magazine, he now began firing randomly into the crowds trying to get into the sanctuary of the classrooms. First seventh graders and then sixth graders all began falling, screaming from being hit and causing an evil grin to alight his face. It no longer mattered whom it was as the whole town was equally guilty of the torment heaped upon him over the past three years and he was finally getting his revenge for it. He briefly saw Nick Higbee and his friends but wasn't sure if he had gotten them, but he never saw the pretty blonde sixth grade girl who fell with a single shot that went straight through her heart.

Against the flow of all the commotion, Gene came towards him offering the hand of friendship. However, his mind flashed back to other times when Gene pretended friendship only to betray him. Such as when he started playing with Mark's ball only to give it to David Fitzpatrick. He wasn't going to let that happen again so the Uzi cut out Gene's legs from under him.

"But I'm your friend," he said between gasps of pain and with a hurt look of betrayal on his face.

"That's why I'm not going to kill you," Mark responded coldly.

By the end of the fifth magazine, only those he

rendered unable to move remained on the playground. The others were all cowering on the floor of their classrooms. Still fearful of being flanked, he kept his vigilance as he bounded over to Mike Sigfried who had been shot in both legs and was still conscious, lying face down.

"I want you to take back every fucking thing you did to me," Mark demanded as he took out the nine-millimetre.

"What did I do to you?" Mike asked in obvious pain but trying to sound innocent.

"Punching me in the back, making fun of me on Friday when I was upset!" Mark yelled and then put a round into Mike's shoulder.

Mike screamed and then said between bouts of pain, "I was just kidding around."

"Well, this is just kidding around," Mark retorted before placing another round in Mike's buttocks. "Now take it all back!"

For a second, it looked as if Mike would remain defiant but suddenly he succumbed. "I take it back."

Mark muttered, "Very good" and took a deep breath. Then suddenly, without warning, fired the pistol again, the shot ricocheting off the ground very close to Mike's head. The instant wetness of his trousers gave Mark the satisfaction he desired.

Lying on the ground nearby, David Fitzpatrick was unable to move but still conscious. Mark leaped over to him holstering the pistol and readying the Uzi. Looking into David's pleading for mercy eyes, he chided, "You could always have me arrested for assault and battery." Then with an evil smile continued, "Or for murder." With those words he proceed to pump half a thirty round magazine into David, laughing as his body was jiggled about by the shots.

Mark knew he didn't have much time left. He took

one last look at the carnage he had caused and smiled victoriously. The sight of dead and wounded pupils lying around him gave his spirits a lift. He had won in the end. There was nothing more to do and the faint sounds of police sirens were becoming louder. Stepping away from David's corpse, he took the nine-millimetre from its holster and unceremoniously securing the muzzle firmly against his temple, Mark ended his torment forever.

Meanwhile

Alan looked at his watch for the fifth time in the last three minutes. "I don't think he's coming," he declared to the two girls who were waiting with him.

Sarah nodded, "He must be late or something, we better go to school."

They hadn't gone half a block when they all heard a series of loud popping noises. "I wonder what that is," Hope speculated on behalf of her two friends. But Alan and Sarah both shook their heads and continued walking. The noises got louder for a few seconds and then seemed to fade. They walked another block before arriving at the front of the school to a site of many kids bent over or sitting or lying on the ground on the grass plot near the front of the building; all out of breath, many looking like they had had the fright of their lives. One boy was even bleeding rather badly from his shoulder. Many of the girls were crying and others were looking down the side of the school from where they came towards the main playground. It was clear that something very horrible had just happened.

Mr Tasker and several teachers came out through the main doors. In a display of generalship, he directed teachers to attend to any wounded and grieving. A first aid kit was produced and the boy with the wounded

319

shoulder was immediately addressed. The principal began making rounds himself, walking among the pupils and reassuring all that they were safe and the police were coming. The ever-increasing sound of sirens backed him up.

Meanwhile, Alan, Sarah and Hope went off in different directions. The girls found a friend named Gail Bunker who through many sobs informed them that a kid with a gun was shooting everybody at the school. Alan had found his older brother Fred, whose darker complexion was lighter from the fright. "He just started shooting everybody," Fred said between gasps. Curiosity got the better of Alan so he asked if Fred knew who it was. "It was your friend who came to your Bar Mitzvah, that Leversee." Alan's shock was overshadowed by the arrival of the police cars.

Assembly

A great sigh of relief went up through the school when the officer announced that the situation was over. "Did you get him?" asked one boy as he followed the principal's instruction to go into the gym. The officer disregarded the question.

"I hope they didn't kill him," stated a girl behind the boy. "Death would be an easy way out for him. He should stand trial for what he's done."

The children who had made it to the front of the school now merged in the hall with those who had found refuge in the classrooms. Very little was said while they were ushered into the gym and seated by class. As they walked through the halls, they noticed the blinds had been pulled down to keep them from seeing the death toll Mark had inflicted on their fellow pupils and more importantly kept them from seeing who among their friends was dead.

"A very tragic thing has just happened at the school and I know many of you will have questions," Mr Tasker began in an attempt to soothe his hysterical pupils. "I will say that the individual responsible for this is also dead." The principal thought it wise not to tell the school how Mark had died although he knew they would all soon find out. His mission now was to reassure his grief-stricken school and get them to cooperate with the police. He continued, "Clipboards, paper and pens will be handed to each one of you and the police would like you to write down anything you saw or heard. The police may want to interview some of you in the next few days."

The pupils in the gym were given plenty of time to write down their accounts of Mark's massacre even though most were finished in a matter of minutes. Sarah, Alan and Hope needed even less time. On advice from the police, Mr Tasker decided to keep everyone in the gym for as long as possible while the police and ambulance crews, some of whom were arriving from as far away as Atlantic City, worked on the casualties outside. Music was played to ease the tension but it was of little help. Since the talent show scheduled for the last day of school was now obviously cancelled, one of the teachers suggested a film, but no one was in the mood for one. No one really cared when it was announced there would be no parties, that was pretty clear now. After an hour, report cards were handed out and the school was told that the year was officially over. Then starting with the back rows, pupils were ushered through a fire door and along the same outside corridor that Mark had used on his very first day at Tye School and out to the front of the building. And that was how the school year ended.

Media Frenzy

321

Only minutes after Mark's final pull of the trigger, news of his great exploit began to circumnavigate the local media. A reporter from the local Downbeach Newspaper arrived at the school in twenty minutes. Immediately the photographer began taking photos of the ambulance and coroner crews at work. The reporter, a young man in his mid twenties, began interviewing police but was not allowed to interview anyone at the school yet. That would come later. However, he and the now steady stream of colleagues who were now arriving missed the big prize. Mark's body and his weapons were the first to be removed from the scene, most likely to avoid any media sensationalism.

Local radio was broadcasting the shooting shortly after as the news rapidly made its way across Southern New Jersey and beyond. Reporters from the larger Atlantic City papers were soon there, as were people from the several radio stations. All now were in competition to get the best angle of the news to their readers and listeners. Just before ten o'clock, the story reached Philadelphia.

The silly game show was going off the air anyway. Still the newsreader at Channel 6 in Philadelphia still apologetically announced, "We interrupt this programme to bring you an Action News special report. We have just learned that there has been a shooting at Bernard Tye Middle School in Ramsgate New Jersey. We now go live to the school where our reporter, Marielen Holt is on the scene."

"Thank you Bob," said the young woman with shoulder-length black hair and wearing a business-like dress as she stood in front of the camera. "This was supposed to be the last day at school for the pupils at Bernard Tye School but it was marred by tragedy," she began sombrely. "Before school started, one of their fellow pupils entered the school grounds with a pistol and an automatic weapon and opened fire on pupils in the playground. His shooting spree lasted for about five minutes but not before he shot at least forty people, fourteen are now known to be dead and several others are on life support, before turning the gun on himself. The gunman's identity is not yet known but he was definitely a pupil here at the school. That's all we know at the moment Bob, but I will keep you posted of further developments. This is Marielen Holt for Action News."

Realisation

Walking home from school, Alan managed to catch up with Sarah and Hope. Normally there would be excitement about the end of school and passing the grade; but there was none. "Do you know what they're saying?" Sarah asked when he caught his breath. With an air of disbelief, she added, "They're saying Mark was the one who shot everybody."

"I know," Alan nodded. "My brother said it was him."

"That explains why he never met us," Hope remarked, stating the obvious but attempting not to be too humorous. "But why did he want to meet us in the first place?"

All three shook their heads at the question and they walked about one hundred feet before Sarah suddenly stopped. Her face bore an expression as if she had just been hit in the back with a bag of bricks. "I think he wanted to get us out of the way," she gasped in horror. "I bet he had been planning this for a long time and because you were his friend and I tried to defend him when Sigfried was picking on him the other day when he was upset. I think because we were one of the few

323

people who were nice to him, he decided he didn't want to shoot us, so he arranged this fake meeting to make sure we didn't get shot."

Now it was Alan and Hope's turn to give looks as if they had been hit with the same bag of bricks. "I think you're right," Alan commented after deciphering Sarah's logic in his mind. Mixed with disbelief and the strange feeling that they should somehow be grateful to Mark, they walked on in silence. Before they parted, the three friends unanimously agreed and made a pact never to mention the arranged meeting that had never taken place that morning.

Unwelcome News

Mark's grandparents first learned about the shooting on the radio. The instant they did, Mr Johnston called his daughter downstairs to listen with them. Mother, grandfather and grandmother didn't move for nearly an hour as more details of the report filtered through, all the time listening for the names of the casualties and praying that Mark wasn't one of them. Their concentration was so intense that the callers at the door had to knock twice before it was answered.

Mr Johnston opened the door to a detective and a uniformed officer. Without waiting for them to be asked to come in, he opened the door for the two officers without hesitation. Once inside, the detective, who Mrs Leversee recognised as the one who had investigated Mark's wrecked bicycle, announced, "We have a warrant to search the property and we would like to ask Mrs Leversee some questions down at the station."

"Has Mark been shot? Is he all right?" Mark's mother asked, the two questions almost sounding as one. Her mind jumbled with many more questions.

The detective put up a hand to silence her. He then reiterated his first statement. "Mrs Leversee, we need you to come down to the station and search the property because your son Mark was the shooter."

Governor's Decision

In his first five months since becoming Governor of New Jersey, Albert Lombardino had seen his approval-rating drop by ten per cent. Many New Jersey voters now thought that he was placating to special interest groups while ignoring their wishes. Furthermore, many living in the Southern part of the state thought he was ignoring them all together. Those thoughts raced around his mind that morning while he prepared himself for a meeting with his advisors. Suddenly a knock at the door and the appearance of his Press Secretary, who didn't even wait to be invited in, disrupted his thoughts.

The secretary's barging in immediately awoke the governor from his deep contemplation. Before he had even got a chance to ask him what the emergency was, the secretary immediately began, "Sir, we've just learned about a school shooting in Ramsgate. They say there's about fourteen maybe fifteen dead and around thirty children wounded."

"Did they catch the person who did the shooting?" Governor Lombardino inquired.

"No sir," the secretary stated. "The reports say that the shooter turned the gun on himself."

He didn't pause a second, this was Albert Lombardino's turn to spring into action. Standing up, he ordered, "Get my helicopter ready, I'm going to Ramsgate." He then left his office; confident his Press Secretary would know what to do. His first task was to cancel the meeting with his advisors. Most were already there when the Governor walked in and he wasted no time. "Gentlemen," he said authoritatively, "I've just been informed of a shooting in a school in Ramsgate. Therefore, I'm cancelling the meeting and heading there now."

Upon hearing their boss's words, the advisors also sprang into action. All the necessary steps were taken; a car was already waiting for the governor by the time he exited the building and when he arrived at the launch site fifteen minutes later, his helicopter was ready to go. Once aboard, the pilot wasted no time in taking off. Albert Lombardino sat back for the hour-long ride, all the time his mind running through what he was going to do and say when he arrived in Ramsgate. Halfway through the trip his thoughts were once again disturbed by his faithful press secretary. Not realising that it had even rung, he was a little surprised when he saw the secretary holding his cell phone out to him. "Sir," the secretary announced, "It's the president."

National Media Frenzy

Throughout the morning TV station vans began to roll into Ramsgate. Roads leading to Tye School became virtually impassable and parking was impossible, even for local residents. Some TV news crews were forced to carry all their equipment from distances over half a mile, not that any of this deterred the determined crews one bit. They had a whale of a story to report to the world. But it wasn't just the cameras and news crews crowding the streets and sidewalks around the school. Swarms of curious onlookers passed by the school hoping to get a glimpse of the carnage Mark had caused.

For the most part, there was little to see especially with all the news crews milling around trying to get the best place for the audiences to view them and the school. Furthermore, the Ramsgate police were very vigilant in making sure spectators didn't get too close and had assistance from the state police as well. The most anybody saw was the two forensic scientists picking up the shell casings from the spot where Mark had begun the morning's festivities, although a couple of people claimed that they could see faint traces of blood on the ground.

Fox News and then CNN, right on their heels, made the people of Ramsgate aware that they were now the focus of national attention. They also realised that this was nothing to be proud of as the events of that morning spread from coast to coast. Each reporter put their own little spin on things, each one trying to sound more sympathetic to the people of Ramsgate than the next one. Still, it did little to take away the misery that many residents were feeling.

Making national headlines prompted many people living around the country to begin phoning friends and relatives living in Ramsgate offering support and condolences. Relatives from Pennsylvania called Mark's grandparents to offer sympathy and to find out if Mark was among the dead or wounded. This left Mark's grandfather in a dilemma. Should he tell them that Mark was believed to be the shooter or should he let them find out on the news? In the end, he thought it would be better for him and his wife and daughter to tell the truth from the start. So his response was, "The police think that Mark was the one who did the shooting," and hope they would understand.

Questioned

Donna Leversee cried the entire time she rode in the police car to the station. In her mind, the police had to be wrong; there was no way that her son could have carried out such an awful thing. The police weren't unsympathetic and when she got to the station, gave her plenty of time to gain her composure. This took over half an hour, which turned out to be a good thing in one respect.

"We have finished our search of your parents' house and we didn't find any guns or ammunition," the tall Detective Cavanaugh stated, sounding a little disappointed, when he entered the interrogation room. When she looked up, she saw that this was the same detective who had questioned Mark Wolfe and his friend over Mark's wrecked bike. He then informed her, "We have confiscated his computer, his CDs and DVDs and a few other items from his bedroom for our investigation. But one of our officers found this note addressed to you and I thought it best you read it before the media see it."

He placed the piece of paper in front of here and she picked it up and began reading. She was completely unprepared for what she read.

Dear Mom,

I am so sorry that I have been such a bad son for you. That I couldn't be like my cousin Tom or Kenny. I'm sorry that I have DAMP and it stopped me from doing well in school and I'm sorry that I didn't fight back against the kids who pick on me. I thought, you would be better off with me not around but I am finally going to fight back against the kids who pick on me and I hope you will be proud of me for this.

Love,

Mark

Once again, she cried uncontrollably. The letter confirmed that her son had committed the dastardly deed. Her mind tried to find the answer to her question as to why he could have done this and that answer came fairly quickly. Managing to wipe away her tears she looked directly at the detective and said, "You know that everybody was always picking on him."

"Before I address that," the detective responded professionally, "I think it's best that I read you your rights. This is just procedure, I'm not arresting you for anything." When Mrs Leversee nodded her acknowledgement, Detective Cavanaugh took out the small police issued card and proceeded to read her the Miranda Rights word for word. After she stated that she understood her rights, the detective continued, "We have many witnesses, including many of the wounded that saw your son with the guns. When our officers found his body, there was a pistol in his hand and an automatic weapon by his side. Our initial investigation concludes that he used the pistol to end his life."

Once again, she broke down into wails and tears. The detective waited several more minutes for her to stop and when she did, he tried to sound as reassuring as possible. He explained, "We are convinced that you had no knowledge of what your son was planning this morning, but do you have any idea where Mark could have gotten the guns?"

Realisation hit her instantly; she knew the answer to that question. Without any hesitation, she answered the detective, "It's my boyfriend, Ted Zimminsky, he keeps guns and taught my son how to shoot. I thought it would be a good way for Ted to get to know Mark. But Ted says he keeps his guns locked in a closet."

"Is there any way your son could have gotten the key to the closet?" Detective Cavanaugh asked, sensing a picture forming in his mind.

She knew the answer to that as well. "Ted was away overnight on business," she explained. "He gave Mark the keys to his apartment so he could look after Ted's dog." Then it hit her, "The key to the gun closet must have been on that set of keys!"

That made perfect sense to the detective. He excused himself and left the interrogation room for several minutes. Mrs Leversee guessed that he was going to issue an arrest warrant for Ted. He said nothing about his actions outside the room when he came back into it. Instead, he asked the question she had been dreading. "Why do you think your son did it?"

She knew the answer to that question immediately; the note had proved it beyond all doubt in her mind. Still she was reluctant to give this answer. It took a further "Any idea at all?" prompt from him to remove this reluctance. Giving the detective a look that pierced his inner soul, she snapped, "Yes, I do, you read the note. He was always getting picked on in school and around the town. Kids were teasing him or punching him in the hall and twice he's had his bike wrecked." Then she seized upon the moment she was waiting for, "If you had questioned those two boys who my son saw wrecking his bike the way you're questioning me now, this whole thing might not have happened."

Mrs Leversee's words struck a chord in Detective Cavanaugh's mind and he reflected back to that time several months ago when he had questioned Mark Wolfe and his friend. Maybe he could have done things better but there was no point worrying about that now. What Mark Leversee had done was far worse. Out loud he said, "Yes, I remember the case. Well, the one boy involved in that, Mark Wolfe, is on life support. He probably won't survive the day, so I think your son got his revenge for the bicycle."

He knew it might not have been the right thing to say as he watched her descend into more tears. Therefore, he concluded that there was no further point in asking her more questions. Her grief must have been unbearable and she would never be able to fully accept the guilt of her son. Besides, he had gotten the main thing he was after; he knew from where Mark had gotten his guns.

As she was leaving, Mrs Leversee turned around and asked, "When can I see my son's body?"

He was prepared for this question. "They'll release it as soon as they're done," the detective responded automatically. He watched the mother leave the station before settling himself back in to the job at hand. Still, something tugged at the back of his mind; perhaps he could have questioned Mark Wolfe a bit more thoroughly.

11:15- Washington D.C.

Every journalist sitting in the conference room knew what this press conference was going to be about. Still they waited with respect and rose when the president walked in and stood behind the podium. He returned the respect and waited for everyone to be seated before he began. Once they were, he looked directly into the camera and spoke:

"We have just learned that there has been a terrible shooting in a junior high school in New Jersey. Our thoughts and prayers are with the victims and their families and I have personally telephoned Governor Lombardino and the Mayor of Ramsgate, Richard Burg to express not only my deepest sympathies but also the sympathies of the entire nation. I have also promised whatever assistance is needed. The FBI will be assisting in the investigation including a team that specialises in investigating school shootings. The Red Cross and other humanitarian agencies have also been dispatched and all will work closely with local law enforcement and officials. May I again, express my deepest sympathies to the people of Ramsgate and I am sure that the American people will join me in expressing their sympathies as well in the light of this awful tragedy; thank you."

After a brief applause, the president answered a few select questions before declaring the press conference over.

Opposites Attract

They may have been members of opposing political parties, but there was no sign of it when Governor Lombardino met Mayor Burg later that morning. Escorted by Chief Gregory, the two men toured the scene of Mark's crimes. They watched with admiration as local, county and now state forensic teams were hard at work collecting and processing the evidence, noted that the casualties had been removed and being politicians, heaped praise upon those men and women doing a thankless job. After viewing the scene, they met and spoke with Mr Tasker. Both men proceeded to heap praise upon the principal for the way he had handled the situation and both reassured him that he couldn't have done it any other way. Afterwards, the three men paused for a few photographs before the mayor informed them that there was going to be a press conference at noon. Albert Lombardino kept his promise about being there.

Released

Glanville Elementary School had been dismissed at

10:30 that morning in order to prepare for the press conference. The children were never told the reason; they just thought it was a special treat for the last day of school. Even before the children were gone, the school gym began to be transformed in preparation for the conference. The belief that the entire nation would be watching motivated everyone into wanting to get things done right. Volunteers worked tirelessly setting up chairs, assisting TV crews and guiding journalists and it was all ready in one hour. All in all, organising the huge press conference turned out to be an amazing feat.

Mayor Richard Burg wasn't a tall man, he stood about five foot seven but he never let that hold him back. He was used to addressing meetings, judges and juries when he was an attorney. The fact that the entire nation would now be watching him didn't faze him in the least. It had been suggested that he let the police chief hold the conference but he vetoed that immediately. This tragedy had happened in his city and it was his duty to tell the nation about it.

He never heard the television stations announce the press conference, so he never heard the universal declaration, "We now go live to Ramsgate New Jersey where the mayor is going to make a statement."

"Today, a very tragic event occurred at Bernard A Tye School This morning, at approximately 8:30, a boy, who was a pupil at the school, entered the school grounds and armed with a Uzi automatic and a nine millimetre pistol and opened fire on his fellow pupils before turning the gun on himself. At the moment, the death toll stands at fifteen dead and thirty wounded, four of whom are in intensive care. The police and ambulance crews have done a marvellous job in light of the horrendous circumstances and I can't praise them enough. I can assure you that the entire incident will be fully investigated and we won't stop until we know how and why someone could have done such a horrible thing."

Immediately, reporters competed with one another to ask the first question. All of them had the same one, "Do you know the name of the shooter?"

When the question was asked, Mayor Burg stepped aside allowing his police chief to take the microphone. "Yes, we do," he informed them. "The shooter's name was Mark Leversee and he was a seventh grader at the school. That's all we are going to say at this time."

Reporters began to clamour for more information, a loud female voice managed to momentarily drown out the others in asking, "Is it true that the boy responsible was a victim of bullying?" The police chief could only respond, "I have no further comment."

Governor Lombardino temporarily halted the uproar by saying a few words and pledging his total support for the town. Like the mayor and the police chief, he too avoided any more questions from the information-starved press in attendance. At the conclusion of the press conference, both governor and mayor were hustled out of a back door and into a couple of waiting cars to go to the hospital in Bridgend where most of the casualties had been taken. When they left, the reporters again tried to press the police chief for more information but none was coming. In spite of their disappointment of not knowing more, the media had gotten the one thing in which they all had come for, the name of the boy who had carried out the shooting. Within minutes, Mark's name was going out to every radio and TV station and Internet site in America.

6:10 GMT/ 1:10 EST

In his best BBC accent, the newscaster had just finished informing many people in Great Britain of the latest goings on in Parliament. "Now, for international news," he followed on as a map of the United States appeared on the screen behind him. "There has been a shooting at a school in New Jersey in the United States. For further details, we go now to Paul Ibbetson, our correspondent in New Jersey. Paul, what can you tell us?"

A distant photo of Ramsgate appeared on British television screens. A man's voice sounded over the monitor. "So far, we know that about 8:30 in the morning local time, a boy went onto the premises of Bernard A. Tye School in Ramsgate, New Jersey. He then opened fire on his fellow pupils with what is believed to have been an Uzi automatic and a nine-millimetre pistol. The shooting spree lasted for about five minutes but not before the gunman shot forty-five people, fifteen of whom are confirmed dead. Teachers were able to open their classroom doors and get many children to safety or the death toll would have been a lot more. The gunman then proceeded to take his own life."

"Have they named the gunman?" asked the newscaster in London.

"Yes, they have. The mayor and the chief of police here in Ramsgate held a press conference about an hour ago with the Governor of New Jersey in attendance. The police chief named the gunman as thirteen-year-old Mark Leversee, who attended the school. Early reports say that the boy was often the victim of bullying. "That's all we know for now, but we will keep you updated as the story unfolds."

"Thank you Paul," the newsreader commented before swiftly progressing to the next story.

French television was next to report on the shooting and very soon after that, the news of Mark's exploits had spread to all of Western Europe, Eastern Europe and beyond. Russian television apparently spent a half an hour on the story alone but no matter what language the news of the shooting was broadcast in, the one constant that remained the same throughout was the name of Mark Leversee.

Hospital Visit

After visiting the hospital in Bridgend, the Mayor of Ramsgate and the Governor of New Jersey parted company. Before they did, there was the obligatory photo shoot and more assurances from Governor Lombardino that he would provide support and resources. The visit to the hospital had been an eye opening experience for both of them. Neither had seen gunshot wounds in real life before and were unprepared for the damage it had caused upon the body. Furthermore, upon their initial arrival, they learned that Mark Wolfe had become the sixteenth fatality and it didn't look good for two of the other three people on the critical list.

Nevertheless, the two men suppressed their queasy stomachs and put on a professional face speaking to some of the wounded who were able to talk. All told the same story; how Mark just appeared and started shooting everybody. Some shed a little light about what sort of person Mark Leversee was. Diane Boreman, who had a bullet go completely through her thigh, took great delight and telling the politicians all about him. She explained, "He was a real weirdo. He had hockey on the brain and told everybody that he played for the Junior Flyers. Everyone knew it was a lie."

"Oh yeah, people picked on him," elaborated Fritz, who had been shot twice in the arm. "That's because he was a pu.., I mean wimp. He did threaten he was going to get a gun and shoot me."

On the ride home from the hospital, a picture of

Mark Leversee began to form in the Mayor's mind. Was it accurate? He decided that before he went to his council meeting, he should go home and speak to his own daughter, Wendy, who was a seventh grader at Tye School. Fortunately, she had been well out of the way when the bullets were flying around. Maybe she could shed some light on the person who had caused so much suffering this day.

Council Meeting

Every councillor made sure that they were at the meeting that took place that afternoon. It was plainly obvious what the meeting was about and all of them wanted to do their part. Therefore, the councillors sitting around a large rectangular table weren't the least bit surprised when the mayor walked into the room in total business mode.

"We know why we're here," he began. "A terrible tragedy has just occurred in our town. We lost many young promising children today; some of them were children of our friends and relatives. Many more will be scarred for life by today's events for a long time to come. This means it is our job to get the town past it so we can all move on and live normal lives again."

The atmosphere was too sober for anyone to applaud the mayor's speech but on the other hand, no one disagreed with it either. He was right, there was a big task ahead. Ears tuned as the mayor continued, "We need to set up committees to deal with all aspects of the situation. First, the governor has promised money and personnel to assist. He then looked to his town treasurer sitting nearby and ordered, "Herb, I need you to come up with a plan on how this extra money is going to be spent."

Herb simply nodded in acceptance while another

337

councillor suddenly chimed in, "With all of the reporters and television crews here, the town's hotels and restaurants have never had such great pre-summer business. I even met a news crew from England."

Mayor Burg gave the councillor a look that warned him he had better not say anymore. Turning to another councillor, he directed, "Theo, you will liase with the chief here in working with state and federal law enforcement. I hear that a team of behavioural specialists from the FBI will be coming."

"What, like on 'Criminal Minds?'" interrupted another councillor.

"I guess so," the mayor responded without missing a step. "We have to make sure there's accommodation for these people, the press can't have it all."

Again, all in the room nodded their agreement as they watched the mayor's face turn even more serious. "As you know, I have a daughter at Tye School who was in the seventh grade, the same grade as the shooter. I'm just grateful she wasn't hurt, but I spoke with her before coming to this meeting and she told me that everybody thought he was weird. She also said that a lot of kids bullied him."

"That's all we fuckin' need," barked an older councillor sitting at the corner of the table to the mayor's right. "The liberal media coming in here and making this kid out to be some sort of victim."

"He's right," another councillor agreed, disregarding his colleague's initial outburst. "We're the victims here! I don't care how much he was picked on, nothing justifies what he's done today."

The councillor's sitting around the table all unanimously began to voice their concurrence to the last two statements. However, one councillor, a younger man added some sense of reality to the situation. "Look," he began, getting everyone's attention. "If this boy was bullied as some people say, then it won't do us any good to ignore it. We can't just pretend it didn't happen if there's evidence to say it had or we might end up looking stupid in the eyes of the world. We've got to find some way to manoeuvre around it, a middle ground perhaps."

The vast majority of people there weren't in the mood to listen to any voice of reason, let alone find a middle ground. Two councillors immediately voiced opposition to the young councillor's idea, one of them saying, "Who cares if we look stupid to some liberal European papers." However, all voices stopped when Chief Gregory, who until then had been sitting silently on the sideline, stood up.

"I have the answer to that already," he declared. "I knew the kid was picked on, my officers had to deal with several complaints from his mother about it and there was the incident of Jeremiah Barrownoski pulling his shorts down. There was even a restraining order in place on one of the kids he shot today, which brings me to my solution. Give the liberals their bullies. We can find out who were the ones who picked on him most from among the dead and use them as sacrificial lambs. He's given us a few already."

The chief smiled as he had the entire room focusing on him their expressions asking for an explanation of his last statement. "The official autopsy reports haven't come back yet, but our initial investigation shows that three boys were shot with a single round, from point blank range in the forehead, execution style. The boy who had the restraining order against him looks as if he was shot initially then was shot with more rounds as he lay on the ground. We found the same with another boy. We will conduct our investigation with the intention of identifying these boys as the main bullies. The liberals will have their scapegoats and it gives us a clear motive behind the shooting."

The meeting room remained silent for a few more seconds before voices indicated their agreement to the chief's idea. After all, it made perfect sense to them. If Mark was bullied, then these bullies should be named. The meeting went on for another hour. Individual tasks were assigned and small groups were formed. When it ended, everyone in the room was clear on what they had to do.

Puerto Rico

Joe Callazone was thoroughly enjoying his time in Puerto Rico. He totally loved the basketball camp he was attending and the family he was staying with in San Juan couldn't do enough for him. He had become good friends with Eduardo who was his own age and a very good basketball player himself. When they walked home together after another invigorating basketball session, Joe was on an absolute high.

Mrs Acquino met Joe and her son Eduardo with a serious look that neither had ever seen before. She might have only stood five feet two inches tall, which was in stark contrast to her fourteen year old son who was nine inches taller but at that moment, she appeared much taller as she motioned for the two boys to sit down. "Joe, your mother called, a terrible thing happened at your school in New Jersey today," she informed him in her thick Spanish accent.

Initially, Joe's response was to ask for more details about what happened but each of his questions was parried with, "Call your mother," by Mrs Acquino. He finally took the hint when she handed him the phone.

He had barely finished dialling when Mrs Callazone started blubbering down the line, "It was terrible! Some boy came into Tye School with a gun and started shooting kids. They say he shot forty-five people!"

When his mother paused to sob some more, Joe quickly inquired, "Did anybody I know get shot?"

"Yes!" she practically screamed down the line and after a few more sobs added, "Oh God! Your friends David Roseman and Jim Nickerson are dead and Matt Barber was wounded but they say he is going to live."

Not yet fully processing the thought of his two dead friends and driven by the desire to know more, Joe asked, "Did they say who did it?"

"Yes," mother answered promptly. "They say it's some seventh grader named Mark Leversee."

Now it was Joe's turn to pause in shock. He immediately regained his composure and as the anger was overcoming him, barked down the phone, "Well, I hope they got him!"

"They didn't have to, after he shot everybody else, he shot himself," she pointed out.

Neither Mrs Acquino nor Eduardo were surprised at Joe's outrage when he got off the phone to his mother. They allowed him to rant, "Some faggot at my school named Leversee went in with a gun and shot some of my friends!"

Knowing nothing they could say would be any help, they let Joe carry on, "He's lucky he shot himself, otherwise I would have rammed the gun up his ass and pulled the trigger myself. If I ever find out where he's buried I will go and piss on his grave." His threats and rants went on for half an hour before they turned into sobs of guilt and mourning.

Face to Name

A school photo taken earlier that year was used to portray Mark's image to the world on the Six O'clock News. He was still wearing the thick horn-rimmed

341

glasses when that picture was taken. In one respect, the picture helped him a lot when the news reporter first broke the news that he had been a target of bullying and suffered from Asperger's Syndrome and DAMP. A few more people might have sympathised with him. Many more might have sympathised with him when a female reporter interviewed an academic who claimed to be an expert on Asperger's Syndrome.

A woman with long, straight, prematurely grey hair and wearing a long flowered dress appeared on television. "People with Asperger's Syndrome and DAMP will perceive the world differently to others," she told those watching in their living rooms. "They have deficiencies in attention, motor skills and perception."

"Would this have caused the boy to carry out the shooting?" the reporter led.

"Not directly," the expert explained. "But the condition would have made him the target of bullies. Plus, he struggled with school and his lack of motor skills would have made playing sports difficult for him. Other children, especially bullies, would have picked up on this and used it against him."

"So you're saying the condition caused him to be bullied, which led to the school shooting?" the reporter asked next.

The reply came with a hard sigh, "I can't say that for sure. The question would be with the Asperger's Syndrome. Many who have it tend to see themselves as victims and they focus inwardly. He might have thought he was the only victim when he fact, he probably wasn't bullied anymore than anyone else."

A second after the female reported had signed off, a male reporter, along with a father, mother and son appeared on television screens. The reporter began, "We're here with the parents of Jimmy Brown who was

342

present at the Tye School shooting today. Turning to Mr Brown, he asked him, "How is your son now?"

Mr Brown replied, "Obviously he is very shaken up, some of his friends were killed today. We're just glad that he's okay."

"Will Jimmy be able to talk to us?" the reporter politely asked Mr Brown.

"Yes, he can," Mr Brown replied in the affirmative. However, Mrs Brown's face bore an expression that said she wasn't so sure.

Without any further prompting, the reporter leaned over towards Jimmy and asked him, "Could you tell us what happened?"

Jimmy immediately stepped into the spotlight for his fifteen minutes. "I didn't really see Mark Leversee with the gun, but I heard the shots and there were kids running and screaming. Then my teacher, Mr Lejeune, opened the door and yelled for us all to get in the classroom, so I did right away. We were told to lie down on the floor, so I couldn't see what was going on in the playground or who got shot. I heard that once everybody was inside, that he went around finishing off some of the wounded before he shot himself."

The reporter took all of what Jimmy said on board and asked without missing a step, "How well did you know Mark Leversee?"

Totally relishing his time in the spotlight, Jimmy responded, "Yeah, I knew Leversee, he was really weird and he used to lie a lot. He said things like his cousin played for the Cincinnati Reds and that he was in a movie."

"Did people pick on him?" the reporter asked earnestly.

"A few people picked on him but he was such a wimp," Jimmy answered.

"Did you ever pick on him?" the reporter suddenly

asked.

"No, I didn't," Jimmy said innocently. "I did tease him a little but everybody did because he was so weird."

The reporter thanked Jimmy and his parents for their time and turned to face the camera where he declared, "That's one view of school shooter, Mark Leversee. This is Corey Blanchard for Eyewitness News."

Bar Whisperings

The Bay Beacon Bar had never been so busy on a Tuesday night and this included the peak summer months. That night, it was full of reporters and other media folk all determined to drink Ramsgate dry after a hard day of reporting the day's big event. Unlike so many of Ramsgate's bars, which catered for the just legal age group, the Bay Beacon was more of a traditional bar. That was probably why so many of the world's media flocked to it that night.

One such person was a young reporter for the South Jersey Current, a fairly large newspaper, more popular with those living more towards the Philadelphia end of South Jersey. Kevin Taylor might have been officially off duty but he kept his nose for news clear just in case. Conversation with the pretty young blonde barmaid was nice but it didn't reveal anything newsworthy. Furthermore, any thoughts of him getting with her after hours were thwarted when she told him she had a boyfriend.

Feeling a little bored, Kevin took out his cell phone and played around with its Internet feature. He looked up the establishment he was in online but it didn't provide too much information about it except that it boasted to have the best cheese steak subs outside of Philly. Many South Jersey eateries made such a boast.

Other than that, it only provided mundane information like hours and location. He was about to go onto another web page when the name of the bar's owner grabbed his attention. Somehow, the name Charles Allen seemed strangely familiar to him.

Seeing an important middle-aged looking man go behind the bar, Kevin decided to strike up a conversation with him as he walked past. "Excuse me," Kevin beckoned getting the man's attention. "This is a very nice bar, are you the owner?"

"No, I'm not, I'm just the bar manager," the man confessed. Then robotically he asked, "Is there a problem?"

"No, no problem, I just wanted to compliment Mr Allen on what a nice place this is," Kevin replied tactfully. "Is he here tonight?"

"No, I'm afraid not," the bar manager answered. "His son Tommy was one of the kids killed today."

The jigsaw puzzle suddenly fit together inside Kevin's mind. He remembered the name Tommy Allen from the list of the dead. Going into full reporter mode, he prompted the manager, "Was Tommy one of the kids who bullied Mark Leversee?"

"Wouldn't surprise me," the manager admitted. "Tommy Allen had a reputation for fighting, always getting into them. A couple of times, Charlie had to bail his son out of trouble with the police. Tommy never got into real trouble because of Charlie being a local businessman here."

The bar manager suddenly stopped. He must have realised that he had said too much. He made quick apologies about having to attend to business and rushed off leaving Kevin alone. Once the manager was out of view, Kevin took out a note pad and made a few notes. The information he had received might not have been much, but it was enough to do some investigative journalism. Maybe Mark Leversee wasn't completely the monster the town was trying to make him out to be and perhaps he was a victim too and some of his victims weren't so innocent.

Apprehended

Ted arrived home after what he thought had been another successful business trip. Like most of the world, he had heard about a school shooting somewhere in South Jersey but didn't know too much about it. His security job that day was so clandestine, he had no access to media during the day and preferred to listen to CDs in the car on the drive home. Therefore, he had no idea what was about to befall him when he returned that night.

"Mark must have taken the keys home," he thought to himself when he didn't see them under the trashcan, which was the usual hiding place. He could hear Mitzi making noises from inside the apartment sounding like she was very distressed. "Didn't Mark feed her or take her out for her walk?" He reached for his cell phone to call Donna but his movements were interrupted by a voice that called out, "Ted Zimminsky."

He turned to see two police officers, one uniformed, one not standing behind him. Their reason for being at his house completely baffled him. "Mr Zimminsky, we need you to come to the station and answer some questions. We also have a warrant to search your apartment," Detective Cavanaugh informed him.

"May I at least know what this is about?" inquired Ted fully prepared to assert his constitutional rights.

"Do you know that there has been a shooting at Tye School today?" the detective asked.

"I knew that there had been a school shooting but I didn't know that it was at Tye School," Ted returned.

"Besides, I still don't know what it has to do with me."

The detective regarded Ted for a moment, fathoming in his mind if Ted was telling to truth or feigning ignorance. He suddenly snapped himself out of his thoughts and asked, "Do you know Mark Leversee?"

Ted confirmed he did straight away but then something clicked his mind, distorting his expression to one of horror. "Did Mark carry out the shooting?" he thought to himself.

Knowing he now had the upper hand, Detective Cavanaugh reached into his pocket and brought out a clear plastic bag containing a set of keys. Ted immediately recognised the keys he had given to Mark the day before. His still horrified expression gave the detective the answer he was looking for. "These are your keys then," he clarified.

Ted nodded and handed himself over to the two officers who were kind enough to let him use the one key to go into his apartment and feed his dog. As he rode in the back of the police car, his mind raced a million miles a second. He couldn't believe that Mark could have done such a deed and yet, he wasn't completely surprised. The kids at school had made Mark's life hell so he didn't blame him if he did do it. Another thought entered his mind totally shocking him. Did Mark use the combat course to plan his massacre? It would explain why he was so ruthless on it. He couldn't answer any of those questions for sure. The one thing Ted was certain about, as the patrol car pulled up to the station, was that he should lawyer up immediately.

Red's Corner

Red Cressman welcomed his listeners to his nightly

phone-in radio programme on the local AM station, "Red's Corner." After his usual welcome to the show, he carried on, "I know everyone will want to talk about the awful tragedy that happened in Ramsgate this morning. But before we start, I would personally like to express my deepest sympathies to all of those who were affected by the tragedy. I see the switchboard is lighting up, so let's have our first caller."

A woman's voice crackled over the airwaves, "It's all down to music and movies kids watch and listen to these days. I bet he listened to stuff like Marilyn Manson and Rob Zombie and then there's all of those horror movies and action films where everything is solved with a gun. That's probably why he thought he could solve his problems by shooting everyone."

"So, you're saying it's all down to movies and music," Red clarified with the caller.

"Yes," the female voice affirmed. "And violent computer games! I mean look at all those games where you go around killing people. There's that game 'Grand Theft Auto,' where you steal cars and kill everyone."

Other callers phoned in with their agreement to the first one. They seemed fully convinced that movies, music and computer games were the sole cause of Mark's atrocities that morning. Even when Red pointed out that there was no evidence to what music he listened to or movies he watched, the caller simply responded, "They will." The one sidedness of the tone of the calls began to slightly depress the host who was hoping for a more open debate.

Relief came halfway through the two-hour show. A male voice, identified as Bob, phoned in with, "I think people are missing the key issue here, Red. It's ridiculous to blame music or movies or even computer games. Don't forget, there is evidence that this boy suffered from a lot of bullying at school and that

348

definitely had something to do with it. He was probably picked on so mercilessly that it was no wonder he snapped."

Red Cressman might or might not have agreed with this caller but he was glad that a different view was now offered. "School bullies may have played a part in why he carried out the shooting but do you think that justifies going into a school and shooting so many people?" he asked Bob.

Bob responded emphatically, "I am in no way condoning what this boy did but I can see how someone who is teased and bullied so mercilessly can snap. It has also been said that the boy had Asperger's Syndrome and that he might perceived the bullying to be so bad, he had no other way to deal with it."

Ducking Bob's statement, Red put the next caller on. "Here we go!" the caller known as Sam ranted. "Another liberal blaming the shooting on bullies. Let me tell you Red, that I was bullied in school and never once thought about getting a gun and shooting up the place. Blaming bullies is just too convenient."

A feeling of delight shot through Red's mind as the debate went in a new direction. Callers siding with either Bob or Sam began to offer their opinions on the bullying issue. However, the tone of the calls became monotonous and Red started getting bored again. So when he had the opportunity, he asked his listeners, "What about America's gun culture? Is that in any way to blame?"

His question was immediately pounced on by a caller called Wanda. "What I want to know Red is how did a thirteen year old boy get a hold of a gun? Today's tragedy proves that we need tougher gun laws or ban gun ownership all together."

The rebuttal to Wanda's view came with the next call. A caller identified as Bud ripped down the line,

349

"Once again, the hippies want to use some unfortunate incident such as this to take away our Second Amendment rights. Instead, what we need is conceal and carry laws like they have in some states. That way some teacher or even a student could have dropped this kid with one shot before he had the chance to shoot so many people."

Bud's statements brought further debate on gun ownership and conceal and carry laws leaving Red slightly regretful that it wasn't brought up until very late in the programme, as it was the theme it ended on. When the two hours were up, Red Cressman had one of the most stimulating shows in recent memory. He just secretly hoped that the day's events would be a talking point for a long time to come.

11 O'clock News- Part 1, Florida

Look most of the world that day; Rusty Leversee had also heard that there had been a shooting in a school in New Jersey. However, he was too caught up in his work and family life to get the full details as to what happened. For Rusty, the late night news was his chance to catch up on the events of the day.

He wasn't surprised when the shooting headlined the news, as it was such a big event that day. A strange intrigue sharpened his desire to know more about it but he couldn't explain why. That intrigue turned to shock when the newscaster announced that it had taken place in Ramsgate, New Jersey. His first thoughts were for the safety of Mark and Leslie. However, that shock turned to sheer horror as father saw the image of his son on the screen and the newscaster reading out "Mark Leversee was responsible for the shooting."

Even the normally reassuring touch from his young wife did nothing to alleviate the feelings he was having at that moment. Every detail of how Mark was alleged to have carried out the shooting and the details of the carnage leading to how his son finally ended his life sliced through Rusty like a jagged knife. He wanted to reach through the television screen and choke the life out of Jimmy Brown when he told the world how weird Mark was. "His son wasn't weird," Rusty thought to himself. "He was just misunderstood and if those pricks in Ramsgate had left him alone, this wouldn't have happened."

The first thing he decided to do once the news story finished was to call his ex-wife. Donna's father answered the phone explaining that Donna was in no fit state to talk; he understood that well. His ex-father in law confirmed all the details of the day, the shooting, Donna being questioned by the police and even Ted's arrest. When the two men finished their conversation, Rusty knew as much as everybody else in the family.

Suddenly, he turned to his wife and said, "I need to go out."

As he went to leave, his twenty-four year old bride pleaded with him not to go. "None of this is your fault, you weren't to know he would do something like this."

He knew she was right but walked out of the door into the muggy night air regardless. With each step came the recurring thought, "I should have let him come live here." Arguments to the contrary from his wife and ex were beaten out of his mind. He was convinced that Mark should have come to live with him. After nearly a mile and a half of walking and the regretful thoughts still in his mind, Rusty found himself outside of Barney's Bar and Grill. Whether he intended to end up here, he couldn't say. He had been on the wagon for eighteen months but this particular night, he fell off of it and it would be another nine months before he was completely back on it again.

11 O'clock News- part 2, Estminston, PA

Just like Rusty Leversee in Florida, Earl and Natalie Farmer in Estminston, Pennsylvania had also heard about a school shooting in New Jersey. Like many people that day, their daily routines prevented them from learning the full details of it. Joined by their sixteen-year-old daughter, Stacy, they sat down to watch the eleven o'clock news together. As expected, the shooting led the news that night. Earl was intrigued in the same way Rusty was while Natalie could only sympathise with the families of the victims in a way only a mother could. However, it was Stacy who had the shock of her sixteen-year life when the news portrayed Mark's image on the screen and confirmed his name.

"Oh my God!" she practically screamed. When her parents looked at her, she explained more quietly, "That's the kid that Lisa met at Three Streams last summer!"

"Are you sure?" Natalie asked. But as she reflected back on the life of her younger daughter, she realised that she didn't need the confirmation her elder daughter was now giving. Without thinking about it, she asked out loud, "What do we say to Lisa?"

"We tell her," Earl stated plainly. Seeing the puzzled looks from the two ladies in the room he explained further, "It's better we tell her first before she finds out some other way and the consequences made worse for her."

"Do you want me to tell her?" Stacy volunteered.

"We'll all tell her tomorrow morning," Earl answered with assertion.

Husband and wife drew closer together on the sofa while they watched the rest of the news, each secretly hoping some detail of the shooting would aid them in their task the next morning. The report gave each some base on which to talk to Lisa about. Furthermore, they were all relieved when her name wasn't mentioned. One thing was clear, when the Farmers, along with the rest of the world, went to bed that night, they all knew about Mark's exploits. Mark Leversee truly was pop star for the day and most of the world had tuned in and watched.

Chapter 26

Declarations, Heroes and Villains

She was still in the process of waking up when she went downstairs that morning. Lisa was somewhat perplexed to see her father still at the breakfast table and he, her mother and sister were all smiling at her. Her mother motioned for her to sit down, which she obeyed. However, it dawned on her that there was something odd about the whole scene. For one, her brother was still playing in his bedroom and the only time their parents were like this was when one of them was in trouble. But she thought that couldn't be right because her older sister was present.

"We need to talk to you about something," Natalie said trying not to sound urgent. Her statement snapped Lisa out of her thoughts.

A feeling a dread loomed over her. She gulped and wondered what she had done to cause this particular scene. Earl must have sensed her anxiety because he immediately assured her, "You're not in any trouble but we need to talk to you about something. As she lent her ears to her father, he continued, "Do you know that there was a school shooting in New Jersey yesterday?"

She shook her head and said, "No" at the same time.

"I think you should read this," her father instructed putting a newspaper in front of her.

Mark's picture on the front page under the banner heading, "Massacre in Ramsgate" began to fill her with horror. She began reading while somehow hoping Mark's photo was nothing to do with the shooting. The second sentence of the news story confirmed her fears. Tears began rolling down her cheeks as she read the details about Mark's mayhem. When she came to the part of the article where it said Mark ended his own life, Lisa pushed the paper to one side and put her head down into her arms that were folded on the table and began crying uncontrollably.

"It's not your fault, you've done nothing wrong," Stacy cited in attempted consolation.

Mother gave eldest daughter a look indicating not to say any more. All three wanted to say something that would help Lisa but none could find the magic words that would make it all go away. Instead, they silently agreed to let her cry herself out. Seeing she was the spotlight of attention, Lisa excused herself and went back to her room where she cried for another three quarters of an hour. She simply wanted to make sense of it all.

Deep down she knew her big sister was right, that it wasn't her fault. Still she kept asking herself, "Did breaking up with him send him over the edge?" In her mind, she kept trying to reason that it didn't but the spectre of doubt kept reappearing in the back of her brain. Like her, he was having problems with kids being horrible to him, she saw that on Facebook. Strangely, she secretly admired him for having the fortitude to do something about it, even if it was the wrong way of doing things. Conflicts in her mind came and went and even after two hours of deep contemplation and heavy prayer, she was none the clearer about things.

Needing to do something, she asked her sister if she could log onto her Facebook account. Stacy understood her little sister's reasons, so she agreed without argument. Logging on as Stacy, Lisa immediately went onto Mark's profile page grateful that he hadn't disabled his account. She didn't know what she expected to find but had to look anyway. Her original intention was an apology but what she read posted on his wall astounded her. With morbid interest and sadness, she read his last post:

"I, Mark Joseph Leversee, thirteen years old from Ramsgate, New Jersey truly believe that I am going to die today. This is my dying declaration and everything I am about to say is the total truth. Ever since I moved to Ramsgate nearly three years ago, I have had grief and misery from the kids living there. You all abused me physically, mentally and emotionally. You teased and humiliated me and insisted on calling me by my former name even though my name has been legally changed for more than two years. And don't say that you didn't know, you all knew my name, you just wanted to use it as a source of amusement. Everybody knew that I had Asperger's Syndrome and DAMP but you used it against me to make my life worse.

Some of you are playing innocent, saying "I didn't do anything to you." So in fairness, I will mention the kids who were the worst to me:

1. Tommy Allen- you kept punching me saying your hand slipped, well today, my finger is going to slip.
2. Joe Kellerman- you kept punching me and body checking me into the walls.
3. Jim Nickerson- I had to get a restraining order against you, that won't be a problem anymore.
4. David Roseman- you kept calling me a faggot and encouraging others to humiliate me. Today you're going to be my bitch.
5. Jim Friend- you got everyone to side with Smiley after he abused me. Your uncle can't save you today.
6. Mike Sigfried- you punched me in the back and constantly and rubbed in the fact I was upset.

Today, you'll be the one upset.

7. David Fitzpatrick- you wrecked my bike and got your lawyer daddy to get you out of replacing it and then bragged about it. Daddy can't save you today

8. Mark Wolfe- I know you wrecked my bike, I just can't prove it. You had to keep picking on me, so I'll have justice today.

9. Joe Gerberwitz- you picked on me in sixth grade. You're my victim today.

10. Andrew Blumenthaw- you wouldn't let me join in games because you thought I sucked. I'm going to show you something I'm good at.

The rest of you are guilty too. After all, you let it happen and you laughed while it was going on. None of you tried to stop it and it was all a big joke to all of you but today I will have the last laugh. Besides, if I was guilty for the things that Gene Lancaster said because I was his friend, then the same is true with all of you. By the way, Gene was no friend because he let it happen too and didn't mind when I took the beatings for things he did. However, I hope he will learn from this.

The kids of Ramsgate have taken everything from me. If I ever had anything good, you would crush it before my eyes and this includes Lisa. You have made me feel worthless and I have suffered so much, I don't see any point to living. But because you're all responsible, I am going to make all of you suffer too.

P.S. Lisa, if you are reading this, none of this is your fault."

Her first reaction was relief that he didn't blame her and she could fully embrace her sister's words that none of it was her fault. She agreed with Mark as to whose fault it really was. To her surprise, she observed that his declaration had 317 likes and many comments underneath. Most were against him saying things like "Burn in hell, Leversee" and "God will not have mercy on your soul." There was even a more childish response from Mark Rossman; "I hope the devil calls you Marvin for all eternity."

Mark's Declaration had its fair share of supporters and well-wishers as well. Many simply wrote, "Rest in peace" but there was a boy from Georgia who posted, "I wish I had your balls" and a post from North Dakota that read, "If more people did what you did, there wouldn't be any bullies in the world." There was even a post from Worcester, England that read, "I wish we had guns here, then I would show some people not to bully me." After reading each and every comment, Lisa made a post of her own, "Rest in peace, Mark. You didn't deserve to have any of those awful things happen to you."

Even before Lisa read Mark's Facebook declaration, the media and police had already discovered it and the former had begun to broadcast it to the world. One newspaper printed the entire posting under the headlines, "Killer's Final Words."

The people of Ramsgate were taken completely by surprise by the posting. Most kids thought Mark was too dumb to say something like that, in spite of the fact that they had said the same thing about his capability of carrying out the previous day's atrocity. When most of the children were approached about it, they simply tried to dismiss it as more of his lies although they didn't have any answers when questioned about it being a dying declaration. Adults just shouted at the media for trying to make Mark out to be the victim.

"I taught Mark Leversee when he was in fifth grade and he gave me a lot of problems," Miss Erichetti declared to the camera on the noontime news. "Yes, it was true that kids bullied him but he always invited trouble because he let his imagination run away with him and the other children picked up on that. As for his so-called Asperger's Syndrome, his mother did no favours trying to play on it. Asperger's Syndrome just happens to be the condition of the moment, used as an excuse by parents when their precious child doesn't do well in school. Even so, the other children didn't care because he was such an easy victim but I never dreamed he would do something like this."

Watching at home, Donna Leversee wanted to reach through the screen and bash Miss Erichetti's face in with a large blunt instrument. Furthermore, she wouldn't have shown any less mercy to some of the other interviewees who corroborated the idea that her son was some kind of freak. No one wanted to admit to Mark's Asperger's and DAMP, just portray him as a psycho to the world nor did they want to admit how badly bullied he was. In a fit of temper, she shut off the television.

Her father came inside almost immediately after from his work outside. He had spent much of the morning cleaning up the word "Murderer," which had been spray-painted across their front door sometime in the night. Both Donna and her mother had lent assistance cleaning the egg and animal excrement that had been thrown at the house. However, after discovering the damage that morning and reporting it to the police, they realised they weren't going to be shown any mercy for Mark's actions. The literal response of the police was, "We don't have the manpower to spare at the moment, your grandson saw to that."

At 1 PM on the day after, Mayor Burg and Chief Gregory again became the focus of media attention when they held a press conference to update the world on their investigation. The mayor, already comfortable with such events, once again expressed his sympathies

359

to the victims and their families as well as the entire town. He also heaped more deserved praise upon the police and ambulance services for all their outstanding work in extreme dire circumstances the day before.

He was not exaggerating. When calls of the shooting began jamming emergency phone lines, the ambulance crews responded magnificently. Both of the Ramsgate crews were at the school in a flash and when they realised when viewing the scale of the carnage that more assistance was needed, they sent out calls for assistance from the neighbouring towns. Vincent, Bridgend, Bay City and offshore towns Winters Reach, Lincoln and Southmoor all responded. Even Atlantic City sent two crews to the beleaguered town. All crews worked tirelessly on wounded victims and probably saved many lives despite the fact that except for Atlantic City, none of the crews had any actual experience with gunshot victims. The Ramsgate police did marvellous job in coordinating ambulance crews and keeping nosy press and onlookers away. Had it not been for these heroic efforts, the death toll inflicted by Mark would have been much higher.

At the conclusion of the speech, journalists competed to ask the same first question, "What do you think of the boy's declaration on Facebook?"

Mayor Burg hesitated for a moment. "I have read it," he said, "And to me it shows that Mark Leversee was indeed a troubled kid and his attack was premeditated. With that, I will turn you over to Chief Gregory who can shed more light about it."

The mayor stepped out of the spotlight allowing the chief of police to step into it. He began with the sad news that just a half an hour earlier, Steven McGuire had become the seventeenth death at Mark's hands and the official casualty count to seventeen dead and twenty-eight wounded." Although he didn't mention it, no one was holding out much hope for Andrew Blumenthaw who was in a deep coma. The chief further explained, "We have made considerable progress in our investigation of the shooting. We can say that we are questioning the person who owned the guns that Leversee used and he is giving us his full cooperation. Also we are pursuing other lines of inquiry like the alleged bullying. We also ask people to keep calm and not to take matters into their own hands."

"Do you mean the vandalism of the Leversee family home?" one reporter asked.

"Yes, I do," Chief Gregory answered. "I ask everybody to remember that it was Mark Leversee who carried out the attack, not his family. We can safely say that his family had no involvement or knowledge of his deeds and they definitely did not give him access to the guns he used."

While the crowd of reporters was digesting this, Kevin Taylor decided to ask, "Do you have the names of any of his bullies?"

The chief regarded him for a second before answering, "We are pursuing those lines of inquiry but we aren't at a stage where we can release names."

When Kevin pressed further, "What about the names he listed on Facebook?" Chief Gregory only responded with, "I am not at liberty to say anything at the moment, but my officers are looking into that too."

Kevin wasn't finished yet. "Is it true that one of the kids killed, your nephew Jim Friend, was one of Mark Leversee's bullies?"

Kevin's question definitely made the man at the microphone feel uncomfortable. He managed to stumble out, "I can't comment on that right now," before abruptly ending the news conference.

In spite of getting a lawyer, Ted Zimminsky found that he had little room to manoeuvre when the police finally questioned him. The guns and ammo were certainly his and he was surprised to see his bandoliers. As a result and on advice from his attorney, he cooperated fully with the police. He was released after two hours of questioning but given a stark warning from his lawyer. "They'll probably charge you with criminal negligence or a similar charge. They're looking for heads to roll over this and since they can't have the boy who did it, your scalp will do just nicely. If it is the case, I will get you the best deal that I can." Ted hoped that he could.

That evening the six o'clock news echoed more of the mayor's praise for the police and ambulance services. It showed their work in more detail with interviews from those on the front line. One paramedic gave his colourful account of how he single-handedly brought Ron O'Malley back from the dead. In contrast, another paramedic had to give the sad account of how he battled in vain to save the life of sixth grader Billy Northwick, who was pronounced DOA.

Of all the accounts of heroism given that day, the most noteworthy one was the account given by Ramsgate patrolman Randy Kelly. He was the officer who first discovered Mark's body; pistol still gripped tightly in the right hand and told of his in trepidation over the prospect of facing a young boy with a gun. Officer Kelly stated that he was both angry and relieved when he found him dead; angry that Mark would not be alive to answer for his horrible crimes and relieved that he didn't have to shoot a thirteen-year-old boy. Once he deduced the threat was over, the officer radioed in for as many ambulances as possible before doing what he could for the wounded. When the ambulances arrived, he directed them to the casualties who were in most need of medical attention, thus saving more lives. To many people, he was the biggest hero of the day.

Interviews with the victims' families began almost as soon as news of the shooting broke out. However, on this particular news programme, there were more detailed interviews with the families of some of the children who had died.

It was often joked that the reason why the school was called Tye School was because every time you turned around, another child surnamed Tye was going to the school. On the news that evening, viewers saw Don and Ann Tye, along with their five other children, four boys and a girl, all-grieving for their youngest sister/daughter Renee. "Our Renee was a sweet girl," Ann Tye sobbed into the microphone. Her husband put his arm around her shoulder giving her strength to continue, "She loved swimming and had lots of friends."

Don tightened his hold on his wife and added, "This should have never happened to our daughter or anyone else's kid," as his eyes began to moisten.

Suddenly, the now youngest of the Tye family, Tim, stepped in front of his parents. "I hope the kid who did this rots in hell," he growled down the microphone.

"Did you know Mark Leversee?" the reporter asked.

"Yeah, I knew him," Tim spat. "He was really weird."

"Did people bully him?"

"A lot of people teased him," Tim stated curtly, "But he asked for it. He wasn't picked on as much as what he said on Facebook."

Next to appear on the screens was the Fitzpatrick family. David Senior stood by a female reporter with his wife and ten year old daughter Patty in the background. "I am very angry at how this boy was able to come into the school with guns and shoot my son and others the way he did. I am also mad about how you people in the media are making this Leversee kid out to be the victim because some kids picked on him," David Senior pontificated.

"He listed your son as one of the kids who picked on him," the reporter stated. Did David pick on him like he said on his Facebook posting?"

"Let me tell you about that," he spewed. "When they were in fifth grade, another kid beat Leversee up and David kicked his bicycle seat causing it to fall off. Well, this kid's mother came into the school the next day, dragging in me and the other boy's mother and wanting both boys hanged, threatening to press charges against them. Then they expected us to buy him a new bike when all it needed was the seat repaired! So, I had to take it home and fix it for them. Obviously, his family are a bunch of money grabbers. The sort of people who will use anything to get what they can out of people."

Cameras then shot over to the Roseman family. Mrs Roseman cried into the interviewer's microphone, "My David didn't deserve this! He might have teased the boy but nothing excuses this senseless taking of David's life."

The final cut was the most potent of all the family interviews. The Cherisso family, mother, father and elder and younger brother all stood in front of the camera brandishing photos of their sister/daughter Lydia, the pretty blonde sixth grader who was slain by a single bullet.

"My daughter didn't even know this boy!" Al Cherisso yelled into the camera.

Wife Sandra Cherisso added her two cents, "Our Lydia was a sweet innocent girl and she would have never picked on this boy. In fact, she was so caring that she would have tried to be his friend or at least taken pity on him."

The reporter showed silent sympathy towards the

Cherisso family while the camera zoomed in on one of the pictures of Lydia. For the first time, the world got to see the pretty young face of Lydia Cherisso. Her infectious smile radiated hope in the dark gloom of the tragic event. This wouldn't be the last time her face would be seen. From that moment on, the innocent face of Lydia Cherisso would always be the one connected to the massacre in Ramsgate.

Red Cressman had no need to worry whether the momentum from the previous night's show would fade. The Ramsgate shooting was still the hot topic of his phone in radio show. From the very beginning, lines were jammed with callers wanting to give their views on the incident, the main focus seemed to be on Mark's Facebook posting.

"Okay, I grant you the kid was bullied," stated one caller. "This doesn't excuse what he did, nothing excuses murder."

Some man calling himself Texas Joe railed down the line, "The kid wanted to kill himself. Sure, he was going through hell but why couldn't he just shoot himself and left all the others alone?"

"What sickens me is all those sick people on Facebook who think this psycho kid is some kind of hero," a caller named Paul chimed in. "Next thing you know, there will be every kid who thinks he's being bullied picking up a gun and shooting people. These people got the wrong idea, it's wrong to take someone's life senselessly no matter how bad they think they got it."

Most of the callers seemed to agree with Paul and then a caller calling herself Sarah came on the line. "I knew Mark Leversee and he was bullied and teased terribly all the time. The kids at Tye School never let up on him, so it's no wonder he snapped."

Intrigued by this caller, Red responded, "I don't

think he was a psycho and perhaps the bullying did cause him to snap. But do you think that justifies what he's done?"

"No, it doesn't justify it," Sarah replied. "I'm not trying to justify, just make sense of it in my own mind. I can sympathise with someone who is picked on so badly to the point where he just can't take it anymore."

All Red could say was "Good point" before opening the line up to more callers, most of whom were quick to denounce Sarah. One very adamantly declared, "All school shooters say they were bullied, it's just a convenient excuse for them."

Red was glad the programme changed direction when it was well into its second hour. Callers followed the mayor's example of heaping praise upon the police and ambulance services. More than one caller thought police officer Randy Kelly deserved a medal. Another caller went further by praising Mr Tasker for the way he had handled the situation on the day and then there was the account of how the girl Nadine Salvatino tried to save her two friends who were shot. With the help of a passing driver, she was able to get a wounded girl off the road for the ambulance. While every caller praised the work of all the men and women who worked tirelessly that day, very few had any sympathy towards Mark.

Chapter 27

Life Goes On, Kind Of

Only grandfather ventured out in the first three days after the shooting. He knew his daughter wouldn't be able to face the people of Ramsgate. Even if nobody said anything to her directly, there would be the looks and under the breath comments and that would have been cataclysmic for her. Then there were all the people from the media milling around outside their property in the hopes of getting an interview from the shooter's family. No one inside the house wanted to talk to them. They also ignored all contact attempts from Ted; he might have been truly remorseful for what happened, but it wasn't a good idea for him to talk to Donna. He did let Mark's father speak to her on the phone three times but other than that, his daughter just wanted to curl up and die.

Watching the television news over the past three days had become unbearable in the Johnston/Leversee household to the point that they all stopped watching it. The final straw came when Keith Wenger was interviewed on the news. Being Mark's friend, they thought he would have said some good things about him. Instead, he wore his other face when he told the world how weird Mark was and how his overactive imagination got him into trouble all of the time by telling lots of fantasy stories. Keith was just one of many who took great delight in talking about Mark's weirdness while failing to mention his Asperger's and DAMP conditions.

Radio didn't seem to carry the news in so much detail so Mark's mother and grandparents listened to it more often. The local station did carry a story about how the Levine family in Ramsgate had their house vandalised one evening because the thirteen-year-old daughter, Sarah, apparently defended Mark on a phone in programme on the radio. The report said that the house had been bombarded with eggs, tomatoes and even excrement and that a larger banner reading, "Murderer Lover" had been hung across the front door. Naturally, the police claimed they were investigating the incident. Mrs Leversee sympathised with the family. They didn't deserve bad treatment just because their daughter had spoken her mind and stood up for her beliefs, stood up for Mark. She was glad that someone was willing to.

The Levine story might have dented her resolve to leave the house that day save for one other variable: They were finally going to let her see her son. Purposefully, she headed for the county morgue in Stargell some fifteen miles away. On arrival, there was no out of the ordinary action by any of the morgue officials, in spite of the "celebrity" status of Mark Leversee. Instead they very professionally allowed her in and took her to see Mark.

As soon as his face was revealed, Mrs Leversee couldn't help but to let the tears out. "How could somebody who now looks so innocent and peaceful have extracted so much violence?" she asked herself. She already knew the answer to that as she lifted his head and cradled it against her in a mother loving way, continuing to weep. Whether or not it was intentional, she wasn't sure, she felt for the entry point of his self-inflicted fatal wound. This increased the volume of her wails for several more minutes before she finally cried herself out. When she was done, she simply thanked the morgue officials and left.

Empowered by finally seeing her son, Donna

Leversee knew that she had much to do. Sitting in the house crying wasn't going to bring Mark back no matter how much she wanted it to and she now understood what had driven him to commit his atrocities even if the authorities and media chose to ignore it. An itinerary of tasks began forming in her mind as she drove back home. The first of which was to stop off in Vincent and see Pastor Bachman about Mark's funeral.

The pastor was extremely sympathetic to Mrs Leversee when they met that afternoon. He told her what a good student Mark had been in Confirmation Class and it was sad that he would never be confirmed. He had high hopes that he would have been a good servant of the Lord had not the incident happened. He also offered his full support and reassured her that she had the support of the entire congregation and that he would be happy to conduct the funeral at St James Church. When she left, Mrs Leversee was feeling even more uplifted about things.

Still on a high when she got home, She decided to take Leslie out shopping with her. Her daughter had also spent a lot of time crying over the loss of her big brother. Although she didn't understand the full details, she did know that he had shot some people. Therefore, she got into the car with her mother and both ignoring the reporters gathered outside, headed for the supermarket.

Donna felt slightly relieved when she didn't notice anyone staring at her or whispering to others as she went past. The few familiar faces she did recognise did not seem to recognise her and she preferred it that way. It allowed her and Leslie to carry on with their shopping. Things looked very optimistic as they neared the end of the shopping trip.

That was until they got to the frozen food section.

Leslie spied her classmate Debbie Lornstein, a younger sister of Amy, who was likewise shopping with her mother. The mothers said nothing, as they didn't know each other and Leslie said a soft "Hi" to Debbie when they went past. Neither mother nor daughter was in any way prepared for what came next.

"Your brother's a murderer!" Debbie loudly declared so that half the shoppers in the aisle heard her. Immediately, Leslie burst out in tears and all eyes turned on Mrs Leversee and her daughter. Donna could hear the wheels turning inside people's heads as they began to work out that the mother and sister of that horrible boy who caused so much misery was standing in the same store as them. Instinctively, she grabbed her daughter and headed for the nearest checkout before anymore was said. While the cashier put the purchases through the till, she felt her ears burning and inwardly willed the cashier to hurry up. After paying for her shopping, she grabbed Leslie again and they made a mad dash for the exit, then the car and then home realising things would never be better for her or her family while they remained in Ramsgate.

There was no further backlash from the shopping incident although it was decided that Mrs Johnston should do the family shopping from then on. In the days that followed, interest in the shooting began to wane, at least in the national and international news as more current events occurred. Whenever news about the shooting was mentioned on television or Internet news, it always seemed that the face of Lydia Cherisso would appear with it making hers the face of Mark's massacre. Fortunately, Mark's family had stopped watching the television news days earlier but that didn't lessen the number of reporters still camped out in front of the house hoping to get a comment from the shooter's family.

Two days after hearing about what had happened at the supermarket, Abe Johnston decided it was time for action. He stepped outside onto his front porch and waited for the assembled members of the media to acknowledge him. It didn't take long for them to do so and then began competing for Mr Johnston's attention. He stood silent for a few more seconds before lifting his hand to gain the media's silence. When he had it, he announced, "I would like to call a press conference for four o'clock, right here." Naturally, the reporters renewed their clamour for detail but he just went back inside.

By four o'clock that afternoon, the number of reporters outside had quadrupled. A small podium with three microphones had been erected as the assembled media waited with baited breath for the big exclusive: Somebody from the Leversee family was going to speak. They didn't have to wait long as at the stroke of four, Abraham Johnston and his daughter Donna Leversee came out of the house and stood by the podium.

A respectful silence prevailed as Mr Johnston began, "Let me begin by expression our deepest regrets for everything that has happened. If we had any inclination that Mark was going to do anything like this, we would have stopped him. We would have never allowed Ted Zimminsky to give him access to his guns or teach him how to shoot. But it's too late to think about what we could have or should have done nor is it any use to point fingers of blame. Too many have suffered and what we do believe is that it is no longer right for our family to remain in Ramsgate. Therefore, we are putting the house up for sale and moving out as soon as possible, thank you."

Father and daughter stood close together in preparation for the questions to come. The many reporters climbed over each other to ask the first question. Abe pointed to one at random who asked, "Do you hold Ted Zimminsky responsible for the shooting?"

Shaking his head, Mark's grandfather replied, "No we don't, no one was to know that my grandson would use those guns to carry out his shooting."

Acknowledging the answer, the reporter then asked, "What do you think of Ted Zimminsky being arrested for Criminal Negligence?"

If was honest with himself, Abraham Johnston had not given any thought to Ted's arrest. Looking directly at the reporter, he honestly responded, "I have no comment on that."

Suddenly, his daughter stepped beside her father and spoke into the microphone, "If the police had made a similar effort with the boys who wrecked my son's bike, the boy who had the restraining order on him and that Barrownoski fellow, then none of this would have happened."

The brief hesitation brought about by Donna Leversee's words allowed Kevin Taylor to wriggle his way through the crowd into position. It allowed him to get noticed when he raised his voice over the general noise and ask, "Do you think it was because one of the boys who bullied your son was the chief of police's nephew?"

Both people standing at the podium reflected back to the incident with Smiley. They both remembered the chief of police saying that his nephew told him that Mark was a liar and a troublemaker and how he basically believed his nephew over Mark. Maybe there was a connection. However, they had no proof so Abe simply answered, "We can't say."

Again the assembled press competed to get their question asked next. The sea of faces must have looked daunting to the two people standing at the podium. If Mark had been there, the sight would have certainly sent him into overload. Mr Johnston must have sensed this too for he decided to end the news conference right then and there. He simply leaned into the mike and announced, "That is all we're going to say at this time, thank you all for coming" before going back inside. The abrupt ending of the conference left many journalists feeling more than frustrated, as many of them would have liked to know more insight into the decision to leave Ramsgate.

Two hours later, the brief news conference in front of the Johnston/Leversee home was broadcast to the nation on the six o'clock news. Those who watched it got to hear the short address from Mr Johnston in its entirety. Many people respected their decision to move out of the town. On the screen, he had seemed deeply remorseful about the deeds of his grandson and many silently sympathised with him. Unfortunately, most television news stations focused more on Donna Leversee's outburst. On many news reports, it was shown before her father's address manipulating many into thinking that she was some crazed psycho or at least a blind mother who refused to acknowledge her son's guilt and was just looking for someone else to blame. After all, Smiley had been brought to justice for his indecent assault on her son. As for the boy with the restraining order, what was the police supposed to do, put a guard on Mark?

Sympathy for Mark's family was dampened down further by the time of the eleven o'clock news. Reporters interviewed people in Ramsgate where the common response was, "Of course they're going to say that." Many claimed they agreed with the decision to move out of Ramsgate although when asked, Don Tye sinisterly spouted, "If they hadn't moved of their own volition, we would have persuaded them."

Many more were critical of Mrs Leversee. "She's blaming the police because they didn't lock up the kids who supposedly bullied her son. Well bullying is not a crime," one respondent ranted.

Predictably, the Cherissos were interviewed. Mrs Cherisso took the microphone and stated, "As a mother, I can see her grief but I can never forgive her son for killing my Lydia."

Nobody in Ramsgate sympathised with Donna Leversee. To many she was just as crazy as her son who had done the deed, her outburst proved that. Some even said that she should be jailed in spite of the fact the overwhelming evidence concluded that she had no prior knowledge of what Mark was going to do. Had it not been for her father's decision to leave Ramsgate, some residents might have taken matters into their own hands.

The news conference proved to a climax in many ways. Having gotten some sort of statement from the shooter's family, many media personnel ended their camp out of the family's front door and life in Ramsgate began to return to some sort of normality. Any worry by the town's Chamber of Commerce that the shooting would kill the tourist trade that summer went away after the first few weeks. Most tourists were simply interested in the beach and bay activities and went nowhere near Tye School. There were a few curious folk who wanted to visit the site of all the bloodshed but they were disappointed as all they saw was some new gates being installed and if they looked real hard, some faint traces of blood.

One day Mrs Cherisso had a knock at her front door. She wasn't surprised to see a police officer standing outside it but she was surprised when the officer handed her a plain brown envelope politely declaring,

"This belonged to your daughter, it was recovered at the site of the shooting and had traces of her blood on it."

She accepted the envelope and thanked the officer, allowing him to carry on with his duties. Extremely curious of the contents, she tore open the envelope and reached in, pulling out a set of rosary beads. While she examined them, Sandra Cherisso thought to herself, "Lydia never took rosary beads to school that she knew of." Intrigued, she went upstairs to her daughter's room, now untouched since that fateful day. She conducted a brief search and didn't have to look hard before she discovered her daughter's beads on top of the dresser. The ones she had been given definitely were not Lydia's. Thinking nothing more on it, Mrs Cherisso put the beads down on the same dresser and made a mental note to try to find out whom they belonged to.

Lisa seemed to be coping well with the news of the shooting. It was true she hadn't left the house since but her family gave her all the support they could. One evening, the Farmers heard the doorbell ring. Mr Farmer opened it to two men who were obviously journalists. Before he could react, one of them asked, "We have word that your daughter Lisa was the girlfriend of Ramsgate shooter Mark Leversee. Do you have any comments on that?"

Earl growled a sharp, "No!" before slamming the door.

Chapter 28

Deeply Departed

Blessed Mary Virgin Church hadn't been that full for many years, not even at the Christmas and Easter masses. On this particular day, nearly every Catholic believer and a few non-Catholic ones, in Ramsgate wanted to be there to pay their respects to Lydia Cherisso, the sweet young girl so cruelly gunned down by that psycho Mark Leversee. Therefore, the church was full to bursting with people, much to the delight of the priest. The downside was that it took more than an hour for everyone to pass by the casket to view the pretty, innocent young girl in the pink dress lying in it.

Father Ted O'Bannon didn't mind the longer delay in letting everyone view the casket. In the twenty-one years he had been the priest of the church, he couldn't remember the last time his pews were that full. With that in mind, the 62-year-old priest began conducting the funeral of Lydia Cherisso. He didn't even mind having to talk over the many in the congregation who expressed their grief through loud wails. On several occasions, he repeated what a sweet and innocent girl Lydia had been and that her death was a tragic loss for the world. While he never mentioned Mark's name, Father O'Bannon did declare that those who commit vile deeds would receive their eternal damnation.

More weeping followed on after the funeral as many of the assembled wanted to directly express their sorrow to the Cherisso family. Like the viewing before the service, this also took more than an hour. There were many utterances of, "We're so sorry" and "She was such a lovely girl" repeated to them a hundred times over. One boy even informed them, "I knew that kid and he was a real weirdo. He said he was going to sue us for his glasses." Mr and Mrs Cherisso gladly acknowledged the boy's comment as they did all of the others. They seemed to enjoy their moment in the spotlight in spite of the grim circumstances that had put them in it.

Although they didn't get the turnout or attention as the funeral for Lydia Cherisso, fifteen more funerals took place for those who had fallen victim to Mark's marksmanship skills. It might not have been as grand, but the funeral service for David Roseman at the Beth-el-Synagogue rivalled Lydia's in outpourings of grief. Many tears were shed as the rabbi spoke about David's promising athletic career and what a good kid he was. The rabbi blamed David's teasing of Mark down to his sense of humour and that Mark had been too troubled a kid to understand that. Those sitting in the congregation agreed. It was also said that the funeral for David Fitzpatrick went very much the same way. The main difference was that everybody seemed to ignore younger daughter Patty Fitzpatrick while they wept for her older brother.

The reason why only sixteen funerals took place for the seventeen deaths was because Joe and Liz Clover's funerals were held jointly due to them being siblings. Theirs took place in a small Lutheran Church in Ramsgate. The turnout was smaller and a lot less vocal but that didn't deter the minister when he conducted it. He praised Mrs Clover on how she had to work two jobs to support her children after their father walked out on them when Liz and Joe were very young. Therefore he was sympathetic to the fact that the children had lacked adult influence in their life and while they weren't angels, they could have been worse. Furthermore, he too went on to declare that Liz and Joe didn't deserve to die and they had just fallen in with the wrong crowd. They may have picked on Mark but that didn't justify their deaths.

Mother Noreen Clover reinforced the minister's words when interviewed after the funeral. "I know that I wasn't always there for my kids," she half screamed and half sobbed. "But I taught my kids to be tough and to fend for themselves. It's obvious that this Leversee kid didn't have that. I heard that his family got money off the government because of some condition he had. Therefore, he was weak and that is why Liz and Joe teased him. But because he thought he was entitled to everything, he couldn't take it and ended up shooting everybody."

All of the other funerals for the dead of Tye School followed the same pattern. Rabbis, priests and ministers all described how innocent the victim was and what a troubled kid Mark must have been, even in the cases of Joe Kellerman and Jim Nickerson. The minister at Billy Northwick's funeral insisted that Billy was in the wrong place at the wrong time, which was probably true. However, the most crocodile tears were shed at Tommy Allen's funeral. Nothing was said about Tommy being in constant trouble at school or his brushes with the law; just what a good kid he was and that he couldn't have possibly done all the things Mark said he had.

Around the same time but intentionally unknown to many in Ramsgate, Mark's funeral took place at St James Church in Vincent. Pastor Bachman suggested that the funeral be kept as low key as possible. Most likely, he didn't want a load of protesters outside his church spoiling the funeral. He believed that Mark didn't deserve that. Therefore, the announcement of it was kept within the walls of the church and only family invited from the outside.

Protesters at her son's funeral was the last thing on Mrs Leversee's mind, there was far too much to do. Finding places to stay for relatives, who included Mark's father and new family, was the main problem. Some had to stay as far away as Atlantic City but at least the problem was solved. Then there was a small number of people she didn't recognise knocking the door to enquire about Mark's funeral. Thinking they might be reporters or worse, she told them that the funeral would be a private one. However, she did regret turning Sarah Levine and Alan Green away after she had opened their card.

Cards were another thing she had been swamped with; she must have received over a hundred. Many offered sincere condolences to her and the rest of the family although there were some nasty ones wishing that Mark burn in hell etc. Of all the cards, the one she treasured the most was the one sent by Lisa. Seeing the card and reading her letter saying how she never meant to hurt Mark brought on the water works. She knew that Lisa was a special girl and made a mental note to write to her after the funeral.

Someone at St James Church must have leaked the time, date and location of the funeral because as the family car pulled up, they saw five individuals standing outside of the church. Three of them were holding a large banner that read, "Burn in Hell, Murderer!" A fourth person held a small cardboard sign that read, "Don't mourn a killer," while the fifth person actively tried to stop anyone who walked past telling them not to go into the church. Most of the people weren't going to the funeral anyway and the few who were, paid no attention.

Fortunately, Pastor Bachman and other church leaders must have had some premonition that something like this might happen. It was pre-arranged for Mark's casket to brought in through a side door and his immediate family go in through the same door. Therefore, there were no attacks on the coffin or the family and both were in place to greet those who had come to mourn Mark.

Mark's peaceful, lifeless body lay in its casket for all who wanted to see it. In many ways, he looked more handsome in death than he ever had in life. No glasses were on his face and the smart powder blue suit jacket and black tie went well with it. His trousers were also black and long enough not to be called flood pants. The image made by those who gazed upon it had them asking themselves, "How could he be the monster the city of Ramsgate and the media were making him out to be?"

There was no security or screening of people who came into the church, so none challenged him when he walked in. He showed no ill intention as he watched relatives and people from the church shed tears as they passed by the body to pay their respects. Many mourners stood by the casket several minutes longer than expected so it was nothing out of the ordinary when he stood there a couple of extra seconds staring at the body in the casket.

Seizing his moment, Joe Callazone suddenly leaned over the casket and struck Mark's face with his fist. He delivered another blow only this time he screeched, "That was for my friends!"

"Stop!" yelled a middle aged woman standing near him but Joe ignored her delivering yet another blow to the corpse. She yelled again for him to stop but again he ignored her as Joe continued to vent his anger at Mark. Finally, the dumbstruck congregation reacted. Mark's uncle and two men from the church subdued Joe, pinning his right arm behind him in a chicken wing and proceeding to march him away from the coffin. Joe struggled screaming, "He's a killer! He killed my friends!" But the three men frog marched him up the aisle to the front doors ignoring his threats to sue them all for assault. Only when they had gotten him out of the church, did they let him go.

He made no attempt to go back in but stood there questioning the three men, "How can you have a funeral for someone who killed so many kids?" The now self-appointed sentries didn't answer but stood at their posts. Frustrated, Joe flipped his middle finger at them growling, "Fuck you," before heading off towards the five protesters. The three men at the door didn't see it but he gave a thumbs up to the protesters before commencing to boast how he got to punch Mark's dead body.

Even with the incident with Joe, the viewing of Mark's body wasn't half as long as Lydia Cherisso's. Still, Pastor Bachman was pleasantly surprised to see more people sitting in his pews than he had expected. He was especially glad that so many of his own parishioners had turned up to pay their respects. The sight uplifted him as he began the funeral service.

"I am not here to justify what Mark has done," he began. "But I will say that I know what a good Christian he was. I can still see him sitting in Confirmation class trying to glean the information. Sure, he sometimes had problems paying attention but that was part of his condition. However, when there was an important point to be learnt, the Lord removed that barrier for him. He had great potential for the Lord, I, Mr Crockett his Sunday school teacher and several others here at St James saw that. Unfortunately, Satan saw it too and that is why he heaped so much misery on Mark throughout his short life. So much so, that he found it impossible to forgive those who Satan used as his tools against him. Satan also used scripture to further twist his mind because Mark thought that he was doing the Lord's work, citing the passage in Deuteronomy. But one thing I do know is that even God, in his infinite mercy, will forgive Mark for his sins and that through the sacrifice of Jesus, will have his place in heaven."

Scanning the faces in the congregation, the pastor delighted in the belief that his words seemed to be hitting home, giving them comfort. It spurred him on to talk more about forgiveness and Mark's potential as a Christian and that Satan still hasn't won. His talk continued to hold that audience that only he noticed the father, mother and baby arriving late. When he concluded, he was certain that his message had the uplifting feel he had intended.

The very second after the funeral was over, the late arriving father made a direct line for the casket. Mrs Leversee recognised the man right away, even through her tears, as did her parents. However, it was eight-year-old Leslie who made the vocal recognition of him. With outstretched arms, she sprinted towards him shouting, "Daddy!" as she ran. Rusty Leversee stopped looking at his son's body long enough to pick up and hug his daughter whispering, "You're getting big," as he did so.

Mr Johnston shook his hand and thanked him for coming. Donna said nothing to her former husband but stood beside him at the coffin prompting Rusty's new wife to join him on his other side. As the coffin lid closed, Mr and Mrs Leversee were united in their grief in the life that they had created together ending so young, so tragically. As a family, they followed the coffin back out of the side door and watched it being put into the hearse. When it was loaded, they too followed behind it to its final destination, the crematorium. The rest of the congregation left via the front door and were forced to dodge the small army of journalists that had somehow swiftly assembled during the service.

Final partings and weeping took place as Mark's body was put into the incinerator. When it was all done, his ashes were given to both of his parents. Mrs Leversee thought cremation was the best alternative as a marked grave would have been a target for vengeful vandals or a shrine to some of the followers his actions had attracted on Facebook. Even at this time, her mind still wasn't sure to be proud or ashamed that before it had been finally removed from Facebook, his dying declaration had accumulated 1,028 likes. Besides by having him cremated, she could at least have her son with her always.

Chapter 29

Because They Called Him Marvin

Thus far, the Ramsgate police were somewhat frustrated over the lack of clear motive behind the Ramsgate shooting. They were further frustrated when their search of the Leversee/Johnston house didn't yield the evidence they were hoping to find. There were no Marilyn Manson CD's or any other subversive music. In fact, Mark only owned two CD's, both Christian rock bands. The one band, The Guiding Lights, were a commercial sounding pop/rock band whose lyrics like, "I love thee, Saviour," couldn't have possibly influenced Mark into shooting up the school. The other band, Demonslayer, sounded a little more promising, at first. Their thrash metal overtones had the police thinking that this was it, but even with the heavy riffs, the lyrics about serving Jesus, proved otherwise.

Computer games were just as unfulfilling. Mark didn't own any of the expected games like "Call of Duty," "Metal of Honour" or even "Grand Theft Auto." The closest he came to any of those was the "Age of Empires" games and "Empire Earth." Other than that, all he had was a hockey game called "NHL Star." He didn't own any DVD's outright and the two that were found, "Saving Private Ryan" and "A Bridge Too Far" had been borrowed from Ted. As a result, the police were more and more being forced to accept that bullying was the reason behind the shooting.

The FBI conducted interviews and they had more substantial theories behind the shooting. Special Agents Glen Ainsworth and Dexter Williams were also eager to dispel the bullying myth and interviewed many people with that aim. However, most interviewed said the same thing. It was no different with the girl they were interviewing at that moment. Sharon Lieberwitz had been in Mark's class for both sixth and seventh grades and admitted to teasing him. She also stated, "Yea, his name was Mark but everybody called him Marvin." When asked why she explained, "Because everyone knew it got to him."

It then occurred to Special Agent Ainsworth, a more slender figure in sharp contrast to his larger African American partner, to ask Sharon, "Do you think people calling him Marvin is what led him to shoot everyone?"

"I don't know," Sharon stuttered shifting her weight on her chair. "A lot of people picked on him because he was so weird. He lived in this fantasy world where he said he was some kind of hockey player. We all knew he was lying."

Sharon left shortly after that. The FBI was getting some idea of who Mark Leversee was and what he went through. They did take Sharon's telling about the hockey fantasy on board and looked at "NHL Star" in more detail. That was where they discovered Mark's fantasy league and relived his game winning assist in the first game of the final against the Junior Flyers.

After that, more of the people alleged to have bullied Mark were interviewed. Nick Higbee was one such person. "He was a total pussy," he cheerfully chortled when asked. "I used to pick on him because I knew I could and if he was here, I would kill him because he killed my friend, Billy."

"You mean Billy Northwick," Special Agent Ainsworth confirmed with Nick nodding in agreement.

As the interview continued, Nick's boastful arrogance began about how he picked on Mark began to rub adversely on Special Agent Williams. He had spent most of his life dealing with what he called "punk ass white boys" who thought they were hard. Therefore, after Nick had recounted how Mark had pulled his hair in a fight and stating further about Billy's death, the agent decided to tell Nick a home truth.

"You owe your life to Billy Northwick," he identified. "Our investigation shows that if Billy hadn't been where he was when he was hit, those bullets that killed him would have definitely killed you and it would have been you buried in a grave and not Billy Northwick." The words and the agent's tone was enough to silence Nick.

As they began to regain their health, more of those wounded on that fateful day were also interviewed. Terry Cratt spewed, "Yeah, Tommy used to pick on him because he was such a faggot. I was pissed off with him too because his friend Lancaster couldn't keep his mouth shut and thought he was being funny. But Leversee laughed at it. Now because of him, I'm going to have problems with my shoulder for the rest of my life."

Many of the wounded tried to act more innocent. Darlene Kinney, the eighth grade girl who had been shot through the shoulder as she tried to flee explained, "Some of the eighth grade boys used to pick on him a lot because he quit the football team, but I never said anything to him."

When the agents interviewed Mike Sigfried, they hoped to get a reason as to why Mark had let him live. Mike's experience had been so traumatic, it was believed he would need therapy for many years. It didn't stop him from an attempt at bravado. "Maybe he was too afraid I would kick his ass," he boasted to the agents. Special Agent Williams gave him a look saying that he wasn't impressed.

Special Agent Ainsworth knew his partner too well

and stepped in to assist Mike in removing his foot from his mouth. "Mark Leversee shot three kids in the head at point blank range after he had wounded them. We know that all of these boys bullied him as much or more than what you did. So I don't think it was because he was afraid of you kicking his ass."

Mike acknowledged this and at the instruction of the agents, recounted his experience of how Mark wounded him and shot him each time he refused Mark's request of taking everything back.

"Did you take it back?" Williams asked and when Mike answered in the affirmative, he asked, "Did you mean it?"

At first, the temptation to act macho briefly crossed his mind but realisation then hit him. He did mean it at the time. His life was in jeopardy and would have said anything to stay alive. Therefore, he answered, "Yes."

Conducting their interviews, the two FBI agents not only gained a picture of Mark but statements were also giving them an idea of what type of person Gene Lancaster was. They mentally took this picture into the room the day they went to interview him. It would seem obvious that the reason Mark left him alive was that he was supposed to be his friend but some accounts told a darker story. Gene would sometimes join in or even lead others in humiliating Mark and if it got physical, he would not offer any help. That was probably the more likely reason why Leversee had shot his legs out from under him without hesitation.

Gene provided a further explanation of his wounding when interviewed. He explained that he was trying to stop Mark from killing everybody and was hoping he would hand his gun over to him. He claimed he was surprised and hurt when Mark shot him.

"He probably knew you were trying to make him stop his slaughter, that's why he shot you," Ainsworth suggested. Gene muttered an "Oh" and the agent went on, "We have statements from people saying that even though you were his friend, you also made fun of him and bossed him around. Also we have reports that saying that when he was getting physically bullied, you never once came to his aid and sometimes you were the one who started it."

"That's not true, he was my friend," Gene protested in attempted rebuttal.

A sinister smile formed on Glen Ainsworth's face. "So you're saying that everyone else is lying," he inferred.

When Gene nodded, he pressed, "So you never teased him or took his ball and gave it to other kids."

Flustered, Gene protested further, "That was just kidding around. I never meant anything by it."

The agent smiled that same smile at him and declared, "Obviously, Mark Leversee didn't see it as kidding around."

Most of the state and federal law enforcement personnel sent to assist left Ramsgate within a month following the shooting. Special Agents Ainsworth and Williams also concluded their investigation and informed Chief Gregory that a full report would be out three weeks later. However, the chief didn't want to wait that long as he believed his city wanted answers as soon as possible. Therefore, he took the information the agents and others had shared with his police force and called a press conference.

Many journalists were on hand to listen to the chief's report. Addressing the assembly, he started, "After working closely with state and federal law enforcement officials, we have discovered these findings about the events that occurred at Bernard A Tye School back in June. First, let me address the issue of bullies. Yes, Mark Leversee was bullied and our investigation has told us who those bullies were. Our evidence also shows that he was not bullied any more than the average child but because of his Asperger's Syndrome, he perceived that he was. One instance that clearly underlines this is the fact that many students used to call him by his former name, Marvin. Most kids would know this as a joke but his condition made him think that he was the victim of much worse."

Chief Gregory touched on other aspects that might have led to the shooting like the Smiley incident. Even there, he absolved the police or people of Ramsgate from any blame and that Mark was an unbalanced person. Still, it was no surprise that the first question asked by any of the reporters was, "Are you saying that the whole reason Mark Leversee shot up the school was because kids used to call him Marvin?"

The chief looked at the reporter as if he had two heads before responding, "Of course not, that alone would not have caused him to do it. But of all the bullying and teasing he believed he suffered, being called Marvin is the most consistent occurrence."

The next reporter made the predictable request for the names of the bullies. The chief wasted no time in obliging. "We know the main bullies to be Tommy Allen, Joe Kellerman and as you probably already know, Jim Nickerson. We also know that Joe Gerberwitz had bullied Leversee when they were in sixth grade."

"Was there any evidence that Mark Leversee was influenced by music or computer games?" a separate reporter asked.

"No, we didn't find any evidence of that," Chief Gregory had to admit. "However, he was hooked on military strategy games and while these games didn't cause him to go out and shoot people, there is evidence of military knowledge in the way he carried it out.

There is a link between that and the games, so they might have aided his planning of the shooting."

Question and answer time lasted another ten minutes before the chief called time on it. The reporters were at least satisfied that they could name some of the bullies for their next edition or broadcast. However, it left Kevin Taylor feeling frustrated about not being able to ask about Tommy Allen being allowed to escape justice for his petty crimes on account of his father. He would have like an answer for that and for some of the other things he was finding out in his own investigation.

The FBI's official report on the shooting came out three weeks later. It began by stating, "Our investigation concludes that Mark Leversee was not influenced by music, films, computer games or drugs when he carried out his shooting at Bernard A Tye School in Ramsgate, New Jersey. School bullies may have justified his actions in his own mind; we don't believe that this was the cause behind his actions.

Having interviewed many people and read reports from school and other officials, we concur that he suffered from Asperger's Syndrome and the condition of DAMP. One of the traits of these conditions is to take what is said literally. In one of these cases, we know that he had strong religious beliefs. The bible verses he cited on the Three Streams Facebook page, where he stated that he was going to do "the Lord's work," were also highlighted in his bible. We believe that he used the passage, "Save none alive that breatheth" as his inspiration.

Another trait of his condition was the lack of social skills. We have found this to be consistent with the behaviour of Mark Leversee. His lack of social skills would have also facilitated his retreat into a fantasy world where he believed he was a star hockey player.

However, we have seen few cases of fantasies that were as advanced as his.

The rest of the report continued in this vein. It concurred with the chief's assertion that Mark had been a troubled individual but it stop short of saying that the bullying he suffered was a cause. It just said that it played a part. Furthermore, it never said anything about the fact that kids called him Marvin.

Most of the people in Ramsgate never read the report. What the chief had said at the press conference was good enough for them. After all, it seemed plausible to them that the fact that many kids called him Marvin was enough reason for Mark's shooting spree. Especially if it removed any real blame from the town of Ramsgate.

Chapter 30

The Crocodiles Descend

In the weeks followed, this advertisement was often heard on local radio stations:

"Were you affected by the terrible tragedy that befell Bernard Tye School? Was your child among the casualties? Were they one of the ones who were wounded and will need ongoing medical care? If the answer to any of those questions is yes, then we may be able to help you. We, at the law firm of Silverman and Pizzano, can help you get the justice you are entitled to. Our dedicated team of lawyers will fight for you to make sure you are fairly compensated. Our no win, no fee scheme means that if you are not compensated, you pay nothing in costs. So call us now and get the justice you deserve. That's Silverman and Pizzano working for you."

Howard Bernstein looked at the distraught mother and father sitting across from him. He did his best to try to reassure them. "Mr and Mrs Cherisso," he began, "I know it doesn't seem right not to sue the parents of Mark Leversee, but I know we wouldn't get a decent payout and naturally, we will sue the man who gave him the access to the guns. But there are others higher up who are just as responsible: the school knew that the Leversee boy was bullied and did little to stop it. They also failed in their duty of care to protect your daughter so we should definitely go after them as well as the police. I know that the Leversee family had a restraining order against one of his bullies, who constantly broke the restraining order, yet the police did nothing. I also know that another of the bullies was the nephew of the chief of police, so they didn't act effectively on account of that. It's these people who failed your daughter and it is they who should pay."

Al and Sandra Cherisso still weren't sure about it. Al inquired, "Are you sure we would be successful if we sued the police and the school and what would the town think of us?" He had heard of cases like this where cities and large corporations were sued for large amounts of money but he wasn't sure it was actually true.

Prepared for that question, the lawyer replied, "I can't guarantee 100% that we would win but we have an excellent chance. As for the town, I think most people would sympathise with you because after all, your daughter was killed needlessly."

It took a little more discussion and persuasion from the attorney but the Cherisso's agreed to sue the school and the police department for a total of three million dollars. They knew it wouldn't bring Lydia back but they believed Howard Bernstein when he said it would bring them closure.

The Cherissos weren't the only family looking for closure and compensation nor was Silverman and Pizzano the only law firm encouraging bereaved families to finance the legal profession. More victims' families looked for the opportunity to cash in. Ramsgate soon became overrun with litigation crocodiles salivating at the fresh meat that Mark's exploits had provided. One such lawyer was Malcolm Provowitz, an attorney in Vincent, who was known for his ruthlessness.

It was on account of that ruthless reputation why the parents of Darlene Kinney contacted him. Darlene might not have been killed but one of Mark's bullets had gone through her right shoulder chipping the scapula. She would recover but she feared that she would never be able to be a cheerleader again. Mr Provowitz recognised this and explained that it was definitely grounds for compensation. Like with the Cherisso's lawyer, he also thought the school and police were responsible but he had other targets in his sights as well.

"Your daughter saw the eighth grade boys pick on the Leversee boy and we know the names of these bullies," he explained. "We also know that in the case of the Nickerson boy, that some of the parents knew their sons were bullying the kid and it may have caused him to snap. Therefore, the parents were negligent in not stopping their sons from picking on this kid and we should sue them as well."

Unlike the Cherissos, Mr and Mrs Kinney didn't need much persuasion. They wholeheartedly agreed to feed the hungry crocodile that was Malcolm Provowitz. At his recommendation, the Kinneys sued the school, the police and also the parents of Jim Nickerson, Brian Cullen and Tommy Allen.

Other lawyers went after the parents of some Mark's other tormentors. The parents of Joe Kellerman, Joe Gerberwitz, David Roseman, David Fitzpatrick and Mark Wolfe also found themselves being served with litigation papers. Many parents also sued Smiley and at the same time, Smiley unsuccessfully tried to use the fact Mark had done this terrible deed to get his ban from working with minors reduced. And although Diane Boreman had found it amusing when Mike Sigfried had picked on Mark, it didn't stop her parents from suing his.

Lawyers looked outside of Ramsgate to further feed their compensation hunger. Ned's Shooting Range was a prime target and one family even tried to sue Microsoft, citing that the Age of Empires games gave Mark the knowledge to carry out his shooting. The

Callazones sued St James Church for the manhandling of Joe at the funeral. Just about every lawyer in and around Ramsgate was able to fill their pockets courtesy of Mark's extravaganza as they promised their clients that compensation would bring them closure.

Eventually, about fifteen million dollars of compensation money would be paid out, greatly enriching the legal profession in the area. More than half of that was paid out by Tye School in out of court settlements and the police paid out nearly three million. Combined, it financially crippled the city of Ramsgate who had to ask for emergency funds from the state.

However, the fiercest courtroom battles were fought between the families. Parents suing parents had a knock on effect with the children thus severing many childhood friendships. To the world, the people of Ramsgate may have looked united in grief over the shooting but behind the picture, it was a town deeply divided with people tearing each other apart through litigation. If he had still been alive, Mark would have rejoiced in the fact that Ramsgate was in such a mess on account of him.

The city attempted to recoup some of its lost revenue by launching their own lawsuit against the South Jersey Current newspaper for an article written by the reporter Kevin Taylor. His article exposed the police's covering up of some of the petty crimes committed by Tommy Allen because his father was a local businessman and that Tommy felt himself untouchable. It also told of how the police ignored Mark's family's pleas for help and how Smiley escaped jail because one of Mark's antagonists was the chief's own nephew. What really drove the nail home was the interview with the Longley family.

In the interview, Mr and Mrs Longley described the suffering of their son Daniel when they had lived in

Ramsgate ten years earlier. Daniel had been diagnosed with autism when he was seven but that didn't stop kids from teasing and bullying him when he was at school. The school did little to stop it and eventually agreed that Daniel should attend a special school in order to shift the problem. Most ironic though was that Daniel's chief bullies were Bobby Allen and Donnie Friend, older brothers of Tommy and Jim.

Fortunately for Kevin, had been able to back up his findings thus crushing any case for libel. When the paper couldn't be sued, there was a citywide call for a boycott of the Current, although a few citizens took it one step further and burnt some copies in a public spectacle. That didn't hurt the paper too much because not many people in Ramsgate ever read it in the first place.

Chapter 31

Conventions and Revivals

Some said that they came as a result of the Ramsgate shooting. Others would claim that their convention had been booked well in advance, no one was sure either way. Whichever the case, one month after the shooting, the New Jersey Chapter of the National Rifle Association held a convention in Atlantic City.

Theo Stevens was a promising young actor who had appeared in a few major films. It was said that his very good looks and acting talent got him far in the film industry in spite of his conservative views and open support for the Republican Party. He often boasted that he had made it in Hollywood despite its liberal intolerance. Stevens was also a huge supporter of the gun lobby and was therefore asked to speak at many NRA Conventions.

All eyes in the convention centre were on the chiselled face of the black haired heartthrob as he stood at the podium holding a .22 calibre rifle aloft. Gasps filled the hall as he boldly declared, "Like Charlton Heston used to say, from my cold dead hands!" Raucous applause followed immediately and he waited for it to die down. Once it became quiet again, he continued, "Once again, the liberals in America want to use an unfortunate tragedy to take away our Second Amendment Right, our right to bear arms."

More applause followed before the actor delved into the meat of his speech. He admitted that the Ramsgate school shooting was a tragedy but quick to refute the argument that guns were to blame. He was quick to point out Mark's problems, including the bullying, and citing those as the cause. Most of his talk was an appeal for conceal and carry laws, suggesting that if teachers had guns, they could have neutralised the threat before too much carnage had been caused. He went onto say that if teachers were too liberal to carry guns, then all schools should have armed security guards. When his speech was over, the two thousand strong audience were on their feet in rapturous cheering.

Outside the convention centre, fifty protestors, many relatives of Mark's victims, picketed. They resented that an organisation that glorified guns would dare come within one hundred miles of Ramsgate so soon after a horrific shooting. Signs of "Go Home Gun Nuts" and "No Guns Here" and even "Guns Killed My Child" dotted the sidewalk outside the main entrance. Their numbers might have been small but many people who passed by sympathised with them. To avoid confrontation, the convention attendees were made to go in and out another door. There was no meeting of the two groups during the two days of the convention but it was clear that the gun debate would go on for much longer.

Sandra Cherisso never attempted to find the true owner of the rosary beads the police officer had brought to her thinking they had belonged to her daughter. Any intention to do so went out of the window the day Father O'Bannon came to visit. He told her of a large interfaith Christian revival that was taking place just outside of Philadelphia at the coming weekend and how uplifting it might be if the Cherissos could share the tragic story of their daughter. Instantly, the thought of the rosary beads came to her mind. Maybe this was a sign from God. Without further thought or even wondering what her husband would say, she agreed to it. A plan was already forming in her mind.

Al Cherisso needed no persuasion as he thought all should hear his daughter's tragic story. So on the Saturday, Mr and Mrs Cherisso, their kids, Father O'Bannon and about twenty members of Blessed Mary Virgin Church, went to the large outdoor theatre with 2,500 other people representing all the local Christian faiths. Unbeknown to the party from the Catholic Church in Ramsgate, Barbara North, Gerhard and several others who had been staff or counsellors at Three Streams the previous summer were also in attendance.

Plenty of music, inspiring messages and activities for the children took place that day. In spite of the different faiths, the outdoor theatre was brimming with Christian fellowship. Five thousand eyes watched as Sandra Cherisso stepped into the spotlight and held the rosary beads high in the air. Ears tuned in as she spoke. "These beads belonged to our daughter, Lydia, who was tragically killed in cold blood during the shooting at Tye School in Ramsgate, New Jersey. The police handed them back to me several weeks ago. They told me that these beads were found by Lydia's body and were covered in her blood. It proves to us that even though her life was about to end, she was still willing to pray. She remained true to her faith, true to Jesus even as she was shot. We can only say that we are very proud of her for this."

Shouts of "Praise the Lord!" and "Hallelujah!" and "Amen!" momentarily disrupted her momentum. She got it back straight away as she told her audience how humbled she was at her daughter's show of faith on that tragic day. Furthermore, she said that they prayed to God to have mercy on the shooter, although they never mentioned Mark by name. If that had, it might have stirred the contingent from Three Streams into saying something because they remembered Mark differently.

The conclusion of Sandra's speech had the two and a half thousand assembled on their feet and fanatically praising God. Shrewdly, the organisers seized this opportunity and passed around the collection plates, it paid off big time. With all the coffers full and a hysterical crowd, the organisers invited the Cherissos to share their message at other rallies, they immediately agreed. For the next four weeks, the Cherisso family went to rallies in Northern Pennsylvania, Northern New Jersey, New York, Delaware and Maryland telling all how their precious Lydia was the one praying to God when she got shot and displaying the rosary beads that weren't hers to prove it.

Back at Blessed Mary Virgin Church in Ramsgate, the Cherissos were given celebrity status. Most in the church complimented them on how brave they were in telling their daughter's tragic story and how wonderful it was for them to be doing God's work. So when it came time for them to tell their daughter's story at their home church, the pews were nearly as full as they had been at Lydia's funeral.

As always, Sandra began by holding up the rosary beads for all to see. That was when a girl named Sherry Satriano, who had been in Lydia's class, recognised her rosary beads. She stared at them through the whole of Sandra's talk, oblivious to what she was saying. That wasn't important anyway. Sherry had been there as well. She remembered how she had taken the beads out to beg God and the Virgin Mary for her life but then dropped them in the crush to get inside the classroom and escape the bullets that were flying around. Therefore, she knew that those rosary beads belonged to her.

Immediately, when the mass was over, Sherry whispered to her mother, "I think those are my rosary beads."

Maria Satriano regarded her twelve-year-old daughter and knew she wouldn't lie about something like this. She reflected back to the day of the shooting. At the time, she was grateful that Sherry wasn't among the casualties and she had genuine deep sympathy for the Cherissos. When her daughter reported that she lost her beads in all the hysteria, it was cancelled out by the knowledge that she was safe. Now though, she wasn't going to let Sandra Cherisso use something that belonged to Sherry to pimp her own daughter's tragic tale.

With Sherry in tow, Maria waited for the crowd of awe-struck fans to disperse away from the Cherissos before making her move. When it did, she made a beeline straight for the sainted mother and politely asked to see the famous beads. Sandra, thinking that Maria was just another admirer, handed them over.

Maria turned to her daughter and showing her the beads asked, "Are these yours?"

Sherry simply nodded and shyly affirmed, "Yes" and reaffirmed when her mother asked, "Are you sure?"

Sandra Cherisso's face turned a lovely shade of scarlet. Al, who was next to her, angrily stormed in, "What are you doing saying that these beads are your daughter's?" He then accused, "Your just trying to use our daughter to get your fifteen minutes of fame. These are our daughter's beads." He hesitated for a moment as a tinge of doubt entered his mind. Then turning to Sandra, he asked, "They are Lydia's beads aren't they?"

At first, she wanted to lie; instead, she broke down in tears at her husband's question. Before any more could be said, Father O'Bannon rushed in and quickly herded all involved into a side room. Obviously, he saw that his star attraction was upset so he acted quickly to avoid a scene. When all were in, Sandra Cherisso tearfully revealed all.

"The police brought them to me, they thought the beads belonged to Lydia because they had found traces of her blood on them. When I took them to Lydia's room, I saw they weren't hers because her beads were on the dresser. I was going to find out whom they belonged to, and then you asked me to speak at the revival. I thought it was a sign from God and I thought it wouldn't hurt anybody to say they were Lydia's."

Al put his arm around his wife's shoulder in a bid to comfort her. He wasn't sure how to react to what she had just divulged. Father O'Bannon quickly offered a solution. Sounding reassuring, he said to Sandra, "No, you didn't mean any harm and you were simply trying to do what you thought was best, the best way you knew how." Noticing the unimpressed face of Maria Satriano, he offered, "Why don't you join us? I'm sure people would be inspired by your daughter's story of how God answered her prayer and saved her life."

Mrs Satriano wasn't interested in using her daughter's story to financially enrich the church. "I just want my daughter's beads back," she said abruptly.

Sandra willingly handed over the beads to Mrs Satriano, who thanked her and left. However, Father O'Bannon became suddenly worried that he was going to lose his cash cow, especially now that more revivals were asking to hear the Cherisso's story. Therefore, he suggested, "No one knows that those weren't your daughter's beads. You have an inspiring message to give to people. We can just use Lydia's beads and no one will be the wiser, but I'll give you time to think."

It didn't take long for Sandra to agree to the priest's suggestion. She and Al had enjoyed their time in the limelight and wanted it to continue. Besides, Father O'Bannon was right, no one would be any wiser.

Therefore, it was decided that the Cherisso family would continue to go on tour of religious revivals and tell about their daughter's sad but inspiring story of how she was praying to God just as her life was ended.

Chapter 32

The Summer and New Beginnings

By the beginning of August, summer life in Ramsgate was largely back to what was considered normal. The tourists still came for the beach, bay and the bars at night. However, some indications of the big event that had taken place in June remained. Charlie Allen hoped that the summer trade would aid him with the legal costs he was now facing. Unfortunately it wouldn't be enough and he was forced to sell his bar at the end of the summer and move the rest of his family to New York. For many of the other businesses though, summer takings were normal.

Not only was he sued by practically every casualty from the shooting, Ted also faced criminal charges of negligence. On advice from his attorney, he pleaded guilty to these charges and his attorney worked out a deal with the D.A. He was banned from owning guns for life and although he and his lawyer hoped otherwise, the judge still thought it necessary to pass a custodial sentence, even if it was only six months in a minimum-security prison. The judge explained that the only reason he was this lenient was due to the fact Ted had cooperated fully with the police and his service to his country.

Only Father O'Bannon and Maria and Sherry Satriano would know the truth about the rosary beads outside of the Cherisso family. The Cherissos went on a summer long tour of religious revivals in the eastern part of the United States telling congregations about how their precious Lydia prayed to God just before she was shot. Sandra would now hold her daughter's rosary beads out for all to see as proof. They also appeared on several local radio stations during their tour and a television talk show in Charleston, West Virginia. They also spoke at religious summer camps for children and even offered to come to Three Streams. However, for some unknown reason, Three Streams politely declined their offer.

For the Johnston/Leversee household, it was a different story. Their house sold surprisingly quickly, mainly due to the enormous efforts of the people who worked at Callazone Realtors. Mr Johnston even got close to his asking price. The realtors on the other side were almost as good and they had help from relatives living in the area. Therefore, they found a suitable house in Scottsburg, Pennsylvania. It was also fortunate that a house in Central Pennsylvania sold cheaper than a house in New Jersey that was two blocks from the sea front.

All the formalities were finalised by the third week in August allowing the family to make the move. None of them even looked back as the cars drove over the Ramsgate Bridge onto the causeway. They weren't sad that they were leaving the town; Ramsgate had nothing but heartache for them and took their son, grandson, and brother. Mrs Leversee was forced to keep her hands in a vice like grip on the steering wheel and look straight ahead or else she would have succumbed to the temptation to flip a parting gesture back at the town as she drove out of it.

It would also be the final time she would think of herself as Donna Leversee. When they got to Scottsburg, she would revert back to her maiden name and Leslie and Douglas would take that name too. From then on, they would all be called Johnston. It was her way of wiping the slate clean.

About one hundred miles away from the Johnston's

new home, the Farmers decided to spend the summer away from Estminston. The press were still hounding them in the hope of getting some news about their daughter's relationship with the Ramsgate school shooter to the point where Earl finally gave a brief statement:

"Last summer, my daughter, Lisa, met Mark Leversee at Three Streams Camp where they became friends. They did keep in touch on the Internet after their week at the camp but that was all. He might have read more into their relationship, maybe because of his condition but Lisa was never his girlfriend. We are dreadfully sorry for what happened at the school in New Jersey and our deepest sympathies go out to all the families. Now we just want to be left alone."

Not trusting the media. The Farmers arranged to stay with some of Natalie's relatives on Long Island in New York. The move was proven to be the right one as no media followed them. All they hoped for was when they returned to Estminston in the September was the whole affair to be over and they could move on with their lives.

Chapter 33

Back to School

Changes made at Tye School over the summer manifested themselves the on first day back. Metal detectors and security guards now manned every entrance to the schoolyard. All pupils were required to pass through the metal detectors and their property searched by the security guards. Naturally, as it was the first day, teething problems arose. Long lines of pupils were forced to wait to get in delaying the start of school and as a result; it served to annoy pupils and teachers. Of course, everybody knew who to blame for the new measures and more than one complained, "It's all because of that prick Leversee."

Inside the school gates, great efforts had been made to ensure that all traces of Mark's June escapades were thoroughly erased. Some more diligent students still managed to find some faint traces of blood on walls and steps. For most kids, however, the idea of normality was still lost. The cosmetic efforts of the school to patch over what happened on the last day of the previous term weren't enough.

Familiar gatherings of groups reformed as always but in many cases among the new seventh and eighth graders, there was someone missing. With Nancy Greenwood and Janice Ricardo both dead, Laurie Swords had to find another group of friends. Fortunately, her popularity made that easy for her. Other reminders were also present, like John Lodge hobbling in on crutches and the seventh grader who was in a wheelchair and might be in it permanently. Even Diane Boreman got into the act when she moaned that she hardly went to the beach that summer and doubted that she could ever wear shorts again because of the scar on her thigh. Her complaints only angered Mike Sigfried as he limped by. Diane had suffered nothing in comparison to what he had but it was her parents that were suing his. The lawsuits added a further dimension to the atmosphere at the school as some children were in open hostility with each other as their parents sued one another.

Teachers at Tye School had their summer vacation cut short by two days in order to undergo training in profiling pupils. Experts in the field gave instruction on what to look for in potential troublemakers and how to help them. Many of the characteristics stated wouldn't have fitted Mark. He would have been put on the other list, potential victims. By the end of the two days, the teachers were given knowledge on how to spot and help a troubled kid and names were being suggested for both lists. Terry Cratt now topped the troublemaker's list while John Bettis and Chris Rawlings were main ones for the other list. What they didn't realise was that Mark had rid them of some of the worst troublemakers among the eighth graders.

Mr Fluyt had survived an attempt to remove him that summer. Some parents believed that his allowing pupils to play what they called "warlike games" had given Mark the ideas for his shooting spree. Therefore, they started a petition for his dismissal. To his good fortune, many parents didn't want to lose someone who they thought was a good teacher and neither did Mr Tasker. Furthermore, he had the full backing from his union and therefore, the petition failed. Some of the disgruntled parents blamed the teaching unions for having too much power but Mr Fluyt was there with the rest of the staff to greet his new sixth grade class that morning.

All of the staff at the school put on masks as the children entered the gymnasium. After welcoming everybody back, Mr Tasker called for a moment of silence for the seventh and eighth graders who wouldn't be joining them. He also announced that there would be a special assembly held that Friday. Then as normal, the children were all assigned to their classes. Only a few eighth graders noticed the absence of Sarah Levine. She was asked not to attend that first week because it might cause unnecessary trouble for her, especially at the Friday assembly. Her parents were assured that the absences wouldn't count against her.

School also began at Arlen Spectre Junior High School in Estminston, Pennsylvania. The normal dreads of going back to school filled the head of thirteen-year-old Lisa. The month spent in Long Island seemed to do her and her family a world of good. For all appearances, she had put Mark's tragic death and all that had gone with it behind her and she could go on with her life. She was growing up in many ways. Physically, the peaches were beginning to ripen and although she was wearing long trousers on account of the dismal weather and her mother's lectures about modesty, her legs would have still given Mark a big reaction.

Upon entering the grounds of the school, which were in many ways similar to Tye School, except for the metal detectors and security guards, she endeavoured to look for her friends. To her dismay, the first familiar faces were Amelia Brackington and her two accomplices. Amelia had begun developing the previous year causing her to ego to grow even faster that her breasts. She got plenty of notice from the boys and there were rumours that she had been de-flowered by a fifteen-year-old. It was this plastic model with highlighted hair and wearing a short skirt despite the weather and mirrored by her look alike friends who confronted Lisa.

"Hey skank!" Amelia called out, "I see you're still as hairy and stinky as last year."

Lisa was in no mood for any of this. She blurted out, "Leave me alone," before trying to go past the plastic trio. Accomplice number two barred her path.

"Leave me alone," Amelia imitated in a screechy voice. "What are you gong to do? Get a gun and shoot me like your boyfriend did in New Jersey."

Something inside Lisa snapped. Before she even realised it, she lunged with full force at Amelia executing the same tackle she had done on Mark just over a year earlier and like Mark, Amelia too went down like a felled tree. This time, however, Lisa wasn't looking for intimacy; she was looking for blood. Instead of a full body pin, she opted for the schoolgirl pin, straddling her chest and trapping Amelia's arms with her knees before unleashing a torrent of rights onto her agitator's made up face.

The two accomplices were too dumbstruck to come to their friend's aid and a crowd began to assemble to watch the show. Shouts of "Chick fight!" were echoed by several males, prompting more males and some females to observe the spectacle. Many hormones became excited at the site of two young ladies on the ground and many simply stared at the legs of the girl on the bottom. Lisa's barrage lasted for two minutes before a teacher of each gender managed to wade through the crowd and pull Lisa off of her beaten foe, who was now bleeding from the lip.

Parents were called into the school later that morning. Dennis Brackington was an influential local businessman and he demanded that Lisa be expelled for the vicious, unprovoked attack on his daughter. Natalie Farmer quickly pointed out that his "precious" Amelia had been harassing Lisa for the previous year at school and on Facebook and she brought in some examples to prove it.

Mr Brackington remained unconvinced. He barked, "You're just trying to play the bullying card like that boyfriend of your daughter's did when he shot up his school in New Jersey. Well my Amelia wouldn't do something like that and there's no proof she made those comments." He then threatened the principal that he would use his influence with the town's business community to not sponsor any school activities if Lisa wasn't properly punished.

Only her Christian charity kept Natalie from going for the man herself. "You don't have to worry about that," she snapped. "I will be taking Lisa out of the school and home schooling her." For her, this was the final blow to her faith in the public school system. So she, in spite of pleas from the principal, began teaching her daughter at home. This way she could ensure that Lisa had a good Christian education.

Fights were also something that marred the first week at Tye School. Six had broken out in that week, nearly as many that took place in the whole school year. Mr Tasker was forced to address the issue in the first Friday assembly. He firmly stated that fights would not be tolerated, even among the girls, and punishments would be swift and harsh. One of the fights was between two girls, Sherry Satriano and a friend of Lydia Cherisso's. The debated rosary beads had been the cause and it led to shouting and then slapping and hair pulling. It wasn't the start to school everyone had been hoping for.

Following the dressing down from the principal, the remembrance service took place. Mayor Burg was a guest and he gave an award to Mr Tasker for his outstanding leadership during the crisis. Another award was given to Nadine Salvatino whose efforts had saved the life of another pupil, even if it was known troublemaker Linda Boston. After giving the awards, he spoke about how the school and the city needed to come together and move on from the terrible tragedy. He called it a "healing process." His words might have had some outward effect but inwardly the school was deeply divided and tearing itself apart. Mark would have been proud.

Chapter 34

Miracles and Shrinks

Dr Ojeda couldn't help feeling sympathetic yet frustrated with his colleague sitting across from him. No matter what the doctor said to him, his colleague continued to beat himself up over it. He tried another approach, "No one, not even you or I could have foreseen what happened. I don't think anyone could have thought that Mark Leversee would get a gun and go into school and shoot so many kids."

Deep down, Dr Fred Walton knew that his friend and colleague was right and if the situation was reversed, he'd be saying the same thing. His mind, however, still refused to accept it. "Maybe if I had argued more for him and his mother at that meeting, put forward a better case that he would have been better out of Ramsgate, not let that teacher steamroll the others, then it might not have happened." Even as he put his explanation forward, he already knew what the response was going to be.

"Even if you had, it is doubtful that his mother would have moved anyway," Dr Ojeda explained. Then to head off the predictable, "I could have tried" response, he added, "Even if you had spoken up at that meeting, it most likely wouldn't have mattered. Anyway, the town is trying to rid itself of any blame. Many people would have seen you advising the Leversees to move out of Ramsgate as trying to blame the town. You wouldn't have wanted your house vandalised."

Dr Walton knew that he wasn't going to win the debate and his friend's argument of beating himself up over it being a waste of time managed to break down some barriers in his mind. It had given him a lifeline. Clinically, he knew he made no mistakes regarding Mark Leversee and saying he should have moved out of Ramsgate wasn't practical and they probably wouldn't have done so anyway. Therefore, he should stop the second-guessing. He took courage in that as he went back to work, giving himself a much needed confidence boost. Still the little gremlin, hiding in the dark recesses of his mind and whispering doubts in his ear, would never go away.

Next to legal bills, psychiatry and counselling bills came in second in the expenditure race from Mark's fallout. Like the litigation crocodiles, the mental health vultures also swooped down on the carnage offering their services to help the distressed folk of Ramsgate find closure. A few even offered their services for free saying that it was to help the beleaguered town. The real reason was so they could use it to advertise their services elsewhere. Many of the afflicted took up the offers, some looking for genuine help, others in a bid to push up the compensation claim. Many shrinks would take great pride in claiming that they restored sanity to a city that was victim to an insane tragedy.

It was determined by the professionals that Mike Sigfried would need the most attention. He had been wounded at point blank range and forced to apologise for his supposed wrongs and that is why the city graciously offered to pay for a leading psychiatrist from New York to come down and work with him.

Dr Samuel Horriman lived up to his reputation. He worked extensively with Mike, starting by pointing out that he was a victim of Mark's perceived persecution by him and that the best thing he could do was to show that it wasn't going to get to him. Dr Horriman also explained that Mike had been in the wrong place at the

414

wrong time and had it have been anyone else in that situation, Mark would have done the same thing, or worse, to them. Mike's mind would gradually heal but the trauma he sustained would never completely go away.

For almost four months, Andrew Blumenthaw lay in a coma while everyone waited to see if he would truly become the eighteenth fatality at Mark's hands. Then one sunny day in October, Andrew regained consciousness. The nurse nearby was so excited; she almost fell over a trolley as she went to proclaim the good news. Doctors and nurses rushed in from everywhere to see Andrew awake and asking, "Where am I?"

Parents were told immediately and his entire family got to the hospital as fast as they could. Their joy was overwhelming and they shared it with the ward, the floor and then the entire hospital. Staff and patients who were able to, made it a point to go to where Andrew had slept for four months and observe the miracle for themselves. Someone alerted the media and before anyone realised, the hospital was swamped with press trying to get a picture of the boy who had survived the Tye School massacre. Therefore, most teachers and students already knew about the miracle when Mr Tasker announced it to the school the next morning. It still didn't stop many pupils, especially the eighth graders, from rejoicing.

Andrew's recovery was almost as miraculous as his awakening. He spent another month in hospital undergoing physiotherapy and counselling, which he responded to both very well. Nevertheless, he would still be confined to a wheelchair for the rest of his life, paralysed from the chest down. On top of that, he would never be able to father children; two of Mark's bullets had shattered his spinal cord and for all the skill of the surgeons, it couldn't be repaired. It just made Andrew more determined not to let it beat him.

He returned to Tye School a hero. Pupils cheered him as he wheeled his chair through the corridors. Children competed with each other over the opportunity to push him in his wheelchair but Andrew had another idea. With the help of some of his friends, he was able to force the weaker kids to wheel him around. Gene was definitely targeted for the task. At first, Gene succeeded with his usual tactic of running immediately but eventually he was caught and forced into servitude, with Andrew explaining to him, "Your buddy Leversee isn't around to take the heat for you anymore." Of course, being Gene, he managed to find a replacement. At the beginning of the year, he had befriended John Bettis and as he had done with Mark, used him to be his fall guy. Nothing was done or said about this forced slavery because of Andrew's hero status. It was clear that Mark's actions hadn't changed everything.

Chapter 35

One Year On, Tears For Tye School

Once again, to her mother's exasperation, Leslie had come home in tears. Donna could easily guess the cause behind her daughter's distress, the two girls who lived on the street and were supposed to be her friends. It was always the same. When it was just one of the girls, they got along fine but when it was both of them together, they would gang up on her, saying nasty things to her. This was such a day.

In between cries and sobs, Leslie relayed the latest happening. "They were calling me fat and an ugly witch!" she wailed. "And they kept pushing me." Mother tried he best to calm her distressed daughter but was having little success. Leslie continued crying, screaming, "I hate it here, I want to move!"

Donna hugged her daughter tightly as memories flooded her mind. Since that terrible day a year ago, when she lost Mark, she continued to beat herself up over not moving out of Ramsgate sooner. Her parents, a psychiatrist and a counsellor all tried to tell her that no one could have known that Mark was going to do what he did. That even if she had moved out of Ramsgate, it might not have solved the problem.

She liked Scottsburg and settled in nicely, which had helped to put the recent past behind her. The school Leslie was going to was very good and she was doing very well in it. She was also able to get Douglas into a nursery school and that allowed her to work part time. The only problem was the one her daughter was having with these two girls. Ms Johnston did try to resolve the situation by speaking to the parents but it seemed to have little effect. Inviting friends she had made at school over did relieve the problem somewhat but didn't solve it. Besides, Donna knew in her mind that what Leslie was experiencing wasn't nearly as bad as what Mark had gone through. The dilemma caused her to say out loud, "We had to move out of Ramsgate because of your brother, now it looks like we'll have to move from here because of you." She regretted saying them the instant the words had left her mouth.

Bernard A Tye School's gymnasium was packed beyond capacity for the service commemorating the one-year anniversary of the Tye School shooting. All of the expected families were there, the Cherissos and the Tyes among the most noted. Many of the other victim's families were also in attendance, as well as many others who weren't directly affected by the shooting. The only victim's families who weren't there were the Allens, the Kellermans and the Nickersons. The parents of all three families had been forced to sell their homes and move out on account of the lawsuits against them.

A sombre atmosphere permeated the gymnasium the moment the service commenced. Starting with Sandra Cherisso and then Ann Tye, families of the victims told the sorrowful tale of how they had lost their son, daughter, brother or sister. Some of those who were wounded and survived told of their pain and how they were rebuilding their lives bringing a small feeling of joy to the service.

Not surprisingly, Andrew Blumenthaw got the loudest applause as he wheeled himself across the stage to the microphone that had already been lowered for him. There was a gasp of silence as he spoke: "Why is everyone so sad? The shooting was a year ago and now it's time for moving on. Sitting here acting all sad is the last thing we should be doing because if we do, then he's won and we don't want Marvin Leversee to win.

That's right, I called him Marvin and I don't care. That was the reason why he shot everybody and so I'm going to call him Marvin just to show him that he didn't win."

He paused for a moment to bask in the thunderous applause from his audience. His hero status meant that he could have said anything and achieved the same result. He carried on, "People have said that we picked on him, bullied him. I was supposedly one of them because I wouldn't let him play sports with us. Well that was because he was so bad at them."

This time he had to pause to allow the loud laughter that followed his last statement "No matter what we did to him, it wasn't nearly as bad as what he did to us, to me. Not letting him join in doesn't justify shooting me and putting me in this wheelchair for the rest of my life. But I'm not going to let him beat me. I'm still going to live my life to the full and when I die, I'm going to have put on my grave, "Leversee, you didn't win.""

The applause nearly blew the roof off the gymnasium and lifted the gloom clouds. Andrew's speech set the perfect scene for the next part of the service. An award was given to a girl named Barbara Henry, who was an eighth grader that day and now finishing her freshman year at Downbeach High School. It was she who, when the bullets began flying, managed to get into the school through an unlocked classroom door and run to the teacher's room to raise the alarm. This action probably saved the lives of many pupils, especially those who were in kill zone two that day. Her bravery and quick action was proudly spoken of by Mr Tasker. Obviously, he must have forgotten that one year earlier, when she came to the staff room to inform him that there was some kid with a gun shooting everyone, she was extremely pale and barely able to get the words out due to her fright.

The service moved from the gymnasium to outside at the front of the school for the expected unveiling of the plaque ceremony. It took much longer than expected for the ceremony to begin due to the large crowd in attendance but the nice weather made the wait bearable. All eyes were on Mr Tasker and Mayor Burg as they stood by the main doors near a part of the wall, which had been purposely covered. When it was believed that everyone had made the move to the outdoors, the mayor addressed the crowd:

"One year ago a terrible tragedy befell this school and our city. We lost friends, sons and daughters and brothers and sisters on that horrendous day. Today we pay tribute to those who tragically lost their lives."

Without further procrastination, the two men removed the cover revealing a large plaque with gold lettering. The inscription read, "In loving memory of the seventeen pupils who tragically lost their lives in the shooting that occurred at Bernard A Tye School." Underneath that inscription were the names of the dead, listed in alphabetical order. Mark's name was not among them. Below the names of the dead, another inscription read, "We also dedicate this plaque to those who were wounded but survived that day." Another alphabetical list of the wounded appeared below it.

It bothered some of the teachers that Tommy Allen's name was at the top of the list, remembering what a troublesome kid he was. Mr and Mrs Cherisso had also launched an appeal stating that Lydia's name should have been first on account of her being the most well known of the dead. They used their celebrity status to back up their point and when that didn't work, threatened legal action and withdrawing the financial contribution to the plaque. The mayor stepped in to resolve the situation pointing out that with the names being in alphabetical order, Lydia's would be second and that the letters used for her name on it would be slightly larger. This satisfied the Cherissos but it demonstrated that all was still not rosy in Ramsgate.

Chapter 36

Five Year On, No Escape

Many people in Ramsgate were looking towards the memorial service commemorating the five-year anniversary of the shooting at Bernard A Tye School. The Cherissos were definitely looking forward to it. Their fifteen minutes of fame had long since disappeared and they weren't even considered celebrities at Blessed Mary Virgin Church any longer. This was their chance to step back into the limelight.

Others too were hoping for similar opportunities at the service. Andrew Blumenthaw was looking to boast of how much he had accomplished since that tragic day. He had graduated twelfth in his class at Downbeach High School and had been offered a scholarship at St Joseph's University in Philadelphia. Furthermore, he was considered one of the top wheelchair basketball players in the state. So, no one could really blame him if he wanted to boast to the world of all the achievements he made in spite of his handicap.

The organisers agreed that their decision to hold the service outdoors was a wise one. Not only did the month of June provide great weather, there was also plenty of room for additional chairs to cater for the larger than expected crowd. Chairs were laid out in many long rows in the courtyard in front of a small portable stage. The podium, which had been taken out from the gym, was placed in the centre of it.

Even though none of them had attended Tye School at the time of the shooting, all of the current student body was required to attend as were the teachers, most of whom were there on the day. Naturally, many of the former pupils who had been there on the day came back for the service as well as many in the community who thought it their duty to attend the memorial.

Mr Tasker presided over a service that went as anyone could have predicted. There were the usual talks about the day when seventeen children needlessly lost their lives and many others who would be forever scarred. There was more deserved praise for the police and ambulance services as the audience was reminded of their heroics and special recognition for Randy Kelly who was now a sergeant on the force. The longest but at the same time most interesting speech came from Mayor Burg who had been re-elected as mayor by a landslide two years earlier, unlike Albert Lombardino who became a one-term governor. He said pretty much the same as the previous speakers, recounting the tragedy and how well the city had moved on from it; but he just said it in a more interesting way. When he finished, the mayor introduced the next speaker, Andrew Blumenthaw.

Andrew wheeled himself out onto the stage to rapturous applause. He shook the hands of the mayor and principal before going to the microphone that had been lowered for him. Holding an old copy of Time magazine in the air, he spoke, "This edition of Time magazine came out when I was in the coma. Some of you might remember it, the cover says, 'Ramsgate shooter Mark Leversee, villain or victim?'"

The photo of Mark's face on the cover jogged a few memories. Andrew continued, "Even after five years, there are some who say that the boy on this cover, who put me in this chair and robbed you of a friend or a loved one, is the victim. During all my four years at Downbeach High School, there were kids and adults who told us that we brought this tragedy on ourselves for the way we treated him. We sometimes had to show them otherwise. Maybe some kids did pick on him but it still doesn't justify what he did to us and I wish that reporter from the South Jersey Current, the one who said the town was corrupt, was here. I would tell him a few things. No, we're the victims here but unlike that boy, I won't use it as an excuse."

Andrew left the stage to more thunderous applause, making the next speaker a tough act to follow. The organisers had planned it that way in the form of the next speaker who was fifteen-year-old Patty Fitzpatrick, David's younger sister. Patty was already becoming a beautiful young woman. Her long light brown hair, that was tied back, and her light blue eyes seemed to punctuate her small round face. Even though it was a hot day, she wore nothing revealing but instead loose fitting clothes that disguised, but not fully concealed, her gorgeous body. However, she was more than just physically attractive. She had a gift for acting and in her first year at Downbeach High became the first freshman ever to get a major role in a school production. She was also a gifted singer and it was her oratory skills and her father's influence that got her chosen to address the audience on this day.

Her modest beauty had the majority of the males looking at her before she began speaking and her skills as an actress grabbed the attention of the rest when she did. She told the assembled, "I lost my brother that day. David was always good to me. He was the only brother I had so I can't compare him to others- but to me, he was a good brother. I do remember when he supposedly wrecked this boy's bike and my father had to fix it for him. The reason why my father had to fix it was because the family of the boy who is responsible for all of us being here today thought that we should buy him a new bike. My father was right, they were the type that

424

tried to get what they could from people."

What Patty said in the rest of her speech and the way she said it had the audience completely mesmerised. Her acting skills definitely paid off because no one could see that underneath the articulate thoughtful girl, Patty Fitzpatrick was drowning in the wake of her parent's mourning over her dead brother.

Sandra Cherisso thought she should have been higher up the order but being at the very end had its advantages. She was able to completely scan the audience for any evidence of Mario Satriano or her daughter in attendance, she found none. As a result, she confidently ascended the stage and stopping at the podium, shamelessly held the infamous rosary beads out for all to see.

"Five years on and I still think of Lydia everyday," she told those sitting in the audience. "I think of how she dropped these beads because she was following her faith when the bullet struck her." Her words brought back memories of the revival tour and she spoke them with a renewed purpose. The story might have been the same but for her, it never got old. She made sure everybody remembered that. It didn't matter what had changed since the shooting, the fact that she was now wealthy from the lawsuits and the revival tour that first summer or the fact that she had a three year old daughter after becoming pregnant in the months following the tour. All that mattered was that everyone remembered her grief.

What she didn't know was that sitting in the audience with his class was thirteen-year-old Paul Satriano. At the conclusion of the service, he went home and told his mother about the lady with the rosary beads speaking at the service and how her daughter dropped them when she got shot. All Maria said to her son was "Oh really," but inwardly she renewed her five year vow not to talk to Sandra Cherisso.

Ramsgate wasn't the only place where the Tye School shooting was remembered. Nearly 170 miles away in Scottsburg, Pennsylvania, Donna Johnston was having her own private remembrance. Like Andrew Blumenthaw, Mark would have graduated from high school. She inwardly shed some tears about the son who she would never see graduate high school and become a man.

What kept her going was the amount she had accomplished in the past five years. She no longer had to rely on her parents as she got a job and worked her way into a better one. That meant she was able to move out of her parents' home and find a place for her and her two children. It also meant that Leslie was able to escape from the "mean girls" and that made her daughter much happier. For those reasons alone, Donna could focus on the positive.

When she wasn't working or spending time with her children, she was involved in her group. Peace In Our Time or PIOT was a group dedicated against violence and war and she was very active in it. They were often thought of as a bunch of hippy radicals by many people even though the group was proven to be harmless and they assisted in many local projects; she found solace in the group.

Recently, she had attracted the attention of a new member of the group, a man by the name of John Peddlemore. John was nothing like Ted or Rusty. He hadn't served in the military, which he was told was the main obstacle to winning the attention of Donna Johnston. He was told by another member of the group how Donna had walked out in the middle of a date because the man had said he had been in the army. John not only stated that he hadn't been in the service, he looked like it too. He had long hair that went almost to his neckline and always seemed to have two days stubble on his face. Furthermore, he always wore faded jeans, which were sometimes ripped. This and the energy he gave to the cause was what attracted him to Donna.

They had been on three dates and things seemed to be going well. John was so much the opposite of Ted and nothing like her ex-husband, Donna longed for it to grow into something more. That was the reason why on their fourth date, she made plans to invite him into her inner sanctum.

It had been a lovely evening. They had a nice dinner at a Hungarian restaurant in a town ten miles away from Scottsburg. After the meal, they went dancing at a nearby nightspot where they danced fairly late into the night. The situation couldn't help but invite romance into it making the rest of the night a foregone conclusion.

The lovely evening turned into a magical night. John discovered there were some definite advantages to joining the group and Donna got something she had secretly missed for five years. Therefore, it was a great night for both of them and both went to sleep feeling fulfilled and contented.

When John awoke the next morning, the space in the bed next to him was empty. He could hear Donna downstairs making breakfast for her children and their voices as well. This gave him time to wake up properly and that was when he saw it. On a small table near her bureau was a shrine to her late eldest son. He already knew that she had a son named Mark who died when a drunk driver had knocked him off his bike and that he was only thirteen when he died. He wasn't surprised that she would have so many pictures of him around the urn that contained his ashes on the table. However, as he studied Mark's face in the photos, he couldn't rid himself of the thought that there was something hauntingly familiar about him.

Donna felt like a giddy schoolgirl when she saw John at the next meeting. She was glad that he had followed her advice to be clean-shaven because he looked so much better without the stubble. The next time they went out, he asked a lot of questions about Mark, although nothing intrusive. Thinking he was just trying to get to know her more, she told John about his Asperger's Syndrome and DAMP conditions and stated that was why the drunk driver who knocked him off his bike only got six months in jail. He listened with great interest.

He said he had to go away for work so the fledgling couple didn't see each other for a week. The next time they did was at the PIOT meeting, only this time, John looked totally different. Gone were the faded jeans and t-shirt and in their place was a black suit and matching tie. He had also gotten a haircut. Donna almost didn't recognise him and when they did speak, he seemed a little standoffish with her.

John didn't sit down when the meeting was called to order but stood next to an unknown man who was similarly dressed. It was obvious the two men knew each other. The bespectacled chairman, a tall thin man with a long nose and long grey hair that was tied back in a ponytail and a beard of the same colour, turned the podium over to John.

"I have a confession to make," he began. "My name isn't John Peddlemore, I am Special Agent Robert Pitcairn of Homeland Security." Observing the surprised and even enraged faces of members in the audience, he continued, "I was assigned to work undercover to investigate the group to determine if it was a threat to national security. I can safely say that Peace In Our Time poses no threat to the security of the nation. I would like to apologise for my deception and can only say that it was in the interest of our country that I did it. However, I am not the only person here who has been dishonest with you. With me here is Special Agent Glenn Ainsworth from the FBI who will tell you more."

Donna was sure that the infiltrator had been looking directly at her during his last few sentences. She looked back at him with fury, feeling used and betrayed and continued watching him as he walked away from the microphone. She was so focused on him, she didn't notice Glenn Ainsworth ascend to the microphone, nor would she have ever known that he had put on a considerable amount of weight in the past five years.

The FBI agent absorbed the icy stares form those sitting in front of him, cleared his throat and started, "Five years ago, I investigated a school shooting in Ramsgate, New Jersey."

He paused briefly to allow his audience to recall ancient history. "You probably don't remember, but the shooting was carried out by a thirteen year old boy named Mark Leversee. Leversee went into Bernard A Tye Middle School with an Uzi and a nine millimetre pistol and opened fire on his classmates, killing seventeen of them and wounding twenty eight more before turning the gun on himself."

While Glenn was speaking, no one noticed the former John Peddlemore manoeuvring his way back to the microphone and standing behind his friend. Glenn stepped aside to let John take the mike again. John declared, "The mother of Mark Leversee is sitting here among you. You know her by her maiden name, Johnston, but when she was married, she was Donna Leversee. So, you know now that her son wasn't killed by a motorist while riding his bike, he shot himself after murdering seventeen other children."

Murmurs in the crowd were overshadowed by a scream of "You bastard!" from a highly enraged Donna. Without hesitation, she rushed up to where the man she had let inside her stood and hit him with a vicious slap that jerked his head violently to the right. Special Agent Ainsworth moved in to restrain her but Robert called him off. Donna turned and faced the now dumbfounded audience, not realising that some of them were actually applauding her, and shouted, "My son was bullied, picked on, teased mercilessly!" Not knowing what else to say, she turned and exited the hall.

The two government agents left shortly after that. Robert Pitcairn had accomplished his mission and was now feeling very glib. He had destroyed the credibility of a potential subversive organisation and had sown discord in their ranks. The fallout, of course, was in the form of Donna Johnston, whose past had now caught up with her and was now in tatters. However, he wasn't totally unsympathetic. He really liked her and would have loved to have had a relationship with her. But how could he trust someone who couldn't be honest about her son? For Donna, it was now clear that she would never be fully able to escape the past.

Chapter 37

Nine And a Quarter Years On, Leslie's Story

It was the second week of Leslie's final year of high school and Donna Johnston watched with pride as her daughter left the house. In spite of all that had happened, Leslie was turning out to be a well-adjusted young lady. She was set to graduate in the top ten of her class and was a major figure in the school's anti-bullying campaign. Furthermore, she was getting offers from major universities to allow her to pursue her interest in chemical engineering. Donna couldn't have been prouder.

She too, had come out the other end very well after all that she had been through. To her surprise, PIOT had stuck by her. They deeply resented the fact that the government had sent somebody to spy on their peaceful little group. As for Mark, the chairman explained that most in the group understood how a traumatic event such as her son's shooting spree would make her so opposed to violence in any form. They were also sympathetic to the way Mark had been treated in Ramsgate. On top of that, the group also dealt with the fallout. When the local newspaper ran the story about it, PIOT was quick to come out with a rebuttal; so stories about her being the mother of the devil's child were soon forgotten. It was no wonder she had every reason to be happy, although this didn't stop her from lamenting over Mark at times.

She did have one concern and that was with her youngest son, Douglas. Now twelve, it seemed he was the complete opposite of Mark in one respect, dealing with bullies. He wasn't a bully himself, but unlike the older brother he hardly got to know, he stood up to the slightest hint of any physical or verbal aggression directed towards him. As a result, he had gotten into many fights, eight in sixth grade alone, none of which he started. The situation became more aggravated when one boy, Douglas's version of David Fitzpatrick, would get others to start trouble with Douglas in the hopes there would be a fight. When he was asked the reason, he would respond with, "I don't want to end up like my brother." Obviously, the school became concerned with his anger issues.

The top school officials also knew about Mark but they only gave that information out on a need to know basis. Nothing about it was ever mentioned when Leslie had attended the school because she went through with flying colours. It was hoped that the same would hold true for Douglas; that hope was proven to be rather naïve. Douglas seemed to react to the slightest threat of intimidation or bullying with violence. It resulted in him being sent to Anger Management classes and given training on how to stand up for himself without resorting to violence.

Leslie too was brought in to help her younger brother. Ever since she was in seventh grade, she was active in school anti-bullying groups. Now a senior, many assumed she would be elected president of the Anti-Bullying Coalition at Scottsburg-Eppindale High School. But a fly in the ointment had appeared at the start of the term. While she laboured hard to address bullying at her high school, her efforts also made her enemies with certain elements. Jocks and Barbie Dolls and others who thought they had the right to throw their privileged weight around accused Leslie of strictly targeting them. In response, they chose one from among their ranks to oppose her in the election for president of the Anti-Bullying Coalition. Straight away, they began a smear campaign against her stating that the reason she targeted jocks and cheerleaders was because she hated the school and had no school spirit. They also tried to hint that she was a lesbian. Leslie's response was to challenge her opponent to a debate.

Normally, the matter would have remained inside the coalition but Leslie suggested the debate be held in front of the entire student body. The opposition, thinking she was playing straight into their hands, agreed. She knew her opponent's supporters would try to discredit her in front of the entire school and she also knew that her opponent, Candy Owens, wasn't just some dumb blonde; she had some brains as well. Therefore, Leslie prepared for battle on two fronts.

Leslie Johnston was by no means unattractive. She had long dark hair that hung down to the middle of her back. She just chose to tie it back most of the time and her body could rival that of any cheerleader. She didn't feel the need to expose her flesh or wear anything that advertised that she hadn't been cheated in the upper body department. This didn't stop her from spending a few extra minutes in front of the mirror or deciding not to tie her hair back on the day of the debate.

Predictably, Candy Owens came into the debate wearing a cleavage exposing top and a very short skirt. Her appearance might have given her the initial advantage with most of the males as they watched the two candidates shake hands and go to their respective podiums for the big showdown. Leslie just hoped that all of her mental preparation would win the day for her.

Just like presidential candidates, both young women braced for the first question from the panel of two students and two teachers. The male student on the panel, a football player, directed his question at Candy. "What will you do to end bullying at Scottsburg-

Eppindale High School?"

Candy smiled to the students in the auditorium and answered, "I would address the fact that all students can be bullies or victims of it. For too long, certain groups of students have been singled out as bullies for no other reason than the fact they're successful and unfairly blamed for all of the bullying at the school. I will address all bullying no matter who does it."

Applause followed her response, most of it from her jock following. Leslie didn't have to wait long for it to die down before she had her chance to redirect. She was expecting Candy's answer so she countered, "The current anti-bullying policies do not target any particular group of students nor is there any zeal among the members of the anti-bullying coalition to do so. All reported cases are dealt with on an individual basis and I would ensure that continues to be the case. However, I will say that of the seventy five percent of reported cases of bullying among the boys, those considered to be jocks or of the so-called privileged group were identified as being the bullies."

She paused for a second to let her audience digest the statistics and then suggested, "It seems like my opponent is suggesting that we either turn a blind eye to jocks who bully or tell children of other social groups to bully more so we can even out the numbers a bit."

The student body laughed at her quip and Leslie saw that she was now one up on Candy. The girl on the panel directed her question at her "Are there certain groups of kids who are more likely to be victims of bullying than others?"

Leslie responded, "First, anyone can be a bully or a victim of bullying. Statistically, most victims tend not to belong to any group but be loners and considered outcasts by the "popular" kids. Now, it has been said that we give special attention to stoners when they

434

become a victim. They say that with they're chosen lifestyle, they deserve what they get. Nobody deserves to be bullied! While I don't condone what the stoners might do, I also know that is not a justification for bullying them."

Because Leslie's answer seemed to cover all bases, Candy could only give a waffled rebuttal. Likewise, when the teachers on the panel asked their questions asked their questions, Leslie came out on top with both of her responses. The result was sending the jock on the panel into a desperate panic. Fearful that the stooge his comrades had planted was going to get slaughtered on points, he decided to go on a more personal offensive. He asked, "Leslie Johnston, why do you have such a fanaticism against bullying? I've never seen anyone bullying you."

She knew that he was right; no one actually ever openly bullied her. She often saw girls whispering behind her back but nothing in the open. Still, she was cautious about her answer. "I just hate bullying in any form."

That answer didn't satisfy the boy who asked the question. He probed further, "There must be something in your past. I mean no one is committed to a cause such as this unless there's some sort of history behind it."

Things she had buried deep down inside her now found their way back to her brain and were now bursting to come out of her. There definitely was a history behind her anti-bullying zeal and she knew it and knew why. At first, she fought to suppress it but she knew that doing so would result in her giving some garbled, disingenuous response. She was also aware that telling the truth might lose her the election and make her an outcast, but she believed that it was a risk she would have to take. The jocks wanted a reason; she would give it to them with both barrels.

"The reason why I hate bullying so much is that I have seen the harm it can do. My name wasn't always Leslie Johnston. Originally, my name was Leslie Leversee; Johnston is my mother's maiden name. My brother was Mark Leversee who, when we lived in Ramsgate, New Jersey ten years ago, was bullied so bad, that he felt he had no other option than to get a gun and shoot seventeen kids dead and wound many more. The reason why he felt he had no other option was because the school and even the police did nothing about the bullying he was suffering. I believe that if that school had a group such as ours, then my brother would still be alive today and so would all of those other kids. That's why I hate bullying so much; it took my brother."

Deathly silence, mixed with whisperings of "Oh my God," reverberated through the school auditorium. Candy weakly tried to capitalise on it, but all she could say was, "She's doing it because of her dead brother." The atmosphere during the rest of the debate wasn't the same after that. Somehow empowered by her admission, the final three questions came easy for her and she wiped the floor with Candy Owens in the final rounds. She could only hope that she could win the election so easily.

She expected the stares that greeted her over the next couple of days. Even her closest friends didn't know what to say. Pondering the debate at her locker at the end of school, her thoughts were disrupted by a vaguely familiar male voice calling out, "Hi Leslie."

She turned around to see a boy known as Chuck Hearns standing behind her. Chuck was captain of the cross-country team but wasn't considered a real jock. At least he didn't have the arrogant attitude of the football and basketball players and wrestlers, many of whom viewed cross-country with the same lack of regard schools the world over view the minority sports. Leslie and her friends secretly considered him a heartthrob because he stood six feet tall and was thin but not bony. He had straight blonde hair that Leslie remembered blowing wildly in the wind when he ran and sparkling blue eyes. All of this made her wonder why he was talking to her.

"That was a very brave thing you said at the debate," he told her. "I don't think I could have said that."

She shyly smiled at him and explained; "I don't think most of the school is going to agree with you on that first bit."

"You might be surprised," he replied reassuringly. Seeing her blush but not reply, Chuck decided to seize the day. "Do you want to go out this weekend?"

Without even pausing a second to think about it, she accepted his offer. This would mark the beginning of a series of fortunate events for her. The next one came the following week, when she was elected president of the Anti-Bullying Coalition by a sixty percent to forty percent margin.

Chapter 38

Ten Years On, A Reconciliation of Sorts

"Why was she so determined to bring up the past?" Donna thought to herself as she watched her daughter. It had been bad enough that nine months earlier, Leslie had revealed the identity of her infamous brother to her entire high school, now she was planning to go back to Ramsgate for the remembrance service commemorating the tenth anniversary of the shooting. She tried to reason with her daughter, "All they're going to do is say what an evil kid your brother was and how weird he was, conveniently forgetting his condition. Even if you do say something in his defence, no one gonna like it. They'll take it all out on you."

"I'm not doing this to hurt you, mother," Leslie tried to reassure. "I'm going there for me, I need to go to Ramsgate and see things for myself."

Mother opened her mouth to ask, "What things?" but the words never came out. She knew that she couldn't stop her daughter from going. Leslie was eighteen now and had just graduated eighth in her class from high school. In September, she would be heading off to Penn State University. She was now a grown woman. So mother only advised, "Be careful" to her as Leslie met the young man who had just turned up at the door for her.

After giving Chuck a kiss on the lips, she turned back to her mother and reassured her, "Don't worry mom, I'll be okay."

Chuck reinforced it with, "I'll look after her."

Ms Johnston couldn't help but feel worried for her daughter as she watched the happy couple walk towards Chuck's car. The sight caused her to turn her head to the mantle where their prom photo stood. Her first thought was that they should have been prom king and queen. After all, they did make a lovely couple, but as the car drove away, the thoughts changed to the belief that Leslie was going to be all right.

A thousand thoughts warred in Leslie's mind as her boyfriend's car sped down the Expressway. They temporarily called a cease-fire when the car pulled into a service stop. While she squared herself away in front of a mirror in the ladies' toilet after performing the necessities, a young woman engaged in the same tasks struck up a conversation with her.

"Are you heading to the shore?" the woman asked in a straightforward manner.

"Yes, my boyfriend and I are going to Ramsgate for a couple of days," Leslie replied.

"What, you're not going to the tenth anniversary of the shooting service, are you?" he woman asked, perplexed.

Leslie thought about her answer for a second before coming up with, "No, we're just going for a couple of days on the beach. "Why, is it going to be a big thing?"

"Oh yeah," the woman answered. "The town will use it as a big excuse to feel sorry for themselves and act all the victim over it. They still do when it's appropriate." Without further prompting she carried on, "I'm from Bridgend, which is near Ramsgate and we go to the same high school as the kids from there. I was just starting my freshman year in the September after it all happened. Before school started on the first day, they got all the kids from Bridgend and Vincent, who went to the school, into the auditorium and explained to us that we had to be sympathetic to the kids from Ramsgate after what they had been through. Let me tell you, the kids from Ramsgate came into the school expecting everyone to feel sorry for them, even the kids who had already been in high school when it happened. Any time there was trouble involving a kid from Ramsgate, they would play the "I'm suffering from a trauma" card and no one would say anything. If anyone offered an alternative viewpoint to their side of the story, they would get shit for it. I mean a kid from my town once said he heard that the kid who shot them all was bullied. Well, all the kids from Ramsgate took immediate offence and put in a complaint against him and this one kid named Joe Callazone beat him up over it. Nothing was done about it because it was concluded that the kid from my town was telling lies about the shooting.

I did go out with a boy from Ramsgate named Matt Barber for two weeks in my sophomore year. He used to show off the wound he received to his abdomen that day and expected everyone to either feel sorry for him or think he was some great survivor. He also used to moan about how the kid got him fired from the school newspaper because he ran a story in it saying the kid was gay. I'll tell you what, I think they did bully that kid to the point where he snapped, they just don't want to admit it."

She let out a sigh of relief after divulging all that information, which Leslie took on board with a smile. Leslie filed it away in a compartment in her brain in case she needed to call upon it later on. Outwardly, she said nervously, "I guess I'll stay away from there."

Anxieties returned as Chuck's car entered Ramsgate's city limits. She was slightly surprised to find how much of the town she recognised after being away for ten years. But that wasn't important, what was important was the event going on at Tye School. The words from the woman she had met at the rest stop still remained with her and acted as a buffer against the things she was going to hear at the service.

She had only seen Bernard A Tye School on a handful of occasions when she was with her mother picking Mark up. The building didn't look any different as she approached it on foot. It was when she got to the main doors that she spotted something she knew was going to be different, the plaque commemorating Mark's atrocity, or was it revenge? It was only out of dumb optimism she stopped to read it and she wasn't in the least surprised when she didn't see her brother's name listed among the dead. She also stored that fact in her brain as she passed through the metal detectors and the main doors.

Pupils helped guide the assembling throng from the main doors, around a corner and then out another set of doors. This didn't stop her from surveying the school she might have gone to if things had been different. She followed the crowd out of the second set of doors and that was when she saw three boys picking on and teasing another boy, who looked vulnerable. Always intolerant of bullying in any form, Leslie went over to them and demanded to know, "What gives you the right to gang up on this boy?"

The self-appointed spokesman for the three gruffly retorted, "But he's weird." Expecting that sort of comment, she replied, "That's no reason to bully somebody. Don't you know that this was what today's all about? Someone who got picked on because kids said he was weird to the point where he couldn't take it anymore and ended up getting a gun and shooting up the school."

A second boy responded with, "I heard that he did it because his name was Mark and everyone called him Marvin."

Leslie had to pause a second to fight back the rage now bubbling inside her. Had the town of Ramsgate trivialised the shooting down to that? She wanted to roar her reaction at these misinformed children, but she knew that it wasn't their fault. Therefore, she reiterated, "No, he was bullied badly, so badly that he felt he had no other choice than to get a gun and shoot his tormentors." It became instantly clear that Mark's actions hadn't changed everything.

She didn't have time to gauge the three boys' reactions as a voice from behind distracter her. "What, you believe all that crap about the kid being picked on?"

Leslie turned around to see a young man in his early twenties in a wheelchair with very short black hair and two days stubble on his face. A blue basketball shirt with USA in red lettering across the front fitted tightly over his muscular upper body that was most likely developed from spending years in the chair. She didn't have to guess that this man was in the wheelchair on account of Mark. Coming face to face with this reality made her hesitate a moment.

Not letting his disability intimidate her, she looked him in the eye and answered with the question, "What other reason would he have for carrying out such an act?"

"Cause he was weird," the young man boldly stated. She felt that she shouldn't even qualify that answer with a response. Instead, she grabbed Chuck from off the sideline and went to find a seat.

Like the five-year anniversary, the playground was filled with many seats arranged in long rows, set before a small stage with that same podium in the centre. Mr Tasker, still the principal but looking noticeably older, welcomed the audience to the service. "Ten years ago today, a terrible tragedy occurred at Tye School, which affected many of us here today. On that day, ten years ago, a former pupil came into our school with a couple of guns and shot many of his classmates. Seventeen children lost their lives that day."

"No, eighteen," Leslie thought to herself fighting off her desire to shout it.

Mr Tasker was still speaking, "Twenty eight more were wounded and many more of us were mentally or emotionally scarred by the event. For the tenth anniversary service, we have decided to do things a little different. After we hear from the first and only scheduled speaker, we will leave the microphone open to anyone who wants to come up and share their thoughts. So without any further delay, here's our first speaker. He was wounded on that tragic day and has been confined to a wheelchair ever since. But he hasn't let that stop him from getting a degree from St Joseph's University and has now completed his first year of law school. On top of that, he will be playing on the US wheelchair basketball team at the next paralympics. Please welcome to the stage, Andrew Blumenthaw."

Leslie watched the man she had just debated with wheel himself across the stage to the podium while basking in the applause. Taking the microphone, which had been positioned for him, he addressed the audience, "I have just had a conversation with a young lady who says that the boy who caused us to be here today was a victim. Okay, I agree, many people picked on him and maybe we should have cut him some more slack and if he hadn't done what he did and was here today, I would apologise to him for the way we treated him. But I can't because he's not here, just like so many of my friends who aren't here because of him. I am reminded of that every day because I have to use this wheelchair every day. Anything I, or others, might have done to him, he more than got us back for. Reflecting back, I couldn't have been one of the ones he wanted dead because those he shot in the head at point blank range after he wounded them. Then I think of my friend David Fitzpatrick who he shot full of holes as David lay on the ground. So, I guess you can say I was lucky. The best thing we can do now is to go on with our lives and achieve something. That's what I did and I'm sure that is what those who died that day would have wanted."

Like all of the previous remembrance services, Andrew left the stage to a huge standing ovation. Any thoughts about long periods of people watching an empty microphone were quickly erased as Sandra Cherisso took to the stage as Andrew was leaving it. Predictably, she held out her daughter's rosary beads. "Ten years later and not a day goes by where I don't think about my Lydia," she began. "These rosary beads remind me of her every day and the faith she showed just before she died holding these beads and praying. It continues to give me strength even after ten years." Suddenly, she found herself unable to say anymore; she broke down in tears and quickly exited the stage.

Sandra's quick and sorrowful departure from the stage meant that she never noticed Maria Satriano taking the microphone next. Unlike the speaker before her, she wasn't accustomed to speaking to large audiences, so she felt a little nervous at first. But what she wanted to say had built up in her for nearly ten years and it was now time to get it off her chest.

"My daughter wasn't killed or wounded that day," she began. "She managed to get safely inside the classroom when the bullets began flying. In all the confusion, she dropped her rosary beads. Obviously, her prayers were answered because she escaped unharmed and I thank God everyday for that. Apparently, days after the shooting, the police took my daughter's beads to the home of the previous speaker assuming they belonged to their daughter. It was an easy mistake to make because after all, they were found by her body. But instead of returning them, the last speaker decided to take them to religious revivals and use them to tell of their daughter's tragic story. We only found out the truth when she displayed them at our own church and my Sherry recognised her rosary beads. So, the beads you just saw a few minutes ago do belong to her daughter, only they weren't being used to pray when she got shot.

Now, I don't want to demean anyone who lost their child on the horrific day. What happened will live with all of us for the rest of our lives and my sympathies go out to all the families who lost children that day or were wounded. What I can't abide are people who want to dishonestly use what happened for their own gain."

Maria's speech left the audience in silence while Leslie inwardly rejoiced in the thought that Ramsgate wasn't as squeaky-clean as it made itself out to be. She sat back and eagerly awaited any backlash. It wasn't dramatic but all of the assembled got to see Sandra Cherisso leave the service crying fiercely with her husband following behind her.

The next few speakers all blended in together. All of them talked about the tragic event and how their child was needlessly killed or wounded and while none of them openly attacked Mark, they made some nasty insinuations about him. Then a middle- aged woman calling herself Gladys Sigfried stepped in front of the microphone.

"My son Mike wasn't killed that day but he often feels some days that it would have been better if he had. Many of his friends died that day and he has never fully recovered from the trauma the Leversee boy put him through. He shot my son in the legs and then as he lay on the ground, he came over and shot him in the shoulder and then the buttocks demanding he take back all the supposed wrongs Mike had committed against him. Even when he took it all back, Leversee shot another bullet that bounced off the ground near his head to scare him more. Mike has never really recovered from that day in spite of all of the psychiatrist intervention and counselling. He can only work part time because the stress makes it too much for him. But what really makes me mad is that after the shooting, we were sued by the parents of another child who was wounded on that day because my son was said to have bullied him. So for us, it was like getting shot twice."

The anguish of Gladys Sigfried was plain for all to see even more so than any of the previous speakers. However, she wasn't fooling Leslie. She must have read Mark's dying declaration ten thousand times over and knew the things that Mike Sigfried had done to him. She did think that whoever sued the Sigfrieds went over the top a bit because the entire school was guilty of the sufferings inflicted upon her brother. It didn't stop her feeling uneasy when she heard the details of how Mark exacted his revenge on Mike.

Thoughts of Candy Owens entered Leslie's mind as she watched the next speaker walk across the stage. She observed that the young woman with short brown hair and wearing a short black dress had Chuck's attention as well, but inwardly wondered if her eloquence as a speaker would match her looks. Her first thought was that this young lady was the younger sister of one of Mark's victims and was going to say how they innocently lost their life to her weird, psycho brother. As a result, she prepared herself to listen to more bullshit.

Patty Fitzpatrick proved the first part of Leslie's theory to be correct as she introduced herself to the audience. She declared to all, "I'm not going to repeat the things I said five years ago. That's not the point of this service and I'm reminded all the time about my brother David. It's been ten years and his memory still lives on and always will in my parents' house and my mind. For the past ten years, we've been telling ourselves that we should hate the boy responsible for all of us being here today and we should hate his family. Well, I can't hate him; I hate what he did but I don't hate him anymore. You see, hate is what caused all of this to happen. He thought that everybody hated him because of how some people picked on him. He, in turn, hated everybody else and that hate led him to go out and murder people. Now we all hate him because of the sorrow he caused.

I say that it's time to break that cycle of hatred. We need to forgive him, forgive each other and most importantly, forgive ourselves. This is truly the only way we can really move on and put it all behind us; finally healing those who were wounded in body and soul. It's what those who died that day would have wanted.

Patty's speech lasted a few minutes longer. That gave Leslie plenty of time to rise from her seat and take her place to be next on stage. While she waited, her anxiety made her unable to listen to the rest of what Patty was saying. That anxiety rose further when Patty finished and started walking towards her. A force from somewhere inside her got Leslie up onto the stage and as she passed Patty, she whispered to her, "You might want to listen to this."

As she looked out into the crowd, she realised that this was nothing like the debate she had won nine months earlier. The crowd was going to be hostile to what she was going to say but she still had to say it. Therefore, she leaned into the microphone and orated, "What the last speaker has just said is right, we do have to stop hating. You don't know me but for the past ten years, I've hated all of you for taking away the eighteenth person who died on this day ten years ago, my brother Mark Leversee."

A chorus of boos began and then came the expected shouts of "Get off the stage!" from people in the audience, one unknown person adding "Bitch" to his command. Mr Tasker, several teachers and two police officers, one of them Lieutenant Randy Kelly, positioned themselves between the front row and the stage to head off anyone who thought of rushing it. Leslie feared it too, so she quickly continued.

"I'm not here to praise my brother or to justify what he did ten years ago. There is no justification for it. Originally, I was going to explain about his Asperger's Syndrome and DAMP conditions, which everyone seems to have forgotten about. It was his conditions that caused him to do the things that people called "weird." Some people said that he made up stories about him being a hockey player and that he was a liar. Yes, he did make it up but I can still remember him playing the games in the backyard or if the weather was bad, on the computer, leading his team to victory. I didn't see the harm in it and for him; it provided an escape from all of his suffering. But to many people, that was a license to brand him a weirdo. That was one of the reasons he was singled out and picked on so much.

When he or my mother complained to the schools and even the police, they seemed powerless or unwilling to do anything. When an adult abused him, he was the one made out to be the troublemaker and kids bullied him for getting the adult who abused him into trouble. I know you are all aware of these facts because I read that many of them were widely used in the many lawsuits that were filed after the shooting.

What changed for me was before the service when I

448

came face to face with one of Mark's victims, your first speaker. All I could think afterwards was that my brother had put him in that chair and I felt bad about that. Three days after the shooting, while shopping with my mother, one of my school friends said to me, "Your brother's a murderer." I cried my eyes out at the time but she's right, my brother was a murderer. He killed eighteen people that day, including himself, and wounded many more. Plus, there are all the mental and emotional scars left behind. Two words describe what caused that day: hate and intolerance. People were intolerant of my brother's condition and showed that intolerance through mental and physical abuse. As a result, he hated the people who were picking on him. That hate caused him to get two guns and shoot forty-five kids and then himself. Now all of you hate him for doing that and some of you hate each other as well. The young woman who spoke before me was right; it's time to break that cycle of hate. It's time to say, 'I'm sorry' and move on. I will start things off by saying "Sorry" on Mark's behalf. I wish I could go back in time to that morning. I would say to him, "No, you don't need to do this, there is another way and together we can help you." But I can't, all I can do is to try to understand, make sense of it all and move on and finally forgive.

Less than a second after Leslie had finished speaking, Patty was back on stage making a beeline for the podium. Leslie stepped aside, letting Patty take the microphone. "She's absolutely right," Patty said into the mike, "We do need to forgive and I forgive your brother."

It was now Leslie's turn. She went back to the microphone and declared, "I forgive your brother and everybody else in Ramsgate."

The two young ladies faced each other. After a brief second, Leslie extended her hand forward, which Patty accepted and shook hands before Patty and Leslie proceeded to walk off the stage together. Applause started as a few splutters but with each step they took grew more substantial, so by the time the girls had left the stage, the Tye School playground was deafened by the thunderous clapping of hands.

Things settled down almost immediately after Patty and Leslie left the stage and returned to their respective seats. Attention was now turned on the heavily pregnant woman with long brown hair, round glasses and wearing a long green dress with yellow flowers waddling across the stage to the podium. Like with all speakers, the audience quietened down to listen to what she had to say.

With a look of sincerity, she spoke, "The last two speakers are right, it's time to stop hating and forgive. I've remained silent for ten years now. The one time I did say something, my parents' house was vandalised. So, I'm going to say it now. I witnessed the hell that Mark Leversee went through when he was in school. He would walk down the hall and either get punched by Tommy Allen or pushed into the wall by Joe Kellerman, so part of me doesn't blame Mark for the way he killed them. And I'm sorry Mrs Sigfried, but your son Mike did bully him, always punching him in the back and twisting the knife when he was upset. I don't condone what Mark Leversee did that day. The idea of him shooting all of those kids still makes my blood curdle.

But I also know that he wasn't a total psycho either. That is why I'm going to break a pact I made with two friends ten years ago today. We agreed never to speak about this but I think it's time I did. On the day before Mark committed his carnage, he asked my two friends and me to meet him before school the next day. On the next day, we waited for him but he never turned up,

450

now we know why. The three of us believe that he wanted us out of the way when he went to the school to commit his horrible act. I think the reason why he saved us was because we were good to him and even defended him at times. Therefore, I am sure he wanted to save us. That proves to me that he wasn't some monster; he was human and vulnerable. This is why we need to stop hating and forgive."

Sarah Einhorn (formerly Levine) left the stage to half hearted applause. She was just glad that there were no openly hostile comments directed at her when she went to sit down. No one recognised the next young lady ascending to the stage, especially as she was accompanied by a toddler whose coffee coloured skin and frizzy hair gave away his dual ethnicity. However, had he been there, Mark would have still recognised his angel right away. The ebony black hair now had blonde highlights and the peaches had grown to full fruition and then some and the legs that extended below the smart tan shorts would have continued to work their hypnotic magic upon him.

Lisa addressed the crowd: "None of you here have ever met me before, although ten years ago some of you contacted me on Facebook. You wrote to me telling me how weird Mark Leversee was, that he was a liar, that his real name was Marvin and that he was gay. I only knew him in the flesh for a week but it was enough for me to know that none of that stuff was true, especially the last one. I also remember him as a strong Christian who wanted to do nothing more than to serve his God. He told me about the things he was suffering, especially that teacher who had indecently assaulted him. The problem was that I was so caught up in my own problems that I couldn't help him. I still feel guilty about that now because I sometimes think that if I hadn't let him go, then none of this would have happened."

She paused a moment to fight back the impending tears before continuing, "It all has given me doubt whether or not there is a God. I mean, how could any loving God have someone like Mark, who wanted nothing more than to love and serve him, and heap so much misery on him that he felt the only way out was to go out and shoot people? I don't know- but the last three speakers are right. We need to stop seeing Mark as some monster and stop all the hate."

Generic applause accompanied Lisa as she left the stage. Like Sarah, she was just glad that there were no open attacks on her. She was also glad that she had the courage to say something on Mark's behalf and hopefully make sense out of all her mixed feelings over the past ten years. Because none of the religion that her parents had tried to pound into her head throughout her youth ever did.

Mr Tasker followed on after Lisa signifying the end of the service, though some believed it was to stop the relaying of any more sympathies towards Mark. He thanked everybody for attending and those who spoke before concluding with his final thoughts: "I remember both sides of Mark Leversee. I still have nightmares over all of the destruction he caused ten years ago, I saw it first hand. The casualties he inflicted make it very easy for me to see him as a monster. It also makes it difficult to remember what he was like before the shooting. I dealt with the many instances he was picked on and I can just as easily see him as a victim. My mind is still tortured by the question I keep asking myself, "Could I have handled things better?" Maybe if I had, we wouldn't need to be here today. I remain torn by both sides of the argument and I believe that had he not taken his own life and stood trial in court, then both sides of his tragic story would have come out, but it never fully will.

One thing I do know is that time does heal all wounds and scars eventually fade although they never go away. The one thing we can take away with us today is that it is time to stop hating and forgive. It was hate that caused this to happen and by getting rid of the hate, we can make sure that something like this never happens again."

The principal's words were greeted with enthusiastic applause that died down to the end of the service. As the congregation readied themselves to leave, Leslie dragged Chuck with her, as she became a woman on a mission. Her first objective came to her as Patty, who was likewise dragging her boyfriend with her, came face to face with her. Executing a flanking manoeuvre that would have made her brother proud, she cut through the departing crowd to where the heavily pregnant Sarah was struggling to stand up. Her fears of missing her final objective went unfounded as Lisa appeared before them with her toddler in her arms.

"They're probably all going to dyke out now," a male voice called out callously. All four ladies and the two men gave the young man who had said it disdainful looks as he went past. Leslie continued to observe him, as she was sure there was something familiar about him and spent a minute filtering through memories of her past. It came to her: he was the boy who had come to Mark's funeral and repeatedly punched his dead body. Watching him walk away, she concluded that some people would never stop hating.

Turning to Sarah, she said, "Thank you so much for saying those things about Mark. I'm glad there are some people who don't see him as a total monster."

Sarah smiled and replied, "It needed to be said, and your brother wasn't a psycho, just misunderstood and a victim of that misunderstanding. I only hope that if

453

Alan Green or Hope Anderton find out, they will forgive me."

Leslie then turned her attention towards Lisa. "I'm so glad that I finally get to meet you," she informed her. "You were the one really good thing in my brother's short life."

Lisa blushed for a moment and stated, "I'm glad I was. He didn't deserve what had happened to him and I didn't deserve him."

With that said, all four ladies engaged in a group hug. The two boyfriends watched from the sidelines with mixed feelings. Patty's boyfriend whispered to Chuck, "Maybe we should go grab a beer." Chuck laughed at this but his cheer changed to concern as he observed Andrew Blumenthaw wheeling his way to the huddled ladies.

Andrew must have sensed Chuck's concern as he stopped in front of them. Looking directly at Leslie, he complimented her by declaring, "You got a lot of guts to come here and speak for your brother, I respect that. I don't know if I can ever forgive him for what he's done, but I can stop hating him. I realise that he couldn't always help the way he was and I should have paid more attention to his Asperger's."

Leslie smiled at him and offered her hand, which he accepted without hesitation. As they shook hands, a clicking sound, similar to a camera, was heard to the side of them. At the same time, hundreds of possible responses reverberated through her head. Every one of them sounded inappropriate, corny or clichéd. In the end, she settled for a safe, "Thank you."

The source of the camera sound became clear as two men walked up to the group. The much younger man, with long hair and holding a camera, stayed in the background as the middle-aged man stepped forward. Flashing an ID, he introduced himself as Kevin Taylor, a reporter from the New York Times.

"Ten years ago, the town tried to sue me and the paper I was working for at the time because I encountered evidence that authorities turned a blind eye to some of kids who had bullied Mark Leversee," he informed them. "I also interviewed a family who had lived in Ramsgate at one time and had a son who had Asperger's Syndrome. He too, suffered in the same way Mark did." Turning to Andrew, he offered, "Five years ago, you told everyone at that service that you would have liked to tell me a few things, now here's your chance."

Andrew looked at the ground and muttered, "There's no point now."

Kevin regarded him for a moment and explained, "From what I discovered when I covered the shooting for the South Jersey Current, I have always believed that Mark Leversee was just as much of a victim as those he shot that day. I also uncovered how little was done to help him and part of that was down to one of his aggressors being the nephew of the chief of police and another being the son of a local businessman. The articles I have written since about the shooting continue to state my belief. It seems that Ramsgate just doesn't want to accept it, that's understandable in a way. When I came here today, I expected to hear the town still wallowing in self-pity, denying its failings that led up to the tragedy. There was some of that today, but what surprised me was seeing you four young ladies speaking on his behalf and calling for the hate to end and forgive. I think that is a good theme for today and that is what my article is going to say in the New York Times tomorrow."

As they all soaked up the reporter's words, Kevin seized the moment to bring in the photographer to take photos. Most were taken with just the four ladies but a couple included Andrew and the last one included the two boyfriends as well. Once the photo session was complete, Kevin bade farewell, reminding them all to buy the next day's New York Times.

After Kevin and his photographer left, Andrew decided to go as well after once again commending Leslie on her bravery. Lisa was the first to speak following his departure. "I finally understand what he went through, it must have been hell for him," she admitted. "People, especially my parents, all used to say that I had a lucky escape, but I never felt that way. I will always remember Mark for what a great guy he was and," she added blushing, "a good kisser too." Her last comment brought smiles to the surrounding faces.

Sarah then piped in, "I'm glad I got to say today what I couldn't say ten years ago. He wasn't a monster, but a victim as much as anybody else. I always knew there was more to him that what people gave him credit for and I'll always be grateful that he saved my life that day."

Leslie hugged Lisa and Sarah; then turning to Patty, she told her, "I owe you the biggest thanks. It was your speech that began to break the cycle of hate and gave me the courage to get up on that stage and speak for my brother."

Patty went coy for a moment and then responded, "It needed to be said. It was this hate that was tearing this town apart."

The two women hugged; the playground was nearly empty now, so they decided it was time they went too. Once out of the main doors, they all exchanged email addresses and promises to keep in touch before getting back to the rest of their lives.

As they started to walk towards his car, Chuck slipped his arm around Leslie's waist, giving her a kiss on the top of her head and whispering, "I'm proud of

456

you." She put her arm around his waist and they walked together, all the while her mind racing one thousand miles a minute. If closure did exist, she had it now or at least the closest thing to it. She had met some of her brother's tormentors and victims and she knew that he had inflicted as much pain on them as they had on him. She also rejoiced in the fact that she was able to speak for him and there were some who no longer wanted to hate him and actually thought good of him and tried to understand him. They didn't think he was a complete weirdo. Finally, she hoped that wherever his soul was now, it could be free from the hate and intolerance he had suffered so much and that he too could stop hating and forgive.

The End

Or is it?

Points or Ponder

Asperger's Syndrome/DAMP: In spite of the fact that much more is known about Asperger's Syndrome than a decade ago, there is still much about it that remains unknown. Even less is known about DAMP. There are many common traits in both conditions. What can be discussed is whether or not Mark's struggles with these conditions are typical of the average person who is diagnosed with them.

Attitudes towards Asperger's Syndrome and DAMP: Many people are still ignorant and intolerant towards sufferers, especially if the sufferer appears "normal." How far does the story go in reflecting people's attitudes? Was Jim Friend's assessment that Mark was no better than a welfare cheat in chapter eighteen an accurate one in regards to people's attitudes? What steps can be taken to promote greater tolerance to those who suffer from Asperger's Syndrome and DAMP?

Bullying: Ignored from the beginning of time, it's refreshing that bullying is finally being taken more seriously. Some may argue that Mark's experiences in the story were more the exception than the rule, but were they? Some will say that no matter what we do, bullying will never be fully wiped out. However, can we take steps to drastically reduce it?

Guns: Every gun tragedy brings about the gun debate. Would tougher gun laws have stopped Mark from getting his hands on them for the big day? Would armed security guards, allowing teachers to carry guns or conceal and carry laws have prevented or reduced the bloodshed? When I wrote "He Was Weird," it was never my intention to go into a detailed debate on guns, as I believed it wasn't the point of the story. Saying that, it is a serious point that a thirteen-year-old boy is able to get his hands on them. That itself is reason why it should be discussed.

Other points to ponder: There are many other topics from the story that could be brought up as points of discussion. Some of these include:

Relationships
Religion
Influence of music and computer games
Fantasies

All of these can be debated alone or in reference to people who suffer from Asperger's Syndrome and DAMP, but I'll leave it for you to decide.

www.ingramcontent.com/pod-product-compliance
Lightning Source LLC
Chambersburg PA
CBHW031026030726
47497CB00004B/1030